Alexandria Bellefleur is a bestselling and award-winning author of swoony contemporary romance often featuring lovable grumps and the sunshine characters who bring them to their knees. A Pacific Northwesterner at heart, Alexandria now lives in New York City with her cats, Mills and Boon. Her special skills include finding the best pad thai in every city she visits, remembering faces but not names, falling asleep in movie theaters, and keeping cool while reading smutty books in public. Her debut novel, *Written in the Stars*, was a 2021 Lambda Literary Award winner and a 2020 winner of The Ripped Bodice Awards for Excellence in Romantic Fiction.

Also by Alexandria Bellefleur

Written in the Stars Series
Written in the Stars
Hang the Moon
Count Your Lucky Stars

Standalones
The Fiancée Farce
Truly, Madly, Deeply

Playing For Keeps

ALEXANDRIA BELLEFLEUR

PIATKUS

PIATKUS

First published in the US in 2026 by Avon,
An imprint HarperCollins Publishers
Published in Great Britain in 2026 by Piatkus

1 3 5 7 9 10 8 6 4 2

Copyright © 2026 by Alexandria Bellefleur

The moral right of the author has been asserted.

*All characters and events in this publication, other than those
clearly in the public domain, are fictitious and any resemblance
to real persons, living or dead, is purely coincidental.*

All rights reserved.
No part of this publication may be reproduced, stored in a
retrieval system, or transmitted in any form or by any means, without
the prior permission in writing of the publisher, nor be otherwise circulated
in any form of binding or cover other than that in which it is published
and without a similar condition including this condition being
imposed on the subsequent purchaser.

A CIP catalogue record for this book
is available from the British Library.

ISBN 978-0-349-43564-0

Printed and bound in Great Britain by Clays Ltd, Elcograf S.p.A.

Papers used by Piatkus are from well-managed forests
and other responsible sources.

Piatkus
An imprint of
Little, Brown Book Group
Carmelite House
50 Victoria Embankment
London EC4Y 0DZ

The authorised representative
in the EEA is
Hachette Ireland
8 Castlecourt Centre,
Dublin 15, D15 XTP3, Ireland
(email: info@hbgi.ie)

An Hachette UK Company
www.hachette.co.uk

www.littlebrown.co.uk

To Millie and Boon

Prologue

The Domestic Noir Plot drummer Ansel Daily and pop superstar Lyric Adair split after two years

by Dominique Eisenstadt
published on July 6

A source close to the drummer confirmed to *Notoriety Magazine* that the pair have gone their separate ways. "Officially, the breakup happened a month ago, but the relationship was rocky for a lot longer. Ultimately, they wanted very different things."

In June, rumors that Daily had been unfaithful to the singer sent the internet into a frenzy after a blind item was posted to a popular gossip blog alleging the drummer has an affinity for hooking up with fans.

"It's f——ing disrespectful is what it is," Daily said, directly addressing the rumors in an Instagram Live. "I didn't do s——."

Two years ago, Adair and Daily were first spotted together in Amsterdam, holding hands outside the Rijksmuseum. Later that summer, the pop star attended the Domestic Noir Plot's tour shows in New Orleans and New York, hard launching their relationship with an onstage kiss after joining the band for an encore performance of their hit song "Gone Girl, Gone" at Madison Square Garden.

Last week, Adair announced her next album, *Santa Ana*, which is set to release on October 26.

Notoriety Magazine has reached out to Lyric Adair's rep for comment.

Update (July 6, 5 p.m.): While Adair's publicist, Rosaline Sinclair, did not reply to our request at the time of this article's publication, she did make an unrelated statement on X (formerly known as Twitter).

ROSALINE SINCLAIR @rosalinesinclair • 3h
Congratulations, @lyricadair, on your single "Santa Ana" setting the single day streaming record for any song on Spotify! Couldn't be prouder of you. 😊

Chapter One

August 28

CASH CURRAN @cashcurran • 2h
@lyricadair
Are you a Hail Mary? Because you seem like a long shot, but I'm willing to take a chance. 🏈🙏

Poppy loved Cash, no doubt about it, but on occasion she wanted to throttle him.

"What in God's name possessed you to make a public pass at Lyric *freaking* Adair?" Poppy paced the perimeter of the patio, bare feet wearing a path in the grass. "Short of literal possession, I can't fathom why you would type—" She tugged her phone from the pocket of her overalls so she could recite the tweet verbatim, going so far as to deepen her voice in her best impression of Cash, "*'Are you a Hail Mary? Because you seem like a long shot, but I'm willing to take a chance.'* On what planet did you think that was a good idea?"

At the rate they were going, Poppy would develop an ulcer before her twenty-sixth birthday.

Cash lobbed a cheeky smile at her and pointed at the ground. "Uh, this one? Planet Earth?"

Poppy picked up one of his outdoor throw pillows and hurled it at his head. Unfortunately, her aim sucked, and they both watched as it sailed over his shoulder and straight into the uncovered pool behind him.

"Ow," Cash said deadpan.

"Do you think this is funny?" She put her hands on her hips. "I'm serious. Tell me."

"You're always serious these days." He laughed. "You're stressing over nothing, Pop-Tart. Chill."

"I will not *chill*. Do you know how many impressions your tweet had?"

"I don't know." He shrugged. "A few?"

Poppy pressed her teeth into her tongue, swallowing a scream. "Try fifteen *million*."

He whistled, brows rising over his sunglasses. "Damn."

More like damn *it*.

She threw herself down on the other end of the wicker love seat with a sigh. Sometimes it was like Cash forgot he was famous. Like he thought he was some random football player and not easily the best quarterback in the NFC West, maybe even the whole league.

"You have millions of people watching you and not just when you're on the field. You're a celebrity now. You can't shitpost and thirst tweet like you did when we were in college and expect to fly under the radar."

"Geez, Poppy." He groaned like she was killing him when it was the other way around. "I asked a girl out. It's hardly the PR crisis you seem to think it is."

"Look." She pivoted, knees knocking his thigh. "As your publicist, you've entrusted me with maintaining and protecting your public image, and it's not a responsibility I take lightly. But I can't do it, let alone do a good job at it, if you keep going rogue and tweeting every thought that pops into your head."

"It's hardly *every* thought."

She threw her head back and stared up at the sky, silently praying for strength. "Cash."

"Isn't this what I pay you the big bucks for? To watch my back?"

Yeah, well, preventing fires from starting was preferable to putting them out in her book.

"You know I'd watch your back even if it wasn't for the, quite frankly, absurd amount of money you insist on paying me, but—"

"Don't sell yourself short." Cash knocked his shoulder against hers and grinned. "We're both playing in the big leagues now. Have you seen what they're paying me? I'd be a dick if I didn't pay you what I do. It's, like, market value."

Market value or not, what she wasn't about to do was coast on their friendship and take advantage of his generosity. No, Poppy was going to be the best damn publicist Cash Curran could ask for, but she couldn't do it with him constantly placing obstacles in her path.

How could she put this in a way that would get through to him? "The best offense is a good defense, yeah?"

Cash frowned thoughtfully. "That's true."

"All I'm asking is for you to exert a little impulse control. Look next time before you leap. Because, you're right, these *are* the big leagues. Lyric Adair isn't just some girl. She's reached a level of superstardom that most people can't even dream of attaining and she's got a legion of loyal fans who will eat you alive if—"

"Her *fans*, sure. That's who you're worried about." His lips twitched. "This has nothing to do with the fear boner you've got for her publicist."

Poppy pointedly ignored the heat gathering in her cheeks and rolled her eyes. "Real mature, Cash."

"And yet I don't hear you denying it."

"I do *not* have a fear boner for Rosaline Sinclair. What I have is a great deal of respect and—and deep admiration for a highly skilled industry veteran with a clear mastery of marketing and strategy."

The lore surrounding the pop star's publicist was vast, the woman a legend among Lyric's fans and industry insiders alike. She was a force to be reckoned with, an utter PR mastermind who was capable and competent and unflinchingly cool under pressure. Everything Poppy aspired to be as a publicist, and fine, yeah, Poppy had eyes—Rosaline Sinclair was hotter than sin.

But that was neither here nor there. To cross her was to commit career suicide. Just ask Gavin Daniels. He dated Lyric Adair for four months when she was only seventeen, then went on some late-night talk show and claimed to have—barf—*popped her cherry*. Rumor had it not even film students at USC would work with him. All because Rosaline Sinclair had called in favors and pulled strings, quietly and ruthlessly working her magic behind the scenes to make Gavin Daniels a persona non grata in Hollywood.

"I don't know," Cash teased. "That sounds like a fancy way of saying *fear boner* to me."

"For the love of God," Poppy groaned. "Stop saying the word *boner* and stop trying to change the subject. Lyric Adair is not someone you mess around with."

Cash's mouth flattened into a grim line, his expression stricken. "Gee, that's a real charitable interpretation of my intentions."

Ah, shit. "You know that's not what I—"

"No, seriously. I love knowing my best friend assumes the worst of me." His smile didn't come close to reaching his eyes. "Makes me feel all warm and fuzzy inside."

Double shit. That was *so* not what she meant. "I'm sorry, okay? You know you're not the only one whose foot lives in their mouth."

Cash harrumphed and crossed his arms. Apparently, he was really going to make her work for it. Grovel and everything.

"*I* know you're a great guy with a heart of gold." And a terrible romantic with an awful habit of believing everyone he dated was *the one*, leading to a string of short-lived relationships and a trail of broken hearts. Saying so would only dig the hole Poppy had tripped in deeper. "I only meant the optics might not be—"

"Fuck the optics." Cash scoffed. "Isn't that what you said when my parents were worried about me losing endorsement deals earlier this year? *Fuck the optics*?"

No one was suggesting Cash couldn't do what he wanted, *date* who he wanted, definitely not Poppy. But his actions, well intentioned as they might have been, were going to have repercussions and it was her job as his publicist to consider them. She wasn't just his best friend anymore. "I only wish you would've talked to me first or—or I don't know, messaged her privately." But what's done was done. "There's going to be a postgame press conference on Thursday. When someone asks about Lyric, and they're going to, you should say—"

"Let me guess. No comment? Contrary to popular belief, I'm not a complete moron."

"You're not," she agreed. "And screw anyone who says otherwise. But if you go with *no comment*, people are going to think you have something to hide. Instead, you should say . . ." What would Rosaline Sinclair have a client say? Something complimentary that couldn't be misconstrued. Something like, "*I admire her work ethic and I strive to embody the same dedication on the field.*"

"Won't be hard to remember considering it's the truth." He sighed and turned, finally meeting her eyes. "I'm sorry, okay? I'm not trying to be a dick or make your job harder."

"I happen to like a challenge," she said, ribbing him gently, relieved that he wasn't still mad at her for implying he was some kind of playboy. "Makes me feel like I'm earning my keep around here."

He rolled his eyes. "Now who's being ridiculous?"

Not her. Not only had Cash taken a risk on her when he could've easily hired a more seasoned publicist—someone with more than just a college internship and a few measly years spent working at a midsize agency under their belt, followed by an embarrassing firing Poppy desperately didn't want to think about—he was also letting her live in his guest room, rent free. There wasn't anything ridiculous about wanting to square up, even the score.

Never would she let it be said that Poppy Peterson was a mooch.

"Honestly? I'm probably making this into a bigger deal than it is. Give it a week or two and I'm sure it'll blow over."

The news cycle was endless, attention spans short, and fresh gossip constantly emerging. Bored by the lack of drama, people would move on to the next celebrity spectacle, preferably *not* involving Cash Curran.

He stared into the middle distance and sighed, shoulders slumping. "It was a long shot anyway."

She frowned. "What do you mean?"

He slipped his sunglasses down the bridge of his nose and looked at her like she'd lost her mind. "What do you mean what do I mean? Lyric Adair probably gets hundreds, if not thousands, of DMs a day. What are the chances she reads any of 'em?" His laugh was all kinds of self-deprecating and it made Poppy's chest ache. "Odds of her responding to a public tweet aren't any better, but I just wanted her attention, you know?"

Far be it for her to judge when she'd acted far, *far* dumber for attention. At least Cash's gaffe was harmless. "I get it."

He slouched deeper into the love seat, letting his head loll against the back of the couch. "Have you ever—" He cut himself off, scrubbing a hand roughly over his face, skewing his sunglasses. "Never mind. It's stupid."

Poppy dug her toes into his thigh. "Tell me."

His hand fell to his side with a heavy sigh. "Have you ever felt it down in your bones that you were meant to meet someone?"

What she wouldn't give to feel that sure about anything, that confident. That a day could go by where she didn't second-guess every decision she made. "This is one massive crush you have, huh?"

"Nah," he said, breezy tone at odds with the set of his jaw. "I don't even know her. I just wanted . . ." He trailed off with another of those resigned laughs. "Doesn't matter what I wanted. She's so far out of my league, it's like we're not even playing the same fucking sport."

Outside of sports, leagues were stupid and juvenile and even if they weren't . . . "Did you forget you're Cash *freaking* Curran? Come on. They wanted you to be the next Bachelor."

And he could've been had filming not conflicted with training camp.

"That shit's not real and you know it." He shook his head. "Have you seen the guys she dates? Half those dudes have Emmys. Or Oscars. Grammys? Fuck if I know."

"And you've got a Heisman. Two National Championships. A Super Bowl ring." She ticked off his accomplishments on her fingers. "You're no slouch yourself." She poked him in the chest, impressing upon him her sincerity. "In fact, you, Cash Anthony Curran, are a total catch, a determination I feel uniquely qualified to make as someone who knew you before you were a mega-famous football player. I knew you when you had gross neon-green rubber bands on your braces and went three weeks thinking Axe was a stand-in for deodorant."

"Don't remind me," he muttered. "Also? I'm pretty sure you're, like, contractually obligated to say that."

They didn't *have* a contract. "When have you ever known me to bullshit you?"

"Doesn't matter. This whole thing was a dumb idea." He lifted his hips and slipped his phone from his pocket, thumb flying across the screen. "There. I deleted the tweet. I know it's not the same thing as never having put it out there in the first place, but it should help things blow over. Right?"

Now she felt bad. "Cash—"

"Poppy." The look he shot her was of fond exasperation. "I'm good. Seriously."

The bubbly, slightly breathy vocal stylings of Carly Rae Jepsen filled the air, putting the conversation on a pause. Poppy pulled her phone from her pocket and frowned at the screen.

Restricted. "Hello?"

"Is this Penelope Peterson?" The caller's voice was clipped, professional, and slightly gravelly while still sounding distinctly feminine.

"This is her. I mean, *she*." Cash snickered and Poppy flipped him off. She hated talking on the phone, always felt like she was doing it wrong. Like some script existed that everyone else knew except for her. "It's Poppy, though. Poppy Peterson."

A soft but not quite silent sigh came over the line and Poppy didn't know who was calling but she had the strangest feeling that she'd already failed some kind of test. "This is Rosaline Sinclair of Rarity PR. Is now an okay time?"

Shut the front door, no it was *not*.

"Who is it?"

Poppy flailed, slapping a hand over Cash's mouth. "*Shh!*"

Rosaline Sinclair—holy shit it was *Rosaline Sinclair*—let out a disbelieving laugh. "Did you just shush me?"

"No!" Poppy shouted, horrified. "*God* no. I—sorry. Definitely not. And now is a great time. I can talk."

Cash snickered, shoulders shaking with barely restrained laughter. "Can you?" he whispered. "Because I'm not so sure."

"*Asshole*," she mouthed, digging her toes harder into his thigh in warning.

The sound of shuffling papers carried through the phone. "Just to be clear, you *are* Cash Curran's public relations agent, are you not?"

She wiped the sweat from her hands on her thighs, palms disgustingly clammy. "I am?"

"Are you asking or are you telling me?" Rosaline sounded amused.

"Telling you?" Poppy wanted to punch herself in the face. "I'm telling you. I—shit, is this about the tweet? Because Cash is *super* sorry about that." Her words caught up with her and her stomach sank. "And I'm sorry for swearing."

Cash threw himself dramatically onto the ground, lying face down in the grass. Big baby. Poppy was the one about to get her ass reamed by the scariest publicist in the business, not him.

The line was silent for a beat. "So, he wasn't serious?"

Poppy winced. "Well, no, not exactly. He *definitely* meant what he said. It was more the, uh, method with which he chose to say what he said that he's sorry about."

"Hm. Lyric found it . . . charming."

Charming? "Seriously?"

"No one is more baffled than I am, trust me." Rosaline sighed. "Assuming he hasn't lost interest, Lyric is available for a call Tuesday evening, eight p.m. Pacific. I'll email you a nondisclosure agreement for both you and your client to sign prior to the call. Upon receipt of the signed agreement, I'll then email you the meeting ID and text you the passcode separately. Is this acceptable?"

Toto, Poppy had a feeling they were not in Kansas anymore.

"Wow, uh, NDAs and two-factor authentication. I guess I've been out of the dating game awhile, huh?"

Poppy laughed to fill the awkward, stomach-churning silence.

"Let's get one thing straight," Rosaline said, her voice chilly. "This isn't a game."

"No, I know it's not. I only meant—"

"I know what you meant, but I need you to understand what *I* mean when I say this isn't a joke. To be perfectly frank, I would have let your client's madcap tweet go quietly into the good night if not for the fact that *my* client requested I reach out on her behalf. If we're going to proceed, we're going to do it on my terms. Which is to say, properly. Are we understood?"

"Yes, ma'am," Poppy blurted, her voice horrifyingly breathy, the words *fear boner* flashing through her mind. Ma'am? *Ma'am?* Someone fucking lobotomize her. "I mean, uh . . ."

An agonizing beat of silence passed, a pause so pregnant Poppy debated flinging her phone into the pool and herself off the nearest tall object. After another moment, Rosaline delicately cleared her throat. "Good. So, Tuesday?"

Poppy covered the phone with her hand and kicked Cash in the side. "Look alive, Curran. Lyric Adair wants to talk to you."

"What?" Blades of grass stuck to his cheek when he lifted his head. "Now? Holy fuck, give me the phone."

"No. Tuesday at eight," she said, still covering the receiver. "What do you want me to say?"

Cash staggered forward on his knees and clasped her upper arms.

"For the love of God, Poppy," he implored. "Say yes."

"*Hello?*" Rosaline prompted. "Did I lose you?"

"No, no, I'm here. Um, eight on Tuesday. NDA. Got it." She wiggled free from Cash's hold. "Do you need my email address?"

"No need. I have it."

Of course she did. Considering the mysterious means with which Rosaline had gotten ahold of Poppy's phone number, Poppy really shouldn't have been surprised. "Is there anything else you need from me?"

Her social security number maybe? Her blood type?

"That's it for now," Rosaline said. "I'll be in touch."

Chapter Two

September 21

Lyric Adair reposted
CASH CURRAN @cashcurran • 16h
RAIN OR SHINE, HOME OR AWAY, YOU KNOW THE
@portlandpathfinders ALWAYS COME TO PLAY, BABY! ONE
MORE SLEEP TIL WE SHOW UP AND SHOW OFF #PDXvsLAC
♡🖤⊘#PathfindersNation

VICTORIA @pdxprincess • 16h
um is no one going to talk about the fact that @lyricadair is
now following @cashcurran?!?

PAIGELA @infrontofmysalad • 16h
besties who wants to bet lyric adair is gonna be at the
#PDXvsLAC game?

CHERRY 🤍 @polinlover96 • 16h
replying to @infrontofmysalad
unhinged behavior 😂 who tf am i kidding, unhinged is
practically that girl's middle name. she's totally gonna be there.

MAYA @cantevenparallelpark • 4h
The camera just panned to the VIP box. I don't see Lyric 👻
#PDXvsLAC

PORTLAND PATHFINDERS @portlandpathfinders • 1h
27–19 FINAL SCORE! ANOTHER WIN FOR THE
#PathfindersNation 🏈♡🖤🏈 SEE YOU NEXT WEEK, MIAMI.

Los Angeles was weird.

There was a whole boulevard of stars and not a single one in the sky. None that Poppy could see. It was eerie that there was this great, big, black blanket of nothingness over their heads, visible through the sunroof of the Ranger Rover they were currently cruising in down Nightingale Drive.

"We're just about there, Miss Peterson," their driver said, eyes meeting hers in the rearview mirror.

She pressed a hand to her stomach, the quasi-queasiness she'd been experiencing since she'd touched down at LAX yesterday increasing exponentially. "Thank you."

Cash squeezed her knee and rocked his shoulder into hers. "I'm starting to think you're more nervous for my date than I am."

Cash's call-slash-interview-slash–chemistry test with Lyric had earned him her phone number. Almost three weeks of nonstop texting later, they were now en route to the first date.

"I'm not nervous," she denied, perhaps a touch too vehemently to be believed. "I just . . . want to make a good impression. Is that so bad?"

"Let me get this straight. *You*," he pointed at Poppy, "are worried about making a good impression during *my*," he pointed at himself, "date."

"When you put it like that, it sounds silly," she groused.

Cash let out a curt snicker that had her wishing they were kids again so she could reach out and tweak his nipple through his ridiculously garish silk Gucci shirt. "Because it *is* silly. You're hopeless, Pop-Tart."

She sputtered out an indignant laugh and swiveled in her seat to face him. "*Me? Hopeless?* Have you met me? I am a fucking ray of sunshine. I am the opposite of hopeless. I am—I am *full* of hope."

He grinned, teeth glinting in the dim light of the back seat. "Full of something."

She narrowed her eyes. "Do not test me. I will turn this car around."

From the front, the driver snorted, quickly covering the sound with a cough. Poppy's face warmed.

"I will have the driver turn this car around," she amended.

"No, you won't. Because you want to make a good impression on *Rosaline Sinclair*," Cash teased, voice annoyingly singsongy.

"Cash," she warned, far from in the mood to be teased.

"Relax. It'll be great. Lyric and I'll . . ." He trailed off with a vague sweep of his hand that had her wrinkling her nose.

She hadn't asked about their plans and quite frankly the less she knew the better. "And you'll, what? Make small talk for a few hours?" He stretched out his big, dumb hands and gave her even dumber spirit fingers. "Oooh, so scary."

She smacked his chest. "Shut up."

"I wouldn't bet against me if I were you," he said. "My gut's telling me tonight's going to be a total success."

Of course it was. *He* was going to get to spend the evening charming a pretty girl. Poppy, on the other hand, was going to spend the evening—actually, she didn't *know* how she was going to spend the evening. She and Rosaline hadn't discussed the specifics, only the logistics. Location (Rosaline's house as it was private and secure), time (here Rosaline had offered a little grace given the chance of the game going into overtime and the knowledge that LA traffic was notoriously a bitch), and a warning not to breathe a word to a single soul. A touch overkill considering the brand spankin' new NDA Poppy and Cash had signed, but Poppy wasn't about to begrudge Rosaline her precautions if they provided her and Lyric with peace of mind.

The car briefly idled in front of a wrought iron gate that looked as elaborate as it did secure before passing through, stopping in front of a two-story Spanish colonial with a windowless half-round carriage-house-style front door surrounded by a half arch of bright pink bougainvillea.

Cash whistled as he opened his car door. "Nice place."

The butterflies in her stomach transformed into bees and her pulse pounded painfully in her throat. Go time. "Before we head in—"

"It's a date. *My* date, not a press conference or some public appearance. I don't need a briefing and I definitely don't need my hand held." Cash stepped out of the car, turned, and ducked, green eyes full of mirth. "I love you, I do, but I've got this."

"I'm sure you *think* you've got this, but—"

The door shut in her face.

Poppy scrambled out after him, moving slower, her pleated A-line skirt bunching awkwardly around her hips as she slid across the leather, tossing a quick thanks at the driver before shutting the door and hurrying after Cash, hoping to corral him before—

Too late. The door swung upon and suddenly Cash had his arms full of pop star.

All perfect, light brown skin and warm brown eyes, springy coils of hair held back from her face with a tangerine knotted headband, Lyric Adair was even prettier in person. The gold bangles on her dainty wrist clanged noisily as she threw her arms around Cash and buried her face in his neck, her laughter bright and airy as Cash crushed her against his chest with a deep, booming laugh and swung her in a wide circle.

It felt a little like Poppy was watching a rom-com play out before her eyes. She wasn't sure she believed in anything as fickle as fate or soulmates, but maybe, just maybe, Cash had been on to something when he'd talked about that feeling of surety, that he and Lyric were meant to meet. That maybe this time *was* different.

"Hi," Lyric breathed when her feet were finally back on the ground, her face tipped up, staring at Cash, still clinging close, her hands holding tight to his biceps.

Cash sounded equally as breathless as he stared down at her, cheeks pink and throat working hard with each swallow. No nerves, her ass. "Hi. I, uh, got these for you." He thrust a bouquet of slightly smushed four-leaf clovers he had special ordered from a fancy florist shop they'd had to detour to after the game.

"Are these—oh my god, you got me a bouquet of four-leaf clovers? I didn't even know they sold those," Lyric gushed, eyes full of hearts.

Cash ducked his head and gripped the back of his neck, which had turned red. "I might've read in an old interview that they're your favorite. And they're supposed to bring good luck, so I made it happen."

"You did your homework, huh?" Lyric teased.

The moment was ridiculous and cheesy and Poppy didn't know whether to laugh or cry or roll her eyes, maybe do some combination of all three as Lyric and Cash continued to stare at each other like they were the only two people in the world, like Poppy didn't even exist.

"You played your ass off tonight," Lyric praised and Cash's flush deepened, the tips of his ears going crimson, clashing with his lavender shirt.

"You watched?"

"You're not the only one willing to do their homework." Lyric cuffed him playfully on the shoulder. "That play where you threw the ball, ran, *and* caught it in the end zone? That was—*insane.*"

"*Insane* might be a bit of an overstatement." Rosaline leaned against the front doorjamb, watching the scene play out with wary eyes at odds with her inviting smile. "But it was a decent game."

She was shorter than Poppy expected. Which was probably a weird thing to think upon first meeting someone in person, but she'd always exuded such confidence on the red carpet that Poppy had figured she'd be taller than the five-foot-two, *maybe* five-foot-three inches she stood. Short compared to Poppy's flatfooted five-seven inches, even shorter considering her special game day sneakers had platforms.

With cheekbones that could cut glass and a soft, generous mouth, Rosaline Sinclair was a mix of one contradiction after another. Her dark brown hair had begun to escape the fishtail braid that hung over her right shoulder, loose strands framing her face and softening her features, drawing Poppy's gaze to her eyes, piercing shards of green bottle glass lined with black in the inner and outer corners. Glints of metal ran up her ears and a small stud in her nose sparkled in the warm glow of the porch light. She was Disney-princess gorgeous and covered in tattoos, like an alternative pinup girl.

"*Decent?*" Lyric lobbed a disbelieving look at her publicist. "Don't act like you weren't screaming at the television during the last quarter. Cash, don't listen to her. You were amazing."

"I was all right." He ran a hand over the top of his head, a nervous tick he'd had since they were kids. "I mean, there were ten other guys with me on the field. It was a team effort."

Rosaline sighed and pushed off the doorjamb. Her gray, acid-washed, oversize shirt had some band Poppy had never heard of on the front, a band she was absolutely going to google the second she got back to the hotel. The cotton looked worn and soft, the hem raw and ragged, and the neckline hung off one of Rosaline's slender shoulders, elaborate grayscale floral ink creeping up her toned arms. "You were the recipient of the Davey O'Brien Award, Walter Camp Award, Maxwell Award, Manning Award, Heisman Trophy, named Associated Press Player of the Year, Pac-12 Offensive Player of the Year, and that's just your college career. False modesty doesn't suit you, Curran."

Cash chuckled awkwardly and threw a wide-eyed look at Poppy that screamed *save me*. "Poppy warned me you'd, uh, do your research, but hell, that's thorough."

Rosaline's eyes flitted past Cash, her gaze landing on Poppy, who, for a moment, forgot how to breathe. It was patently unfair to be that attractive. Save some good looks for the rest of the planet. "I require a warning, do I?"

As if she didn't already know she was terrifying, as if she didn't relish the fact, as if she hadn't constructed a fearsome reputation with intention.

"To be honest?" Poppy's heart could outpace a hummingbird and only half the reason was because Rosaline terrified her, the other half because it had been a minute since Poppy had been around someone so beautiful and it was throwing her off her game. "I think we both know you do."

"*Poppy*," Cash hissed through his teeth. "*The fuck?*"

What? She shrugged. She was just being truthful, something she hoped Rosaline would appreciate.

Rosaline gave her an incredibly amused look before turning back to Cash. "I'm thorough, don't get me wrong, but digging up the highlight reel of your college career was hardly necessary considering you've been a hometown favorite for over a decade. Be glad you were a Duck, Curran, and not a Beaver, otherwise I might've decided not to let you darken my door."

Poppy frowned. "Hometown favorite?"

"Rosaline's from Portland," Lyric said as if it were common knowledge. She reached around Cash and held out her hand to Poppy. "It's really great to meet you, by the way. Cash has told me so much about you."

Poppy shook Lyric's hand. "Likewise."

"It's such a nice night that I was thinking we could spend some time out on the patio." Lyric wrapped her hand around Cash's elbow with a casual sort of comfort most couples didn't exhibit after three dates, let alone the one they had yet to actually go on. "Did you two want to join us?"

Poppy opened her mouth to tell Lyric her offer was incredibly kind, but no way was she going to impose when Rosaline beat her to the punch.

"You have fun." Rosaline's stare clashed with Poppy's, the corners of her mouth twitching upward, not quite a smile but close. "Poppy and I are going to spend a little time getting to know each other."

Chapter Three

"Wine?" Rosaline had breezed into the kitchen on bare feet, plucking an already-open bottle of red wine off the butcher-block counter. Two short-stemmed, wide-bowled wineglasses sat nearby.

Poppy hovered in the doorway, eyeing the bottle in Rosaline's hand longingly. A glass of wine would take the edge off, but it was never *just* one glass. Not for Poppy. "Water would be great, thank you."

Rosaline filled one glass before recorking the bottle. "You sure? I've got . . ." She turned, tongue clicking against the back of her teeth as she surveyed the inside of her sleek glass front refrigerator. "Kombucha, coconut water, Olipop, LaCroix, and . . . iced tea. Peppermint, I believe."

The contents of her refrigerator couldn't have been more different from the Gatorade and Muscle Milk that filled Cash's.

"Uh, a soda would be nice. Any flavor."

Rosaline retrieved a can of cherry vanilla Olipop from the fridge, which just so happened to be Poppy's favorite. She cracked open the can and poured it into the empty wineglass before nodding to one of the tall barstools in front of the island. "Make yourself comfortable. I have a feeling we're going to be here awhile."

Poppy hauled herself onto the stool as smoothly as possible. "Your place is beautiful. Very midcentury Spanish eclectic. I love it."

Set behind that grand carriage-style door was a veritable oasis. Bird-of-paradise sprouted proudly from the enormous terra-cotta planter by the door, magenta orchids and African violets dotting the long entry table. The floors were octagonal Saltillo tile overlaid with a colorful Moroccan rug, and the textured walls were painted a vibrant saffron from the foyer all the way down the hall leading to a kitchen even Nancy Meyers would covet with its ginormous island and emerald glass-front cabinets, peacock-colored backsplash, bevy of copper pots and pans hanging from the ceiling, and cream-colored, retro-style appliances.

The place was a cozy, colorful jewel box, so different from the austerity of Cash's bachelor pad that Poppy could weep. Cash had given her free reign to redecorate as she pleased, but staying with him was only ever meant to be a pit stop, not permanent.

Rosaline looked at her curiously across the island. "Design buff?"

"Unless religiously watching *Zillow Gone Wild* counts, hardly." She gave a self-effacing laugh. "But I know what I like when I see it."

Rosaline's eyes raked down the length of Poppy's body. "Something we have in common."

Poppy blinked, startled, breath hitching. For a wild second, it almost seemed like . . .

Ha, no. No, Poppy was totally imagining things. Except, what if . . . no, no, she was *definitely* imagining things. Rosaline Sinclair had *not* just checked her out. She'd probably just been . . . hell if Poppy knew, sizing her up?

Historically, Poppy had not always made the best choices, good ones even, but she was trying to turn over a new leaf. Flirting with Rosaline Sinclair would be stupid. Right?

Right. "So Portland, huh?"

"Lake Oswego, if you want to get specific." Rosaline sipped her wine. "You seem surprised."

"I mean, Portland is big but it's not *that* big. I guess I just figured I would've, I don't know, read it somewhere."

Rosaline cocked her head, braid falling over shoulder, more of that dark, glossy hair slipping free from the loose plait. Poppy had the strangest impulse to tuck it behind Rosaline's ear, maybe trace the plains of Rosaline's face with her fingertips while she was at it. To follow the slope of her nose down to the curve of her cupid's bow.

Poppy tucked her hands underneath her ass, sitting on them instead.

"Read about it?" Rosaline's lips twitched. "So you're admitting I'm not the only one who did her research?"

"I don't think I need to tell you that you're nearly as famous as Lyric."

For crying out loud, the woman had her own Wikipedia page. A lengthy one at that.

Rosaline huffed out a soft laugh. "*Infamous* would be the word most would use, but sure."

Poppy tapped her socked toes against the bottom rung of the stool, hands still tucked under her. "Right. So, I watched that *E! True Hollywood Story* about Lyric when I was in college, and you were featured in it."

"You really haven't been doing this for very long, have you?" Rosaline asked over the rim of her wineglass, bursting Poppy's bubble, and bringing her back down to earth with a whopping case of imposter syndrome.

Poppy nibbled on the inside of her lip. "Is it that obvious?"

"You're not much older than Lyric is what I meant."

Oh. "Well, sure. But I'm guessing you already knew that."

"Curran's one thing; bold of you to assume I bothered to look you up beyond your contact info."

"I think it would be bolder of me to assume you didn't," Poppy volleyed back.

Rosaline had a certain perspicacity that lent itself to an unparalleled competency that Poppy couldn't help but admire. She might not be in possession of her own Wiki page, but she would have to be stupid to believe for a single second Rosaline Sinclair didn't know more about her than she was letting on.

"I'm starting to think I'm not the only one who should come with a warning." Rosaline gave her an appraising sidelong glance, her left brow rising sharply. "You've been Curran's publicity manager for a little over a year."

It wasn't a question, but Poppy nodded anyway. "Mhmm. About a year and two months." Since the recent expansion draft brought Cash home to Portland to play for the Pathfinders, the NFL's newest enfranchised team.

Rosaline's expression turned thoughtful. "In the last year alone, you've had your work cut out for you, haven't you?"

Poppy frowned. "What do you mean?"

Rosaline shrugged. "I can't imagine it was a walk in the park, orchestrating the public coming out of a professional athlete as bisexual. A football player no less. That couldn't have been easy."

It wasn't about what was easy, it was about what was right. If Poppy cared about easy, she'd have taken Rosaline up on that glass of wine when she'd had the chance. If Poppy cared about easy, she'd have given up a long time ago. "I don't care about easy; I care about Cash. And coming out was important to him, so it was important to me."

As his friend she'd wholeheartedly supported him and as his publicist she'd helped him strategize a game plan that accounted for as many outcomes as could be predicted. Easy? No. A hardship? Never.

"Risky," Rosaline said, unnecessarily stating the obvious.

Of course it had been a risk. But any brand that distanced themself because Cash was queer could kick rocks.

"Some risks are worth it." Poppy lifted her chin, staring Rosaline down, daring her to say otherwise. "Some things are more important than brand deals or endorsements or public opinion. And maybe it makes me a bad publicist to admit it, but people are always going to be more important to me than getting good PR."

Cash's being able to live authentically and be a visible role model to young, queer athletes was infinitely more important than appealing to a few Brads, Chads, and Dads who were pissy their favorite quarterback was bisexual and not afraid to say it with his whole chest. The face of the NFL was changing—albeit at a snail's pace—and as far as Poppy was concerned, those small-minded fuckers could change the channel if they were so butthurt over it.

"It wasn't an indictment," Rosaline said, giving her a soft look she couldn't quite parse. "The opposite, in fact."

Opposite of indictment could mean a lot of things. "I guess it didn't seem right that I could date whomever I wanted, and Cash couldn't."

Her parents might not understand her for a whole host of reasons, only a few of which were related to her being bisexual, but she'd never faced any real discrimination for liking who she liked. Not the way Cash could've, the way he could've lost everything he'd worked tirelessly for. Mercifully, it hadn't come to the worst.

"What I'm trying to say is that it was very brave of him." Rosaline's eyes shone, green as sea glass, their sharpness blunted by sincerity. "Curran is lucky to have someone like you in his corner."

Cash Curran was *good* in a way Poppy had found so few people were, there for her when no one else was, not even her family—*especially* not her family. Even when she'd given him every reason not to, he'd believed in her. Twenty years they'd been looking out for each other; Poppy wasn't about to stop now that fame and money were in the mix.

"Like I said, he's my best friend," she demurred. "I'd have his back even if I wasn't working for him."

"Well, for whatever it's worth, I'm sure it wasn't simple, but together you made the entire rollout look, quite frankly, effortless," Rosaline praised. "I doubt I could've handled it any better myself."

Poppy exhaled slowly, shoulders falling from where she'd inadvertently had them hiked up to her ears.

For as long as she could remember, she'd been chasing the high of the first gold star she'd gotten, a shiny foil sticker stuck to the corner of a spelling test, indelible proof that she was *good*. It had driven her to do things she wasn't proud of, desperate for the attention she was missing at home, starved for validation. Affection. It had taken a year of therapy to recognize it for what it was, to accept that she didn't *need* anyone to tell her she had value for it to be intrinsically true, but it was also okay for her to want to hear it from time to time, normal even. There was still a lot she was working to unpack, a lot she'd probably always be working to unpack, the destination the journey.

She didn't need a gold star like a first grader anymore, but that didn't stop her breath from vanishing when Rosaline said exactly what she hadn't known she'd needed to hear tonight. She wasn't totally fucking up this job the way she had everything else in her life. Cash could count on her. She was capable. She could do this.

"Timing it with Pride Month just made sense and Cash was already planning on donating to The Trevor Project so really, it wasn't—"

"Poppy." A tiny thrill shot through her at the way her name sounded when Rosaline said it in that trademark Lauren Bacall–style rasp, her lips pressing and parting before coming back together as her mouth shaped the word. "Take the compliment. I don't give them out very often."

Poppy felt like she was glowing, like she'd swallowed the sun, the rarity of Rosaline's praise making it all the more precious. "Thank you. That—that means a lot. Especially coming from you."

Rosaline's lips parted as she sucked in a stuttered breath, her face frustratingly unreadable as she rested her forearms against the counter. "Be honest with me, one professional to another. What's your angle right now?"

"Angle?" Poppy frowned. "I don't have an angle."

Rosaline sighed and shook her head, looking the picture of disappointment. It was a look Poppy knew well. "And here you were doing so well, Poppy."

If that was meant to be a compliment, it sure as hell didn't feel like one. "Seriously. I don't—I don't know what you're talking about." Hair escaped the bun at the nape of her neck when she shook her head. "I don't—you told me to take the compliment and I meant what I said. You're so clearly amazing at your job and so—so confident and I . . . I admire you, I guess." Her cheeks burned, but she soldiered on, needing to get this out, needing Rosaline to understand. "That sounds annoyingly juvenile when I say it out loud, but I do. I don't have an angle; I just genuinely appreciate you saying what you said. It meant a lot." Even if the praise felt tainted now, all tangled with sour uncertainty.

Rosaline stared, eyes wide and mouth agape, looking as wrong-footed as Poppy felt. "I was talking about Cash and Lyric, but okay? Thank you."

Oh. "Well. I don't have an angle there, either."

Rosaline tipped her face up to the ceiling, lips moving as if silently praying for strength. "Look," she said, lowering her head and assessing Poppy, expression pinched. "I said I wanted you to be honest with me—"

"I am," Poppy blurted. Painfully honest was all she'd been since the moment she stepped out of the car. "I have been. I have no ulterior motives and neither does Cash."

Rosaline scoffed softly. "Forgive me if I'm struggling to believe he wasn't chasing clout with that public tweet."

Poppy sat straighter, hackles rising, and glared. "He's got 1.4 million followers. He doesn't *need* clout."

"And Lyric has 95 million. Do the math."

Poppy didn't need to do any math to know the numbers were irrelevant to what Rosaline was implying. "You're suggesting Cash is using Lyric."

"I'm not *suggesting* anything," Rosaline said, matter of fact. "It's happened before and I'm not so naive as to believe someone won't try it again. Operative word being *try* this time."

"And I'm telling you Cash isn't that kind of guy. I've known him since I was five. I think that makes me uniquely qualified to speak on his character."

"Or uniquely biased," Rosaline argued, and Poppy rolled her eyes. Figures she'd have a rebuttal. "Even you have to admit Cash Curran doesn't have the greatest track record when it comes to relationships." She braced her hands against the countertop, slightly farther than shoulder width apart. "Has he ever been in a relationship that's lasted longer than a year?"

"Has Lyric?"

Rosaline's lips flattened into a hard line and a muscle in her jaw jumped. "We're not talking about Lyric."

"If my client's relationship history is fair game, I don't see why yours shouldn't be either," Poppy demanded. "Sure, Cash has an Adriana and a Misha and a Rachel and a Blake in his past, but last time I checked, Lyric had a Gavin and an Alex and a Bryce and a Conner and a Nate in hers."

Lyric wasn't some wide-eyed ingenue and Cash wasn't a mustachioed villain looking to steal her virtue or tie her to a set of train tracks. They were both adults and this was far from a first relationship for either of them.

"The difference is that the press calls your client a heartbreaker and makes cute quips about him playing the field, but the same outlets speculate on Lyric's body count and write think pieces about why she can't keep a man. They denigrate Lyric for doing the same thing they praise Cash for in the same breath. Don't even get me started on the rumors. Lyric's sleeping with all her friends. She's secretly married. She's having a baby. It's brutal out there, even more so because Lyric isn't just a woman, she's a Black woman. So, no, we are *not* talking about Lyric. Not when your client will come out of this smelling fresh as a fucking daisy, and I will be forced to not only clean up the mess he made but also put Lyric back together after suffering yet another heartbreak at the hands of a guy who claimed to be different."

Dating was difficult enough. Doing it while the whole world watched? Poppy shivered. No, thank you. To think that Lyric had been living that nightmare since she was fourteen? Poppy's heart went out to her. "I'm not going to pretend to understand the level of scrutiny Lyric faces on a daily basis. I'm definitely not claiming Lyric and Cash are going to be treated remotely similar by the press. But it's not fair to act like Cash holds all the cards here."

Her brows rose. "Meaning?"

"Ninety-five million followers." Poppy tried to mimic Rosaline by arching a single brow. "*You* do the math."

"Lyric's follower count isn't going to spare her the pain of heartbreak."

Poppy rolled her eyes. "No, but in the court of public opinion, Cash is going to get crucified by Lyric's legion of diehard fans if the blame for a potential breakup gets placed on his shoulders. Even if it's not true, you and I both know perception is reality. You're telling me he won't get absolutely inundated with hate mail? That his notifications won't be flooded, that some of Lyric's especially loyal fans won't buy tickets to his games just to heckle him? That some Pathfinders fans who are also fans of Lyric won't cancel their season tickets, that the team won't lose money, that Cash might not get released from his contract early if management thinks he's more trouble than he's worth?"

That Poppy, consequently, might not lose her job.

"Dating someone as high-profile as Lyric isn't without its risks." Rosaline shrugged, as good as confirming that she had the power to ruin Cash and, by association, Poppy. All in a day's work for Rosaline Sinclair. "Just like being an athlete isn't without risks. Cash could tear his ACL tomorrow and never play football again and yet he gets out on the field every Sunday. In ten years, he could be a washed-up nobody sitting in a bar talking about how he used to be someone. Most athletes have some sort of backup plan."

"And Lyric could develop vocal nodes and lose her four-octave range." If looks could kill, Poppy would've slumped over dead atop the kitchen island. "My point is, I could just as easily ask you if being the wife of a professional athlete is Lyric's backup plan, but I won't because—"

"—it would be patently ridiculous?" Rosaline laughed.

"*Because* I have more respect for her than to assume she's a cleat chaser." Not that there was anything wrong with exclusively looking to date athletes. "I'm not saying you have to like Cash. Hell, I'm not saying you can't have your own private thoughts and opinions about whether this relationship is going to last, whether you *want* it to last. I'm only asking that you afford Cash and me that same respect. Don't start us—*him* off at a disadvantage. Please."

Her heart hurled itself against the wall of her chest and her hands shook as she reached for her soda. She, Poppy Peterson, had just looked Rosaline Sinclair in the eye and asked Rosaline to respect her. Her voice didn't even quiver. Maybe she didn't need one, but for that alone, Poppy *totally* deserved a gold star.

"That girl out there?" Rosaline said, jerking her chin toward the hall where the rest of the house was and the presumed door leading to the back patio. "She is *the* single most important person on this planet to me. She's been through more than most people twice her age and she has achieved more than most people could dream of achieving in *two* lifetimes. But the fact of the matter is the higher you climb, the harder you fall, and there are people out there looking for any excuse to tear her down. This life? It's not for the faint of heart. Most people? Can't handle it. They think they can, but after a while it all gets to be too much. Lyric deserves someone who won't exploit her fame but isn't afraid of it either. Someone who's ready to be there with her, every step of the way, through the good and the bad." She pinned Poppy with a hard stare. "Can you tell me, honestly, that you believe Cash is that person? It's a lot to ask of someone, I know, but if Cash can't handle this, he needs to get out now before Lyric is in too deep and gets her hopes up that maybe this time is going to be different."

Poppy couldn't make any promises, but she knew the type of man Cash was. He didn't do things by halves. "When Cash is in? He's all in." Sometimes to a fault. Not that she was going to say that. She'd put her foot in her mouth enough times tonight already. "I've never seen him back down from a challenge and he isn't afraid to work his ass off. Unless you've got a crystal ball, your guess is as good as mine whether this time is going to be different. The rest? That's up to Cash and Lyric."

Rosaline looked up at Poppy through her long, dark lashes and sighed. "Unless you've been living under a rock, I'm sure you know Lyric has an album coming out in a month. We already discussed it before you got here, but she and I have agreed that—if tonight goes as well as she hopes it will—it would be prudent to keep focus on the album. I don't want its release overshadowed by a relationship that could very well be a flash in the pan."

"Keep focus on the album," Poppy parroted. They could save so much time if Rosaline just said what she meant instead of speaking in riddles. "Meaning what exactly? Wait—don't tell me. It involves another NDA."

By the time this was all said and done, Poppy would be able to recite the verbiage of Rosaline's NDAs verbatim.

Rosaline crossed her arms. "Until the album drops, I don't want to hear any whispers about Lyric's love life, only buzz about her music. For the next month, discretion will be of the utmost importance. That means no public outings or dates, no online exchanges anyone can pick apart, and absolutely no pictures. Cash Curran will keep Lyric Adair's name out of his mouth. He will not tweet about her. He will not talk about her. He will not wear her merch. Interview questions will be vetted ahead of time by yourself well in advance. If a situation arises where you *cannot* vet the questions, such as during a postgame press conference, Cash will answer any and all questions pertaining to Lyric in an appropriately vague manner. Do you think he can handle that?"

"I don't foresee any of that posing a problem for Cash."

"And you?"

"Don't worry." Poppy shot Rosaline her flattest stare. "I promise not to go on any public dates with your client."

"Cute." Rosaline's lips twitched like she was trying not to smile, and Poppy counted it as a victory. "But I was talking about whether or not you're prepared for the road that lies ahead of you if this relationship between our clients pans out."

"Can you ever *really* be prepared in this line of work?" Poppy mused, reaching for her soda. "I mean, half the job's about rolling with the punches, right?"

"There is a certain degree of improvisation required," Rosaline conceded with a tip of her chin. "But rolling with the punches doesn't mean failing to prepare. A failure to prepare is to—"

"Prepare for failure." Poppy hid her smile behind her wineglass when Rosaline frowned. "That's like *live, laugh, love* for athletes. I'm pretty sure Cash has it on a poster in his home gym. Hell, I think one of his teammates might have it tattooed on his ass."

Rosaline snorted. "Charming."

"You *really* don't need to underscore the importance of preparedness to me," Poppy promised. "Trust me when I say I take this job seriously. I know I've only been doing this *specific* job for a little over a year, but—"

"I'm not talking about sending a few press releases or working with the team's public relations coordinator. Chances are very good your client is about to be thrust into the spotlight."

"Cash is the best quarterback in the NFC West. He's already—"

"Portland famous. He's Pacific Northwest famous. And while Cash might look like he got dressed in a thrift shop in the dark, Lyric's not going to be the Ryan Lewis to his Macklemore, okay? She's a superstar. She sets records and then she breaks them. If Cash is going to be in her orbit, he is going to experience fame on a scale you can't fathom. And you? You're not just going to be along for the ride, you're going to be helping to steer the ship. Can you handle that?"

Honestly? She didn't know. How could she when this was all uncharted territory? There was hardly a *For Dummies* guidebook written for this.

"I welcome any words of wisdom you want to give, but you should know that Cash isn't the only one who isn't afraid of a challenge."

Maybe she didn't know what she could handle until she was handed it, but she'd never know if she didn't try.

Poppy held her breath as Rosaline gazed at her appraisingly from across the kitchen island, fingers tapping idly against the stem of her empty wineglass.

After an excruciating moment of silence, Rosaline sighed and offered Poppy a ghost of a smile. "I look forward to being impressed by you."

Chapter Four

Portland Pathfinders star quarterback Cash Curran spotted leaving home of Lyric Adair's publicist hours after game against the Chargers

---

**by Avery Michaels
published on September 22**

The Santa Ana winds are blowing, but is love in the air for America's favorite pop star?

A source exclusively told *Notoriety Magazine* that Curran was spotted leaving the Hollywood Hills home of the pop superstar's illustrious publicist, Rosaline Sinclair, hours after the Portland Pathfinders cinched a 27–19 victory over the Los Angeles Chargers at SoFi Stadium. This was the team's fourth win and overall game of the season.

According to the insider, Curran was seen leaving in a black Range Rover that took him and an unknown woman back to the Pathfinders' hotel, arriving shortly after one in the morning.

This comes less than two weeks after Cash Curran tweeted, publicly propositioning the pop star.

CASH CURRAN @cashcurran • 8/28
@lyricadair
Are you a Hail Mary? Because you seem like a long shot, but I'm willing to take a chance. 🏈🕷

Okay, Romeo, we see you! We can only imagine Adair's answer was a resounding yes given Friday's rendezvous. Only time will tell if this is a fling or if the romance is real, but we can't imagine Lyric's formidable friend and publicist would open her home to just anyone.

Rosaline Sinclair, the PR mastermind behind Adair's success for the last eight years since the star became emancipated at sixteen and switched management, is well known for being a cutthroat advocate for the star.

"I wouldn't want to cross her," a source who spoke on the condition of anonymity said. "Rosaline Sinclair is f——king scary. She could snap her fingers and Thanos your career out of existence."

Santa Ana, Adair's sixth studio album, releases in a month and after two years without a new album, fans are feral to know how the star really feels about her relationship and subsequent split from the Domestic Noir Plot drummer Ansel Daily. If her tryst with NFL's most eligible bachelor is anything to read into, Adair is definitely ready to move on.

The quarterback split from his model girlfriend, Ashley Tibbey, in January of this year. The pair were together for just over six months. More recently, Curran made waves in June when he released a statement on his Instagram account, coming out as bisexual. He was met with resounding support from the Portland Pathfinders and the NFL, both of whom matched his generous donation to The Trevor Project.

Curran, known as much for his fearless fashion statements as his brazen moves on the field, rocked a bright pink-and-purple-patterned silk Gucci button-up with white, double pleated AMIRI trousers. He flexed his sneaker game in a highly coveted pair of SB Dunk Low x Ben & Jerry's Chunky Dunky. As a note, *Notoriety Magazine* may collect a share of sales from the links on this page.

Time to place your bets on whether we'll be seeing our favorite pop star at a Pathfinders game!

At the time of publication, reps for Adair and Curran did not respond to *Notoriety Magazine*'s request for comment.

Comment? *No one* had reached out to Poppy for a comment.

This was a nightmare.

Any second now, Poppy was going to wake up in a cold sweat and this whole *fiasco* was going to have been nothing more than a bad dream, stress disrupting her sleep. Any second now. Any second . . .

"Fuck."

She pressed the heels of her hands into her eyes, a negative image of the photo she'd spent the better part of the last five minutes staring at in horror appearing behind her lids. This? This was bad, *so* bad. The only way this could get any worse would be if—

Her phone rang.

Poppy whimpered against the skin of her wrist, pulse pounding against her lips. She peeled her eyes open. Just as she'd feared, Rosaline's contact lit up her screen and not even the vocal stylings of Carly Rae Jepsen could calm her nerves. She was going to die. Rosaline Sinclair was going to charter a private plane and fly to Portland to personally see to it that Poppy's head rolled.

"Hi, Rosaline."

"Poppy," Rosaline greeted calmly. *Too* calmly. "How are you this morning?"

Poppy gulped. "I've, uh, been better."

Rosaline tutted. "I'm sorry to hear that. Though, I suppose I wouldn't be having a very good day if *Notoriety Magazine* called *me* an unknown woman, either."

Poppy winced. "You saw it."

"I saw it," Rosaline confirmed her fears. "What I want to know is how it happened."

How the hell was she supposed to know? "I'm guessing we were followed?"

"You're guessing?" Rosaline huffed. "Do you get paid for guesswork, Peterson? Must be nice."

Poppy sucked in a sharp breath and gripped her knees, nails biting into her bare skin, the sting grounding her, keeping her from apologizing for something she hadn't done. "No, of course not. But—"

"Maybe I should call you Jessica Fletcher considering your penchant for amateur sleuthing."

She said it like that was an insult, but Poppy would be *honored* to be compared to the best detective produced by network TV. "What do you want me to say?"

"I want you to tell me who Curran told so I can figure out who else I need to put the fear of God into today."

"No one." She rose from her bed on wobbling legs and made her way to the door so she could find Cash. "He didn't tell anyone."

He'd signed an NDA. They both had. Even if he hadn't, he knew what was at stake here.

"Not a teammate or a trainer?" Rosaline pressed. "A family member, maybe? Someone looking to make a quick buck?"

The fuck? That was just—*no*. "Absolutely not."

"Are you sure?"

Kissing and telling had never been Cash's style, *especially* not when he really liked someone the way he clearly liked Lyric, hearts practically appearing in his eyes each time he talked about her. But was it outside the realm of possibility that Cash, in all his excitement, had accidentally let something slip?

Poppy didn't know but she was going to find out.

"Let me call you right back."

"*No*, Poppy, don't you dare—"

She ended the call and took off for the basement Cash had converted into a home gym that put the Pathfinders practice center to shame. "Cash! Cash, are you down here?"

She skidded to a stop at the bottom of the stairs, eyes sweeping the room. Cash's back was to her as he straddled a weight bench, a dumbbell in each hand, grunting softly with each repetition.

Poppy sighed. "Seriously, Cash? Could you not hear me yelling?"

He kept at it, muttering—no, *singing* under his breath. Singing along to Lyric freaking Adair. Of course.

She stalked across the room and snatched the AirPod from his left ear. He jerked and swore.

"Jesus!" He glared hotly over his shoulder. "I could've dropped one of these."

She tossed the AirPod on the bench between his legs. "I've been saying your name."

Cash set the weights down and reached for the towel draped over the end of the bench. "I couldn't hear you."

She closed her eyes and bit back a sigh. No shit. "Look, just give it to me straight. Did you tell anyone?"

He mopped the sweat off his brow and looked blankly at her. "Tell anyone what?"

"*Yesterday*, Cash." Adrenaline coursed through her body, making her jittery. She knocked the hard-shell case of her phone against her thigh. "Did you tell anyone about last night?"

"Of course not." He tossed the towel over his shoulder and shrugged. "I promised not to."

"No one? None of the guys on the team? Not even DeAndre? In the locker room, after the game? Maybe you got excited, and you accidentally said something you—"

"De knows that I'm interested, but beyond that, no one knows I was talking to her, let alone that we had plans to meet up." He frowned sharply. "What's this about?"

"It's—" Her phone rang, vibrating in her hand. She groaned. "I'll fill you in later." She answered the call. "Hello?"

"You hung up on me." Rosaline sounded torn between shock and awe, as if the entire idea that someone might end a call before her was foreign.

"I told you I'd call you back and if you'd have waited two more minutes, I would have."

"Patience isn't a virtue I possess, Poppy."

No shit. "I talked to Cash, and he didn't tell anyone. Needless to say, neither did I."

"Needless to say," Rosaline said, sounding like it did, in fact, need to be said. "Well, the leak sure as hell didn't come from our camp."

Of course not. Because Rosaline was perfect and never messed up a day in her life. She probably came out of the womb walking, talking, and knowing how to handle a PR crisis. Whereas Poppy was just a fuckup waiting to happen. Got it.

"I know it's not what you want to hear, but it's not exactly a stretch that someone could've seen Cash get in a car outside SoFi and followed us. We also stopped at a florist so Cash could pick up flowers. It could've happened then."

A heavy, staticky sigh came over the line. "Fine."

Her phone beeped twice, and she pulled it away from her ear. The screen was black, the call disconnected.

Without warning, without reason, Rosaline had hung up on her. Unbelievable.

With a growl of frustration, Poppy turned and drove her fist into the standing punching bag behind her. Pain exploded in her knuckles, and she whimpered softly, quickly cradling her hand against her chest. The stupid bag barely wobbled.

"You okay there, Pop?" Cash asked, sounding concerned.

"Fine," she grumbled, shaking out her hand. *Goddamn* that hurt.

"You might want to put some ice on that."

Ice, huh? She could probably just chip some off Rosaline and call it a day.

Poppy was far from perfect, a fact she accepted with only a small amount of self-castigation on a good day. She wasn't afraid to own up to her mistakes when she made them, but this time she hadn't done a damn thing wrong. She might respect the hell out of Rosaline as a publicist, but she wasn't some punching bag for her to take out her anger.

Rosaline needed to understand that.

She answered on the third ring. "What."

Poppy cradled the phone against her ear with the hand not currently throbbing in time with her heartbeat. "I wasn't finished."

"Well," Rosaline said simply. "I was."

"You are impossible, you know that?"

"Excuse me?"

Fuck it. She was too stressed to mince words or care about the potential repercussions of giving Rosaline Sinclair a piece of her mind. She already thought Poppy was a hack who wasn't cut out for the responsibility that came with having a high-profile client; what harm could come from being forthright with her feelings?

"You heard me." Poppy punted a stray football out of her path, pacing the length of the gym. "I get that you're frustrated. I am too. But you don't get to be mad at me for something outside of my control and you *definitely* don't get to blame me for it."

"*You're* frustrated?" Rosaline scoffed. "In a single article, your client was praised for his prowess on the field, applauded for his daring fashion choices, and exalted for his philanthropy. The writer's lips were so firmly affixed to Curran's ass that a crowbar couldn't pry them free. And you're *frustrated*?"

It wasn't about what the article said, it was that the article existed at all. That they had been followed, that some creep had been hiding out across the street, lurking in the dark, surveilling them, waiting to snap a photo, to invade Cash's privacy and blast his personal business all over the internet. *That's* what pissed her off. "Cash deserved a say in how and when this got out too."

"And Lyric deserved better than having her upcoming album release reduced to relationship fodder in some rag sheet. *Again*," Rosaline grumbled. "*This* is what I was worried about. *This* is what I wanted to avoid. Her new single debuted at the top of the *Billboard* Hot 100 with sixty million streams, fourteen thousand digital downloads sold, and an airplay audience of thirty-three million, but did the article mention any of that? Of course not. Why would they laud her for her accomplishments when they could speculate on her love life instead?"

No one was suggesting Lyric deserved to have a major career moment undermined. She and Cash both deserved better. None of this was right and none of it was fair, but treating it like a competition for the shorter end of the stick was going to get them nowhere. "This sucks."

"You can say that again."

Poppy slid down the wall until her butt hit the rubber mat covering the concrete floor. It wasn't even noon, and she was ready to crawl back under the covers and call it a day. "What are we going to do? I mean, what's our plan now that people know?"

"You know, I was thinking we'd hard launch with a billboard on Hollywood and Highland."

"Okay, let's say we don't do that. What are we actually going to do?"

"Pivot, Peterson. That's what we're going to do. We're going to pivot. When's the next Pathfinders' home game?"

"It's a bye week," she said. "The game is next Sunday. Why?"

"Because." Rosaline sighed, deeply aggrieved. "Lyric's going to be there."

Chapter Five

"Pop-Tart?" Cash called out from the hall. "Can I come in?"

Poppy stared morosely at the bedroom door. "If you want."

The door opened, and Cash slipped inside the room, hair still wet from his shower. "I, uh, made your favorite." He lifted the glass in his hand, showing off the smoothie he'd made. "Strawberry matcha, which I stand by tasting like dirt, but you like it, so ..."

"You didn't need to do that." She held out a hand for the smoothie. "But thank you."

Cash hovered awkwardly beside the bed. "I just got off the phone with my folks. They'll be at the game. They're on board."

Part one of Rosaline's master plan to hard launch Lyric and Cash's relationship was in motion. If they couldn't stop people from talking, the next best strategy would be to make sure they were talking about Lyric and Cash's relationship the way they—Rosaline—wanted. By hard launching at an NFL game, not only would their relationship automatically have an international spotlight shined on it, but so would Lyric's upcoming album. And if Lyric was seen publicly interacting with Cash's parents, the relationship wouldn't look like some rebound; Lyric wouldn't look like a girlfriend—she'd look like potential daughter-in-law material.

She'd have to be blind not to see the plan's positives, but there were also a boatload of cons, most of which would befall Cash should the relationship go south. How was it Rosaline had put it? The higher you climb, the harder you fall? The more serious the relationship appeared, the more Lyric's fans would be crushed for her if they split. The blame would fall squarely on Cash's shoulders, and he'd have to face the fallout of breaking the heart of America's sweetheart pop star.

She couldn't help but worry.

Cash took a seat on the edge of the bed. "I know you're upset. That article blindsided all of us, but we talked, Lyric and I, and she's on board with this new plan. She doesn't want to hide—not me, not this, not any of it. And honestly? Neither do I. She's *amazing*, Poppy, and she deserves someone who isn't afraid to be all in with her. To—to walk in the sun with her."

Walk in the sun? "Have you been listening to Cyndi Lauper?" she teased.

He ducked his head, trying to hide the blush that crept up his jaw and turned his ears red. "Lyric likes her."

Her heart squeezed, affection swelling up inside her. Listening to new-wave pop? He really must be smitten.

"That's sweet." She squeezed his fingers. "And I'm not trying to discredit either of your feelings. I'm just nervous? It's—it's been less than a month, Cash, and you're already planning on going public."

He tugged his hand free and scowled petulantly. "It's a football game, not a marriage proposal. Would you be telling me I was moving too fast if some regular girl was coming to one of my games?"

"But that's just it. She's not a regular girl. She's *Lyric Adair*. A football game isn't just a football game—it's a declaration. You're going to be inviting the whole world into your brand-new relationship," she warned. "Are you ready for that?"

"This isn't a game to me," he swore. "Or if it is? I'm playing for keeps. I appreciate the concern, I do, but this is something Lyric and I need to figure out. Together. Because you're right about one thing—she's not a regular girl. This is her life and if I want to be a part of it, I need to get used to everything that entails, the good and the bad, the hard and the messy. Our relationship won't be real if we build it in a bubble. If we're gonna make it, we've got to learn how to drown out the noise."

When Cash put his mind to something, there was no deterring him. She knew better than to try. "If you say so."

"I do." He gave her a chuck on the chin and smiled. "Chin up, Pop-Tart. And don't let Rosaline Sinclair get in your head."

She rubbed her eyes and groaned. "You didn't hear the way she spoke to me on the phone. She thinks I'm a total hack."

A strange look passed over his face, his mouth opening and closing without saying a word.

She straightened and frowned. Nothing good ever came from a quiet Cash. He was kind of like a cat or a toddler that way. Silence usually spelled trouble. "What?"

"Nothing," he said, too breezy to be unfeigned.

"*Cash.*"

He scrubbed a hand over his face and sighed. "Okay, I didn't want to make it weird, but you work for *me*, Poppy. Not Rosaline. And for what it's worth, I couldn't be happier with your performance."

She snorted. "Right, sure. My inability to protect your privacy and keep your relationship hidden from the press really *screams* capable."

"I know you're not apologizing for something we both know damn well wasn't your fault. What's this really about?"

She gave her smoothie a stir, jabbing the straw through a piece of fruit that hadn't been totally obliterated by the blender's blades. "It's stupid."

"Lucky for you I'm fluent in dumbass." He gave her a lopsided smile and bumped her shoulder, jostling her lightly. "Come on. Lay it on me."

Can't say she didn't warn him. "I just wanted her to be impressed, you know?"

"Rosaline?"

"No, the Easter Bunny." She rolled her eyes. "Yes, Rosaline."

His brow furrowed. "Since when is the Easter Bunny a girl?"

She stared. "God love you, Cash, but when you said you were fluent in dumbass, I didn't need you to prove it."

"Off topic, right." He winced. "I can't say I love this, Pop. You twisting yourself in knots to win someone's approval."

She looked away, fiddling with her straw.

No one had ever taught her how to make friends and she'd definitely not been a natural at it. Eventually, she'd learned a cheat code, a way to fake it until she made it: mimicry. All she had to do was look around and imitate the people around her, do what they did. Watch the same shows, feign interest in the same silly gossip, shop at the same stores, and wear the same clothes. After a while, it wasn't too hard to secure invitations to the same parties where she learned to drink the same beer and play the same drinking games and fool around in the same closets. She'd learned how to fit in, but it had required constant vigilance. Poppy had never not been thinking, never not analyzing the behaviors of everyone around her and weighing her own against them. She could never drop her guard, never be herself and, after a while, she'd forgotten what being herself even looked like.

Who was Poppy Peterson anyway?

College had been a breath of fresh air, granting her the freedom to figure out who she was without all the bullshit artifice getting in her way, without worrying constantly what everyone thought of her. Classes had been challenging, work-study jobs had kept her busy, and the campus had offered a plethora of clubs, all opportunities for her to discover the beat of her own drum and learn to dance to it. Life had been good, and she had been happy, and then she'd graduated and got a job working at a midsize PR firm in Portland, which had been fine, and reconnected with a few old classmates, which had been ... less fine. Overnight, it had been like all the work she'd done on herself was erased and she was right back in high school, feeling wrongfooted and second-guessing her every move. Only this time, she had all the responsibilities that came with being an adult. All the stress.

Suddenly, Poppy had been unmoored. Cash, her best friend and the only person she'd never felt like she had to fake it around, was in Seattle, playing for the Seahawks. She was lonely and—it wasn't an excuse—she fell into some really terrible habits. A glass of wine to unwind after work all too easily became a bottle, and a beer with friends meant blacking out. Soon, she hadn't been able to function without a drink, a little something to take the edge off and relieve the near constant stress she was under. Stress that, in hindsight, was mostly of her own making.

The after-work and weekend drinks turned into a splash of vodka in her morning cappuccino and that splash became a shot and that shot became a heavy-handed pour that had her slurring in a meeting, and suddenly, Poppy was packing up her desk, fired. She'd gone to a local bar and—she'd already fucked up, why not drown her sorrows and numb the pain?

She'd woken up in the hospital missing the last twelve hours. Her parents had been called, her emergency contact, and they'd looked at her with such abject disappointment, as if they didn't recognize her. Not much of a shock considering they hardly ever spoke and when they did the conversations were little more than perfunctory, surface-level "how are you?" questions that were never intended to be answered honestly or deeply, Poppy already too much of a burden by simply existing, let alone requiring actual nurturing.

The real problem was that Poppy hadn't been able to recognize herself. She'd needed help, help that Cash had been eager to provide when he heard through the grapevine, from his grandparents, that she'd been in the hospital and later, when she spilled her guts to him on the phone and he learned the full extent of how not okay she was. He'd gotten on the first flight he could, helping her pack a bag and bringing her back to Seattle with him. A few short months later, Cash was the first player selected in the NFL's expansion draft and they were headed back to Portland. He'd needed a new publicist, Poppy had desperately needed a job, and the rest was history.

Cash was her rock, picking her up when she was at her lowest and helping her put herself back together, giving her a job and a place to live, helping her find a purpose. He'd saved her life and she'd never stop owing him for that.

So she understood his concern, but this wasn't history repeating itself. Approval wasn't what she was seeking from Rosaline or anyone else. She wasn't trying to be someone she wasn't, only the best version of herself. Whatever that looked like.

"It's not like that. I'm not tying myself in any knots, promise. I just—" She blew out her breath. Right now Cash was looking at her like he didn't quite believe her. "Do you remember how nervous you were before your first training camp?"

At three in the morning, he had called her, too keyed up to sleep. She'd kept him company all night, distracting him by forcing him to quiz her for her Gender, Media, and Diversity midterm.

He chuckled under his breath. "I thought I was going to hurl." He wrinkled his nose. "I think I did, actually."

"You knew you were good, that you were a first-round draft pick for a reason. But you wanted the coaches and the other guys who'd been playing for longer to see that you were good. You wanted them to give you a slap on the ass and tell you, *Good job out there, Curran*."

Cash burst out laughing. "Way to make it sound homoerotic."

She raised both brows.

"Okay, fine," he conceded, tipping his head. "It's a little homoerotic."

"Thank you."

"So what you're saying is, you want Rosaline Sinclair to smack you on the ass and tell you you're doing a good job?" He smirked. "Sounds kinky."

Her cheeks burned. "*No*, but she's the best of the best at what she does. She's the GOAT. It would be like if . . . Johnny Unitas told you that you played a great game."

"Johnny Unitas died in 2002, Pop. If he told me I played a great game I'd get my head checked."

She rolled her eyes. "Fine, it would be like if, God, I don't know, Peyton Manning told you that you played your ass off on the field. You'd have no doubt that you'd played a great game."

Unlike Cash, Poppy wasn't a first-round draft pick. Not even close. She'd been the equivalent of a free agent, hired only because Cash had needed someone, and she was there, with the bare minimum qualifications required to do the job. She didn't have a track record of being great, just a burning desire to be more than a pity hire.

So, no, it wasn't about approval or jumping through hoops to prove herself to Rosaline; it was about affirmation. She didn't *need* Rosaline or anyone else to tell her she was doing a good job. She just really, *really* wanted to hear it so that maybe that awful, insidious little voice in her head, the one that whispered that just because she hadn't yet didn't mean she still might not fuck up Cash's career the way she had her own, would shut the hell up for once. She hated that voice, would drown it if she could because . . . sometimes she worried it would drown her. The ultimate kill or be killed battle, only it was her against herself.

"I get it." The corner of his mouth twitched like he was trying not to smile. "There's nothing wrong with having a praise kink."

A—seriously? "Why are you so obsessed with my sex life?"

"How can I be when you don't have one?"

She set the glass down on her nightstand and snatched the nearest pillow, whacking Cash in the face. "This is bi-on-bi crime."

He snickered and stole the pillow. "Oh come on. I don't hear you denying it."

"I am a professional."

"A professional what?" he teased. "Simp?"

Without her pillow, she had to resort to using her fists, punching him in the shoulder.

"Watch the throwing arm!" He laughed.

"I can't believe a guy who started listening to Cyndi Lauper for his girlfriend called *me* a simp."

"Guilty." He grinned, unrepentant.

"*As I was saying.*" She narrowed her eyes. "I am a professional. Rosaline Sinclair is my—my *colleague.*"

She wasn't about to jeopardize her job or Cash's career because of an all too unfortunate crush. And dear *lord*, was it unfortunate, lusting after someone who thought the worst of her when they even thought of her at all. But what else was new? She'd never wanted what was easy or good for her. She was probably destined to die single and alone. Maybe with a few cats who loved her if she was lucky.

"It's hardly like you report to each other. And not that you need it, but if you're looking for it, as your technical boss, I give you blanket permission to bump uglies with Lyric's publicist should the occasion ever arise."

"*Bump uglies?*" Poppy wrinkled her nose. "What are you, twelve?"

"What do you want me to call it? Enjoy a little bangity-bang-bang? Shake the sheets? Cash in the Kegels? Partake in some hand-to-gland combat?"

"Hand to—*oh my god.*" She stared, jaw hanging, horrified. "You're a child. I cannot *believe* you bagged a girl like Lyric Adair."

He smiled soppily. "She likes my dumb jokes."

Like her grandmother used to say, there was a lid for every pot. "Well, whatever weird slang you want to call it? It's never going to happen."

She wished she could say she had enough self-respect that today had quashed her crush, but if anything, she just wanted to work that much harder to prove Rosaline wrong. Probably not the healthiest of motivations, but Poppy was nothing if not a perpetual work in progress.

"Stranger things have happened," he said. "I thought the same thing about Lyric and look at us."

He was the exception, not the rule, drawing from a seemingly indelible well of good fortune, one of those rare people who were lucky in life. Whereas Poppy didn't so much have a well as she had a shallow puddle that was dry most months of the year.

"The point is moot. I don't even know if she likes girls." For all she knew, Rosaline could be straighter than a two-by-four.

"You want me to ask Lyric?"

"You can't just ask if someone's queer, Cash."

He rolled his eyes. "I was going to, you know, be subtle about it."

Unfortunately, Cash wouldn't know subtlety if it bit him on the ass. "Your offer is both sweet and incredibly unnecessary." The last thing she needed was him meddling in her nonexistent love life and causing Rosaline to look at her like she was even more pathetic. "I just want her to take me seriously. That's it."

He scooted closer, knee touching hers. "Don't take it personally. Lyric says Rosaline is like this with everyone."

But Poppy didn't *want* to be everyone.

She was Poppy Peterson, damn it. She might not be the best or the brightest, but knock her down nine times and she'd—eventually—stand up ten.

Chapter Six

Sunday, October 7

PORTLAND PATHFINDERS @portlandpathfinders • 8h
WAKE UP, PATHFINDERS NATION! IT'S GAME DAY!! 🏟
#ATLvsPDX #PathfindersNation

CASH CURRAN @cashcurran • 4h
PUMPED AF! LF GOOOOOO!!! 🤘 #ATLvsPDX
#PathfindersNation

LIANA LIN-KATU CHANNEL 2 NEWS @lianalin • 35m
Currently at Pathfinders Stadium and there's a noticeable
heightened security presence. We were just stopped going into
the tunnel and told no photos. All press was made to put away
phones and cameras. More to come. #ATLvsPDX

CHELS @chelsyeah • 5m
you guys are never going to believe this but i'm working
concessions at the pathfinders game and lyric adair just walked
past me. wtf is happening rn 🫠

Poppy chewed on her thumb, shredding her nail, watching as the clock on the jumbotron counted down the minutes until kickoff.

Down on the field, the players were finishing their pregame warm-ups, some of them already headed for the locker room. In the end zone, Cash tossed a football back and forth with Pathfinders' tight end DeAndre Jones, who said something that made Cash laugh so hard he doubled over, hands braced on his knees.

"*Holy shit,*" Cassidy, DeAndre's wife, gasped and Poppy whipped her head to the side, mildly terrified that at nearly nine months pregnant, Cassidy's water had broken. Cassidy stared down at her phone, jaw hanging open. "Oh. My. God."

"What is it?"

She practically shoved the iPhone in Poppy's face. "Lyric Adair was just spotted inside the stadium. *This* stadium. Holy shit, what is she doing here?"

Someone had snapped a picture of Lyric entering the stadium, flanked on either side by plainclothes security guards.

"Wait." Cassidy pinched the screen to zoom in on the photo. "Number three." She looked at Poppy, eyes bulging. "She's wearing Cash's number."

It wasn't just his number—it was his jersey. An actual game-worn jersey the league would fine him at *least* five hundred dollars for giving away. It dwarfed Lyric's petite frame, the sleeves, even rolled, hanging down past her elbows and the hem grazing the middle of her thighs.

"Wow." Poppy tugged on her earring. "Huh, that's, uh . . . that's crazy."

"No fucking way." Cassidy scoffed. "You *knew*. You knew and you didn't tell me. The fuck, Poppy?"

Poppy winced. "I plead the fifth."

Cassidy smacked her arm. "Your constitutional rights aren't going to keep me from kicking your ass. I can't believe you kept this from me." She paused, eyes flitting to the field and narrowing. "Wait. Did DeAndre know about this? Oh my God, I am going to *murder* that man."

"De didn't know," Poppy promised. "No one did."

Other than Cash's parents, who were picking at the buffet on the other side of the suite, the only people who'd been told Lyric would be at today's game were the Pathfinders' and stadium's security teams. Even they had only been apprised of the situation on a need-to-know basis, liaising with the pop star's personal security detail to keep her safe going in and out of the stadium.

Poppy had *personally* put Lyric's management in contact with both the Pathfinders' director of security and the facilities manager, a task that, as Cash's publicist, really hadn't been her responsibility. But she'd gone the extra mile, cc'ing Rosaline on every email, Poppy's way of silently thumbing her nose at her. *Suck on that, Rosaline Sinclair.* That would teach her to underestimate Poppy Peterson's work ethic.

Cassidy grabbed Poppy by the arm, looking her dead in the eye. "Tell me *everything*."

Poppy shrugged out of her hold. "I kind of *can't* say anything."

Cassidy gave her an incredulous stare. "You had to sign an NDA?" She laughed softly and shook her head. "Who am I kidding? Of course you had to sign an NDA. It's Lyric freaking Adair. Holy shit." She glanced at the suite's door then back at Poppy. "Is she coming *here*?"

Poppy didn't see the harm in confirming that much when any minute now Lyric was going to walk through that very door. "Mhmm."

"*God*," Cassidy breathed and patted the top of her head. "How's my hair?"

Poppy smiled. "You look fine, promise."

Cassidy rested a hand on her bump and sighed. "If I'd have known this was going to happen, I'd have gotten induced last week." She pouted. "DeAndre's giant-ass baby is pressing on my bladder, but I don't want to be in the bathroom when she gets here."

Not five seconds later, the door to the suite opened, and in stepped one of the burly, plainclothes security guards Poppy recognized from the photo. He performed a quick visual sweep of the suite from the doorway before stepping to the side, whispers rising from the fringes of the room as Lyric stepped inside, Cash's number splashed across her chest like a mutual claim.

She spotted Poppy almost instantly, her megawatt smile lighting up the room as she ignored the stares and crossed the suite, throwing her arms around Poppy's shoulders. She smelled like vanilla birthday cake, marshmallowy sweet.

"It's so good to see you," she breathed against Poppy's ear. "I've been so nervous all morning, I thought I was going to throw up."

Grammy-winning superstar Lyric Adair, who'd performed sold out shows inside arenas much larger than Pathfinders Stadium, was nervous to—what? Meet a few players' wives? Poppy bit back a smile. That was actually really endearing. No wonder Cash was head over heels for this girl. "It's good to see you too. I'm glad you're here."

"Me too." Her gaze drifted over Poppy's shoulder, scanning the field, undoubtedly trying to spot Cash. "I didn't miss anything, did I?"

"Kickoff's not for another five." Cassidy waved. "Cassidy Jones, DeAndre's wife."

Lyric's eyes lit up with recognition. "Cash's friend! Tight end, right? Number . . . eighty-nine?"

"You got it." Cassidy grinned. "And clearly *you* need no introduction."

"Well, it feels bizarre not introducing myself, so . . ." She stuck out her hand. "I'm Lyric, Cash's girlfriend."

Cassidy's brows disappeared beneath her bangs. "Girlfriend, huh?" She darted a quick glance at Poppy before reaching out and shaking Lyric's hand. "Welcome. I was about to head to the bathroom, but you want me to introduce you to a few of the other players' partners?"

Lyric beamed. "I'd love that."

Cassidy linked her elbow with Lyric's, setting off across the suite.

As if sensing Poppy wasn't following, Lyric paused after a few steps and looked over her shoulder. "Poppy? You coming?"

Across the suite, Nina and Alexis, wives of Devon and Jerome Daniels, brothers and both linebackers who'd been drafted from Miami and Tampa respectively, waved at Lyric.

"You go ahead." Poppy wasn't a WAG—a wife or girlfriend of one of the players—and sometimes it felt a little like some of the wives were humoring her. Like, if she wasn't dating Cash, they didn't quite understand what she was doing hanging around. "I'll catch up with you later, okay?"

A soft, skeptical frown creased Lyric's forehead. "Are you sure?"

"Positive." Poppy pasted on a smile. "Have fun."

Lyric, who was originally from not far outside of Orlando, could bond with Alexis and Nina over . . . hurricanes and humidity, sinkholes, and . . . falling iguanas. Poppy didn't know. The farthest east she'd traveled was Denver. Florida was as foreign to her as the moons of Jupiter.

"Pathfinders are favored by three points."

Poppy jumped, elbow knocking the waist-high table in front of her, a frisson of pain shooting down her arm to her wrist. "*Jesus Christ.*" Her hand flew to her chest, heart fluttering frantically under her palm. Rosaline stood beside her, staring out at the field, arms crossed over her black-and-green plaid shacket. Poppy blinked at her. "Where did you come from?"

Rosaline looked at her askance. "The door?"

Poppy rolled her eyes. No shit. "You took me by surprise, is what I mean."

Rosaline turned slightly, pivoting to face Poppy. "You knew I was coming."

Again, not what she meant. "You could've, I don't know, walked less like a freaking jungle cat."

The corner of her mouth twitched. "I'll make sure to announce my presence next time." She gestured to the field. "I'll borrow a megaphone from one of the cheerleaders, maybe."

Cheerleaders in the NFL were dancers, really. "They don't use megaphones."

Rosaline's stare bore into the side of her face. "I was joking."

Poppy tugged the sleeves of her sweatshirt down over her wrists. "Funny."

"Question: Are you going to ice me out over our phone call all game?"

That was rich, coming from her. "The game hasn't started yet." Hurt bled into her voice, words wobbling and mortifyingly reedy.

Rosaline heaved a sigh. "You want to talk this out right now?" Her brows rose. "Really?"

You know what? "Forget it." Rosaline was right. Now wasn't the time to be having this conversation, assuming there was even a conversation to be had at all. "The game's about to start."

The Falcons had already taken to the field along with the Pathfinders, the captains heading to midfield for the coin toss.

"Poppy." The way Rosaline said her name, almost plaintive, made Poppy sigh and, against her better judgment, turn, reluctantly meeting Rosaline's eyes. Her gaze was already trained on Poppy, piercing and inscrutable, the rest of her expression equally hard to read, giving Poppy nothing. "I'm sorry, okay? I don't often find myself in a position of needing to apologize." She shrugged tightly, her voice dropping not to a whisper, but close. "Clearly, I don't really know what I'm doing."

"Something Rosaline Sinclair *doesn't* excel at?" Poppy scoffed under her breath. "Alert the presses."

Rosaline flinched, a flicker of hurt flitting across her face. "That's less of an anomaly than you seem to think." Her jaw shifted, her tongue pressing against the inside of her cheek. "Trust me."

Poppy's stomach twisted unpleasantly. "Okay, look, I'm—"

"No, you look." Rosaline darted a quick glance over her shoulder before stepping closer, standing hip to hip with Poppy. Her perfume tickled Poppy's nose, woodsy and sweet, citrus and patchouli. "I have been Lyric's publicist for the better part of a decade, during which time I have seen everyone from her parents to the media to guys she's dated, even people who have called themselves her friends, try to exploit her. Her own *parents*, Poppy." Rosaline pursed her lips. "I have very low expectations of most people, and for good reason. When I saw that article, I assumed history was repeating itself. Most of the time the most obvious explanation is the right one. You can't blame me for being cautious."

Caution was one thing, condemnation another. "No, but you can't blame me every time something goes wrong and then—then *stonewall* me. You aren't the only one with a job to do here."

A crease appeared between her brows. "You're right. A lot of what I said to you on the phone was reactionary. I was a bitch to you and for that, there's no excuse. I should've brought my concerns to you in a more . . ." She shook her head, lashes fluttering as she seemed to struggle to find the right word. "I don't know. Diplomatic manner. We should be working together, not against each other. I'm sorry."

Poppy let her breath out slowly, shoulders falling, the fight draining from her, Rosaline's words a better balm than she could've imagined. "I—okay."

Rosaline frowned. "Okay?"

"Yeah." She shrugged. "I accept your apology."

Rosaline looked at her askance, green eyes wary. "Just like that?"

"What? You want me to make you grovel or something?" She offered a tentative smile. "That's not really my style. Just promise you won't do it again and we're square."

"Okay." Her eyes flitted over Poppy's face, making her warm all over. "I promise."

Poppy released a breath through her nose and turned back to the field. The Pathfinders won the coin toss and elected to kick. "Favored by three points, you said? You know the over/under?"

"Forty-seven." Rosaline joined Poppy in watching the field. "Should be a good game."

"For Cash's sake, I'm hoping for a shutout."

"With the way the Falcons' offense has been looking so far this year? I wouldn't hold my breath."

Unfortunately, Rosaline was right, the odds of a shutout were slim to none. "As long as they win, I guess the score doesn't really matter."

Cash had never wanted to win a game as badly as this one. Not even the Super Bowl, he'd said.

Rosaline hummed in agreement as Lamar Reynolds, the Pathfinders' kicker, sent the ball soaring, the Falcons fielding it in the end zone for a touchback.

"By the way, I tried, but I couldn't get Cash out of today's postgame interviews." Under the league rules, players were required to be available to the media after every game and at least once during the practice week. Avoiding the media came with a hefty price, a $50,000 fine for not abiding by the NFL's policy. Players diagnosed with concussions were exempt from mandatory media obligations until cleared per concussion protocol, but that was about it as far as exceptions went. She'd checked, but unless Cash wanted to fork over a cool fifty grand, he was SOL. He was doing well for himself, but not well enough to throw around that kind of money. He wasn't that frivolous either. "But don't worry; we've rehearsed what he should say if he's asked about Lyric, and he knows to block and bridge to generate intrigue instead of outright—"

"Poppy." Rosaline sighed and Poppy could've sworn it sounded almost fond. "It's Sunday. We are at a football game. Do you really want to talk about work?"

Well, no, but—what else were they going to talk about? The weather?

"Besides," Rosaline added. "I trust that you've properly prepared Curran to handle the media."

"You do? I mean—" She cleared her throat. "Good. I'm glad. Because I have."

"Good," Rosaline echoed, sounding amused. "Now, nix the work talk. Barring a crisis, Lyric has made me promise not to talk about work today under threat of bodily harm, and seeing as how I take my promises seriously . . ."

"Is that why you're here then?" Poppy asked. "In case of a crisis?"

"If that's your way of asking if I'm suggesting you couldn't handle a crisis on your own should one arise, I'm not. I'm here as Lyric's friend, not her publicist."

"She's your only client, right?"

"Mhmm."

"How'd that happen?"

Rosaline let out a short laugh. "I'm pretty sure this conversation falls under the purview of *work talk*, Poppy. In fact, I'm positive it does."

"It's work talk adjacent," she argued. "I'm hardly asking you for your opinion on cultivating media relations or reputation management. It's called getting to know each other."

Poppy loved football as much as the next person who'd attended a Division I college, but there was still only so many stats she could discuss before running out of things to say.

Rosaline gave another of those fond-sounding sighs. "I was working at Avalon Records, overseeing publicity for their folk and rock divisions. Our offices were in the same building as a production company that was interested in developing a reality series starring Lyric. Lo and behold, I wandered into the bathroom on my break and stumbled on Lyric sobbing her eyes out because she wasn't interested in being a reality television star. She was miserable. Overworked and exhausted and the very definition of burned out, sixteen with three studio albums and a world tour under her belt, ready to retire." Rosaline shot her a look. "I didn't poach Lyric from her previous publicist, no matter what the rumor mill likes to say. I just gave her my business card and told her to call me if she ever needed a shoulder to cry on because it seemed like she might. A week later, my phone rang. Lyric told me she wanted to file for emancipation, that her parents were mismanaging her money. Spending all of it, really. I helped her find a lawyer and a new manager and when she needed a place to stay, I moved her in with me. A few months later, I left my job and started Rarity PR, working solely as her publicity manager."

No wonder Rosaline was so protective of Lyric. She'd practically raised her. Acted as a big sister, at least. "What you're saying is, you basically adopted a sixteen-year-old." When Rosaline was only what? Twenty-three? Twenty-four?

"A sixteen-year-old who'd been forced to grow up way too fast. She's more like a little sister to me than a client," Rosaline said, confirming her suspicions.

It wasn't like any sibling relationship Poppy was familiar with, but then again, her relationship with her brother and sister was . . . calling it unique would be an understatement. "Do you have any siblings? *Other* siblings, I mean."

"Two sisters."

"Let me guess. You're the oldest."

"No, actually." Rosaline flashed a wide smile and for the first time Poppy noticed her right incisor was pointier than the left. A cute little fang that gave her otherwise perfect smile character. "I happen to be the baby of the Sinclair family."

Poppy jerked her head back. "Get out. You are not."

"I am." Rosaline drew an *x* across her chest with her index finger. "Though, Helen and Bianca are twins, so they have that whole infamous twin telepathy connection working in their favor. They're only two years older than me, but they're closer to each other than I am to either of them. Growing up, sometimes it felt like I was an only child."

"Same. I mean, not with the twin telepathy thing, but my brother was a junior in college and my sister was a senior in high school when I was born."

Rosaline gave her the same horrified look everyone did when she told them about the age gap between her and her siblings.

"It's weird, I know. Trust me." However bizarre it sounded, the reality was weirder. Poppy didn't have enough fingers to count the number of times her parents had been mistaken for her grandparents. "My mom and dad were done having kids. I mean, I don't think my mom thought she could even *have* any more." At forty-five, Mom had assumed her childbearing years were behind her. "It ended up being like that show that used to be on TLC, *I Didn't Know I Was Pregnant*. Mom thought she'd put on some weight over the holidays and then she thought her appendix had ruptured and," Poppy said, waggling her fingers, "surprise! I was born a perfectly healthy six pounds eleven ounces."

"Jesus," Rosaline breathed. "I don't even know what to say."

She shrugged. "It wasn't all bad. It's how I met Cash. My parents aren't much younger than his grandparents. His parents lived—well, they still do—not far from Lake Oswego, down in Dunthorpe. But he'd visit his grandparents on the weekends, and we were neighbors." She smiled. "Not to brag, but I don't think very many people can say that Cash Curran taught them how to play football."

"Oh yeah? You take the powder-puff world by storm?"

"God no." Poppy laughed. "I was awful."

"You couldn't have been *that* bad."

"This isn't me being humble. Balls and Poppy? Do *not* mix."

Rosaline snickered and Poppy played back what she'd said, full-body cringing when her words caught up with her.

"*Sports* balls," she stressed. "It's my hand-eye coordination. It sucks."

"Mhmm, sure." Rosaline's lips folded in, the corners of her mouth twitching and her eyes crinkling like she was trying not to laugh. "You just say things, don't you?"

Poppy sighed. No use denying it. "My mouth does tend to get me in trouble sometimes."

Rosaline's gaze dropped, her eyes lingering on Poppy's lips. "I bet."

A frenzy of butterflies filled her stomach and her heart sped, beating an almost painful tattoo against the cage of her chest.

Poppy didn't know what the hell was going through Rosaline's mind, but she definitely hadn't imagined *that*. No way, no how could Poppy pretend she was seeing things when Rosaline was staring at her mouth like it was an answer to a question she'd forgotten to ask. A question maybe Poppy hadn't heard. She didn't *know*, and that was the crux of it all—she couldn't just *ask*.

"Hey." Lyric appeared beside them, all but vibrating with excitement. "Mind if steal Rosaline for a sec? I want you to meet Cash's parents."

Poppy pasted on a smile she prayed didn't look manic. "Go! Have fun!"

Lyric was already moving, cutting back across the suite to where Cash's parents stood waiting. Rosaline lingered, half smile fixed even as her eyes traveled from Poppy's head down to her feet, a slow, full-body perusal that left Poppy lightheaded. "I think you and I have different definitions of *fun*."

Chapter Seven

By the time halftime rolled around, Poppy's stomach was well on its way to trying to cannibalize itself.

She'd skipped breakfast and lunch, too nervous to choke down more than a handful of popcorn and three stale Altoids that had lost their signature cinnamony kick. Now it was nearly six thirty and Poppy was starving.

She eyed the buffet table with a growing frown. She didn't want miso-glazed salmon or chicken cordon bleu from a chafing dish. She wanted nachos. *Pulled pork* nachos. Slathered in sour cream and queso blanco, covered in pickled jalapeños and pico de gallo. Or some loaded jojos maybe. *Ooh,* with bacon bits. Real, greasy stadium food, the kind she had to trek to one of the concession stands to find.

Poppy slipped the strap of her purse over her shoulder.

"Going somewhere?"

"*Jesus,*" she yelped, hand flying to her chest, heart slingshot into her throat. "You have *got* to start wearing a bell."

Rosaline snorted softly. "Hate to break it to you, but collars aren't really my style." She cocked her head, dark hair spilling over her shoulder like ink. "Besides, that noise you make when I sneak up on you? Extremely amusing."

Poppy swallowed hard, toes curling inside her sneakers. She

could think of a few other noises she could make that Rosaline might find equally as diverting, but she wasn't going to because it would only make her feel crazier than she already did. "Well then, for your sake, I hope it will be a funny heart attack."

Poppy's stomach took that moment to unleash another ungodly growl. Not one of the noises she had in mind, but Rosaline laughed anyway.

"Hungry?"

"Starved." Poppy pressed a hand against her stomach. "I'm going to find food."

Rosaline arched a brow. "You realize there's a whole table of food behind you, right?"

"Yeah, well, I don't want chilled asparagus swimming in lemon aioli or a tuna niçoise salad board." She liked asparagus as much as the next person but . . . "It's a football game. I want nachos."

She wouldn't go to an expensive steak house and order a hot dog any more than she wanted to eat shrimp cocktail and ahi poke while watching guys in tights tackle each other.

Rosaline pursed her lips. "Okay." She turned on her heel and marched straight for the door.

Poppy stared for a moment before her feet got with the program and she hurried after Rosaline. "Where are you going?"

"If I have to smile and pretend to be nice to one more person who just wants to pick my brain about Lyric, I'm going to commit homicide." Her lips twitched. "That and you kind of sold me on the nachos."

"You're saying you don't think you could manage Lyric's PR from prison?"

"It's more that I look god awful in orange than my lack of faith in my ability to do my job from inside a cell."

Oh, bullshit. Rosaline was one of those people who could make a paper bag look like haute couture. "I don't know. I bet you'd rock a prison jumpsuit. Very, uh, *Orange Is the New Black*, you know?"

A surprised laugh burst from Rosaline's lips. "Don't get me wrong, Taylor Schilling's pretty and all, but I, for one, am kind of hoping I never have to find out how well I'd fare in a penitentiary."

Pretty. Poppy tried hard not to make a face at Rosaline's use of the ultimate ambiguous compliment. *Pretty* could mean everything from the straightest of flattery to *that dress would look better on my floor*.

Rosaline's footsteps slowed as they reached the end of the hall. "Left or right? I have no clue where I'm going."

To be fair, the place was a maze, not helped by the fact that the halls all looked the same, the walls identical cement block painted light charcoal, the floors throughout the stadium all the same forest green stamped with the Pathfinders logo, two interlocking capital *P*s.

"Unless you want to wind up in the visiting team's locker room? Left."

"I think I'll skip that part of the tour if you don't mind." Rosaline wrinkled her nose. "Eau de sweaty football player doesn't really appeal to me."

"I think you mean *ew* de sweaty football player."

Rosaline laughed. "Touché."

Poppy tugged her ponytail in front of her mouth, hiding her smile behind her hair. Every laugh from Rosaline was a windfall, an unexpected boon that put a bounce in her step, mirroring the lightness in her chest. "Aside from narrowly avoiding a felony charge, are you enjoying the game?"

"I am. And to be fair, it was mostly only Cash's mother who tried to pump me for information."

"Ah." Poppy winced. "Yeah, Eileen can be a bit of a, uh . . . mother hen."

"That's certainly one way of putting it."

That sounded ominous. "What did she say?"

If Eileen said something truly egregious, Poppy would have to pass it on to Cash. He'd want to know.

Rosaline sighed and pressed her fingertips to the space between her brows. "She asked me if Lyric plans to retire after having children."

Oof. That was—bad, putting the cart *way* in front of the horse. "I wish I could say I'm surprised, but Cash's parents are kind of—"

"Fossilized?"

"I was going to say *traditional*, but yeah, that works." Poppy rolled her eyes. "It took forever to convince them that there was nothing going on between me and Cash, that contrary to whatever old-fashioned notions they had, guys and girls could be just friends."

Rosaline cast her a sidelong glance. "So you and Curran never . . . ?"

Poppy shuddered so hard she almost crashed into the wall. "God, no. Cash is—he's like my *brother*. No offense to him or whatever, but *definitely* not."

Rosaline's shoulders relaxed, rolling down and settling low, arms loose at her sides. "Jocks not your type?"

"Not really?" Poppy hedged as they stepped out onto the crowded concourse on the western side of the stadium. "To be fair, I don't think I have a type."

The only thing any of the people she'd dated—and she used that term loosely—had in common was that they'd all eventually dumped her, leaving Poppy for greener pastures.

"Maybe you just haven't found what you're looking for."

"Maybe." Though looking implied she was putting actual effort into trying to find someone and Poppy hadn't been out on a date in over a year. "What about you?"

They joined the line outside PDX Grille, queuing up behind a guy who'd foregone a shirt, half his torso painted green, the other half black, the colors in the middle muddied by the sweat dripping down his back. Rosaline squinted up at the menu. "Football players aren't really my type, either."

"Darn," Poppy joked. "And to think Cash wanted to introduce you to Goliath."

Rosaline whipped her head toward Poppy, her eyes comically wide. "*Goliath?*"

She bit the inside of her cheek, trying not to smile. "Yeah. Robert Haverford. Number fifty-four, offensive tackle. They call him Goliath because he's six eight and weighs, like, three hundred and eighty pounds. Cash thought you'd make a cute couple."

Rosaline's eyes narrowed. "See, I know you're fucking with me, but in case Curran ever gets the bright idea to play Cupid? Tell him he can save his breath."

"Oh? Are you, uh, seeing someone?"

It was a fair question, perfectly within the realm of polite get-to-know-you conversation.

"No." She shot Poppy another sideways look. "But I don't have any problems procuring my own dates."

Somehow, Poppy had no trouble believing that. "That makes sense."

The corner of Rosaline's mouth dimpled. "Does it?"

Heat crept up Poppy's throat and into her cheeks. "I mean, you're . . . you know."

Gorgeous. Confident. Sexy. Successful. Practically a celebrity in her own right. Rosaline could take her pick of adjectives and she wouldn't be wrong.

"I don't, actually." She arched a brow. "Enlighten me."

Poppy pretended to study the menu despite already knowing exactly what she planned to order. "You just . . . strike me as a person who knows what they want and isn't afraid to go after it. That's all."

Rosaline hummed softly and their shoulders accidentally bumped together as the line moved forward. Poppy was ready to move away, worried she'd invaded Rosaline's personal space when she swayed, seeming to purposefully bump into Poppy. "You're not wrong. I am rather—"

"The fuck you mean you don't take cash?!"

Beside her, Rosaline froze, and Poppy did the same, eyes trained on the guy sweating off his body paint and bitching at the harried-looking worker behind the concessions counter.

The woman offered him an apologetic grimace as she set a plastic cup full of foamy beer on the counter. "Sorry, sir. We went cashless at the start of the season. But there are cash-to-card kiosks located throughout the stadium if you need one."

"'s fucking ridiculous 's what it is," he slurred, obvious that this beer was far from his first. He flicked his credit card across the counter and didn't even try to stifle his laughter when it hit the worker in the chest and fell to the floor, forcing her to bend down to pick it up.

Rosaline's lips flattened into a thin line, her nostrils flaring delicately. "Prick."

The man stiffened, drawing up to his full height, a hulking six-foot-four, easy. Poppy cringed and stepped back. Shit.

He glared over his green-painted shoulder. "What did you just call me?"

"You heard me." Rosaline stood her ground, unflinching. "She's undoubtedly underpaid, overworked, and doesn't make the rules; lay the fuck off."

A stale, beer-soaked sigh exploded from his lips and—it was like watching a car wreck happen in slow motion. One second, he was twisting around and the next his glassy eyes were widening as he stumbled and lost his footing on a souvenir football someone had dropped, the beer he held sloshing up the sides of the cup and over the rim, spilling onto and instantly soaking through Poppy's sweatshirt all the way to her skin.

He gaped at her, then frowned at the empty cup in his hand. "Fuck that. I'm not paying for this."

He tossed the cup to the ground and staggered off, disappearing into the sea of fans, forgetting all about his credit card.

"What a *fucking* moron." Rosaline's scowl softened as her eyes swept over Poppy's beer-soaked body. "Are you okay?"

Poppy smelled like a dive bar, like sour citrus and skunky hops and it made her head swim and her eyes sting. She couldn't go back to the suite smelling like this. Everyone would think—*Eileen* would—

"Poppy?"

"I'm fine." Her voice sounded far away, faint and garbled like she was ten feet underwater.

Rosaline watched her with a sort of intensity that suggested she didn't believe her, the sort of intensity that would normally make Poppy shiver, but right now just made her want to curl in on herself. "Would you like to try that again?"

She swallowed twice, tongue fat and uncooperative inside her mouth, and plucked at the pocket of her hoodie, pulling the sodden sweatshirt away from her skin. "I just—I need to get this off." She scanned the concourse with eyes that failed to focus, the hall a dizzying blur of black and green with the occasional splash of red thrown in. Her stomach churned and her lower lip wobbled. Fuck. "I need to find a—a merch stand."

A hand wrapped around her wrist, grip gentle but firm, Rosaline's touch grounding, real in a way nothing else felt right now. "Come on."

Rosaline tugged, giving Poppy no choice but to follow her down the hall and into the restroom, where she bullied Poppy into the big stall all the way at the back. She locked the door and dropped her hand, reaching for the hem of her beer-soaked sweatshirt.

Poppy's breath hitched in her chest. "What are you doing?"

"What's it look like?" Rosaline's eyes flickered to hers, her steady gaze a lifeline Poppy desperately clung to. "Arms up."

She didn't hesitate; she lifted her arms over her head and held still, letting Rosaline drag her ruined sweatshirt up her body and over her head, leaving her in nothing but a thin blue T-shirt bra and her denim cutoffs. Goose bumps erupted across her skin the second the chilly, air-conditioned air hit her damp skin. A shiver lashed up Poppy's spine and she crossed her arms over her chest.

Rosaline let the sweatshirt fall to the floor with a soft splat before turning to the sink inside the stall and turning the tap all the way to the left, as hot as it would go. She ripped one, two, three paper towels from the dispenser on the wall and ran them under the steaming stream of water, soaking them before squeezing them out. She turned back to Poppy, soggy paper fisted in her hand. "Is it okay if I touch you?"

"Yeah." Poppy uncrossed her arms and let them hang limp at her sides. "Okay."

Carefully, almost as if she were afraid Poppy might spook,

Rosaline stepped closer and reached out, brushing the warm, wet paper towel against Poppy's stomach.

She held impossibly still, breath trapped in her chest as Rosaline wiped the remnants of beer off her skin, eyes flitting to Poppy's face every few seconds as if checking in, making sure that this, *she*, was still all right.

Poppy was not okay.

Sour spit filled her mouth and no matter how many times she swallowed she couldn't get rid of it, the smell of beer stuck in her nose, so cloying she swore she could taste it on the back of her tongue. The paper towels Rosaline was using to wipe her down were scratchy and rough, like sandpaper against her skin, but she wasn't—she wasn't scrubbing hard enough. Each too-gentle stroke might as well have been a lash butterflying Poppy open, all the tender bits she painstakingly kept tucked away on display beneath the harsh light of a flickering fluorescent bulb.

She wanted to snatch the paper towels from Rosaline's hands and scrub until the skin of her stomach turned red and raw and angry, until she was *clean*, but she couldn't move, pinned in place by Rosaline's stare and the free hand she'd curved around Poppy's waist, her palm a brand against Poppy's bare skin.

"Your bra looks dry," Rosaline said, voice no louder than a whisper. "I think it's fine."

Poppy opened her mouth to say that was a relief, that bras were expensive, and this was one of her favorites, basic but pretty, so it was a good thing she wasn't going to have to trash it or beg a vendor for a bag to stick it in, but instead a sob burst from her lips like a gunshot in the quiet of the restroom.

Under any other circumstance it might've been comical how fast Rosaline's eyes widened, going as big as saucers, but there was nothing funny about any of this.

"*Sorry.*" She pressed the heels of her hands against her eyes, trying to stave off the tears burning the backs of her lids. "This is—*God*, this is so embarrassing. I'm so sorry."

Mortifying, more like it. Never before had Poppy wanted so badly to just—disappear.

"Hey, no." Rosaline gently tugged Poppy's hands away from her face. "You're fine."

She shook her head and Rosaline sighed. She hadn't let go, her thumbs sweeping against the back of Poppy's knuckles where the skin was stretched taut over bone, Poppy's fingers curled tight against her palms into fists. It took a moment for her fingers to unclench and when they did, her knuckles ached all the way to her wrists.

"Shit happens," Rosaline said, the corner of her mouth quirking. "No use crying over spilled beer, right?"

When people talked about how even the most mundane places could feel holy, the sentiment had never resonated with Poppy. Communing with nature might've been one thing, but it wasn't like Poppy had ever felt God in the middle of a Trader Joe's cheese aisle.

But maybe she did get it, because standing here shirtless and shivering inside the handicap stall felt a lot like being tucked away inside a confessional. Which was the only logical explanation for why she opened her mouth, sins spilling out like soda from a can that had been shaken. "Maybe. But I don't, uh, I don't drink. Not—not anymore. Not since I . . ." She let the sentence hang, trailing off with a stiff shrug. "I smell like beer and Cash's parents, they'd, um, they'd think I—" Poppy had to pause to swallow and catch her breath. "They might not say it, but they'd assume."

Assume she'd fucked up. And they'd talk to her parents, who would assume the same, everyone except for Cash waiting for the inevitable moment when Poppy would drop the ball and prove them right. How could Cash think it was smart to trust Poppy with the responsibility of managing and maintaining his public image when she wasn't even capable of keeping her own life on track?

"Well." Rosaline's voice was measured, careful in a way that Poppy hated. "You know what they say about assuming."

Poppy scoffed and dragged the pad of her thumb under her eyes, flakes of mascara smearing against her skin. "It's not even like they'd be wrong."

Rosaline frowned and Poppy sighed.

"Not about—" She pressed her palms against the bare skin of her stomach, and it dawned on her with a dizzying rush of blood to her head that she was standing there, almost half naked. She quickly crossed her arms. "*That*. But look at me." Who was she kidding? This wasn't a confessional, it was a stadium bathroom that smelled like Fabuloso and that generic pink soap that was in all public restrooms. Rosaline was no priest, she was Lyric Adair's publicist, and even though Poppy hadn't said the word, she had basically just told Rosaline she was an alcoholic. Brilliant. Fuck flirting; Poppy was doing a stellar job of selling herself *professionally*. "They didn't want Cash to hire me. They didn't think I was cut out for this." And maybe they were right. Maybe she wasn't. "I mean, here I am, having a panic attack in a bathroom stall because some asshole spilled beer on me, spilling my guts to *you*, and—you didn't sign on for this. Hell, you already think I'm a total hack so maybe they're right. Maybe it is only a matter of time before I fuck up."

Again, just like always, her capacity for screwing up and disappointing the people who mattered to her most knowing no bounds.

The longer she rambled, the more pinched Rosaline's face became, her eyes flinty and her mouth drawn into a scowl. "I am looking at you." Her chin rose. "And you want to know what I see?"

Not particularly and not now when it felt like she was made of spun sugar. Like with one wrong word she might shatter into hundreds of thousands of tiny shards like mirror ball glass. She swallowed hard and braced for impact. "What's that?"

Rosaline's scowl softened. "I see someone who cares a great deal about the people she loves. Someone who is tenacious and clearly isn't afraid to speak her mind." Her breath shuddered softly from between her lips, and she took a step closer to Poppy. "Someone who wants *desperately* to do a good job. And anyone who cares that much?" She shrugged. "Everyone stumbles sometimes, but you're not going to fuck up, Poppy."

Her eyes burned with a vengeance, and she hugged her arms around her body, fearing she might fracture, that Rosaline might actually kill her with kindness. She stared at the floor, at Rosaline's black Adidas, and blinked fast. "You can't know that."

"Yes, I can." She tipped Poppy's chin up with two fingers that lingered against her skin even after she had met Rosaline's startlingly green eyes. "You want to know how?"

She couldn't find her voice, so she nodded instead.

"Because . . ." Rosaline said, her hand drifting down, curling to fit against the front of Poppy's throat, thumb notched in the space between her clavicles. Not squeezing, just holding, presence not pressure. Poppy's breath stuttered anyway, her heart rattling against the inside of her ribs. "I said so. Because I *told* you so." Rosaline's thumb swept across the hollow of Poppy's throat. "And you're not going to make me wrong, are you, Poppy?"

Something inside her snapped. Her self-control, her sanity, any guess was as good as any other. She sucked in a breath that felt like breaking the surface of a lake after spending too much time underwater and melted into Rosaline's touch.

A slow, almost imperceptible smile spread across Rosaline's face, a little hitch at the left corner of her mouth. Instantly, Poppy's chest flooded with warmth, the feeling like she'd done something right, incomparable, second to none.

Several stalls away, a toilet flushed, and Rosaline jerked back, hand falling to her side, the little bubble they'd made burst. Poppy immediately mourned the loss of her touch.

"We're, uh." Rosaline shivered as she exhaled, dark lashes fluttering with each blink of her heavy lids, looking more discomposed than Poppy had ever seen her. "The game. We're missing the game."

"Right," Poppy croaked. The reason they were here. "The game."

"You can't go out there wearing nothing but a bra." Rosaline shrugged out of her plaid shacket. Her black bodysuit hugged her curves, fitting her like a second skin. "Not that anyone in their right mind would complain."

Poppy goggled at her. "What?"

Rosaline blinked back. "Did I stutter?"

This was officially the weirdest day of Poppy's life. Maybe she was hallucinating? "Um."

"Here." Rosaline tossed Poppy her top before bending to pick Poppy's beer-soaked sweatshirt up off the floor. "Put that on and let's go." She unlocked the stall door. "I don't know about you, but I still want those nachos."

Chapter Eight

DANI^LA @danianne • 5h
so which oomfs want to teach me about football because this game makes no sense 👉🙄👈

VICTORIA @pdxprincess • 3h
so you're telling me that not only is cash curran the goat, he's also the master of turning delulu into trululu? hats off my king 🫡

NFL UPDATES @unofficialnflupdates • 3h
The @portlandpathfinders and @nfl official accounts are now following @lyricadair.

LYRIC ADAIR UPDATES @lyricadairupdatesunofficial • 3h
Lyric Adair's publicist @rosalinesinclair is now following @cashcurran.

PORTLAND PATHFINDERS @portlandpathfinders • 2h
Another day, another win for the Pathfinders!! 🏈 #ATLvsPDX #PathfindersNation

MAYA ANA @mayaana • 2h
This has got to be the most obvious example of a PR relationship I've seen in my life.

AVA @avababy • 1h
My friend is working at xport tonight and Lyric Adair is there with Cash Curran and a bunch of other Pathfinders players. They're all over each other, apparently

They didn't talk about it.

Not in the suite and not after the game when they slipped out with Lyric to wait for Cash outside the locker room. Poppy would've thought the whole thing was a fever dream, a delusion cooked up by all the cortisol floating around inside her brain, except she still had Rosaline's shacket and Rosaline's words were imprinted in her memory.

Because I said so. Because I told you so. And you're not going to make me wrong, are you, Poppy?

Today might've been a shit show, and she might've spent a decent portion of it doubting herself and driving herself batty by reading into every word and glance of Rosaline's, but like Rosaline had said, Poppy cared too much to fuck this up. It didn't matter that she couldn't remember the last time anyone had been that gentle with her or touched her with half as much care as Rosaline had inside that bathroom stall.

Enough was enough. The moment had been charged, no doubt, Poppy had a job to do, and she wasn't about to ruin the progress she'd made with Rosaline by mistaking kindness for interest or seeing signs of a connection where there had been . . . civility.

It was getting late. She had spent the better part of the last two hours on X, trying to keep her finger on the pulse of what people were saying about today's full-throttle, real-life hard launch of Cash and Lyric's relationship. Not easy to do considering everyone and their brother was talking about it. Cash and Lyric were trending on every platform, news site, and search engine, Lyric's appearance at the game having generated maximum exposure, captivating her followers, Cash's fans, and sports enthusiasts alike. Poppy was struggling to keep up with it all, her eyes crossing.

It was time to call it a night.

The doorbell rang and she started, laptop sliding off her bent knees and into her lap. She set it on the coffee table and stood, stretching her arms above her head with a yawn that made her jaw pop. The doorbell rang again, making her sigh. "Coming!"

She swore, if Cash forgot his house key again, she was going to suggest he start tying a spare to his shoelaces because, honestly, this would make it the third time in as many weeks, which was a little—

Ridiculous.

Rosaline, not Cash, stood on the front porch holding a Sizzle Pie pizza box in one hand, the other poised to ring the bell for a third time.

She rubbed her tired eyes and—nope, she wasn't seeing things. Rosaline was actually standing there, still wearing that curve-hugging bodysuit tucked into her black leather pants, an amused smile creeping across her face.

"What are you doing here?"

Rosaline held up the pizza as if that answered Poppy's question. "Can I come in?"

She stepped aside, letting Rosaline pass. Rosaline paused to step out of her shoes and as she did, her eyes swept the room, surveying her surroundings.

"Nice place Curran has." She studied the giant abstract fresco on the wall with a curious tilt of her chin. "A little modern for my taste, and it could use some color, but it's hardly the bachelor pad I was expecting." Rosaline glanced at Poppy over her shoulder and arched a brow. "Or did you decorate?"

She shook her head. "He told me I could change whatever I wanted when I moved in, but it's not like I plan on living here forever, so I didn't see the point."

Rosaline hummed. "I imagine you'd stay in Portland?"

Aside from the four years she'd spent living in Eugene, she'd never lived anywhere else. And that was less than a two-hour drive outside the city. It barely counted. "I mean, Cash is here. My job is here. Unless he decides to go somewhere else, which wouldn't happen until his contract's up in another four years, Portland's home." She locked the front door. "Lyric isn't here, by the way. They're still out celebrating with the team, I think."

With its twin rooftop patios, outdoor bar, and amazing view of the Willamette, xport rooftop lounge was the Pathfinders' go-to postgame celebration spot.

"I know." Rosaline made herself at home in the middle of Cash's couch. "I was just there. You weren't."

"Bars aren't really my scene," she said, perching on the arm of the couch.

"I figured," Rosaline said, voice free of judgment, but also absent of condescension. Like she was just stating a fact. The grass was green, and Poppy didn't frequent bars.

Poppy chewed on her lip. "So, you decided to come here? Doesn't your family still live in Portland?"

If she hadn't been staring so intensely at Rosaline, she might've missed the minute pursing of her lips. "My parents do."

"We could've comped them tickets to the game. If you'd wanted."

Rosaline flipped open the pizza box. "Football isn't really their thing." She held out the box. "You want?"

Poppy stole a slice of what looked like Sizzle Pie's Don Caballero pizza—pepperoni, sausage, green peppers, and onion—and settled in on the cushion next to Rosaline. "If football isn't their thing, what is?"

It was hard for her to wrap her brain around anyone in this city not having at least a passing interest in the sport, but that probably had more to do with the circles Poppy ran in than reality.

Rosaline stared up at the ceiling, her tongue pressed against the side of her cheek. "I don't know. Exceptionality?" Her head lolled to the side and whatever she saw on Poppy's face made her snort out a laugh. "My father founded a green architectural design firm here in the city and was recently recognized with the Progressive Architecture Award for outstanding strides made in the field. My mother is a glass sculptor with permanent collections in the Smithsonian and the Musée des Arts Décoratifs in Paris. My sister Helen is principal cello in the New York Philharmonic, and Bianca's doing a stint in Berlin as a guest tattoo artist, but before that she attended RISD, got her BFA in painting, and was awarded the Guggenheim Fellowship." Rosaline paused, frowning slightly. "I think she got the Carnegie Prize too, but I honestly can't remember."

"Damn." Poppy whistled. "And then there's you." Renowned publicist to one of the bestselling artists in the world. Talk about an impressive family.

"And then there's me." Rosaline lowered her eyes, lashes casting a faint shadow on her high cheekbones, her expression shuttering. "I saw my parents last Christmas, and I'll see them again in a few months at Thanksgiving."

She knew an *end of discussion* when she heard one, and she knew better than to press. Families were complicated. No need to tell her that. "So, you came here. How'd you even know where Cash lives?"

"If Curran doesn't want his address on the internet, tell him to buy his next house under an LLC."

Not many things rendered her speechless but learning that Rosaline had scoured the county records for Cash's home address came close. "You realize you could've texted me, right?"

"I could've. But then I'd have probably missed out on seeing you in those delightful sushi pajamas."

"If that's sarcasm, I'm choosing to ignore it."

"As is your right." A flush spread down Poppy's throat as Rosaline's gaze raked over Poppy from top to bottom in another of those dizzying full-body perusals, the second of the day. "They're cute." She grinned. "Very . . . Delia's circa 2008."

Ugh, *cute* was even worse than *pretty*.

Poppy screwed up her face, feigning confusion. "Very what?"

Rosaline arched a brow. "Don't be a brat, Poppy."

Poppy shivered at the soft censure in Rosaline's voice and plucked a pepperoni off her pizza. "You still haven't said what you're doing here."

"I'm sorry, did I interrupt your big Sunday night plans to," Rosaline said, squinting at Poppy's computer screen, "comb through Curran's mentions?"

Poppy stretched forward and closed her computer, hiding her search history from Rosaline's prying eyes. She still hadn't answered Poppy's question. "You mean you *haven't* looked at what people are saying online?"

"Who do you think I am? Of course I have." She set the pizza box down on the coffee table beside Poppy's laptop. "But eventually you've got to know when to call it a day and get some rest. Even I know that."

"Wow." Rosaline Sinclair lecturing *her* on having a work-life balance? "And here I thought you never slept."

"I suppose that's better than the rumor that I sleep in a coffin. You know, with being out for blood. Poaching Lyric and vilifying her exes." She snorted. "Like they don't do a perfectly good job of that themselves."

"I just thought that if you slept, you probably did it with one eye open," she teased.

Rosaline leveled her with a flat glare. "Funny."

Poppy saw straight through her faux consternation and smiled. "I try."

"If you want to know the truth," Rosaline said, tucking her right leg under her, resting her arm along the back of the couch, and facing Poppy, "I came over because I wanted to see how you were doing. I know today was . . . not easy."

"Oh." She blew out her breath. Not easy. That was one way to put it. "Yeah. It was . . . a day." She set her slice of pizza back in the box, no longer hungry. "Aside from being mortified that I treated a public bathroom stall like my own personal confessional?" She shrugged. "I'm okay."

"You shouldn't be. Mortified, I mean. What you told me? Won't ever leave that bathroom stall if that's what you're worried about," she promised.

The thought hadn't even crossed her mind. "I'm not. But I appreciate that."

Rosaline pressed her lips together, pausing for several seconds as if weighing her next words. "You know that you don't have anything to be ashamed of, right? Not for what you said and certainly not for saying it."

She lowered her gaze to her lap. "Not everyone would agree with you on that."

Most people looked at any kind of dependency as a weakness, a personal failing. Her parents did.

"Yes, well, not everyone's as brilliant as I am." Rosaline tossed her hair over her shoulder with a sort of casual confidence Poppy couldn't help but find attractive. "We all have our crosses to bear."

The weight on her shoulders lifted, leaving her lighter than she'd felt all day. "Thanks. Not just for saying that, but I didn't get a chance to thank you for everything you said earlier. For, you know, talking me off the proverbial ledge."

Rosaline's lips quirked at the corners. "Don't mention it. This is a stressful job and, after a while, that stress can take its toll. I've watched a lot of people in this industry burn out, seen a lot of people come and go because they didn't have—"

"*Whoa*, I haven't always had the healthiest of coping methods, sure, but if you're suggesting I can't handle this or that my freak-out earlier was because of work—"

Rosaline pressed a finger to Poppy's lips, silencing her. "If you'd have let me finish," she said, glowering softly, "you'd know I wasn't suggesting that at all. I mean, God, did you not hear a word I said in that bathroom?"

She lowered her hand, giving Poppy permission to speak.

It took a moment to make her mouth work, her lips tingling where Rosaline had touched her. One touch and she was right back in that stadium, dazed and confused courtesy of the woman currently studying her like she was the puzzle and not the other way around. "No, I did. I heard you. I just—sorry, what *were* you suggesting?"

"Honestly?" Her plump bottom lip disappeared between her teeth, a look on her face like she was gearing up to say something. "I was about to propose a mutually beneficial way we could both blow off some steam, but now I'm wondering if I've read this entirely wrong."

Her mouth dried up instantly. "What?"

She waited for the penny to drop, for Rosaline to burst out laughing and take the words back, say it had all been a joke. Only, for the second time today, Rosaline looked utterly discomposed, as lost as Poppy felt, a deep furrow forming between her brows as she stared uncertainly at Poppy. "Am I? Reading this wrong?"

The words *mutually beneficial* and *blow off some steam* echoed through her brain on an endless, maddening loop. "To be clear, when you say reading *this* wrong, you mean . . ."

"Oh my God." Rosaline scrubbed a hand over her face and sighed. "You know what? I'm going to go."

She latched on to Rosaline's wrist. "Wait. You just—you took me by surprise, okay? I wasn't even sure if you—earlier, that thing you said about jocks not being your type . . ."

"Not unless they play powder puff." Rosaline smirked.

"Huh. Okay." Those times she'd wondered whether Rosaline was flirting hadn't been the product of her overactive imagination after all. "To be honest, until today, I kind of thought—I didn't think you thought of me like—well, I didn't think you thought of me much at all."

Rosaline looked at her like she was crazy.

"Hey, in my defense, you're hardly an open book, Rosaline. You're like the—I don't know, like the fucking 'Epic of Gilgamesh.' One second, you're staring at my mouth, and I can't figure out if you want to kiss me or for me to stop talking forever. The next you're asking me what my angle is. You can't blame me for being confused by what you want."

Rosaline scoffed. "Well, suffice it to say, I think of you plenty. It's honestly irritating how often I do."

"You know," she huffed. "If you keep throwing around words like *irritating*, you're going to make me wonder if *I'm* the one reading this wrong."

"Something you need to know about me," Rosaline murmured, low and with purpose, making Poppy's blood hot, "is that I don't like wanting what I can't have. Hence my irritation."

Her breath hitched at the intensity of Rosaline's gaze. "So, when you say *blow off some steam* . . . I think I'm going to need you to be *really* explicit here."

She wasn't entirely convinced Rosaline wasn't talking about playing a rousing game of paintball at this point. Maybe duking it out in some ring. She needed it all spelled out for her, to avoid any sliver of doubt that this was actually happening inside her head.

"Explicit *is* sort of the whole point." Rosaline smiled sharply, teeth flashing white against the dark pink of her mouth. "I've got a capacious imagination and a list as long as my arm of things I've been thinking about doing to you since the moment you stepped through my front door. But if you want me to be specific? Most of them involve stripping you down, laying you out, and taking you apart until you're strung out and shaking." She reached out and, with two fingers, tucked a strand of hair behind Poppy's ear, grazing the bolt of her jaw. "Is that specific enough, or would you like a demonstration?"

Holy shit. She fought the urge to squirm and pressed her knees together, an unignorable ache settling hot and heavy between her thighs. "At least buy a girl dinner first," she joked, a little breathless.

Rosaline looked pointedly at the pizza box, then back at Poppy.

"Oh." She flushed. "Prepared really is your middle name, huh?"

"Look, this job eats up ninety percent of my time. I don't have time to date. Even if I did, do you know how hard it is to find someone who checks even *half* my boxes?" The question was obviously rhetorical. "Discretion is vital considering what I do and who I work for. Then there's the fact that work comes first for me, and most people don't understand that. Or they'll say they do, but they really don't. Factor in my personal preferences—"

"Is this where you tell me your desires are very singular?" Falling back on humor was sort of Poppy's go-to when she felt overwhelmed and this? Was very, *very* overwhelming.

Rosaline rolled her eyes. "I don't want to do anything to you that you don't beg me for. What I actually meant is that I'm not looking for anything serious. No strings. I like you, Poppy. You're smart and you're funny and I don't hate spending time with you."

"That's a real ringing endorsement," Poppy murmured.

Rosaline continued as if she hadn't spoken. "More importantly? We both have skin in this game, and I trust you not to run and blab my business or Lyric's, which *is* my business, to the press. Most importantly?" She placed her hand high on Poppy's thigh, thumb slipping under the soft flannel of Poppy's sleep shorts. "I'm really, *really* dying to hear what you sound like when I make you come." Rosaline's thumb swept an arc along the bare skin of her inner thigh and Poppy couldn't suppress the shudder that rolled through her despite the mild irritation still simmering in her veins. "Does any of this sound like something you might be interested in?"

She was no stranger to the occasional one-night stand, even if that kind of sex usually left her unsatisfied, with an unresolved ache between her thighs and an itch under her skin she couldn't quite scratch. But none of those hookups had ever made Poppy want like this. Want so badly she could barely breathe, barely *think*, her hands shaking, and fingertips tingling with the need to touch and be touched in turn, skin hungry and desperate after only a few heady promises.

Rosaline had made it clear what was—and wasn't—on the table. Even if Poppy wanted more, a year ago her life had been in shambles and today she was still facing the consequences of her choices, still piecing her life back together. Besides a cargo hold's worth of baggage and a full-size bed in a house that wasn't hers, what did she have to offer anyone right now, let alone someone as exceptional as Rosaline Sinclair? At least Poppy was self-aware enough to recognize her own shortcomings.

There was only one problem that made her hesitate, that kept her from blurting out an enthusiastic *hell yes* and launching herself at Rosaline, eagerly accepting everything she had to offer.

"Wouldn't this sort of be a conflict of interest?"

Rosaline's hand went still. "How?"

She shrugged. "I don't know. You work for Lyric and I work for Cash and—"

"You're not going to be thinking about work while I'm fucking you, Poppy." A violent little shiver slithered down Poppy's spine when Rosaline grazed the crease of her thigh with the edge of her thumbnail. Rosaline smirked and did it again to the same effect. "If I'm doing it right, you're not going to be thinking very much at all."

Fuck it. Poppy spread her legs, silently asking for more. "I just don't want you to think I don't take my job seriously."

"Don't worry." Rosaline withdrew her hand from the bottom of Poppy's shorts and reached for the drawstring at her waist. "I promise I'll still respect you in the morning, Peterson."

She had to be able to hear how hard Poppy's heart was beating. Hell, people down in Clackamas County could probably hear it thundering inside her chest as Rosaline's fingers flirted with the scalloped lace at the top of Poppy's panties.

"That's—that's a relief," she stuttered.

"So, are we good?" Rosaline's eyes flitted from where Poppy's sleep shirt was slightly rucked up her stomach to her face. "Because I really want to touch you now."

"Please," Poppy breathed.

Rosaline snapped the elasticized lace band of Poppy's panties and chuckled when another shudder rolled through her, the subtle sting raising goose bumps along the skin of her thighs. "Begging?" She grinned. "Already?"

Poppy's hips canted forward and lifted slightly off the couch, silently asking for Rosaline to stop teasing and to actually touch her. "Is that what you like?" Rosaline's hair had once again fallen loose from the braid tossed over her shoulder and Poppy gave in to the impulse to tuck a strand behind her ear, to let her touch linger, tracing the plains of Rosaline's face, fingers skimming her jaw, a smile tugging at her lips when Rosaline turned her face into the touch, her cheek pressed to Poppy's palm. "You want me to beg you for it?"

Another breathy laugh escaped Rosaline's parted lips, hot air gusting gently across Poppy's wrist. "I'm certainly not going to complain if you do." Her hand slipped lower, palm cupping Poppy, fingers parting Poppy's folds. Her dark lashes fluttered rapidly, and a soft groan fell from her lips. "You're already soaked," Rosaline whispered hoarsely. "You really need this, don't you?"

Poppy nodded jerkily and drank in the look on Rosaline's face, her jaw slightly slack, glossed lips parted, her eyes heavy-lidded, and gaze dark, locked on where her hand was hidden inside Poppy's shorts, looking as wrecked as Poppy felt, and Poppy—Poppy hadn't even touched her.

That needed to change. Poppy cupped Rosaline's cheek with purpose and leaned in, heart pounding as she closed the distance between their faces, ready to finally, *finally* learn what Rosaline's mouth felt like against hers, to find out if Rosaline's lips were as soft as they looked, if—

With a turn of her head, Rosaline swerved, lips brushing Poppy's cheek. "No kissing, okay?"

Poppy tried not to frown.

Kissing was one of her favorite pastimes. In fact, she missed the days where it was the main event rather than a step to sprint past on the way around the rest of the bases. But kissing was intimate, probably why she liked it so much, feral for affection of any kind. Maybe Rosaline had the right idea, kissing a little too intimate for whatever this was. Blowing off steam. Physical release.

Catching feelings for Rosaline Sinclair was the last thing Poppy needed.

Poppy nodded. "No kissing."

Rosaline leaned back in, lips skimming the skin of Poppy's throat, leaving a trail of shivery heat in their wake. Poppy closed her eyes, dizzy with desire, head filled with the spicy sweet scent of Rosaline's perfume.

"Hold on." Rosaline shifted, right hand sliding between Poppy's back and the couch, urging her to turn. With one arm now banded around Poppy's waist, she dragged her closer, Poppy's back pressed against Rosaline's front, her body nestled in the cradle of Rosaline's thighs. She brushed Poppy's hair over her shoulder, giving it a gentle tug that sent pleasant tingles down Poppy's spine. Her head fell back against Rosaline's shoulder.

"What do you like?" Her teeth grazed the underside of Poppy's jaw and Poppy couldn't have swallowed the whimper that rose up in her throat when Rosaline's fingers slipped back inside her panties and dragged up her slit, finding her clit swollen, sensitive. "Tell me."

Her hips shifted restlessly, bare skin of her thighs sticking to the leather. "More."

Rosaline hummed. "More what?"

Just—*more*. All of it. She tried to rub her thighs together, to alleviate this ache even just a little, but Rosaline was quicker. One hand dropped, the one not buried between Poppy's legs, her grip against Poppy's thigh bruising. A sob of frustration slipped out.

Rosaline had the audacity to laugh. "I asked you a question." Her hand returned to Poppy's hair, fingers carding through the strands at the nape of her neck, nails raking against her scalp. Her lips closed around the lobe of Poppy's ear and nipped.

Poppy's breath stuttered, chest heaving. It was hard to think, let alone form words with Rosaline's fingers rubbing her slowly. Up and down Poppy's slit, making a maddening circuit from her clit to where she was dripping. "I can't—can't think when you're touching me."

"I could always stop if you want," she offered, voice sly as if she knew exactly how much Poppy *didn't* want that. Her fingers made light circles around Poppy's clit.

"Please don't." She rocked against Rosaline's hand, seeking the friction she desperately desired. "Please."

"God, you beg so *pretty*." A faint warmth blossomed in Poppy's chest, and she had about three seconds to bask in the glow of Rosaline's praise before two of her fingers were slipping inside Poppy and crooking forward. Rosaline's mouth pressed against the hollow beneath Poppy's ear. "Is this what you wanted?" she asked, lips curving against Poppy's skin.

Poppy arched against Rosaline, trying to get Rosaline to press harder, fuck her faster. "Uh huh."

Rosaline curled her fingers a little harder, giving Poppy almost exactly what she wanted. "You should see yourself. Riding my fingers like you just can't get enough. Like you're desperate for it." Her teeth grazed the side of Poppy's throat, breath ghosting against her skin. "*Are* you desperate for it?"

Her thighs trembled, her insides fluttering. "*Yes.*"

The answer tumbled off her tongue, more breath than word, an almost soundless noise drowned out by the heartbeat inside her head.

Rosaline tightened her fist in Poppy's hair, dragging a whine from her throat. "I want to hear you say it."

Poppy shut her eyes, a wicked blush creeping up her jaw, heat flooding her cheeks. "I'm—" Her voice cracked, and Rosaline huffed a laugh, breath hot against her neck.

"My, my, have I actually rendered Poppy Peterson speechless?" Rosaline nipped at the thin, sensitive skin covering Poppy's collarbone, the sharp sting sending a bolt of pleasure to her center. Rosaline drew reactions from Poppy she couldn't control, the muscles in her calves twitching and her toes curling and back bowing. Each hard, ever quickening curl of her fingers drove Poppy a little closer to the edge, pressure building, pleasure licking up her spine. "So fucked out and you haven't even come yet."

Her words toed the line between condescension and praise, just the right side of mean, setting Poppy's blood on fire. They made her want to work harder, do as Rosaline had asked, chase that feeling she'd gotten when Rosaline told her she begged pretty. She unstuck her tongue from the roof of her mouth and licked her lips. "Can I?"

"Hm." Rosaline licked a stripe up the side of Poppy's throat, soothing the earlier sting. "Can you what?"

Poppy's chin wobbled and she struggled for breath.

Rosaline tsk-tsked softly. "Come on. You can do it."

That. Want turned to need and Poppy threw out a hand, clutching Rosaline's thigh. "Can I come?"

"I don't know." Rosaline smiled against Poppy's neck. "*Can* you?"

Just like that, the hand between her legs stilled and Poppy bit down hard on the side of her tongue, choking on a stifled sob.

Rosaline gave a throaty chuckle followed by a lazy thrust of her fingers, keeping Poppy hovering right there on the edge, her whole body thrumming like a live wire, close but not close enough. "You're desperate now, sure. But I wonder . . . just how desperate can you get?"

This . . . this was either going to be the best thing that ever happened to Poppy, or it was going to kill her. Maybe both, but there'd be no in-between.

"*Please*," she tried, knowing that had worked like a magic word once before.

Rosaline slipped her fingers from Poppy's cunt, making her whimper at the loss, her legs shaking and hands clenching, squirming in Rosaline's lap. "Hm, no. Not yet."

"*Rosaline*," Poppy whined high in the back of her throat, earning another of those soft—*evil*—chuckles.

"You'll come when I want you to come," she said, circling Poppy's clit with a featherlight touch. "You want to know why?"

"Tell me," she begged. Whatever hoop Rosaline wanted Poppy to jump through before she'd let her come, Poppy would eagerly hurl herself through it.

"Because right now?" Her fingers slipped through Poppy's wetness, three pressing inside, the unexpected stretch so good Poppy keened. "When we do this?" Rosaline sank her teeth into the side of Poppy's neck and sucked, no doubt leaving a mark, a bruise that Poppy could press in the morning, a tender reminder of this fever dream of a night. "When we do this, for however long we do this, you're mine, Poppy."

Poppy was past the point of speech; all she could do was steal greedy, gasping gulps of air as Rosaline dragged the pads of her fingers against the front wall of Poppy's cunt as if with a single-minded purpose—to make Poppy lose her goddamn head.

Mine.

She had never belonged to anyone before. Not in any way that counted. Even if it was only temporary, only for a short while, and even if it wasn't *exactly* how Poppy wanted to belong to someone—and wanted someone to belong to her in kind—something inside her swelled, bright, and hot, and hungry. And it had nothing to do with the brink Rosaline was nudging her toward with each relentless stroke of her fingers.

"Poppy?" From the way Rosaline said it, this wasn't the first time she'd called her name, Poppy too lost inside candy-coated thoughts to hear it.

"Mm?"

"Are you?" Rosaline tugged on Poppy's earlobe with her teeth. "Are you mine?"

Poppy nodded so fast her head spun. *"Yes."*

Rosaline released a ragged breath and pressed a kiss against the bare skin where Poppy's sleep shirt had slipped, the place where her shoulder met her neck. Shockingly sweet when her fingers were making filthy slick noises between Poppy's thighs. "Good girl."

Time stopped.

For a moment she didn't even breathe, could've sworn her heart quit beating. Even her thoughts went silent, her head filled with static, perfect pink noise roaring in her ears. She shivered under the praise and—that whine came from *her* throat as she arched, writhing against Rosaline's hand.

She was so fucking close. If Rosaline just pressed a bit harder, a little more—

The heel of her hand ground against Poppy's clit, snatching the breath from her lungs and sending her into orbit. Her lids slammed shut, muscles clenching around Rosaline's fingers as she shattered.

"That's it. I've got you." Rosaline worked her fingers harder, faster and—it was too good, pleasure so sharp it almost hurt. *Almost.* She jerked, blunt nails digging into the leather covering Rosaline's knee, a whimper verging on a sob escaping her lips as she shook so hard her foot almost hit the coffee table. Rosaline shushed her softly. "You're so fucking pretty when you come, I—" Rosaline swore under her breath and her teeth dug into Poppy's neck.

She sounded *wrecked*, her voice hoarse and hushed. Nearly reverent.

But that could've just been her imagining things. A delusion brought on by all the oxytocin racing through her veins, turning her brain to postorgasmic mush.

After a moment, Rosaline's fingers slowed before stopping altogether. Still inside Poppy, but not making any moves as if to prolong the pleasure, just keeping her full in a way that Poppy wasn't used to after sex but definitely appreciated. Normally after she hooked up with someone, *this* wasn't on the menu. Maybe a few seconds of postcoital cuddling happened while everyone caught their breath, but as soon as the sweat started to cool? Someone would roll out of bed or pull away, righting their clothes or making a beeline for the bathroom.

Nine times out of ten, that someone wasn't Poppy.

Rosaline had lowered her arm, a pleasant weight around Poppy's waist, her hand practically a brand against Poppy's sweat-slick skin. Silence stretched between them, fractured only by the sound of their breathing, but unlike most silences, this one didn't make Poppy's skin crawl with an unbridled itch to fill it.

Time passed, how much she couldn't be certain, Poppy floating, brain blank. Thoughts pleasantly quiet, her focus zeroed in on the way Rosaline's pinky swept a soothing arc just above Poppy's hip. Almost hypnotic, grounding in a way that she didn't entirely understand but wasn't about to question.

Another minute passed, maybe two or three before Rosaline withdrew her fingers with a sigh Poppy would swear sounded reluctant. Poppy frowned and pressed her knees together, drawing them a little closer to her chest, empty in a way she really didn't like.

Another of those soft whines she didn't mean to make escaped her lips and—*god*, she wasn't normally like this. She needed to get a grip. Pull herself together before Rosaline got the wrong idea and thought she was a needy mess with a bad habit of taking a mile when someone gave her an inch.

Poppy frowned.

The right idea, maybe.

Rosaline pressed another of those too-sweet-for-what-this-was kisses to the side of Poppy's jaw and stretched out her arm, snagging a slice of forgotten pizza from the box on the coffee table. She brought it to Poppy's mouth. "Eat."

Poppy let go of the passing thought that Rosaline was holding the slice with the hand that had just been down Poppy's panties, those same fingers that had been inside her now pinching the crust, and opened her mouth for a bite. Rosaline held the slice for her until she had made it all the way to the garlic butter–covered crust, which she stole for herself.

Slowly, Poppy came back to planet Earth, blinking back the fog that had wrapped around her mind like her favorite weighted blanket. She tilted her head, letting it loll against Rosaline's shoulder. Rosaline was already staring down at her, lids heavy and pupils eating up all but a thin ring of vibrant green. A smile played at the edges of her lips, very cat that got the cream. Satisfied, even though Poppy was the one who'd just come so hard her brain had leaked out her ears.

"That was really . . . wow."

"*Wow?* Really? That's what you're going with?" Rosaline's pinky continued to sweep against Poppy's skin, driving her to distraction. "Not, I don't know, phenomenal? Spectacular? I mean, Jesus, Poppy, come on. Stroke my ego."

She bit her lip, trying and failing not to smile. "I could always stroke something else?"

Rosaline's expression flattened and she gave Poppy the most deadpan of stares. "That was terrible."

"Sorry." Poppy shrugged. "Guess my brain's still coming back online."

Rosaline grinned. "See? Now, that's more like what I want to hear."

The pizza had been great and all, but between all the gasping and panting, Poppy was parched. Her tongue slipped out, wetting her lips, and Rosaline's eyes flitted downward, following the move with laser sharp focus.

Poppy's breath stuttered and stalled and, for a wild second, it seemed like Rosaline *was* going to kiss her. That she was going to—

Her face was cast in sudden stark relief as too-bright headlights flashed through the gauzy curtains covering the front window. Poppy held her breath, fingers crossed it was just a car turning around in the driveway. The lights blinked out and a car door opened a second later, dashing her hopes.

Rosaline blew out a frustrated breath and scooted backward on the couch, putting a foot of distance between them that felt chasmal. A similar yawning pit opened inside Poppy's stomach. "I'm guessing that's Curran."

She sounded about as happy with his arrival as Poppy felt.

Poppy frowned. "You didn't get to—"

"It's fine," Rosaline said, shifting until her feet were flat on the floor.

Poppy begged to differ.

Her reluctance must've shown on her face because Rosaline said, "Hey. Seriously, it's fine, Poppy." She reached out with her pinky extended and hooked it around Poppy's. She lifted their joined hands and pressed her lips to her own fist, sealing whatever promise they were about to make with a kiss. Something inside Poppy's chest splintered, cracking like a glow stick at just how silly the gesture was *period*, but especially coming from Rosaline. "You'll get me next time."

She tried to laugh, but it came out as a shaky exhale. "So, there *is* going to be a next time?"

Rosaline looked at her incredulously. "What about my having a list as long as my arm of things I'd like to do to you was unclear?" Uncertainty flickered across her face. "Unless *you* don't want to—"

"No. I mean, I'm a little skeptical this isn't all part of some dastardly plan of yours to kill me, but I do. Want to. Again."

Rosaline chuckled, warm and throaty. "But what a way to go, right?"

The front door swung open, and Cash and Lyric stumbled inside joined at the lips, the way she was blindly working to tug Cash's belt through the buckle suggesting they were about three minutes from being joined at the hips too.

He pulled away from Lyric with a gasping laugh and stared down at her borrowed jersey with uncensored awe splashed across his face. More of Lyric's lipstick was smeared on his chin and the tip of his nose than left on her mouth. "God*damn*, girl." He whistled. "Did I tell you how good you look wearing my last name?"

"Lyric!" Rosaline barked.

"Holy shit." She pressed her palm to her chest. "What the fuck, Roz? What are you doing here?"

Rosaline stood and set her hands on her hips. "Where are Ravi and Elliott?"

"I told them to go back to the hotel."

Rosaline made a strangled noise like she'd swallowed her tongue. "Excuse me? I must've misheard you because it sounded like you just said you sent your *security detail* back to the hotel."

"What? It seemed like overkill." Lyric shrugged. "What was I going to do? Ask them to spend the night on Cash's couch? That would've been so weird."

"I wouldn't let anything happen to her." Cash wrapped his arms around Lyric's waist and hooked his chin over her head. "I've got a kick-ass security system."

Rosaline shot him a murderous glare. "Does your '*kick-ass security system*,'" she said, making sure to put that in quotes, "come with a Glock 22, QuikClot Combat Gauze, and military training?"

Cash had the decency to look abashed, regretful even. "Uh—"

"Yeah, I didn't think so," Rosaline said, voice clipped.

"Back off, Rosaline," Lyric snapped. "It was my decision, not

Cash's. And Ravi and Elliott followed us here. Hell, they're probably still outside idling by the curb because they're more terrified of you than they care about listening to me. You're overreacting."

Rosaline pinched the bridge of her nose. "I swear to God, if I go gray before I'm forty, it's going to be your fault."

Lyric looked at Poppy imploringly. "You seem like a logical person. Tell her she's overreacting, please."

All eyes turned to Poppy, putting her on the spot.

"Um, honestly?" She shifted her weight from one foot to the other. "I don't think she is."

Rosaline's eyes widened. Cash just smirked at her from across the room.

Poppy shrugged. "Rosaline made a really good point earlier. Cash, your address is in the county public records. Anyone could look it up. Your security system's nice, sure, but I think we need to see about upgrading it." Especially now. "Get a gate, at least. Maybe get *you* a security detail."

Or consider moving.

Cash frowned down at Lyric. "The security detail might be a bit much for me, but those are good points, babe."

Lyric deflated, shoulders slumping in defeat. "I'll call Ravi and Elliott and tell them to turn around. If they even left."

"You're going to hate me, but it's been a long day and it's late," Rosaline said. "I think it would be for the best if you and I headed back to the hotel."

Lyric pouted. "But we're flying back to LA tomorrow morning."

Rosaline had already pulled her phone from her pocket, her fingers tapping away at the screen. "And you'll see Curran in two weeks at the World Music Awards."

Record scratch.

"Did you just say the World Music Awards?" She glared at Cash. "Why am I always the last one learning about these things?"

He opened his mouth, but Lyric set a hand on his arm. "I wasn't sure if I was going," she said. "They asked me to perform, and I wasn't sure if I was up for it, but—" she said, craning her neck and smiling up at Cash, "I'm proud of this album and I'm happier than I've been in a long time, so I decided I wanted to go. I only asked Cash today if he'd be my date. And he said yes."

Of course he said yes.

"Two weeks." Poppy blew out her breath. "Okay. I'm guessing the awards are on a Sunday? Your game is on Monday, so you'll have to clear it with Coach, but I think we should be able to get you a flight out right after practice. We'll need to figure out what you're going to wear—"

"Poppy." Rosaline did a shit job of hiding her smile behind her fingertips. "Breathe. If you can't find a commercial flight out in time, there are always alternatives. All you need to worry about is what *you'll* be wearing."

What. "Me?"

"Sure." Rosaline arched a brow and gave Poppy another of those sweeping once-overs that made her hot all over. "Unless you were planning on going in the buff."

Across the room, Cash did a poor job of concealing his laughter with a cough.

"I wasn't aware I was going at all."

"I pulled a few strings and managed to procure an extra ticket. It's yours, assuming you want it."

They were the WMAs. Of course Poppy wanted it.

Rosaline skirted the coffee table, making her way over to the door. "We'll talk. Come on, Lyric."

Lyric stretched up onto her tiptoes and gave Cash a lingering, closemouthed kiss. "I'll text you in the morning?"

"'night, baby." Cash brushed his lips against Lyric's forehead and opened the front door. "Good night, Rosaline."

Rosaline gave him a curt nod. "Good night, Curran." She paused in the doorway and tossed a butter-wouldn't-melt smile over her shoulder. The place she'd sunk her teeth into Poppy's neck throbbed in time with her heartbeat. "Have a good night, Poppy."

"You too," she said, doing a superb job of keeping her voice even if she did say so herself.

Cash locked the door and leaned his shoulder against it, smirking. "You want to tell me what Rosaline Sinclair was doing here after midnight?"

"Do *you* want to wipe that shit-eating grin off your face, or should I do it for you?" Poppy sniffed and crossed her arms. "We had things to discuss." She nodded at the coffee table to where the half-eaten pizza lay. "She brought pizza."

"*Things to discuss*, huh?" He kicked off the door and joined Poppy on the couch, taking a seat on the cushion Rosaline had vacated. The leather was probably still warm and something about that made her shiver. "Funny how the WMAs just never came up."

Poppy froze. "Oh. Um."

"That's what I thought." Cash's smile broadened. "Now, why don't you tell me about that massive hickey, hm?"

Chapter Nine

Lyric Adair spotted in Cash Curran's VIP suite at Portland Pathfinders' game amid dating rumors

by Jaimie Xin
published on October 8

It looks like Cash Curran's so-called Hail Mary of a play paid off!

Amid red-hot dating rumors linking the pop superstar, 24, and the Portland Pathfinders quarterback, 28, Adair was spotted cheering for the Pathfinders from inside Curran's VIP suite at Sunday's game against the Atlanta Falcons (26–7). The "Facsimile" singer made quite the bold statement by wearing a Pathfinders' jersey, and not just any old one. The jersey Adair wore was none other than one of Curran's own. Adair was photographed cheering on her rumored beau alongside his parents, Eileen and Jeb Curran. An insider close to Adair confirmed to *People* that this was not the first time the pop star met Curran's parents, suggesting that the relationship might be more than a casual fling.

Following the game, locals spotted the couple at a postgame victory party at xport lounge along with several other Pathfinders players, family, and friends.

A source told *People* that Adair and Curran were extremely affectionate all night.

"I don't think I ever saw them not touching," the source said. "He'd have his arm around her, or she'd have her head on his shoulder. Occasionally, they kissed, but they weren't, like, excessive with the PDA. They just seemed really comfortable with each other."

Adair and Curran were seen leaving xport together shortly after midnight.

This most recent sighting comes two short weeks after Curran was spotted leaving the Hollywood Hills home of Rosaline Sinclair, Adair's publicist. He was photographed leaving with an unknown woman who has now been identified as Penelope Peterson, his publicist and close family friend.

Adair is rumored to be hitting the stage at the World Music Awards for the first time in four years. The show will broadcast live from the Dolby Theatre in Los Angeles on Sunday, October 21 at 8 p.m. ET on CBS and Paramount+. Whether or not Curran will make an appearance has not been confirmed, though the next Pathfinders' game is on Monday night, making his attendance possible.

Representatives for the eleven-time Grammy winner and Super Bowl champion have yet to respond to requests for comment from *People*.

POPPY WOULD ADMIT she was . . . moderately freaking out.

From what she'd gleaned through the grapevine and copious amounts of research, the work that would go into preparing for an award show would normally follow a certain script.

If a client was an A-lister, or highly sought out, say if they'd recently been in a major box office film or just won a gold medal at the Olympics, their publicist would reach out to preferred major media outlets weeks if not months in advance of the show to prearrange interviews. The publicist would request questions in advance and vet those questions with the knowledge that award shows were, by nature, unpredictable, and reporters could go off script.

If a client *wasn't* an A-lister, if they weren't nominated for an award, or if they were nominated in one of those unfortunate non-televised categories, their dutiful publicist would put together a résumé of sorts, a single sheet with an easily digestible list of their client's accomplishments and accolades. These celebrities would usually show up early to the red carpet. Their publicists would approach reporters and hand over their list of accomplishments and ask if the reporters were interested in interviewing their client.

The big celebrities tended to show up late and would navigate the carpet strategically, either approaching outlets for their pre-arranged interviews or deciding on the spot to say yes to an interested journalist knowing that whatever questions they asked hadn't been previously vetted.

Last year, Poppy had attended the ESPYS as Cash's plus-one—his girlfriend at the time, Ashley, was away shooting a campaign for The North Face in the Italian Alps. The World Music Awards wouldn't be her first red carpet rodeo, but it would be her first time attending one of this magnitude and as Cash's publicist.

The night needed to go off without a hitch.

Only, the dance she'd expected suddenly had totally different steps.

In the roughly forty-eight hours since *People* magazine had posted an article linking Cash and Lyric and speculating that he might attend the WMAs, Poppy had received a whopping 132 emails and 49 phone calls. Her inbox and voicemail were flooded with media requests and offers from practically every major fashion house that made menswear to dress Cash for the show.

Lyric had already texted Cash a photo of the stunning canary-yellow satin gown she'd be wearing so they wouldn't clash on the carpet. Despite his fondness for luxury labels, when he could, he'd rather use his platform to bring attention—and business—to queer-owned fashion brands. Poppy was already in contact with one of Cash's favorite labels, trying to finagle expedited alterations.

That left the media requests. Poppy opened her text thread with Rosaline, reread the perfunctory back-and-forth conversation they'd had discussing the logistics, including the private jet company Lyric used, Rosaline knowing it would be next to impossible to book a commercial flight that left Portland after Cash's practice and would arrive in Los Angeles in time for the awards. She lingered on the brief text Rosaline had sent early Monday morning thanking Poppy for an excellent night.

If she had taken a screenshot of that text for posterity, that would remain between her and the private, locked folder she'd saved it in.

She tapped at the screen and started to type.

> **POPPY (11:44 P.M.):** Is Lyric doing press on the carpet?

> **POPPY (11:44 P.M.):** My email inbox is flooded with media requests for Cash.

> **POPPY (11:44 P.M.):** I know he's attending as Lyric's plus-one, so I don't want to arrange or turn down anything without discussing it with you first.

She didn't want to step on Rosaline's toes or for them to get their wires crossed.

> **POPPY (11:45 P.M.):** United front, you know?

POPPY (11:46 P.M.): Are we instituting a moratorium on relationship questions if we do the press line?

POPPY (11:46 P.M.): I can't decide if it would be silly not to address the elephant in the room or if it would be overkill. Show don't tell . . . 😬

ROSALINE (11:54 P.M.): Poppy, are you planning on writing me the next great American novel in 140-character increments?

She cringed.

POPPY (11:55 P.M.): Maybe just the next great American novelette. 😁

POPPY (11:55 P.M.): Sorry. I'm a little over-caffeinated.

Little being the understatement of the century.

ROSALINE (11:56 P.M.): It's nearly midnight. Stop drinking coffee and go to bed.

Poppy pouted at her phone.

POPPY (11:56 P.M.): Rude.

POPPY (11:56 P.M.): I asked you a question??

> **ROSALINE (11:57 P.M.):** I believe you asked me three.

She scrolled back up and counted.

> **POPPY (11:58 P.M.):** One was obviously rhetorical 😳

In the ten minutes it took Rosaline to respond, Poppy finished her iced chocolate macadamia nut breve from Dutch Bros. Her third of the day. Ill-advised? Most definitely. Delicious? No doubt. But her emails weren't going to reply themselves, and if she couldn't sleep after, there was probably some show with eighty-seven seasons on Hulu for her to watch.

> **ROSALINE (12:08 A.M.):** Lyric will be skipping the press line. I did promise a brief exclusive to Rolling Stone under the condition all questions be about her album. I trust they know better than to pull any funny business.

She snorted.

> **POPPY (12:09 A.M.):** You mean they know better than to fuck with you.

> **ROSALINE (12:10 A.M.):** Hey, you said it, not me.

> **ROSALINE (12:10 A.M.):** Obviously, it's up to you if Curran does press, but I think you might

> be right about it being overkill. Always leave them wanting more is usually my motto.

> **POPPY (12:11 A.M.):** Great minds 🤏

She might consider arranging an exclusive like Rosaline had for Lyric, but only so Cash could plug the LGBTQ+ youth sports foundation he was starting here in Portland. No matter what, she'd be putting Cash through his paces, making sure he was prepared for anything a red-carpet correspondent might throw at him. Better to be overprepared and underwhelmed than the alternative. *That* was Poppy's motto.

Poppy was in the middle of drafting a reply to *Out* magazine—they had a history of reporting favorably on Cash—when her phone buzzed against her thigh.

> **ROSALINE (12:20 A.M.):** What are you wearing?

Well, *ho-ly shit*.

Poppy smiled. Fuck email. Her night just got a lot more promising.

Her Taco Bell hot sauce pajamas were far from sexy, but that was easily rectified. She wiggled her shorts down her legs, kicking them across the room, and unbuttoned the short sleeve matching top, leaving her in a pair of—well, they weren't her best underwear, but they were black and bikini-cut and maybe a little basic but inoffensive. And it wasn't like they were going to stay on for long.

She fluffed her stack of pillows—Cash gave her so much shit for sleeping with a veritable mountain of them and, oh my god this was not the time to be thinking about Cash. She straightened her duvet, trying to make it look like she hadn't spent the better part of the day working from bed, and attempted to arrange herself artfully across the covers with her shirt splayed open, revealing most of her stomach but still keeping her breasts covered. She opened her camera, flipped it over to selfie mode, and held the phone up, trying to get as much of her body in the shot as possible while keeping her face out of it because she wasn't a total moron. She snapped a few pictures from a couple of different angles because options were always nice and then opened her gallery.

Maybe not the best near nudes she'd ever taken, but for a spur-of-the-moment photo shoot, not bad. They were . . . far from artistically erotic. More tastefully slutty, exactly the vibe Poppy was going for. Why bother with pretense when they both knew what was about to happen?

Before she could get too nitpicky and start tearing herself apart, finding flaws in the softness around her middle or her skin, which wasn't perfectly smooth, Poppy picked her favorite shot and sent it to Rosaline.

She settled further into the pillows and trailed her fingertips along the waistband of her panties, shivering at her own teasing touch. Right now, a thousand miles away in LA, Rosaline was probably looking at the picture Poppy had sent. Any second now, she was going to text back and god, Poppy didn't know what she wanted more—Rosaline's words or a picture in return, which, knowing Rosaline, *would* be artistically erotic. Black and white, maybe, to complement all that inked skin. Both would be perfect. She dipped her fingers beneath the cotton and exhaled sharply, heat stirring low in her gut, a heavy sort of pulsing that made her hips shift restlessly against the bed.

Her phone rang and she jerked her fingers out of her underwear like she'd been caught with her hand in a cookie jar. Her heart hammered and she fumbled the phone, nearly dropping it, laughing as her hands shook, struggling to switch over to speaker.

"Hi," she answered, as breathless as if she'd sprinted a mile, blood pumping just as hard. "Not that I'm complaining, far, *far* from it, trust me, but I was *not* expecting this."

"That," Rosaline said, clearing her throat, "makes two of us."

Poppy swept her fingertips up and down the valley between her breasts. "Like I said, I'm a big believer in show, don't tell."

"I was asking what you were wearing to the World Music Awards, Poppy."

Her breath left her in a rush, cheeks filling with heat. "*Oh.*" Fuck. Poppy was so stupid. "That's—wow, okay. Sorry. Um. I—I haven't decided yet. I'll probably go to Nordstrom downtown. Buy something off the rack. Don't want to—" Her voice cracked and she squinched her eyes shut. "Stand out."

If there was a God, if they were merciful at all, they'd strike Poppy down now and put her out of her misery.

Rosaline let out a strangled-sounding laugh. "Poppy." The way she said her name managed to be both soft and full of reproach. One more contradiction to add to the ever-growing list. "Do you *really* think I give a damn about that now? I want to talk about that picture."

She seemed bound and determined to give Poppy whiplash. At the very least keep her on her toes.

Poppy gnawed on her thumbnail. "Did you . . . like it?"

"Did I *like* it?" Rosaline laughed, a little mean in a way that sent a shiver down Poppy's spine. "I like sunrises and kittens and horror movies. But that picture you sent? No, Poppy, I *didn't* like it. You want to know why?"

She didn't wait for Poppy to answer.

"Because," she said. "You're there, and I'm here, and do you know how fucking expensive it is to charter a flight at such short notice at this time of night?"

Poppy choked on a laugh. "I know I'm hot and all, but there's no need to buy any carbon credits on my account."

"I beg to differ," Rosaline said loftily. "But I suppose the next best alternative would be if you told me what you were doing dressed like that. *Un*dressed like that?"

She curled her toes into her soft, cotton duvet. "I, uh, was sort of hoping you'd tell me?"

Rosaline chuckled, low and throaty, and a part of Poppy regretted having her on speaker, that she couldn't hear Rosaline's voice directly against her ear. "You're telling me you didn't have anything in mind when you took that picture? I mean, what did you think was going to happen? What did you think I'd say when I saw you like that, posed so pretty, like such—" Her throat clicked. "I—never mind."

"Say it," Poppy pleaded. "What did I look like?"

"You know damn well what you looked like," Rosaline accused sharply. "Don't play with me. Do you think you're being cute? Fingers where I wished mine were, touching you, skin on—" Her throat clicked for the second time and goddamn, Poppy had never, *ever* felt so fucking heady. Dizzy with desire, drunk on—on power. Like even though she was on her back, waiting for Rosaline to give her permission to touch herself, it still somehow felt like she held the cards. *Some* cards, just enough of them. "What did you think was going to happen when you sent me that picture?"

"I thought—"

"You didn't though, did you?" Rosaline chided softly, tongue clicking against the back of those perfect teeth Poppy had yet to taste. Wanted to—to trace. "You just wanted it. Wanted someone to tell you what to do?"

Even though Rosaline couldn't see, Poppy still nodded. "Uh-huh."

"Are you touching yourself?" Rosaline asked.

"No, I—"

"Don't lie to me. I saw that hand."

She shook her head, then remembered she was on the phone and Rosaline couldn't see her. "I didn't. I waited. I wanted—"

She couldn't say it.

"You know what I think you wanted? I think you wanted permission."

Poppy didn't answer.

"My question is, do you think you deserve it?" Rosaline didn't pause long enough for Poppy to answer, not even sure what her honest answer would be. "From those texts you sent me, it sounds like you've been working hard today. I think you deserve it. Go on."

Poppy trailed her fingers down her belly. "How?"

Rosaline seemed to shudder. "You know what pisses me off?"

What the hell kind of answer was that? "Kind of feeling like I am right now, to be honest."

Another of those throaty laughs came through the line. Assuming they'd do this again, Poppy was going to wear earbuds. "The other night, I feel like—" Her throat clicked. "I barely got to learn how you like to be touched."

Being touched at all sounded good right now. "You started slow. I kind of hated that, but I—I also didn't?" she confessed. "And then, when you didn't let me until you said I could."

Rosaline hummed. "Start slow then. Are your breasts sensitive?"

She ghosted her fingers back up front. "Mhmm."

"Circle your nipples for me."

Goose bumps rose up on her skin as she did as Rosaline asked—no, told her, and her nipples pebbled, hardening into points. "Feels nice."

Rosaline scoffed. "If *nice* is where we're at, we need to do better. Pinch them."

She did, pinching her nipples between the pads of her fingers, sucking in a sharp breath at the pleasant sting.

"You make the prettiest fucking noises. Those little whimpers and gasps? Christ, Poppy."

Her tits throbbed, heavy. "You're touching yourself too. Right?"

"What do you think?" She laughed. "Unlike you, I'm not really a fan of *slow*."

Oh god. "Tell me?"

"Pinch yourself again and I will. Harder this time."

Squeezing, Poppy pinched until it hurt and then a little harder because Rosaline had told her to and even though she couldn't see her right now, Poppy really, really wanted to be good. A bolt of pleasure shot from her chest to her core, her pussy clenching. A tiny cry fell off her tongue and Rosaline swore softly.

"I grabbed my vibrator within seconds of getting that photo. I've had it on practically this entire time," she said, panting just a little. "Wishing it was your mouth on me."

Between her thighs, she was already soaked. She rubbed her legs together, trying to get even a little friction. A groan of frustration tumbled off her tongue.

"You like the idea of that, huh? Maybe me putting you on your knees? Shoving your face against me? Ordering you to get me off?"

Iron and salt exploded on her tongue from how hard she bit her lip. "Can I touch myself?"

"I don't know," Rosaline laughed. "Can you?"

Bitch. Poppy loved it. "*May* I touch myself?"

"Ask me nicely."

Poppy squeezed her eyes shut. "*Please.*"

At this rate, Rosaline was going to have come twice before Poppy came at all and—she really didn't hate that.

"Are you still wearing those panties?"

"Yeah."

"Keep them on. Spread your legs and tug them to the side."

Parting her legs, Poppy pulled her underwear to the side. The cotton blend bit into the inside of her thigh from the stretch, and she shivered, the air from the fan cool against where she was soaked.

"I know you said you like slow, but I have something different in mind right now." Rosaline's voice was strained like she was close. "I want you to fuck yourself, Poppy. Three fingers. Pretend they're mine. I wouldn't be gentle."

Poppy dropped her hand between her thighs and—*god*, she was drenched, arousal seeping from her. Even though she was touching herself, she still inhaled sharply when her fingers slipped inside, then stole in a deep breath, bracing herself before following Rosaline's instructions, fucking herself hard, curling her fingers the way Rosaline had. Her back arched and biting her lip couldn't even stop the noises clawing up her throat from slipping out.

"Talk to me," Rosaline demanded. "What was it you said the other night? *I'm going to need you to be really explicit?* Paint a picture for me. Do you always get as wet as you did with me, or has it just been a while? Or was it me?"

Her next gasp came out as a cry. "That's too many questions."

Rosaline's laugh was thready and it made Poppy clench. "I guess you don't really have to answer. I must be on speaker because I can hear how wet you are." The slick sounds coming from between her thighs filled the room, making her flush hotter than she was already, a mottled blush creeping down her chest all the way to her belly button. "Close already?"

She was, rapidly approaching her peak at breakneck speed. "Uh-huh."

"Stop." Rosaline exhaled shakily. "Keep those fingers buried in your cunt but stop moving."

A cry of frustration escaped her. "*God*, I hate you."

"I want to hear you when you come," Rosaline panted. "And—fuck, seeing as *I'm* about to come, I don't want to miss anything."

Her mouth dropped open. Maybe Poppy hated her a little less, a *lot* less when she cried out, Poppy's name on her lips. Poppy's eyes scrunched and her back bowed a little, pussy pulsing around her fingers, not coming but so, *so* fucking close, the sound of Rosaline getting off nearly nudging her over the edge.

Rosaline's soft pants filled the room and a barely-there buzz Poppy hadn't noticed until it was missing disappeared. Her muscles ached from clenching, holding still and holding off at that edge she wasn't allowed to topple over.

"Go on." Rosaline laughed lightly, still breathless, and it straddled the line between the hottest and most beautiful sound Poppy had ever heard. Maybe Poppy hadn't touched her, but it still felt like she'd had a hand in making Rosaline feel good and that was almost better than coming. "I want to hear you."

She closed her eyes and imagined it was Rosaline touching her, the way she would if she were here, the way she said she would, *fucking* her and not gentle, either. Deep and fast, fingers curling hard, pressing, and it was like Poppy's body recognized the earlier interruption had been a *pause* and not a *stop*, because she was there. Pressure built in her core, swelling, walls gripping her fingers tight. At once, she snapped, all that pressure releasing rhythmically as her vision whited out.

Her throat felt raw, ragged from whatever noises she was making but couldn't hear over the sound of her pulse thundering inside her head.

"Holy fuck," Rosaline whispered in that near reverent way she had once before, and Poppy sank back into the sheets with a broken laugh.

"Ditto," she said, still breathing heavily. "In addition to that master's you've got in public relations, do you also have a master's in dirty talk I don't know about?"

Rosaline snorted. "Helps to have some really . . . tempting inspiration."

Poppy beamed up at the ceiling. "I don't think I've ever been called *tempting* before."

"I don't believe that." Rosaline sounded aggrieved.

Sweat was beginning to cool on her skin, so she tugged her shirt closed and righted her underwear into place.

"Eh. Believe it." But it's not like now was the time or Rosaline was the person with whom to talk about her lackluster love life. Lackluster in *many* aspects of her life, really. She'd already embarrassed herself by dumping her feelings on Rosaline . . . once? Twice? Three times would just be pitiful. "Anyway, sorry again. For that picture I sent."

The blades of her ceiling fan whirred noisily.

"What the fuck, Poppy?" Now, there was no mistaking that Rosaline sounded aggrieved. Pissed off, really. "What about the last . . . god, I don't know even know how many minutes would make you think you should be *sorry?*"

She shifted uncomfortably, reached for a pillow, and hugged it to her chest. "It was still unsolicited. It's not what you meant when you asked what I was wearing."

Even though she wasn't mad—not about that—it didn't mean that she might not have been.

"Christ," Rosaline muttered and blew out a noisy breath. "Okay. Consider this blanket permission to send me as many tawdry photos as you'd like." She paused. "As long as they don't have your face in them. Not that your face doesn't do it for me, but the last thing I need is to get hacked and have a PR crisis of my own making on my hands. Do you know how much grief Lyric would give me? I'd never live it down."

Poppy pressed her lips into a thin line, biting back a smile. Her bottom lip still stung from biting it, but she didn't mind, too much. Tomorrow, when it throbbed, she'd think about Rosaline.

Not that she was catching feelings or anything. It would just be a . . . pleasant, potent reminder of the hottest phone sex of her life.

"I'm going to choose to focus on the fact that you said my face does it for you and *not* that you think I'd ever be stupid enough to send a nude with my face in it via text."

"You do that," Rosaline teased. "Though, question—how else would you ever be sending a nude? Carrier pigeon? FedEx overnight?"

Poppy snickered. "Um, it's called Snapchat?"

"Trust a third-party app with my naked body?" Rosaline scoffed. "I think the fuck not."

Poppy threw her head back against the pillow, laughing so hard a totally unbecoming snort slipped out. "But first-party apps are totally fair game?"

Rosaline went quiet. "I think someone I know said some risks are worth it."

Huh. She had said that, hadn't she? "You might regret that. Giving me permission. I might end up spamming you," she teased.

"I guess I better charge my vibrator," Rosaline said, perfectly deadpan. "I should probably go."

Poppy hugged the pillow tighter, chest constricting. "Right. Sure."

The couch thing the other night had been a fluke, Rosaline hand-feeding her pizza and holding her. Even though they were a thousand miles away and it made absolutely no sense, Poppy had been hoping for . . . not the same thing, but maybe something close. That maybe they'd talk for a little while because it turned out talking with Rosaline was pretty fucking awesome, now that she wasn't railroading her and staring at her like she was some accomplice in a devious scheme to break her surrogate little sister's heart. Rosaline was funny, quick-witted, and levelheaded in a way that Poppy really admired. And she listened, *really* listened, when Poppy talked. And she hadn't judged her or made her feel like she was less because of her—

Her heart climbed into her throat.

Shit.

So much for that whole *not catching feelings* thing she'd promised herself she wouldn't do.

"It's just that it's getting late," Rosaline said, and it was probably a figment of Poppy's overly idealistic imagination, the part of her that had accidentally caught feelings for Rosaline, but she almost sounded remorseful.

"Sure," she said, trying and probably failing miserably at injecting a little levity into her voice because she might be a great many things, but an actress was not one of them. She sucked at poker too. "Makes total sense. Go. It's all good."

It was not all good.

"Lyric has a photo shoot with *Vogue* in the morning and an interview after," Rosaline said. "It's a sunrise shoot. Call time is four thirty."

"Oh." Poppy looked at the time and had a minor heart attack. "Holy shit. I am *so* sorry. I can't believe I—"

"Shut up, Poppy," she said, and it might've been the fondest anyone had ever sounded when telling her to be quiet. "I called *you*, remember?"

Okay, that was fair. She had. "I'll try to keep my sexting to reasonable hours next time."

"I don't mind. Really," Rosaline said. "Now, go to sleep, Poppy. And try not to mainline too much caffeine before bed."

"Will do on the first, no promises on the second." She tucked her pillow under her chin, smiling into the fabric. "Good night."

Rosaline ended the call and Poppy pressed the heels of her hands into her eyes. She'd probably have stupid, heart-shaped imprints on her skin if heart-eyes were a real thing that existed outside of old cartoons.

She didn't have a fear boner for Rosaline Sinclair, she had a freaking *heart* boner—same as a crush only stunningly hornier. Words she never in a million years thought would cross her mind, but then again, if someone had asked her even two weeks ago if she'd be having sex with Rosaline Sinclair, she'd have laughed herself into another dimension.

She was buttoning her pajama top, about to make a trip to the bathroom before trying to go to sleep like Rosaline had told her to, when her phone buzzed.

ROSALINE (1:12 A.M.): Sweet dreams, Poppy.

Chapter Ten

Tuesday, October 16

> **ROSALINE (11:32 A.M.):** Change of plans re: the WMAs.

> **POPPY (11:35 A.M.):** Ok?

> **POPPY (11:39 A.M.):** ???

<Incoming call from Rosaline Sinclair>

"If you were in Los Angeles, it would make preparing for the WMAs much simpler," Rosaline said without prelude.

Poppy cradled her phone against her shoulder. "Cash can't fly in until the day of. Mandatory practice, remember?"

"Mandatory for him. You have no such obligation to attend, do you?"

"No, but I assumed I'd fly down with—"

"Then there's no reason you can't get a flight out tonight." The muted click-clack of a keyboard made it past the phone's background noise cancellation. "What do you think about staying at the Beverly Wilshire? CUT is *definitely* overrated as far as restaurants go, but the spa has a eucalyptus steam room that will absolutely change your—"

"Slow down." Poppy laughed. "Rosaline, be real. I can't stay at the Beverly Wilshire."

It was the *Beverly Wilshire*. The Four *freaking* Seasons. A one-night stay probably cost more than Poppy made in two weeks at her old job. She could afford it now, sure, but did she honestly have any business dropping that kind of money on a hotel room she didn't *really* need? Not to mention what a last-minute flight would cost.

"Okaaay." Rosaline drew out the word skeptically. "Would you rather stay at the Beverly Hills Hotel?"

Poppy palmed her face. "Look, I can *maybe* fly down Saturday, but . . . what would I even do for four whole days by myself in LA?"

There was a pause. "Are you being serious right now? I can't tell."

Poppy frowned. "Yes? I'm being serious."

"Jesus Christ," Rosaline muttered, making Poppy frown harder. "Look, if you're so worried about making the trip worth your while, I'm having dinner on Thursday with a few acquaintances from *Vanity Fair* who are in town covering the awards. You are more than welcome to come with me. Plus, you said you still need to find a dress. If ever there were a rack that deserves better than *off*-the-rack, it's yours. We'll go shopping, you and me. There. You have plans. Happy?"

Her brain blue screened. "I—you think I have nice tits?"

"Poppy," Rosaline chided. "Is that the only thing you took away from what I said?"

"No," she denied. "*Vanity Fair* magazine. Shopping for dresses that probably cost more than Cash's mortgage payment. I've got a spectacular rack. I heard you."

Rosaline chuckled, low and throaty, and all the hair stood up on the back of Poppy's arms. "It's up to you, but I personally like the idea of us being in the same city for more than twelve hours." She paused. "Not that I didn't enjoy our call last week, but you're not the only one who's a fan of *show, don't tell*. If you know what I mean."

"Oh." Poppy's stomach erupted into a flurry of butterflies. "You could've led with that."

"I'm saying it now. So? Are you coming or not?"

God, Poppy hoped so. "I'm not flying private."

Wednesday, October 17

POPPY (8:18 A.M.): Landed! I'll text you when I get to the hotel.

CASH (8:22 A.M.): text me from your uber

CASH (8:23 A.M.): share your location

POPPY (8:25 A.M.): Okay, Mom.

You started sharing location with Cash Curran

CASH (8:26 A.M.): 👍

POPPY (8:59 A.M.): Bag secured and I'm in the car! The driver just asked if I want to see pictures of her grandkids. I'll text you after I get checked in.

CASH (9:00 A.M.): kk

POPPY (10:55 A.M.): <image>

POPPY (10:55 A.M.): Holy shit. Cash. Look at this room!

POPPY (10:56 A.M.): <image>

POPPY (10:56 A.M.): Look at the view! I can see all of the Hollywood Hills from my balcony.

POPPY (10:57 A.M.): <image>

POPPY (10:57 A.M.): Look at this bathtub! Sorry. I love you, but I live here now ✌️

CASH (11:00 A.M.): damn that's a nice tub

CASH (11:01 A.M.): how's the gym

POPPY (11:02 A.M.): Of course that's what you care about.

POPPY (11:03 A.M.): And it's nice. Plenty of cardio machines.

CASH (11:05 A.M.): good. can't have you slacking off on marathon prep

POPPY (11:06 A.M.): Yes, coach 😊

CASH (11:08 A.M.): what time is richard gere picking you up

POPPY (11:09 A.M.): Richard Gere????

CASH (11:10 A.M.): you're staying in the pretty woman hotel pop-tart

POPPY (11:10 A.M.): 😞😞😞

POPPY (11:12 A.M.): She's picking me up in a little under an hour and I need to shower off the plane first so 👋

CASH (11:13 A.M.): have fun. don't do anything i wouldn't do

POPPY (11:14 A.M.): Considering your track record, that should be a piece of cake 😊

CASH (11:15 A.M.): 🖕

AT EXACTLY 11:59 a.m. on the dot, a mint-colored Chevrolet Corvette that appeared to be in mint condition pulled up to the curb outside of the Beverly Wilshire.

Poppy slid into the passenger seat with a smile. "Nice car. 1956?"

With one hand on the wheel and the other resting on the gleaming silver stick shift, Rosaline peered at Poppy over the top of her bright green Bottega Veneta cat's-eye sunglasses. She looked like an Old Hollywood starlet, curls pinned in place beneath a white silk scarf. "Hello to you too. And I'd say good guess, but I don't think it was, was it?"

Rosaline's lips twitched in a smile, and it would've been so easy to stretch across the small gap between the seats and find out if they were as soft as they looked.

If kissing were on the table, and it wasn't.

An ache formed in the tender, fleshy spaces between Poppy's ribs, but she ignored it, leaning forward and stroking the dash reverently. "Didn't they only make something like one hundred and fifty of these? In this color, I mean. Cascade green with beige coves?"

Rosaline's brows rose, impressed, and Poppy's smile broadened into a satisfied grin. "One hundred and forty-seven, actually. And only one hundred and eleven with a special high-lift camshaft and dual four-barrel carburetors."

She whistled. No wonder she could feel the engine's purr in her bones. "Nice."

Rosaline waited for Poppy to fasten her seat belt before flipping on her left blinker. "I didn't take you for a car enthusiast."

She wasn't. Not really. "My dad loves cars. Classic ones, mostly."

That she knew anything at all about cars beyond the basics was a credit to her desperate desire to find common ground with her dad, even if it meant forging it herself. After school, she spent time in the detached garage, curled up in a rusty old lawn chair, poring over back issues of *Car and Driver* magazine while her dad tinkered around until Mom yelled at Poppy to do her homework and leave her father alone.

"He a collector?"

"Eh, not unless you count a 1972 Thunderbird he bought off a guy in Coos Bay that turned out to be a total lemon. But he and

Dillon—my brother—used to fly to Pennsylvania every fall for the, uh, what's it called?" She snapped her fingers. "Antique Auto Club of America Eastern Meet, I think?"

"Did you ever go?"

"Um, no." She hoped she was the only one who could hear the decades-old disappointment in her voice, which she tried to cover with a breezy shrug. "It was more of a father-son thing."

Even though Dillon didn't know the difference between a carburetor and a clutch plate and had once fried the electrical system in his Kia Forte by trying to jump-start it with the battery connected backward. No hard feelings.

"You know, there's a big roadster show every February in Pomona." Rosaline made a left onto Beverly Drive. "Maybe next time you can come with me."

Poppy turned, seat belt strap biting into the side of her neck. "Wait—really?"

She cursed Rosaline's sunglasses for making it impossible for Poppy to see her eyes. To gauge what she was thinking. All she saw was surprise splashed across her own face reflected in the mirrored lenses.

"I usually drag Lyric with me," Rosaline said, by way of explanation. "She couldn't care less about cars." She downshifted as the light ahead turned red. "Are you hungry?"

What she really wanted to know was what it meant that Rosaline had invited her to something that was four months away, but sure. "I could eat."

Erewhon was just around the corner. Overpriced and overhyped as the luxury supermarket was, the weather was perfect for a quick picnic on the grocery store's patio and the hot bar meant they'd have a plethora of options to choose from. And Poppy honestly wouldn't mind trying one of those smoothies she kept seeing all over TikTok. The ones made famous by the likes of Hailey Bieber and Bella Hadid and boasted benefits like boosted energy and perfect skin.

Inside, Poppy had to take a second to get her bearings, the store almost as cramped as it was colorful, niche overpriced organic items filling the aesthetically pleasing, Instagrammable shelves.

"Meet you at the café?" Rosaline asked, reaching past her for a basket, fingers brushing Poppy's hip in the process, the touch of her hand fleeting, gone before Poppy could press into it the way she wanted, the way she would've if she'd had the chance. If they weren't in public, where anyone could take a picture and post it on the internet. "I just need to grab something first."

Rosaline disappeared down one of the too-narrow aisles to the left and Poppy set off in the opposite direction.

There were items here she had never heard of. Pure luna sea moss gel and purified reverse osmosis hyper-oxygenated water. Truffle-infused hot sauce and hump fat made from the humps of wild camels, which was apparently an actual thing people ate. Supplements and adaptogens and—what the hell were nootropics? She snapped a few pictures of the most bizarre items to send to Cash before joining the line for the café behind a guy who looked a little like Jesus. If Jesus were white and wore $750 Ferragamo slides and Loewe pave crystal sunglasses indoors and talked too loud into the latest model of an iPhone.

"Can you believe the bitch is actually suing me?"

Holy shit. The guy was Ansel Daily, drummer of the Domestic Noir Plot and more important, Lyric's ex-boyfriend.

His sun-streaked brown hair was longer, his entire aesthetic a little more *I bought a private island in Croatia and started a cult* than Poppy remembered, but it was definitely him.

"I *barely* even tapped her. And you know I drive electric. It's like, I hit one chick with my car, but I'm also saving the planet and shit. It's a wash, you know? Nah, dude, I'm at Erewhon. I went a little hard on the"—Ansel sniffed—"*espresso martinis* at Bird Streets last night, if you catch my drift." He chuckled. "Yeah, yeah, I'm headed to the studio, just need to grab something to, like, detox or shit. Fuck if I know. Mhmm. 'Kay, dude. See you." He pocketed his phone and stepped up to the register. "Yeah, gimme a Chagacinno with mucuna and CBD oil and—make sure it's ceremonial matcha and not the culinary kind. Okay, sweetheart?"

The fresh-faced barista took Ansel's condescension in stride, scribbling his order down on two cups before punching it into the register. "You can insert your card or tap whenever you're ready."

Ansel pulled a black American Express out of his wallet, tapped the card against the reader, hit the *no tip* button, and walked over to the pickup counter, all without so much as a thank-you.

What. A. Prick.

"What can I get for you?"

Poppy schooled her scowl into a smile as she stepped up to the register, placing an uncomplicated order for a Malibu Mango smoothie and tipping double what she normally would to make up for Ansel the Asshole's lack of gratuity.

She was minding her business, debating whether to try a spicy tuna sandwich or get the poke nachos when, to her right, Ansel snapped his fingers.

"Hey, you." He snapped his fingers again. "Do I know you?"

Her mouth dropped open. "Did you just snap at me?"

He squinted at her. "I swear you look familiar."

"I guess I just have one of those faces." She turned back to the cold bar, done with the conversation.

"No, no, I think I—" He started to laugh. "Oh shit. You're Cash Curran's assistant, aren't you?"

"Publicist," she gritted out. "I'm his publicist. Not his assistant."

"That's cool." Ansel leaned his suntanned, sticker-tattooed forearms on the counter, angling his body toward her. "So, tell me—how exactly is he enjoying my sloppy seconds?"

A vein in her temple began to pulse, her blood pressure rising. "You know what? You can go—" His phone was in his hand and maybe Poppy was being paranoid, but the last thing she needed was for some video of her telling Ansel Daily to go fuck himself to go viral. "You sound like a sore loser."

"A sore loser?" He laughed. "That's cute." The barista set his disgusting-sounding, CBD-laden Chagacinno down in front of him. "Tell Cash to enjoy his thirty seconds of fame while it lasts." He turned, only to stop dead in his tracks. "Rosaline."

"Ansel." She stopped beside Poppy and smiled benignly, sweetly even. "I heard your tour got canceled. What a bummer for all twelve of your fans."

Ouch.

"Doesn't it get exhausting?" He snatched his Chagacinno off the bar. "Always being such a cunt?"

Rosaline gave an effortless shrug and snatched Ansel's basket off the floor, shoving it into his chest with a smile. "Why do you think I drink cold brew?"

Ansel sneered, his shoulder knocking hard into Poppy's as he stormed off in the direction of the checkout.

"I cannot believe Lyric actually dated him," Poppy murmured.

"Ansel might be a mediocre drummer, but he's a master manipulator and a narcissist." Rosaline glared at Ansel's retreating form. "As embarrassed as I am to admit it, he even had me snowed for a while."

"Asshole."

Rosaline hummed in agreement. "And karma's a bitch," she said sagely, taking Poppy's hand. "Let's go."

"But my smoothie—"

"We'll come back for it." She started walking, pulling Poppy along. "Trust me."

They joined the line for the register; at least half a dozen shoppers were behind Ansel, whose basket was now empty, his groceries packed into two brown paper bags.

Poppy frowned at Rosaline. "What are we—"

"That's not mine." Ansel's voice carried, loud enough that every head in the store swiveled in his direction.

The cashier, a guy with big arms and an even broader chest, held up a supplement bottle bearing a bright blue label, the words *Load Boost* written in bold, unmissable neon yellow. "It was in your basket?"

"Yeah, well, I didn't put it there." Ansel snatched the bottle from the cashier's hand. "Do I look like I need help with my"—he flipped it around—"semen volume?"

The cashier stared. "I honestly don't know how to answer that."

"Well, I don't," Ansel snapped, glaring at several shoppers who had their phones out, recording his mini meltdown. "There's nothing wrong with my spunk, okay?"

Rosaline's shoulders shook with suppressed laughter.

"Wait." Poppy gaped at her. "Did you—"

"Karma's a bitch," Rosaline repeated, waving at Ansel as he scowled at them from the front of the line. "I just happen to be a bigger one."

No "hard" feelings!
Ansel Daily has a meltdown in Erewhon over male enhancement supplement

by Deuxmoi Editor
published on October 18

The Domestic Noir Plot drummer was spotted at Erewhon yesterday afternoon where, according to a regular at the Beverly Hills location, he hit up the hot bar for Grass-Fed Korean Short Ribs and Garlic Miracle Noodles before heading over to the smoothie bar for a Chagacinno. Also in his cart? Raw ranch kale chips, venison jerky, and . . . Load Boost?

According to multiple onlookers, Daily insisted the supplement that claims to increase ejaculation volume was added to his cart by mistake.

Chapter Eleven

Sunday, October 21

WORLD MUSIC AWARDS @WMAs • 5h
The world's largest fan-voted awards show is tonight! Tune in on @CBS or @paramountplus to see your favorite stars perform including the long-awaited return to the stage of @lyricadair! #WMAs

LYRIC ADAIR @lyricadair • 4h
The secret's out! I can't wait to hit the stage at tonight's #WMAs! The support you all have shown for my first single off the new album has been truly mind-blowing. Your enthusiasm and excitement for Santa Ana has been amazing and the support you've shown me this last year has touched me in ways I can't put into words. Maybe I'll just express my gratitude by playing you all a new song tonight instead

IN MY SANTA ANA ERA @omgahdaaaaavid • 4h
replying to @lyricadair
a new song?! screaming crying throwing up 🎧

VICTORIA @pdxprincess • 3h
replying to @lyricadair
but is @cashcurran going to be there?!?!?!

LILIANA @evanbuckleystan98 • 1h
replying to @pdxprincess
oh my god imagine the red carpet photos 🫠

VICTORIA @pdxprincess • 1h
replying to @ evanbuckleystan98
praying mother and father keep us fed 🙏

'm just saying. I don't kiss my friends on the mouth, and I sure as hell don't have sex with them in dressing rooms."

"Dressing *room*, singular." She glared weakly at Cash from across the back seat of the limo en route to the Hollywood Roosevelt Hotel, where Lyric had been getting red-carpet ready with *Vogue*. "And for the record, Rosaline and I don't kiss on the mouth, either."

He stared blankly at her. "You don't kiss."

Poppy wasn't sure why, but something about the way Cash said it rubbed her the wrong way, putting her on edge. "I told you. What we're doing is casual and kissing is . . . kissing isn't. Kissing is personal."

"And sex isn't?" Cash made an obvious effort to collect himself, pinching the bridge of his nose with a sigh. "You can't seriously tell me you're okay with this. Poppy, I know you and I know you like her more than you're letting on."

She shrugged. "I'll get over it."

"It" being the ever-growing, decidedly *not* shrinking crush she was harboring for Rosaline that her four days in Los Angeles had done nothing to squash.

"You're going to get over it," Cash spoke slowly, "by continuing to fuck her?"

She was done talking about this. Done thinking about it too. "Thank you for your concern, but I knew what I was getting myself into when I agreed to it."

"Have you thought about talking to Rosaline? Maybe you're not the only one who—"

"Nope." Poppy shook her head, hair she'd spent too long trying to curl tickling her bare shoulders. "She was very clear about what she wanted."

The limo pulled to a stop in front of the back entrance of the hotel.

"What about what you want, Poppy?"

"Please, *please* don't say anything in front of Rosaline," she begged. "No mentioning what I told you about the dressing room or making pointed comments about kissing or innuendos or—"

"I get to make one innuendo." He stared at her with narrowed eyes over steepled fingers. "One."

"We're not haggling."

"Two innuendos."

She glared. "I *like* Rosaline, okay? And maybe you think what I'm doing is stupid, and maybe you're right. Maybe this is all going to come back and bite me in the ass, but for tonight, I'm just asking you to be cool, okay? Be cool and don't say anything that's going to send her running for the hills."

"Okay." He shrugged and she was about to breathe a sigh of relief when he added, "*Three* innuendos." He grinned when she scoffed and threw up her hands. "Hey, I *am* your boss, remember? Technically, I call the shots."

At that moment, the back door opened and in slipped Lyric, radiant in her yellow, off-the-shoulder dress with its full tulle skirt. Someone, presumably security, shut the door behind her, leaving it slightly ajar.

Cash's face lit up like he was a kid on Christmas morning and his girlfriend was a pretty wrapped present waiting for him under the tree. "I am one lucky son of a bitch," he said, sounding awed.

Lyric laughed. "Better not let your mother hear that." She greeted him with a kiss and immediately started in on fixing his shirt to her liking, undoing the top button and smoothing down the collar. "You dress up nice." As if remembering they weren't the only two people in the limo, the only two people on the planet, she turned, spotted Poppy, and threw her a blinding smile. "Poppy! You look beautiful. That dress?" Lyric fanned her face.

Poppy tucked her hair behind her ear. "Please, look who's talking. Are you excited for tonight?"

Lyric blew out a breath and laughed softly, waffling her head from side to side. "It's been a hot second since I performed so—"

Once more, the door opened, stealing Poppy's attention. Rosaline slipped into the back seat, shutting the door fully behind her, breathtaking in a black two-piece, single-breasted suit tailored to perfection. The neckline plunged, dipping nearly to her belly button revealing a deep strip of suntanned skin, shimmering delicately from whatever body lotion she'd chosen to wear this evening. Maybe it was the heels, or the cut of the pants, but even though Rosaline wasn't tall, her legs looked miles long.

The lengths Poppy would go to have those legs wrapped around her head were, quite frankly, boundless.

"Evening, Curran," she greeted absently, eyes focused on her phone, fingers swiping furiously at the screen. "Glad you made it to town safely."

She slipped her phone into her clutch and raised her head, gaze sweeping Poppy up and down, eyes lingering on the square neckline of her lilac-colored column dress. Her throat worked on a swallow, and she met Poppy's eyes, her own lidded, looking like she wanted to toss Cash and Lyric out of the car and drag Poppy into her lap. Like she wanted to eat her.

"Pretty dress," she said, as if she hadn't already seen it, hadn't already unzipped it once and watched the silk puddle around Poppy's feet before she took Poppy apart with her mouth right in the fitting room. "You clean up nice."

"*This week on National Geographic Television, Los Angles Edition,*" Cash said in a shitty Australian accent, "*we explore the courting and mating habits of*—ow, *babe!*" His lower lip jutted out as he rubbed his chest, soothing the nipple Lyric had just tweaked through his lace shirt. "That hurt."

Poppy glared at him.

One thing. She'd asked him for *one* damn thing.

"From what Lyric's told me, you're into that kind of thing." Rosaline flashed him a wicked grin. "Let's not get into a pissing contest, Curran. I will always win."

His jaw dropped and a vivid flush crept from his chest up to his eyebrows. Beside him, Lyric clapped a hand over her mouth, muffling a snort.

"What the fuck, babe?" Cash turned to her in horror.

Things she did not need to know for one thousand, Alex.

"It's not like I go into specifics," Lyric argued, stroking his cheek with the backs of her fingers.

He leaned into her touch, a little like a great big puppy looking for pets. Which—no, her brain was not going there. "Wait. Did you tell her about the thing with—"

"Okaaay," Rosaline interrupted, sparing Poppy from either having to plug her ears or experience the horror of learning more about Cash's apparently not-so-vanilla sex life. What she'd heard was already enough. "Here's how tonight's going to work." She paused, turning to look at Poppy. "Actually, why don't you take point?"

She cleared her throat. "Sure. I'll keep it brief—"

"You better, because I can see the theater across the street, Pop-Tart." Cash craned his neck, peering through the tinted window.

She scowled at him. "I *said* I'll keep it brief. And please don't call me that right now." He'd temporarily lost the privilege of using her nickname for his blatant disregard of her one request. "You said it before; you're my boss, remember? We're working tonight."

Cash's smile fell. "Pop—"

"A few reminders." His hangdog expression wasn't going to work on her, not now. "Lyric, this is far from your first rodeo, so I'm sure you already know this. Feel free to ignore me. The show starts at five, we're arriving at, um—"

She reached for her clutch, needing her phone to check the exact time.

"Just after four thirty," Rosaline said, phone already in hand, beating her to the punch.

Poppy shot her a grateful, albeit tight smile. "Thanks. We'll pass through the security tent, Rosaline and I will pick up our publicity credentials, and we'll hit the carpet. You're not doing the press line, but there will be a designated area for photos. At this point, you hardly need an introduction, but I'll be escorting you. We want to move it along. Um." Outside, the limo neared the theater, slowing behind a few other cars, and she paused, stealing a breath, heart racing, mind going a mile a minute. This was fine. She was fine. She could do this. "Even though we aren't doing the press line, we'll be passing through and media will likely try to persuade you, probably through Rosaline and me, for thirty seconds. It's a no. No exceptions. You have one exclusive with *Out* magazine, Cash. I'll stop you when we reach them. Then there will be escorts when we reach the doors to the theater. Rosaline and I have all our tickets so you don't have to worry about that; we'll hand you yours when we reach the doors. After the show, you'll follow an escort to the back where security will have coordinated with the driver to take you to the after-party."

She exhaled shakily. Had she missed anything? Press, photos, exclusive . . . no. She hadn't and if she had—a possibility—Rosaline was here. No way would she let anything slip through the cracks.

Lyric reached across the back seat, setting a hand on Poppy's knee. "Thank you."

"Yeah. Thanks, P—" Cash let out a shuddering breath, dug a knuckle into his right eye. "Thank you."

Her heart crashed into her stomach, breath escaping in a punched-out whoosh that had Rosaline swiveling and studying her with sharp eyes that had her shrinking in her seat.

Poppy had one job tonight—make sure things went off without a hitch. It was a *job*, one that she'd only recently convinced Rosaline she wasn't a total hack at. What they were doing off the clock was meant to alleviate the stress of the job, not add to it. In trying to be professional, Poppy had overcorrected and now Cash was upset and he couldn't go out on the carpet all gloom and doom because the gossip blogs would smell blood in the water and spin a story about how his relationship with Lyric was on the rocks and—

"Curran," Rosaline didn't quite snap, but her tone was demanding enough to make Cash sit up straighter, looking at her with wide eyes. "Apologize to your best friend."

What. "Rosaline, we don't need to—"

Rosaline's hand was on her wrist, just resting there, but the touch was unexpected, making the words dry up in her throat.

"Just do it," Rosaline said in that same take-no-prisoners tone. "Tell Poppy you're sorry for upsetting her." One of her brows rose. "Mean it."

Cash wiped his palms on his thighs and blew out a breath, eyes lifting and meeting hers, stare beseeching. She fidgeted, the fingers of the hand not snared by Rosaline tapping tunelessly against the leather seat. "I'm sorry for not listening to you and for saying what I said when you told me not to talk about it," he said, eyes flickering briefly to Rosaline before returning to hers. "I was a dick for—I was a dick. No excuses."

Tears welled up behind her eyes, which she blinked back as fast as she could, refusing to let them fall and ruin her makeup moments before she stepped out onto the red carpet and into a sea of celebrities and photographers. "Apology accepted. And I'm sorry for being a neurotic hard-ass." She offered him a shaky smile. "It's only because I care."

His shoulders sagged in relief and Lyric, who'd been watching the whole scene play out with big, sad eyes, ran a hand soothingly up the middle of his back. "Don't worry. Cash knows he needs a firm hand sometimes."

Lyric's lips curved impishly and the tension in the limo broke.

"*Ugh.*" Poppy tipped her head back and groaned. "Brain bleach. I need brain bleach *immediately.*"

"Not that this conversation isn't riveting," Rosaline cut in dryly, fingers stroking the fragile, sensitive skin of Poppy's wrist, making her shiver. "But we're here."

Cash clapped his hands together. "Game time, babe."

Lyric booped him on the nose. "I think you mean *showtime*, baby."

"Open the door before I throw up all over my suit. It's dry-clean only," Rosaline demanded, voice strained, sounding as nauseated as Poppy felt.

Cash stepped out of the limo first and immediately turned, offering his hand to Lyric, who beamed up at him as she took it, her smile as bright as the cameras that immediately flashed.

Poppy was closest to the door, logically she should've stepped out next, but she didn't, couldn't. Not until she did something first.

As if sensing her hesitation, Rosaline looked at her curiously. "Poppy?"

"Thank you," she said. "For doing what you did. I know I messed up . . ."

Rosaline's fingers banded around her wrist, her grip gentle but firm. Just right. "You think Lyric and I don't fight sometimes?" She'd also worn her hair down tonight and it fell in perfect, Old Hollywood–style waves around her shoulders, swaying when she shook her head. "Of course we fight. Let me tell you, back when we lived together?" Her lips drew to one side, quirking in a rueful little smile. "But we always get over it. Because we love each other. Cash was going to come to you, with his tail between his legs, and apologize eventually. I just nudged the inevitable along."

"Sure, but the way he felt was written all over his face as clearly as a billboard. He was going to step out on that carpet, and everyone was going to assume there was some sort of trouble brewing in paradise."

People *loved* to assume. Especially if those assumptions made for a good story. Even more so if they made them money.

Rosaline nodded emphatically. "You're right. They absolutely would have." She nudged her knee against Poppy's and smiled. "Which is why part of our job is crisis management. And it's always better to—"

"Prevent fires than have to put them out." Poppy shut her eyes. "I *know* that. Like I said, I—"

"If the next words out of your mouth are some variation of *messed up*, Curran's not going to be the only one in need of a firm hand," Rosaline warned, slightly tightening her grip on Poppy's wrist.

Her breath caught and beneath Rosaline's fingers, her pulse sped.

"Or maybe you'd like that." Heat pooled low in her gut at the scorching look Rosaline sent her, low lids and a smile that promised Poppy would love and hate what Rosaline did to her in equal measure.

She had to swallow before she could speak and even then, her voice still came out strangled, high and thready. "Maybe I would."

Rosaline exhaled sharply, seemingly as affected by the promises she was making as Poppy was. She gave Poppy's wrist another squeeze. "You're the one who helped me realize that we should be working together. You drop a ball, I pick it up. And it goes both ways. Not that I believe you dropped a ball. I think—" She paused, pressing her lips together like she was choosing her next words carefully. "Your feelings on the matter are valid. If you don't want—"

"Um." Cash ducked his head into the limo and Rosaline instantly let go of Poppy's wrist. Poppy tried not to let the snub sting and failed. Miserably. "Not to interrupt what looked like a"—he threw Rosaline a cheeky smile—"*riveting* conversation, but are you two going to, you know, do your jobs?"

Chapter Twelve

"Lyric!"

"Ms. Adair!"

"Cash! Cash!"

"Over here!"

"This way! Lyric!"

"Can we get a photo of you two together?"

"You're stunning!"

"Perfect! Can you just turn . . . ?"

Cameras clicked, photographers shouting over one another, desperate for the perfect picture of Hollywood's new *it* couple.

It was dizzying—the noise, the crowd, the sheer number of faces she'd only ever seen on TV now standing mere feet away. Poppy stood back, out of the way, soaking it all in and trying to blend into the background as much as possible and still—

"Over here! What's your name? Can you turn for me?"

She froze like a deer in the headlights. For some reason they were—they were talking to *her*.

"Just smile," Rosaline whispered, appearing at her side.

She glanced down at the badge dangling from around her neck, making sure she hadn't dropped it. "Can't they see my credentials? I'm not—"

"You're beautiful, Poppy," Rosaline murmured, head tipped

down, lips barely moving. "Who wouldn't want pictures of you?" She glanced up at Poppy through her long, dark lashes and gave her a coy smile. "Bet they'd *die* for the pictures you've promised to send me."

Poppy shuddered softly, breath leaving her body. She swayed on her heels and Rosaline's fingertips pressed into the small of her back, steadying her, keeping her from stumbling in front of what had to be at least a hundred cameras from outlets all over the country.

"Rude," she murmured. "Now I'm going to look like a tomato in every picture."

Rosaline snickered. "A very cute tomato. Now, *smile*."

"Yes, ma'am," Poppy said in a sudden, unexpected burst of cheekiness.

Rosaline's eyes widened and a sharp, too loud laugh popped out of her mouth. She shook her head, grinning. "You, Poppy Peterson, are playing with fire."

With that, she stepped away, striding gracefully down the carpet like it was a runway. Photographers called out to her by name, but she paid them no mind, simply keeping a sort of reserved smile on her face as she followed Lyric, stopping when she stopped, moving when she moved in a dance she had perfected.

Poppy smiled and—no, that was too much teeth. Looking like a rosy little hothouse tomato was one thing; the last thing she wanted was to be likened to a deranged clown. What was that thing Tyra Banks always said? Smile with your eyes? A top model she was not, but she did her best to follow that advice as she hurried after Cash.

For the most part, the two posed for photos together, separating at times for Lyric to step into the spotlight that, tonight, was rightfully hers. Aside from the occasional eye-roll-worthy cajoling request from a photographer for them to *give us a kiss, come on*, so far, the night was off to a promising start. Even those requests, as annoying as they were, could've been worse, but Rosaline still glared, appearing to take mental note of the outlets responsible.

Poppy almost pitied them. Almost.

In seemingly no time at all, they reached the final batch of photographers. Lyric was posing alone, Cash standing off to the side talking to the husband of an R & B singer currently topping the charts. Rosaline had her gaze trained on the sea of photographers, flashing occasionally to Lyric.

Poppy hung back, smile flagging, feet already throbbing, the perils of purchasing a pair of shoes the day before an event and not breaking them in. She shifted her weight from one foot to the other, turning slightly in the direction they'd just come from when—what the fuck was she—there was no way she was seeing . . .

Maybe ten, twelve yards away, only slightly tucked away by a gauzy white partition that separated the photography area from the publicist arrivals waiting tent, stood a white woman wearing the same sort of publicity credentials Poppy had on. She was slipping off her modest kitten heels and reaching up for the halter tie of her unremarkable, unembellished black dress.

Poppy whipped her head around. Was no one seeing this? All of the photographers were so focused on the talent, on getting the perfect shot, that no one but her, playing wallflower, seemed to notice. She quickly turned back to the absolute bizarre spectacle playing out just in time to witness the dress hit the carpet and— *okay*, that was *a lot* of skin.

This was only her second big red carpet, so by no means would she claim to be well-versed in the goings on of what happened behind the scenes at these things, but she was 99.9 percent sure this wasn't normal. Unless it was some kind of performance piece? Art? A *Jackass*-style revival she didn't know about? Guerrilla marketing, for what? No clue. A new album, maybe? Or maybe it was—

No.

Poppy's jaw dropped.

The woman, whoever the hell she was, turned just enough that Poppy could make out the giant tattoo on her stomach.

A giant tattoo of Lyric's *face*.

A full-color, giant tattoo of Lyric's face circled with an even larger heart with script beneath it reading, *Until death do us part.*

Growing up in Portland, Poppy had been around her fair share of *weird*. From naked bike rides to the giant pumpkin regatta to the Freakybuttrue Peculiarium, Portland was *known* for *weird*. But this? This had to take the cake, topping her list of most strange spectacles Poppy had ever seen.

The woman was still tucked far enough away that none of the photographers could see her, and everyone on the carpet was either busy posing or focused on their clients. All of the event staff was congregated at either end of the carpet, nowhere near where she was. They say look to the helpers . . .

Rosaline might not know what was happening any more than Poppy, but she'd know what to do about—

Shit.

The naked woman with Lyric's face tattooed on her stomach stepped out of her puddled dress and took off at a sprint down the carpet, headed straight for *Lyric*.

There was no time to think. Like a middle linebacker rushing a running back who made it past the defensive line, Poppy charged, hurling herself at the streaker. She tucked her head and dove, catching the woman around the waist and dragging her to the carpet, where they landed in a pile of limbs, Poppy's face smushed against the lifelike tattoo of Lyric on the woman's stomach.

Of course *now*, everyone was paying attention, cameras flashing wildly as the woman under Poppy shrieked and thrashed.

"Lyric!" the woman wailed. "Noooo! I have to see Lyric! Lyric!"

Poppy held her down as best she could—Jesus, this girl was strong. Or on something? PCP? Were bath salts still a thing? Poppy grabbed wherever she could and—wow, that was definitely *not* an arm. Spontaneous naked wrestling was *not* on the curriculum back when she was getting her bachelor's in Public Relations at UO. Not unless they counted *expect the unexpected* because there was no way anyone could've expected this, least of all Poppy.

Her own strength was beginning to flag when arms wrapped around her middle from behind and picked her up, lifting her off the woman. She let herself be dragged backward toward the security tent as no fewer than five guards descended on the streaker.

"I love you, Lyric," the streaker sobbed through snotty tears, still naked as the day she was born, while security hauled her away in a different direction. "Just give me a chance and I swear I can make you so happy."

"Holy shit, Poppy." Cash—oh thank God, it was Cash who'd pulled her off the streaker—hugged her. "What the fuck was that?"

She pushed away from his chest, still trying to catch her breath. "I don't—I don't know I just—"

Rosaline stormed through the tent flaps, fury in her eyes.

"Are you insane?" Rosaline hissed, closing the distance between them. "What were you thinking?"

"I—"

"You're not a fucking security guard, Poppy," Rosaline snapped.

Poppy cringed. "I know. I'm sorry."

"Screw security guard." Cash laughed. "She was more like a linebacker out there. Should I start calling you Ray Lewis?"

"This isn't funny, Curran," Rosaline snapped.

He crossed his arms, smile slipping into a scowl to rival hers. "You think I don't know that? Some stalker fanatic creep just tried to rush my girlfriend and I watched my best friend tackle her. Security hauled my girlfriend to a tent on the opposite side of the carpet and who the fuck knows when I'll be able to go see her because it looks like they put the whole theater on lockdown." He jerked his chin at the front of the tent where several event security guards stood blocking the entrance. "If I can't find some tiny shred of humor in this entirely fucked-up situation, I'm gonna go ballistic."

Rosaline pursed her lips. "It *was* a nice tackle."

"Good form, right?"

"I think Poppy lied when she told me she was bad at powder puff."

Cash shook his head. "No, no, she really was terrible."

"Oh my god," Poppy said, voice faint. "I think I have a concussion."

She'd never seen Cash snap into action so fast off the field, grabbing her face in his hands and staring intently into her eyes. "What day is it?"

She slapped his hands away. "I'm kidding. I just feel like I'm experiencing some sort of, I don't know, collective delusion. You two, talking about my latent football talent? Really?"

He frowned. "That's not a day, Pop-Tart."

Rosaline sighed. "Seriously, Poppy? What in god's name possessed you to do that?"

She'd honestly love to know the same. "I don't know. I was standing there, and suddenly, this woman starts stripping. Part of me thought I was seeing things. Then I spot this ginormous tattoo of Lyric on her stomach and there was no one close by to help and there's no protocol for this kind of thing, okay? Then she takes off at a dead run and I just—" She shook her head. "I didn't think, okay? I just—"

"Performed the greatest tackle to ever take place on a red carpet?" Cash chimed in.

"I didn't know how dangerous she might end up being. What kind of threat she posed." In the chaos of it all, that hadn't crossed her mind. Which probably said something about her sense of self-preservation, but that was something to unpack some other time. "All I knew was she was heading straight for Lyric."

Rosaline's face twisted and she turned her head to the side, blinking fast. "Thank you." She sniffed once and turned to Poppy, eyes shining with sincerity. "I should've said that already. That was incredibly brave of you." She huffed out a wet laugh. "Ridiculous and reckless, but incredibly brave."

Okay, yeah. *Definitely* concussed. "You're not mad?"

Rosaline reared back, staring at Poppy like she'd lost her mind, which was an absolute possibility at this point. "You threw yourself in harm's way to protect the woman who is practically my little sister. Why would I be mad?"

"I don't know, maybe because you stomped in here looking like you were on the warpath reminding me that I'm not a security guard?"

Rosaline threw her hands up. "Because you could've gotten hurt, Poppy!"

"Oh." Her shoulders slumped. "You were worried about me?"

Rosaline cupped her forehead, looking as lost as Poppy felt. "Did it seriously not occur to you that—" She broke off with a huff and shook her head, jaw clenched. "Forget it." Rosaline's gaze swept down Poppy's body and her own followed. Her dress had managed to remain mostly unscathed, some pilling on the hips from carpet burns and a small tear down at the hem. Miraculously her shoes had remained on. Probably because her feet were so swollen. "You *aren't* hurt, are you?"

A little bruised and growing more confused by the minute, but otherwise . . . "No, I'm okay."

Rosaline nodded tightly. "Good. I'm glad."

She didn't *sound* glad. She sounded pissed.

Poppy didn't know what she had done, but she wanted desperately to fix it.

"I made a scene," Poppy said. "Everyone's going to—"

"You didn't make a scene. The crazy chick who thought it was a good idea to declare her undying love for my girlfriend buck-ass naked on the red carpet made the scene," Cash said, voice hard, brokering no arguments.

Too bad because Poppy had arguments in spades. "A hundred photographers captured Cash Curran's crazy publicist tackling said streaker and wrestling her to the ground. A picture's worth a thousand words and—"

"You're not crazy, though." Cash paced in a tight circle, tugging at the roots of his hair. "Like Rosaline said, what you did was brave. It was fucking heroic."

No, she could see the headlines now and none of them were good.

This wasn't what they wanted people talking about. The focus was meant to be on Lyric's upcoming album, on Cash's new queer sports initiative in Portland, on his dedication as an athlete, on shining a positive light on their relationship. Not whatever the hell this was.

"You were there. You know what happened. But a picture without context—"

"So let's give them context," Rosaline said.

"How?"

"When they open the carpet back up, you," Rosaline said, a calculating gleam in her eye, "are going to do the press line."

MAYA @cantevenparallelpark • 4h
Lyric and Cash look so in love on the red carpet 🥺😍 #WMAs

IN MY PINING ERA @claudiaxyz92 • 4h
cash and lyric are adorable but i can't be the only one sensing some tension between their two publicists right?? someone tell me I'm not crazy #ISeeSapphicsEverywhere #WMAs

VICTORIA @pdxprincess • 4h
replying to @claudiaxyz92
yeah no something fruity is definitely happening there 👯

LILIANA @evanbuckleystan98 • 4h
replying to @pdxprincess @claudiaxyz92
no guys don't be ridiculous I bet they're just gal pals ✂️

DANI @danidarko • 4h
replying to @evanbuckleystan98 @pdxprincess @claudiaxyz92
anyone know their usernames? asking for a friend 👀

LILIANA @evanbuckleystan98 • 4h
replying to @danidarko @pdxprincess @claudiaxyz92
@/rosalinesinclair and @/poptartpdx 🫡

PAIGELA @infrontofmysalad • 4h
holy shit cash curran's publicist bodied that girl on the carpet
👁️👄👁️ #WMAs

CHERRY 💗 @polinlover96 • 4h
wait that was actually really scary 🫣 how'd that streaker get past security? @WMAs someone could've gotten hurt #WMAs

Breaking news: Potential tragedy prevented on World Music Awards' red carpet thanks to quick thinking by Cash Curran's intrepid publicist, Poppy Peterson

by Nina Breezy
published on October 21, 7 p.m. PT

This story is ongoing.

Tonight's World Music Awards was put on temporary lockdown after a streaker broke onto the red carpet.

The streaker, an individual intent on interacting with Lyric Adair, managed to evade security, and was tackled to the carpet not by Portland Pathfinders' quarterback, Cash Curran, who was in attendance, but by his publicist, Poppy Peterson.

"In this business, you're taught to expect the unexpected, and this was certainly unexpected," Peterson said when we spoke with her before the show, once the area was declared secure and the lockdown was lifted. "It was clear to me this individual posed a threat to Lyric, who is not only extremely important to Cash, but has become a friend of mine as well. Staff security was, unfortunately, not in the vicinity, and while I have every faith that Lyric's personal security would've kept her safe, I did what was necessary to prevent this individual from potentially endangering not only Lyric, but anyone else."

Peterson, fortunately, was unharmed and is being praised on social media for her quick thinking . . . and reflexes.

VICTORIA @pdxprincess • 2h
Cash Curran's publicist did what security couldn't do, and she did it in a dress and three-inch heels. Damn. 👏 #WMAs

Both Adair and Curran have expressed their immense gratitude to Peterson.

"Poppy was so brave tonight and potentially prevented what's been my worst nightmare since I was sixteen. Whether it's a festival, concert, benefit, or award show, these are meant to be safe places to come together to celebrate the music we love and the artistry and hard work that goes into creating it. No one should feel unsafe at these events or feel like they have to exercise constant vigilance," Adair said.

"I can't tell you how scary it was to see my best friend on the ground. She, and I say this with absolute sincerity, is the bravest person I know. I go up against guys who weigh 350 pounds almost every week on the field and I'd still rather tussle with them than go up against Poppy. She's a spitfire and a powerhouse and I'm proud to have her in my corner," Curran said. "But I've got to say that knowing two of the most important people in my life were in potential danger tonight makes me sick. Poppy shouldn't have had to step up, but I'm damn glad she did."

Even the Pathfinders have shown their support.

PORTLAND PATHFINDERS @portlandpathfinders • 2h
that was a hell of a sack @poptartpdxl someone's obviously been attending practices. when you get home, we've got a jersey waiting with your name on it

Rosaline Sinclair, acclaimed publicist to Lyric Adair, provided a comment. "What Poppy Peterson did was immensely brave and extremely selfless, putting herself in the proverbial line of fire. I'm proud to have her as a colleague and to have the privilege of calling her a close friend. What happened tonight should not be downplayed nor should it be trivialized; everyone needs to remember that what will most certainly become an internet meme could've been a tragedy. I'd like to know how this happened, how this individual who most certainly should not have been on the carpet managed to secure credentials and pass through security. Event staff and the private security group for the event absolutely need to answer and be held accountable for their inaction this evening. Do better."

Despite what happened on the carpet tonight, the show must go on. The ceremony proceeded with a slight delay and at the time of publication is currently underway.

Adair, despite being shaken, is confirmed to be hitting the stage. Her album *Santa Ana* releases on October 26.

Representatives for the World Music Awards and Executive Prevention Protection, the group that provides security for the event and others like it, have yet to respond to requests for comment from the *Los Angeles Times*.

Chapter Thirteen

Traffic on I-10 W at this time of night was mercifully light.

Rosaline spent the majority of the drive staring out the window and Poppy spent most of the drive staring at Rosaline.

She'd said maybe fifty words to Poppy since leaving the theater, Cash and Lyric taking a separate car to her house, skipping the after-parties in favor of a quiet night in, savoring their time together before he'd have to leave at the ass crack of dawn to fly back to Portland.

Three blocks down from Poppy's hotel, AKA Beverly Hills was hosting the iHeartRadio after-party. The entire Golden Triangle district would be teeming with paparazzi and rather than deal with that, Rosaline had suggested she stay with her, an invitation Poppy had been all too eager to take her up on.

Only now, sitting and stewing in the silent back seat of the limo, Poppy was beginning to rethink the plan.

"Are you sure you aren't mad?"

"I'm not mad. I'm—" Rosaline pressed her fingertips to the space between her brows and sighed. "When we first met, you told me that people were always going to be more important to you than good publicity. You aren't the only one who feels that way. Maybe I don't always *say* it, but . . . most people—people who don't know me—think I'm Rosaline Sinclair, Machiavellian bitch pulling strings behind the scenes who doesn't care about anything but the narrative." She stared down at her lap. "I don't want you to be most people."

Poppy didn't want to be *most people*, either. She wanted to be more than that. So much more. "I know that. I guess I just hadn't realized that you . . ."

She didn't know how to finish that sentence in a way that wouldn't give her own growing feelings away.

Rosaline's face softened. "I like you, Poppy."

The profession was bittersweet. She liked her, but she didn't like her the way Poppy was growing to like Rosaline. It wasn't the same. But it was good. It was—it was good enough. Close enough.

Not that it needed to be said, but . . . "I like you too."

A wrinkle appeared between her brows. "Do you?"

She looked at Rosaline sharply. "What's that supposed to mean?"

She shrugged a shoulder, eyes fixed on the seat in front of her. "Earlier, in the limo, you seemed uncomfortable with Curran and Lyric knowing about us. If you didn't want me to say anything to Lyric, I'm sorry. She and I, we don't really keep secrets from each other, and considering you told Curran—"

"*Technically*, I didn't tell him. The gigantic love bite you left on my neck did the talking for me."

Rosaline pressed her lips together, eyes dancing with mirth. "Sorry?"

"No, you're not." Poppy laughed.

Rosaline smirked. "No, I'm really not. Lyric had a lot of questions about what you and I were doing together alone after midnight. A lot of extremely pointed questions. So, I suppose I was put in a similar situation."

The car made a left onto Nightingale Drive, the street Rosaline lived on.

"I wasn't uncomfortable earlier. Or, yeah, I was, but only because Cash is, well—I love him, but he's Cash. His sense of humor is, well, you heard him today. And I didn't know if this"—she pointed between them—"was supposed to be like, you know, *Fight Club*."

A laugh burst from between her lips. "*Fight Club*? When I was teasing you earlier about needing a firm hand, I certainly didn't have anything quite that brutal in mind."

"No!" Poppy snickered. "The first rule of *Fight Club* is you don't talk about *Fight Club*?"

Rosaline bit her bottom lip, clearly stifling a laugh. "No, it's not like *Fight Club*. At least not to me. I mean, unlike Lyric—who, for the record, is a big fat liar because she does, in fact, go into specifics, meaning I know entirely too much about your best friend's sex life—I'm a firm believer that *some* things should remain private. That being said"—Rosaline reached out and tucked a strand of hair behind Poppy's ear—"a part of me wants to brag to everyone I know that I get to have you like this."

Rosaline's touch lingered, fingers grazing the shell of Poppy's ear, the lobe, the sensitive spot behind it, before she trailed the back of her knuckles along her neck.

Poppy shivered. "Get to have me like what?"

The wrought iron gate outside of Rosaline's house opened, allowing the car to pass.

Rosaline took her hand away, lips quirking when Poppy arched her neck, chasing Rosaline's touch. "Come inside with me and find out."

Overnight bag slung over her shoulder, Poppy followed Rosaline into the house.

"You can just set that down anywhere," Rosaline said, locking the front door and kicking off her heels, sighing softly as she curled her toes in the plush pile of the colorful runner that stretched down the hall.

Poppy dropped her duffel and clutch near the big planter by the door and steadied herself on the entry table to step out of these godforsaken heels that, at this point, were practically suctioned to her poor feet. She caught a glimpse of her reflection in the gilt bronze Rococo-style mirror hanging on the wall over the table.

For all the stress and rigmarole of the day, including her unfortunate red-carpet audition for *WWE SmackDown!* she didn't look too shabby. Her hair had fallen flat, and her mascara had started to flake, leaving a faint smudge under her eyes, but it wasn't nearly as scary a sight as she'd expected.

"Did I tell you how beautiful you look tonight?" Rosaline swept her hair aside, baring her shoulder, a shoulder which she hooked her chin over, wrapping her arms around Poppy's waist and studying them in the mirror, a small smile flirting at the corners of her lips.

Poppy shook her head and melted back against Rosaline. "You just told me I clean up nice."

"You do." Rosaline pressed her lips against the bare skin of Poppy's shoulder, just behind her dress strap. "Look beautiful."

"Thanks." She tipped her head to the side, baring more skin for Rosaline to explore with her mouth, the gentle sweeping brushes of her lips making Poppy's skin prickle. "But I think we can both agree this dress looks better on the floor."

Rosaline buried her smile against Poppy's skin, pressing a too-soft kiss to the spot where her neck met her shoulder. "Do you trust me?"

Poppy had slept with people before with whom she'd trusted

only so far as to stop if she asked them to, the barest of minimums. On the other hand, she'd told Rosaline things only Cash, her closest friend, knew. Of course she trusted her. Trusted her more than she trusted herself right now, probably.

"Of course."

Rosaline pressed against the small of her back, silently urging her to lean forward.

"I really do like this dress," she said, reaching for the zipper and sliding it halfway down Poppy's back. Taller than Poppy now, with her bent over like this, Rosaline's gaze flickered down, meeting hers in the mirror. "I think maybe it should stay on a little longer."

She slipped her fingers under the straps and tugged them down Poppy's arms, making her shiver. The fabric didn't quite pool, hindered by the zipper. Instead, Rosaline gave the top of the dress a tug until the bodice slipped, baring Poppy's breasts.

Her face flamed, totally on display and in front of a mirror no less.

Rosaline reached around her body and cupped her breasts, lifting them, thumbs brushing her nipples. They felt heavy, her nipples hardened into taut peaks from the cool air and Rosaline's simple touch.

"Every part of you is so fucking *pretty*," Rosaline murmured, letting Poppy's breasts fall, hanging heavy outside her dress. "Can I touch you?" Her hands skirted Poppy's sides, dragging the fabric of her dress up her thighs, and gathering it around her waist.

Poppy braced her hands against the table, palms flat. "I thought you *were* touching me."

A sting against the back of her hip made her gasp and arch her back, Rosaline having snapped the elastic of her underwear against her skin. She shifted restlessly, rubbing her thighs together.

"That's not what I meant, and you know it," Rosaline said, slipping a leg between Poppy's knees and knocking a foot against the inside of hers. Taking the hint, Poppy spread her feet apart, sucking in a startled gasp when Rosaline pressed firmly against her back, bending her over the entry table. Poppy's hands scrambled against the wood, seeking purchase, fingers curling around the back edge closest to the wall as Rosaline slipped a hand under her dress, fingers stroking up the back of her right thigh to the curve of her ass, teasing.

Poppy blinked down at the glossy wood finish, hair spilling over her shoulder in a curtain. "Touch me. Please?"

Rosaline's lips skimmed the back of Poppy's neck, a gentle brush that sent a shiver down her spine. "That's good, Poppy. You're going to keep being good for me, aren't you?"

Poppy trembled, breathing fast. "Yeah."

"Keep your hands on the table, okay? Don't move them."

She nodded, keeping her palms braced and holding still as Rosaline's arms disappeared from around her, the warmth at her back disappearing too. She could've lifted her head and looked in the mirror, but there was something heady about the anticipation, about not knowing what Rosaline was going to do, where she was going to touch that set her blood on—

"*Oh my god.*" Poppy jerked, rising up onto her toes, Rosaline's mouth suddenly between her legs, her breath hot and damp against Poppy's panty-covered core.

Rosaline chuckled against her, fingers dipping beneath the elastic at her hips, tugging her panties down her thighs, letting them pool around her feet. Her laughter morphed into a soft, breathless moan.

"Fuck, Poppy," she rasped, sounding reverent, thumbs parting Poppy's folds, holding her open. Poppy's toes curled harder in the rug, her face on fire. "You're dripping, sweetheart."

The little term of endearment made her heart clench. "*Rosaline.*"

There was no warning, just Rosaline's tongue running up her slit making her jerk hard, one knee knocking into the table.

"Don't hurt yourself," Rosaline teased, and then her mouth was back on Poppy, tongue dipping inside her, curling, avoiding Poppy's clit, driving her crazy.

Poppy mewled and pressed back against her face, one hand rising to steady herself against the mirror. "*Please.*"

Teeth bit into the swell of her ass making her startle, air leaving her lungs. "What did I say, Poppy?"

Her tongue swiped at her bottom lip, mouth dry as she panted. Rosaline had said a lot of things. A lot of really spine-melting, mind-bending, *amazing* things. Put on the spot, she couldn't recall a single one.

She hissed through her teeth when Rosaline bit her on the other cheek, hard enough to sting, maybe even to bruise. She hoped it did.

The ache between her thighs grew more insistent, impossible to ignore.

Rosaline tutted softly. "I told you to keep your hands on the table, baby."

Baby. As if her brain wasn't short-circuited already. "Sorry."

Two of Rosaline's fingers slipped through her folds, sliding inside of her, making her breath hitch. "You can be patient for me, can't you? Just a little longer?"

She trembled, elbows locked, arms quaking. "Uh-huh."

Her fingers dragged almost all the way out before sliding back in, slow little thrusts that made Poppy curl her toes in the rug, trying hard, *so* hard to keep from squirming and pressing back, riding Rosaline's hand, rushing her along.

With her other hand, Rosaline reached between Poppy's legs to strum her clit and she pumped her fingers insider her a little faster. "You're doing so good for me, sweetheart."

A choked sob slipped out, something inside her chest loosening at the praise.

Rosaline swore on a harsh exhale and then her mouth was back on Poppy, warm and wet, licking from where she was dripping all the way up to—*fuck*, Rosaline's tongue swept right over her hole, circling her rim slowly before pressing, spearing Poppy with the very tip of her tongue.

She couldn't help it then, arching and rocking back, riding Rosaline's fingers, her face. Desperate.

"Good," she praised, fingers speeding, curling down and pressing hard, drawing desperate little mewls from Poppy's lips. She pressed a kiss to Poppy's ass cheek. "You're so close. I can feel your cunt fluttering around my fingers."

Pressure built and she pressed her face against the crook of her elbow, spots dancing behind her lids each time she closed her eyes.

Even if it killed her, she refused to tip over the edge. Not until—

"Whenever you want, okay?" Rosaline whispered, teeth grazing her skin as she curled her fingers harder, faster. "Don't hold back."

Everything inside her drew impossibly tight and with one more curl of Rosaline's fingers pressing against that perfect spot, the dam inside her burst, pleasure ripping through her so good she could hardly stand it.

"That's it," Rosaline soothed, letting up on her clit, fingers thrusting a few more times, languid, before easing them from Poppy's cunt. Almost immediately, Poppy's knees buckled, and Rosaline laughed, not unkindly, as Poppy sagged to the floor in a spent, satiated heap. "Are you all right?"

Poppy blew her hair out of her face and looked over her shoulder. Rosaline was kneeling, eyes bright beneath half-mast lids, a smug smile playing at the edges of her lips.

It took her a minute to find her voice. "You know," she panted. "When we talked on the phone last week and you said you were going to put me on my knees, I didn't think you meant like this."

Rosaline chuckled and banded an arm around Poppy beneath her breasts, dragging her back against Rosaline's chest. "The night's young."

Her heart skipped. "Sounds like you have plans for me."

"I did tell you I have a plethora of ideas of what I want to do to you, did I not?"

Her breath, just barely having slowed, quickened, her interest piqued. "A *plethora*, huh?"

"One might even go so far as to say a surplus," Rosaline confirmed, pressing her lips to the hinge of Poppy's jaw. "I highly doubt we'll be able to get through even a fraction of them before the sun comes up."

That just meant there would need to be a next time. "Out of curiosity—do all of these ideas of yours take place just inside your front door?"

Rosaline drew back, one brow arching imperiously. "Are you complaining about what we just did?"

The idea was so ludicrous she couldn't help but laugh. "Not in the slightest." The rug under her was softer than some couches she'd slept on. But she wouldn't mind seeing the rest of Rosaline's house. The bedroom, mostly. "I was just wondering what was on the agenda for the rest of the evening."

"Agenda?" Rosaline asked, hauling herself to standing. Poppy stayed down, unsure if she even *could* stand, knees still weak. "You make it sound like I put together an actual schedule."

"Ten to ten fifteen, fuck Poppy in the foyer," she teased. "Check."

Rosaline's eyes crinkled at the corners, an amused smile tugging at her mouth. "Oh, please. I'm not *that* anal."

She had barely opened her mouth to make a joke when Rosaline, as if sensing what she was about to say, reached down and pressed a finger to her lips, effectively shushing her. Her eyes narrowed, lips twitching, clearly holding back a smile even if she didn't want Poppy to see it. "That was low-hanging fruit. Don't even."

"You have no idea what I was about to say," she protested playfully.

Rosaline's hand cradled Poppy's jaw. "What I know is that you are *entirely* too verbal for someone whose knees I just watched give out."

"You're resourceful." She turned her head and pressed a kiss to Rosaline's palm, looking up at her from beneath her lashes. "I'm sure you can figure out a way to shut me up."

If not, Poppy had an idea or twelve she'd be more than happy to share.

"Can you stand, or are your knees still too weak?"

"Yeah, yeah, yuck it up." She took Rosaline's hand when she offered it, helping Poppy up. "No one likes a braggart, Rosaline."

Rosaline's thumb swept against Poppy's cheekbone. There was a softness in her eyes, a tenderness to her smile, as she stared at Poppy, who had to have looked utterly debauched, tits out and dress hiked up around her waist, face undoubtedly flushed and sweaty and god knew what her makeup looked like now. Yet Rosaline was looking at her like she was the prettiest thing in the room.

"You still trust me?" she asked.

A flippant joke on the tip of her tongue was swiftly swallowed, the look on Rosaline's face a touch too earnest to be met with humor.

"I do."

Rosaline's answering smile was resplendent, making Poppy's stomach swoop with an intensity that stole her breath. Like she was on a roller coaster headed down the drop, all she could do was hold on and enjoy the ride.

With an enviably steady hand, Rosaline cupped her jaw, tipping her chin down, her gaze flickering between Poppy's eyes and her lips. Poppy held her breath as Rosaline leaned in slowly, the distance between their faces dwindling, Poppy all but able to taste the single glass of champagne Rosaline had drunk during the show, the sweet, sharp scent of it mixing with the tang of Poppy's arousal, clinging to Rosaline's warm breath. It fanned against Poppy's face, her lips, lips she parted in anticipation, holding perfectly still save for the rapid rise and fall of her chest.

Rosaline's lips pressed against Poppy's, pillowy soft and hot. Her tongue swept across the seam.

Poppy's lungs burned and her knees shook, threatening to give out again. Rosaline tore her mouth away with a gasp, chest rising and falling against Poppy's.

"I have an idea," Rosaline said as if she hadn't just turned Poppy's world on its head, kissing her like she was starving for it. Starving for her.

"Am I going to like this idea?" she asked, following Rosaline past what looked like a formal living room and down another hall.

"I know I am," Rosaline said, stopping in front of the first door on the left, reaching inside, flipping on the light. She gestured Poppy to go in ahead of her. "You," she said, laughing, "are either going to love it or hate it."

Her heart pounded. That sounded . . . ominous? Promising? She couldn't be sure. "Do I get a hint at least?"

Like the rest of the house, what she'd seen of it, Rosaline's bedroom was outfitted in rich jewel tones. The walls were painted a moody shade of teal, the tray ceiling too, and an amethyst-colored rug covered the dark hardwood floor. In the center of the room, against the wall, was a magnificent brass four-poster bed made up simply with a plush-looking emerald duvet Poppy wanted to roll around on.

Rosaline swept Poppy's hair over her shoulder and reached for the zipper at the middle of her back. "I'll do you one better and tell you everything." She lowered the zipper the rest of the way, satin pooling around Poppy's feet. "How's that?"

Anticipation all but made her vibrate. "I'm listening."

Rosaline's breath ghosted against the shell of her ear. "First, I want you to go lie down. Middle of the bed, on your back. Get comfortable. Think you can do that?"

In that bed? She didn't see how she *couldn't* get comfortable. "I don't know," she teased, padding across the room and kneeling onto the bed. She crawled toward the mountain of pillows piled at the headboard and flopped onto her back, doing as Rosaline had asked, getting comfortable. "That was *quite* the Herculean task."

From the doorway, Rosaline looked at Poppy, eyes sweeping over her from head to toe, gaze hot and hungry. "See, you joke now, but in ten—hell, five—minutes you're not going to be laughing."

"If I'm not laughing," she asked, sitting up slightly, propped on her elbows, watching as Rosaline reached for and undid the single button that held her suit jacket together, "what *am* I going to be doing?"

"I'd say screaming." Rosaline shrugged the jacket off her shoulders and down her arms, letting it fall to the floor, forgotten. "But your mouth is going to be otherwise occupied."

Poppy's mouth went dry.

Stunning and *gorgeous* and *beautiful* were fine words, apt even, but they didn't do Rosaline justice. She was a work of art, a canvas of shimmering golden skin and dark, delicate ink that wrapped around her arms, covering her from shoulder to wrist, a few smaller pieces on her ribs and above her left breast, just over her heart.

Like Poppy, she'd foregone a bra, the plunging neckline of her suit jacket not allowing for one. Now, jacket discarded, she was bare down to the waist, breasts full and high, no more than a handful and *god* did Poppy want her hands full.

"Did no one ever teach you it was impolite to stare?" Rosaline teased, crossing the room, hands dropping to the button of her pants.

Poppy sputtered out a laugh. "Pot, kettle."

Maybe she was gawking, but Rosaline had just been looking at Poppy like she wanted to unhinge her jaw and swallow her whole.

"Well, you're going to give a girl a complex," Rosaline said, sliding her pants over her hips and down her thighs, leaving her in a pair of skimpy red underwear, a scrap of lace that left little to the imagination. A massive floral piece decorated her side, ink curling around the jut of her hip and trailing down to nearly her knee, grayscale like the rest of her tattoos and just as intricate. Poppy wanted to press her mouth to Rosaline's skin, trace each and every swirl of ink on Rosaline's body with the tip of her tongue.

"I was thinking you're more beautiful than any painting I've ever seen." More riveting too.

Rosaline's footsteps faltered and she blushed prettily. "You must not be much of an art connoisseur."

Maybe not, but like she'd told Rosaline once before... "I know what I like when I see it."

Her blush deepened, skin turning the most alluring shade of pink, a flush that swept along the crests of her cheeks and the bridge of her nose. "You're sweet." She rounded the bed and crouched in front of her nightstand, setting her phone on it, and opening the bottom drawer. "For what it's worth, you're prettier than any piece of artwork I've ever seen too." Her smile turned sly. "You're even prettier when you come."

Poppy waited with bated breath as Rosaline turned back to the nightstand, riffling inside the drawer.

Rosaline let out a soft *aha!* and rose from her crouch, a small, hot-pink egg vibrator in her hand.

"Here's what I was thinking," she said, crawling across the bed, kneeling beside Poppy. "Spread your legs for me, sweetheart. I want to see you."

She let her thighs fall open and drew her knees apart, going the extra mile, reaching down and spreading herself open.

Rosaline's eyes darkened as she stared. "So fucking pretty." She reached a hand between Poppy's thighs, sinking three fingers inside her heat, her thumb brushing Poppy's clit. Poppy snapped her thighs together with a whimper.

"Sensitive?" Rosaline grabbed her knee, lifting and pressing it back, holding her open. She removed her thumb from Poppy's oversensitive clit and curled her fingers inside Poppy harder. "Is this okay?"

Her legs shook and she could hear how wet she was, the slick sounds coming from between her thighs making her flush to the roots of her hair. "What happened to me touching you?"

"Patience, Poppy." Rosaline withdrew her hand, fingers sliding out of Poppy's cunt leaving her bereft, making her whimper. She reached for the egg vibrator and glided the silicone toy through Poppy's folds. She pressed the vibrator inside of Poppy. "Still okay?"

She wriggled atop the duvet. "Peachy."

Rosaline rose up onto her knees, tongue sweeping across her lips hungrily. Her thumbs slid under the sides of her panties and wiggled them down her thighs, revealing a dark, neatly trimmed thatch of curls that glistened in the light. "I was thinking I'd spare your poor, weak knees," she said, throwing Poppy a cheeky smile and tossing a leg over her, straddling her chest, "and ride your face instead."

Poppy's mouth watered. Yes. That. She wanted that. She nodded quickly, eagerly, and reached out, skimming her hand up the inside of Rosaline's thigh, skin silky smooth under her fingers. "You come up with the best plans."

"I thought you'd like it," she said, and Poppy tried to drag her down, drag her closer, hands wrapping around her hips. Rosaline covered Poppy's hands with her own and smiled when she groaned impatiently. "You want to be good for me, don't you?"

More than anything. "I do."

Rosaline's hips shifted restlessly above Poppy. The insides of her thighs glistened with arousal. "You're going to make me come with that mouth I haven't been able to stop thinking about since—" She shut one eye like she was thinking back, then huffed out a broken laugh, chin dropping to her chest. She raised her head, tongue swiping against her bottom lip before her mouth quirked in a small smile, her green eyes bright as she stared down at Poppy. "Since you answered the phone and shushed me."

She choked on a laugh. "I didn't. I was—"

Rosaline pressed a finger to Poppy's lips and arched a brow. "*You* are going to make me come with your mouth and until I do—" she reached for her phone, keyed in her passcode, and swiped at the screen, "I am going to make *you* come. As many times as I want."

Rosaline tapped the screen one more time and—

Poppy jolted, fingers spasming against Rosaline's hips as the toy inside her flared to life, rumbling right against her G-spot. Her mouth fell open.

Rosaline set her phone down beside her, within easy reach. "The battery is good for five hours of continuous use." Rosaline smiled deviously. "I made sure it was charged. Theoretically, I could make you come over and over and over again, if I wanted."

Five hours of—Poppy groaned and dug her head into the pillow, fingers scrambling against the comforter for purchase. She was already half out of her mind. Screw five hours; it wouldn't take five minutes to drive her out of her mind entirely.

"For what it's worth, I have the utmost faith that it won't take you five hours to get me off." Rosaline knee-walked farther up the bed, setting her hands on the headboard. "How does all that sound?"

Poppy let out a slow, deliberate exhale and tried to relax. The vibrations weren't intense, but they were distracting, jolts of pleasure licking at her spine. As many times as Rosaline wanted. Christ. She hated to ask, but . . . "What if I can't? What if it's—"

"Snap your fingers and everything stops," Rosaline promised.

"Otherwise, I'll be the one to decide what you can handle." With gentle fingers, she brushed the hair off Poppy's forehead and tucked it behind her ears. "I'm still taking care of you, remember?"

She swallowed past the lump blossoming in her throat, doing her best to put the pressure building in her core out of her mind. Without any friction on her clit, Poppy was trapped, stuck in a holding pattern, a state of limbo so close to the edge she could taste it, but not close enough to fall off. She could always reach down and touch herself, but her clit was swollen to the extent of almost hurting if she touched it. "Can I please make you come now?"

Rosaline shuddered softly, eyes slipping shut. "Well, seeing as you asked so nicely."

Hands braced on the headboard, Rosaline widened her stance, hovering over Poppy's face, so close, but so far and—

Fuck it. Patience fractured, Poppy surged up, the muscles of her stomach burning as she crunched forward slightly, burying her face in Rosaline's cunt, her nose in the neatly trimmed thatch of curls between her thighs. She ran the flat of her tongue up Rosaline's slit, giving her a broad lick.

A breathless laugh escaped Rosaline's lips, hips jerking. "Jesus."

Poppy turned her head, burying a smile against the crease of Rosaline's thigh, the place where her leg met her body, her scent here strong and perfect, perfume faint and fading, mingling with the smell of sex, all muted musk and clean sweat, making Poppy's mouth water and her head swim, dizzy with desire.

Hands wrapping around Rosaline's thighs, skin soft and muscles firm beneath Poppy's fingers, Poppy dragged her down, dragged her close, tongue dipping inside her cunt, earning her the sweetest-sounding gasp for her trouble.

Rosaline had said she'd be the one to decide what Poppy could handle, but she had no idea the depths of Poppy's desperation, how badly she *wanted* the full weight of Rosaline against her, wanted to be wholly and completely at her mercy, to show her just how *good* she could be, wanted, *ached* to hear Rosaline say the words.

With the tip of her tongue, she gave Rosaline's clit a teasing lick.

"Your *mouth*." Rosaline groaned. "I knew it would—would be, but I—I didn't—" Her voice broke when Poppy wrapped her lips around the bundle and sucked. A shudder wracked Rosaline's body, her abdomen tensing, twitching. "*Fuck*."

Inside her, the vibrator sped, the sudden change in intensity tearing a gasp from her throat, the sound muffled against Rosaline's flesh. Sweat beaded along her hairline, the muscles in her thighs and stomach tensing, toes curling, and, with an intensity that stole her breath, her body turned itself inside out, brain short-circuiting. All she could do was close her eyes and ride it out and pray it didn't actually kill her, her heart pounding in a way she was pretty sure wasn't healthy.

She turned her head and whined into the crook of Rosaline's hip. "I can't."

Rosaline shushed her sweetly, one hand leaving the headboard, stroking her hair. "You can. You're okay. You're doing so good." She rolled her hips, dragging her pussy against Poppy's mouth. "*So* good."

Aftershocks of pleasure rippled through her, insides fluttering, clenching around the amazing, *awful*, still-buzzing toy, but it was the praise that made her squirm. Made her want to try harder. Do better. She fastened her lips around Rosaline's clit and flicked her tongue fast and hard, determined to make her come because *she* couldn't. Not again. No matter what Rosaline said, it would wreck her, send her splintering into a million little pieces she'd never, ever be able to put back together.

"You're—*oh*, fucking hell, Poppy, you're—*god*, you're perfect," Rosaline babbled, rocking down against Poppy's mouth. "Feels so—" She sucked in a sharp breath. "Good. I'm so close."

Fuck, so was Poppy. Everything south of her belly button went molten, and the flimsy, gossamer-thin thread holding together snapped, the pleasure rolling through her so good, so sharp it almost hurt. A blissful sort of agony that made her eyes prickle and her vision blur, her fingers digging hard into Rosaline's hips.

Rosaline bolted upright with a sharp cry, hips jerking and thighs quaking. After a moment she listed to the side and reached for her phone with a trembling hand, taking mercy on Poppy and shutting off the vibrator just as she passed the point of oversensitivity.

One hand still on the headboard, Rosaline rose up onto her knees and climbed over Poppy, settling into the space beside her. She leaned in and brushed her mouth against Poppy's, a sweet kiss that curled Poppy's toes and took her breath away. She pressed her lips to the corner of Poppy's mouth, her jaw, the lobe of her ear, the tender space behind it. Chaste little connect-the-dot kisses that made Poppy melt into the mattress. Everywhere her lips could reach without moving down the bed, Rosaline kissed. Task complete, Rosaline flopped back against the pillows with a shuddering sigh. Her lids were heavy and her green eyes soft as she reached out, thumb sweeping against Poppy's cheekbone. "Was that okay?"

Her heart squeezed dangerously. Was it *okay*? Poppy huffed. "I can't believe you're asking me that question." As if Rosaline hadn't made her come so hard she was pretty sure the fabric of the universe had torn, creating a rift in the cosmos, the consequences of which were yet to be discovered. "Shouldn't I be asking you that?"

"Considering my brain may or may not still be leaking out my ears, *okay* is an understatement."

Poppy snorted. "Sexy."

Rosaline tapped the tip of Poppy's nose with her finger, making her go cross-eyed. She chuckled softly. "You realize I wasn't planning on actually *sitting* on your face, right?"

Poppy scooted closer. The pillow under her cheek smelled like citrus and musk, rose and patchouli. Like Rosaline's perfume and sex—if Poppy could bottle the smell she would. Spray it all over her room, bathe in it. Cash would probably have something to say about that, but he could consider it payback for all those times he'd picked her up back in high school with his funky ass, sweat- and sock-smelling gym bag in the back seat instead of the trunk where it belonged.

"It's called face *sitting*, not face *hovering*," Poppy pointed out. "I don't believe in doing things halfway."

"Hm, no. You really don't, do you?" Rosaline grinned and reached out, winding a sweaty strand of Poppy's hair around her finger before tucking it behind Poppy's ear. "I almost crushed you with my thighs. You could've suffocated. What would I have told the police? The *headlines*, Poppy? I'd have an unmitigated PR disaster on my hands all because of your hubris."

"Icarus flew too close to the sun and I, what? Buried my face too deep in your pussy?" She laughed. "Bad press surrounding my hypothetical and untimely demise aside, at least as far as final meals go, I'd have had no complaints."

Rosaline tucked her face into her pillow with a groan. "That was abominable."

It really was god awful. And yet she couldn't help herself. Give her an inch and she was liable to take a mile. "Don't you know, fallen warriors go to Vulva-halla, Rosaline."

Without raising her head or looking at Poppy, she pointed at the door. "Get out. Right now. I mean it."

"*Nooo.*" She laughed and slipped her arm around Rosaline, encircling her waist, breasts mashed against Rosaline's back as she clung to her like a sloth. "I like your bed."

It was warm and soft and that was even without crawling beneath the sheets, which she'd bet her left tit were just as soft, if not softer, than the duvet. But far and above all else, the best thing about Rosaline's bed was that she was currently in it.

Rosaline cracked open one eye, glaring weakly. "I see how it is. I'm nothing more than a glorified Airbnb to you."

"More like a true-blue bed-and-breakfast," she teased, nuzzling the ball of Rosaline's shoulder. "Except, in case it wasn't clear, you're the break—"

Rosaline lurched forward, swallowing her words with a kiss.

"What am I going to do with you?" Rosaline asked, shaking her head, a smile stealing across her face.

Keep her. If she was looking for suggestions, she should absolutely, 100 percent keep Poppy. Keep her in this bed, just—keep her, period.

"I'm going to have to gag you, aren't I?"

Poppy bit her lip and smiled impishly. "Don't threaten me with a good time."

"It's hardly a threat if I intend to make good on it." Rosaline sat up and threw her legs over the side of the bed. Poppy didn't pout, but it was a near thing. "Are you hungry?"

Starving. Aside from a meager table of hors d'oeuvres in the freezing cold publicists' lounge Poppy had only briefly poked her head in, there had been no food, not unless you counted the

Vosges chocolate truffles Lyric had offered Poppy from her gift bag, which she did not accept. Only free-flowing champagne and cocktails that Poppy had obviously not indulged in were served during the show, imbibing encouraged, eating not.

Not that, at the time, she'd had much of an appetite. Now was a different story.

Rosaline padded her way across the room to her dresser and rummaged through the top drawer. She tossed a bundle of fabric at Poppy. "Get dressed." She slipped a T-shirt over her head, white and oversize. "I'll whip you up my specialty."

Chapter Fourteen

"What do you have against peanut butter and jelly?"

Poppy finished chewing and reached for her can of cherry vanilla soda. "Nothing." She hid her smile behind the can. "I guess I wasn't expecting this to be your culinary specialty. That's all."

"I never claimed to be a chef." Rosaline crossed her arms. "I am a publicist."

"A great one," Poppy agreed, trying not to laugh at how Rosaline was getting up in arms, huffy because Poppy had giggled when she'd set the plate down in front of her, peanut butter and jelly sandwich cut into two neat triangles with the crusts removed.

She wasn't laughing *at* her, she was just . . . amused. And bizarrely touched? Her own mother had never gone to such lengths, more the type to tuck a five-dollar bill in her book bag than pack her a sack lunch.

"This is Los Angeles," Rosaline argued. "No one here cooks. Everyone either has a private chef, shops the hot bar at Erewhon, or orders takeout."

She was pretty sure that's what people said about New Yorkers, not Angelinos, and even then, it was a sweeping generalization, probably not true for a decent percentage of people. The grand majority even.

"Or they know how to make a mean PB&J," she teased.

She narrowed her eyes. "Are you implying you can do better?"

As far as quick, low effort, postcoital midnight snacks went? Probably not, nothing quite like a PB&J when the mood struck. But for all her shortcomings, Poppy was no slouch in the kitchen. "Cash got me cooking lessons for my birthday last year. I'm not about to give Gordon Ramsay a run for his money or anything, but I do all right. Not that there's anything wrong with this." She held up her sandwich. "Perfect ratio of peanut butter to jelly *and* you cut it into triangles, which everyone knows makes it taste better. Ten out of ten, no notes. Bonus points for removing the crust."

Rosaline averted her eyes, a blush creeping up the front of her neck. "It's white bread," she muttered. "No one likes white bread crust."

"Exactly." Poppy grinned. "Thank you. It's delicious."

Rosaline picked at her own sandwich, tearing off a corner of the bread and popping it in her mouth, nibbling idly unlike Poppy, who had already devoured half her sandwich, hungrier than she'd even realized. "Cooking is . . . *not* a skill I possess," she admitted with a wince. "Years ago, when Lyric moved in with me, I made—*tried* to make—this five-cheese lasagna I saw someone make on the Food Network. There may or may not have been a minor incident involving a small broiler fire that resulted in the fire department being called." Her wince turned into a chagrined smile. "As Lyric loves to say, it's safer for everyone if I just stick with takeout."

The LAFD might beg to differ, but it was a travesty not to make use of a kitchen this gorgeous, with top-of-the-line appliances.

"And that was what? Eight? Nine years ago? Maybe it's time to get back on the horse."

"Implying I was ever on said horse to begin with." Rosaline rolled her eyes and gave a self-effacing laugh. "Like I said, it's simply not a skill I possess."

She said it as if it were immutable: once a terrible cook, always a terrible cook.

"I started a kitchen fire once."

Rosaline paused, hand hovering over her plate. She looked at Poppy curiously. "Is that why Curran got you the cooking lessons? Cheaper than a full-kitchen remodel?"

She huffed out a quiet laugh. "No, I was, uh, I was six at the time, I think. Maybe seven."

Rosaline frowned. "And your parents were where exactly?"

"Out." Poppy shrugged. "Some work dinner for my dad, I guess." Time had blurred some edges of the memory and sharpened others, setting them in stark relief. She remembered the blue raspberry sucker the very kind fire captain had given her while they waited on the porch for her parents to return. How she'd been so confused when her dad had lied and said the sitter must've run to the store and left Poppy by herself. How later that night Mom had been hysterical, her voice shrill as she cried and demanded to know what in the world Poppy had been thinking using the stove when she knew good and well she wasn't supposed to. That she could've burned down the house and what were they supposed to tell the neighbors who'd all seen the fire trucks parked out on the street? "My babysitter canceled last minute, and my parents figured I was old enough to stay home alone for a few hours. Which would've been fine had I not gotten hungry and tried to make myself mac 'n' cheese. On the stove." She cringed. "I forgot the water."

She hated the way Rosaline looked at her, green eyes full of pity Poppy didn't want, her lips parted like she didn't quite know what to say. It was just a stupid thing that had happened when she was a dumb kid. She knew how it sounded, *bad*, but it's not like she was traumatized by it. She was fine. There was no use crying over burned macaroni from almost two decades ago.

"Poppy—"

"The silver lining was the fire department came to my school two weeks later for a safety demonstration—stop, drop, and roll and all that jazz—and it was the same firehouse that responded to the call at my house. The fire captain remembered me by name, and all my classmates thought it was the coolest thing ever. I was easily the most popular kid in class for the rest of the week."

Rosaline's expression settled into a scowl. "No offense, but I don't think I like your parents very much."

"They're not bad people," she stressed, not wanting to give the wrong idea. "They're just—"

"Bad parents?" Rosaline arched a brow.

Poppy shrugged. "They were just done having kids by the time they had me."

To hear the stories Dillon and Jessica, her brother and sister, told about their respective childhoods, someone would think they'd been raised by entirely different parents from Poppy. Parents who took them camping on the weekends and on fun family summer road trips down the Oregon coast and taught them how to ride their bikes and swim and helped them with their homework and went to all their soccer games.

Poppy had never gotten any of that.

Which was fine. So maybe on occasion they'd forgotten to sign her permission slips and pack her lunches, and maybe there hadn't been any money left in the college savings account after Dillon got his master's, meaning she'd had to take out student loans, but they'd never laid a hand on her, she'd never gone hungry, and her clothes were new and clean. And she'd always had Cash, first to run around the neighborhood with and later to whisk her away in his beat-up Honda Accord. Poppy's childhood might not have been anything to write home about, but she'd turned out okay. Moderately well-adjusted, some might even say.

Rosaline's face was pinched. "That's no excuse to—"

"Let's not talk about my parents." Rosaline wasn't her therapist; she didn't want to hear about Poppy's *woe is me* childhood. It was depressing, too depressing for the casual relationship Rosaline was seeking. The one Poppy was determined not to ruin, especially not with her too-big feelings and not by talking about her parents, either.

Rosaline looked like she wanted to argue but instead dipped her chin in a reluctant nod. "So you can cook. Tell me, what other secret talents does Poppy Peterson possess that I don't know about?"

"I'd hardly call it a talent," she demurred. "The cooking classes did the heavy lifting, trust me."

By nature, she wasn't very talented. Hardly anything came easily or intuitively to her, but what she lacked in natural ability she made up for with a streak of stubbornness a mile wide, unable to take no for an answer, even when the call was coming from inside the house. When her own inaptitude was what held her back.

Rosaline rounded the counter and joined her at the bar, sliding onto the high-back barstool beside her. She turned, facing Poppy, one of her knees slotting between hers. "You should give yourself more credit."

"You haven't tried my food," she joked.

Her hand found Poppy's thigh and squeezed. "I wasn't just talking about your cooking, Poppy." Her gaze had softened, her voice too, and Poppy didn't know what to do with the warmth unfurling inside her chest other than steadfastly ignore it.

"But maybe you can sometime." Rosaline's fingers toyed with the hem of the borrowed, oversize shirt that hit Poppy mid-thigh. Baby pink and with the name of a barre studio printed across the front, it smelled like the lavender sachets Rosaline kept in her dresser and a little like her perfume too.

"Maybe I can what?" she asked stupidly, not even sure what they were talking about anymore. Rosaline's touch was distracting, the way her fingers brushed against Poppy's thigh wreaking havoc on her ability to focus.

"Maybe you can cook for me sometime," Rosaline clarified, letting go of Poppy's shirt and reaching the hand Poppy was resting on the counter. She flipped Poppy's hand over and, with the tip of her finger, traced the lines of her palm leaving shivery tingles in her wake. Her gaze lifted, eyes flitting over Poppy's face. "Show me what I'm missing."

"Oh." Poppy nodded and fought the urge to curl her fingers around Rosaline's. Hold her hand. "Sure. I could—I could do that. How do you feel about Indian? I just learned how to make saag paneer. I could make that."

Rosaline ducked her head and, for whatever reason, smiled at her lap. "I'd like that."

"Cool." Poppy nodded then stopped, worried that she resembled an overeager bobblehead.

"You were going to tell me all about the other secret skills you possess," Rosaline prompted, thumb sweeping an incredibly diverting arc against the inside of Poppy's wrist.

She reached for her soda and took a long sip. "I'm training for a marathon. Or, well, Cash and I are training for a marathon. Cash is training *me* for a marathon." He'd put together a detailed training regimen and everything. "Not that that's a skill, really."

And not that she was particularly good at it. But she woke

up at the ass crack of dawn and ran however many miles Cash told her to and then she did it again the next morning and the next after that. She might not be fast, and her form might not be pretty, but she was dedicated and that counted for something.

"A marathon," Rosaline repeated, nose scrunching adorably. "Wow, your masochistic tendencies run deeper than I realized."

Poppy choked, soda spilling down her chin, droplets dotting the counter. Rosaline cackled and she glared. "I am not a masochist."

"No, you just like beating yourself up for things that aren't your fault." Rosaline stretched across the counter and grabbed a napkin. Rather than hand it over, she dabbed at Poppy's chin, cleaning the cherry vanilla soda off her face. "Why a marathon?"

Poppy puffed out her cheeks. "It's kind of a long story."

Inadvertently, she'd steered them toward another none-too-breezy topic.

Rosaline made a big production of looking around the kitchen. "Does it look like I have somewhere to be," she said, tapping her phone, checking the time, "at eleven twenty-seven at night?"

Poppy picked at her sandwich one-handed and gnawed on her lip. "It was Cash's idea. I guess studies show running reduces stress and improves your mood." She shrugged. "Helps your mental health. And um, last year, I sort of needed all the help I could get with that."

The marathon training and the cooking lessons had both been part of Cash's holistic Get Poppy Better plan. In addition to therapy, obviously, but beyond driving her to her appointments and lending her an ear, Cash wasn't qualified to help her there.

"You're right," Rosaline said, fingers dancing across Poppy's palm. "That *was* a long story."

A snort escaped her. "You think you're hilarious, don't you?"

"I don't *think*," Rosaline said loftily before her whole face softened and she squeezed Poppy's hand. "So it's working then? The running?"

"It's either that or the Lexapro," she joked. "It's not a silver bullet or anything like that—I know better than to believe those exist. But I like it. Well, actually, I hate it while I'm doing it, and sometimes I desperately want to quit, but it does make me feel better afterward. And it's nice to have a goal, something to push myself toward."

"Twenty-six point two miles." Rosaline whistled, nudging Poppy with her knee. "That's kind of badass, Peterson."

Poppy laughed, face warming pleasantly under the praise. "It's running. People have been doing it since the dawn of time."

Rosaline reached out and flicked her between the eyes.

"Hey!" Poppy laughed and rubbed her forehead. "What the fuck was that?"

"Your inability to take a compliment outside of sex is vexing. Stop it."

She laughed harder. "Oh, well if it's *vexing*."

Rosaline gave her a flat glare. "It's annoying as fuck. I don't like it."

"You're not exactly great at taking a compliment, either, you know."

"Well, I guess it's a good thing we're not talking about me then, isn't it?" Rosaline smirked. "So, tell me—when you aren't corralling Curran or training for your marathon, both of which I find admirable in their own right, what does Poppy Peterson like to do in her free time? Any other masochistic hobbies I should know about? Self-flagellation, maybe?"

"Hm," she pretended to think about it. "Does being a Mariners' fan count as self-flagellation?"

Rosaline laughed. "Yes."

"Nah, I'm kidding. Well, not about the Mariners, unfortunately. I am a fan. But as far as other hobbies go? Football, I guess? Watching, not playing. Obviously."

"I don't know," Rosaline teased. "Fifty bucks says your tackle's going to be an ESPN top play of the week."

Poppy shut her eyes and groaned. "Ugh, that means my *dad* is going to see it."

And he'd tell her mom and she'd definitely have something to say about Poppy's red-carpet throw down.

"It'll blow over," Rosaline assured her, which was nice and all, but she didn't know Charlotte Peterson. Issues didn't blow over in the Peterson household as much as they were either swiftly swept under the rug and never talked about again, or they were constantly dredged up. Over and over and over again, never allowed to be forgotten or left in the past. There was no in-between.

"Here's to hoping," Poppy said wryly. "What about you?"

Rosaline's brows rose. "What about me?"

"Talents, skills, hobbies, etcetera?" She nudged her plate aside and rested her chin on the heel of her hand. "Aside from making a mean PB&J."

Rosaline stuck out her tongue and shrugged. "Does having a burner account to live tweet *Love Island* count as having a hobby?"

"Um, yes. And I'm going to need your handle ASAP."

"I don't know." Rosaline's voice turned teasing. "That's privileged information."

Poppy jutted out her lower lip, making Rosaline laugh.

"I don't actually tweet that often. It's really just my weird way of staying in touch with my sister Bianca. We don't have much in common except for, as it turns out, a weakness for trashy reality TV."

"Bianca's the tattoo artist, right?" Poppy ghosted her fingers over a curl of ink at Rosaline's wrist, black lines crisp and clean with minimal bleeding. It was beautiful work. "Did she do this?"

Rosaline nodded. "Most of my tattoos are courtesy of Bianca. Back when she was an apprentice, she needed help building her portfolio, and unlike our sister Helen, who's very vocal in her refusal to get a tattoo because she believes it would be akin to putting a bumper sticker on a Ferrari, I already had several and was more than happy to help."

"Did you give her free rein on the design or . . . ?"

Her lips twisted. "Much to the immense disappointment of my parents, there isn't an artistic bone in my body. I just told her what flowers I wanted and let her run with it." She pointed at the flora, blossoms and vines, a never-wilting, never-dying, unchanging bouquet upon her skin. "Hellebore. Clematis. Dogwood. Delphinium. Ivy." Rosaline's fingers rested just above the crook of her left elbow and an almost shy smile graced her lips. "Poppies."

Something inside her chest fluttered riotously. "They're beautiful."

Poppy didn't believe in fate, knew that the fact Rosaline had her namesake—*nick*-namesake—tattooed on her body was nothing more than a coincidence, that plenty of people had poppy tattoos. They symbolized everything from peace to eternal life to remembrance, beauty and success, death and sleep, messages delivered in dreams. It still put a warm spot behind her breastbone and an ache between her ribs, a foreign yearning that, if she weren't careful, could blossom into something too big for her to contain.

Rosaline's smile grew and her hands rose to cup Poppy's face. "I think so."

Her lips were soft, and she tasted like raspberry jelly, sweet and tart. Poppy pressed closer and grabbed the front of Rosaline's shirt, dragging her as close as the space between the barstools would allow, smiling into the kiss when Rosaline let out a tiny gasp of surprise against her mouth. Now that she'd gotten a taste of Rosaline, she wasn't sure how she was supposed to ever stop. The prospect of boarding a plane back to Portland in the morning put an unsettled pit of anxiety in her stomach rivaled only by the disquiet she felt when she thought about the inevitable day Rosaline would get tired of her, their pseudo-relationship having run its course.

On the counter, Rosaline's phone vibrated, pinging once, twice, three times. With a reluctant groan, she pulled away, pecking Poppy on the mouth before reaching for it. Her eyes flitted across the screen, her expression pinched.

Poppy shifted anxiously on the barstool. "Is everything okay?"

"Other than the fact that Curran is apparently in possession of my phone number?" She arched a brow as her phone pinged again. "Everything's fine."

"Cash is texting you?" She frowned. "Why is he texting you and not me?"

"He said he did and you're not answering."

Right, her phone was still tucked away inside her clutch, which she'd left in the foyer. "Well, it's almost midnight." And Poppy had been busy.

Rosaline snorted, shaking her head softly. Her phone sounded like a slot machine with the way it kept going off in her hand. "They may have skipped the after-parties, but I don't think they skipped the booze." A strange look suddenly flickered across her face, her mouth slightly dropping open. She lifted her head and met Poppy's gaze, the look in her eyes inscrutable. "Um, here. See for yourself."

With no small amount of trepidation, Poppy took Rosaline's phone.

CASH (11:43 P.M.): ROSALINe! Tell potpart to pick up her phone

CASH (11:43 P.M.): Poptart

CASH (11:43 P.M.): I gotta talk to her

CASH (11:43 P.M.): It's important

CASH (11:44 P.M.): 💩 you're trending on twitter

CASH (11:44 P.M.): 😂😂😂

CASH (11:44 P.M.): I wrote poppy and it came out poopy and my phone put the emoji

CASH (11:44 P.M.): Srry pooopy 😂

CASH (11:44 P.M.): People think ur dating rosaline

CASH (11:45 P.M.): On tiwtter

CASH (11:45 P.M.): Because u 2 were making eyes on the carpet before u sacked that chick

CASH (11:45 P.M.): like kapow pow pow 💥

CASH (11:45 P.M.): That was so badass pooptart ur so badass

CASH (11:45 P.M.): I love u

CASH (11:45 P.M.): I'm sorry I ran my mouth in teh limo I'm a dumbass

CASH (11:45 P.M.): I just love u so much and want u to be hppy

CASH (11:45 P.M.): Hapy as I am

CASH (11:46 P.M.): Have you told r4osaline u like like her yet

CASH (11:46 P.M.): Ok m gonna go lyric wants a take a bubblebth wit me bye

Poppy's heart rose into her throat and her hands shook, a tremor she prayed Rosaline wouldn't pick up on. Goddamn it, Cash. She forced a laugh. "He's wasted."

Rosaline hummed and took back her phone. "Clearly." Her lips twitched. "Poopy."

She buried her face in her hands with a groan.

Rosaline chuckled. "It certainly seems like he and Lyric are having a good time. I'm glad."

She dropped her hands and sighed. "He doesn't let loose very often."

"Neither does Lyric." Rosaline swiped across the screen. "He's right, by the way. You are trending."

"Lovely." Poppy rubbed her eyes. "Just tell me—how bad is it?"

"Well," Rosaline said, eyes locked on her phone, index finger intermittently flicking the screen to scroll, "I suppose that depends on your definition of the word."

Poppy slumped over, resting her cheek against the counter, the granite cool against her overheated skin. "So it's badder than bad. Got it."

"Don't be melodramatic," Rosaline chided, nudging Poppy's knee with hers. "You're a meme, but that was to be expected. Most people seem to agree with Cash and think you're a badass." She paused, tongue sweeping out and wetting her bottom lip. "Someone made a fancam edit of us."

Poppy lifted her head. "A *what?*"

"Fancam edit. A montage of clips from the red carpet set to—"

"No, I know what a fancam is. I just . . . I guess I never thought I'd see the day where someone made one of me."

One of her and Rosaline, apparently.

Rosaline's teeth dug into her bottom lip. "People do seem to think you and I are secretly seeing each other."

She curled her fingers around the edge of the counter so they wouldn't shake. "Seeing each other like . . . ?"

Rosaline's eyes flickered to Poppy's face before returning to the screen. "Dating, Poppy. The internet thinks we're secretly dating."

Poppy swallowed thickly, an ache in her throat. "Oh."

The look on Rosaline's face was frustratingly unreadable as she set her phone aside and met Poppy's stare. "You sound upset."

"Well, yeah." She grimaced. "People think we're dating and—we're not."

Poppy must've done a piss poor job of concealing her feelings if people sitting at home, people who didn't even know her, had picked up on them.

Rosaline was unnervingly quiet, staring down at the remnants of her sandwich like they were offensive, her brow knit.

The half a PB&J Poppy had scarfed down sat like a stone in her stomach. She needed to fix this. Say something to . . . God, she didn't know. Assure Rosaline that she wasn't operating under any delusions here. Poppy understood what this was. "Rosaline—"

"We could be."

Poppy froze, heart lodged in her throat. "What?"

"Dating." Rosaline leveled her with a stare from beneath her dark lashes. "We could."

"You and me?" she croaked.

Rosaline's eyes crinkled at the corners as her smile grew. "Yeah, Poppy. You and me."

Her heart skipped several beats. "But you said—" Poppy shook her head. She was so confused. "You said you weren't looking for anything serious. You said—you said no strings."

"Well, I changed my mind," Rosaline said simply.

Poppy very nearly reached down to pinch her thigh and check that she wasn't dreaming. "You changed your mind." She held her breath waiting for the *gotcha*, for Rosaline to burst out laughing. For her to say something like, *You should see your face*.

Except Rosaline wasn't cruel. She wouldn't toy with Poppy, not like that.

"I believe that's what I said." Rosaline's voice was teasing, but her eyes flitted over Poppy's face, searching. "Cards on the table? I really like you, Poppy, and it's—" She hung her head and chuckled weakly. "I honestly believed I could do *no strings*, which, in hindsight was extremely foolish of me because, as Lyric pointed out to me recently, I've never done a damn thing casually in my life." She winced. "Don't get me wrong, it's going to suck if you don't feel the same, but I needed to say something. That there *are* strings. At least, on my end."

Her heart battered against her sternum as if it could beat a hole through her chest. "You like me." The truth started to sink in. "You really like me."

"Okay, Sally Field." Rosaline was beaming as she reached out and pried Poppy's fingers free from the edge of the counter, thumb smoothing over the backs of her knuckles. "You're clever and courageous and you make me laugh and—what's not to like? I could honestly wax poetic about you, Poppy." A blush swept across her cheeks. "You can ask Lyric if you don't believe me. These last few weeks, she's had to put up with my—I personally would call it a recitation of your many merits. But she calls it *mooning*. Like she's one to talk."

"Mooning," Poppy breathed, making Rosaline laugh.

"You can't seriously be surprised," she said, and she couldn't have been more wrong. *Surprise* didn't begin to do Poppy's shock justice. "I don't think I could've done a poorer job of hiding the way I felt. The way I feel. I mean, the internet took one look at us and saw right through me."

"Right through *you?*" Poppy laughed. "More like right through *me.*"

She hadn't even seen the pictures from tonight, but she knew without a fraction of a doubt her feelings would be splashed across her face, plain for anyone to see, legible as a billboard.

Rosaline's smile broadened, lighting up the whole kitchen. "Oh? Tell me more."

"You can't seriously be surprised," she said, throwing Rosaline's words back at her. "I thought you didn't have time to date. Or was that just an excuse?"

Rosaline shrugged. "I think we make time for what matters."

Her heart squeezed and swelled simultaneously inside her chest before, like a pin to a balloon, her bubble burst. "I live in Portland."

"So? It's not like either of us work a traditional nine-to-five or go into an office." Rosaline shrugged easily. "Not to mention, the holidays are right around the corner, and I know Lyric and Cash are making plans to spend them together in Portland. Plus, my parents are there so I'd be flying into town no matter what. I'll be in town from Thanksgiving through the new year. At least."

And after? She wanted to ask, but she didn't want to jump the gun. It was only October, after all.

"I don't know what your plans for the holidays look like, but I was hoping we could spend some time together," Rosaline continued, bringing Poppy's hand to her mouth and brushing a kiss to her knuckles that turned her insides to goo. "If you want."

As if it were even a question.

Chapter Fifteen

Monday, October 22

> **POPPY (12:11 A.M.):** Text me in the morning, please. I want to make sure you didn't drown in Lyric's bathtub. 🖤

CASH (6:45 A.M.): i'm dying

> **POPPY (6:46 A.M.):** You're hungover, you big baby. You're going to be fine.

CASH (6:46 A.M.): no, I need you to listen. in the top drawer of my nightstand is a document. my last will and testament.

> **POPPY (6:46 A.M.):** Oh my god 🙈

CASH (6:47 A.M.): listen. i'm leaving you everything. you're my best friend and I love you. even when i fuck up you always forgive me. i think that's really special

POPPY (6:48 A.M.): So you read through your texts from last night, huh?

CASH (6:49 A.M.): I AM SO SORRY

CASH (6:49 A.M.): I THOUGHT I WAS TEXTING YOU

CASH (6:49 A.M.): PLEASE TELL ME I DIDN'T FUCK THINGS UP FOR YOU ☹

CASH (6:49 A.M.): LYRIC IS GONNA KILL ME

POPPY (6:50 A.M.): Stop texting me in all caps. It feels like you're screaming at me.

POPPY (6:50 A.M.): And no. You didn't fuck things up. The opposite actually.

CASH (6:51 A.M.): ?????????

POPPY (6:52 A.M.): Rosaline and I are now dating.

CASH (6:53 A.M.): FUCK YEAH YOU ARE

CASH (6:53 A.M.): I KNEW IT

CASH (6:53 A.M.): YOU'RE WELCOME

POPPY (6:54 A.M.): ☹

POPPY (6:54 A.M.): Please please tell me you're on your way to the airport. You've got to be at the stadium by 11.

CASH (6:55 A.M.): i'm in the car

POPPY (6:56 A.M.): See you soon.

ROSALINE (12:02 P.M.): I hope you made it home safely. How's Curran feeling?

POPPY (12:09 P.M.): Safe and sound! 🖤

POPPY (12:09 P.M.): And he felt like death warmed over this morning, but he hurled on the plane and feels better now.

ROSALINE (12:10 P.M.): Lovely.

ROSALINE (12:10 P.M.): Glad he's feeling better, though. The Titans have a pretty decent defense this year. Would hate it if his hangover cost us our division standing.

POPPY (12:11 P.M.): He was doing depth drop hurdle jumps when I left to grab a bite to eat. I think he's okay.

POPPY (12:11 P.M.): How's Lyric feeling?

ROSALINE (12:13 P.M.): Sent me a string of skull emojis and a plea for a breakfast burrito. She'll be fine.

POPPY (12:14 P.M.): By the way, Cash was mortified when he saw his texts from last night. He wanted me to tell you he's sorry.

ROSALINE (12:15 P.M.): I know. He texted me. Used proper punctuation and everything.

POPPY (12:16 P.M.): Wow, serious business.

ROSALINE (12:18 P.M.): He also told me not to break your heart.

POPPY (12:19 P.M.): 🙄

POPPY (12:19 P.M.): Ignore him.

ROSALINE (12:21 P.M.): He threatened to make my life a PR nightmare. Told me he'd pull a Tom Cruise and declare his love for Lyric by jumping on a couch on national television if I hurt you.

POPPY (12:22 P.M.): I'm going to murder him.

ROSALINE (12:23 P.M.): To be fair, I did tell him I'd remove his kneecaps with an ice cream scoop if he hurt Lyric.

POPPY (12:24 P.M.): 🙄

ROSALINE (12:26 P.M.): Credit where it's due, his threat was rather imaginative. If not wholly unnecessary.

POPPY (12:28 P.M.): Oh?

ROSALINE (12:29 P.M.): I don't plan on breaking your heart, Poppy.

Romance rumors abound amid investigation into red-carpet stunt at the World Music Awards

by Avery Michaels
published on October 22

Lyric Adair and Cash Curran are red-carpet official!

The pop star, 24, and the football player, 28, confirmed their relationship, making their red-carpet debut at the World Music Awards Sunday evening before Adair took to the stage, performing "A Minute to Midnight," the second single off her upcoming album, *Santa Ana*.

Adair dazzled in a yellow, off-the-shoulder dress from Christian Siriano, accessorizing with Bea Bongiasca jewelry and Mach & Mach heels. Curran wore a sheer black lace shirt and black pants, both from queer-owned brand ORTTU. He sported a pair of limited edition Craig Sager Air Jordan 1s.

However, it wasn't Curran's daring fashion choices that made waves on the carpet, but rather the presence of a streaker intent on interacting with Adair. Like the 1974 Oscars' streaker who posed as a journalist to gain entry to the stage, the woman who stripped down last night similarly posed as a publicist to gain access to the carpet.

Executive Prevention Protection shared a statement to Instagram and X (formerly known as Twitter).

"We take our responsibility to protect event attendees at the shows we provide security for seriously. We are currently working with event staff and the LAPD to investigate what transpired at last night's show. Updates to come."

It was none other than Cash Curran's publicist, Poppy Peterson, who tackled the streaker to the carpet. Before Peterson, 25, a Portland native and longtime friend of Curran's, saved the day, many sitting at home watching the red carpet picked up on the palpable chemistry between her and Rosaline Sinclair, 34, Lyric Adair's own publicist, who also happens to hail from Stumptown. Their easy rapport, lingering touches, and flirtatious glances on the red carpet have sparked rumors of a romance between the two publicists.

Sinclair, notoriously private, has never spoken publicly about her sexuality, but has long been an avid advocate for the LGBTQIA+ community.

Sinclair and Peterson were seen leaving the show together; Adair and Curran left in a separate car.

Sinclair and Peterson did not immediately return *Notoriety Magazine*'s request for comment.

> **POPPY (10:57 P.M.):** Did you see the article Notoriety published?

> **POPPY (10:57 P.M.):** It's about us.

ROSALINE (11:02 P.M.): They're the worst. I called them out publicly years ago for being sexist. They've had it out for me ever since.

ROSALINE (11:02 P.M.): Am I going to have to send a cease-and-desist letter?

POPPY (11:05 P.M.): It shockingly wasn't . . . uncharitable? But there's this line at the end of the article that . . . one sec.

POPPY (11:06 P.M.): "Sinclair, notoriously private, has never spoken publicly about her sexuality, but has long been an avid advocate for the LGBTQIA+ community."

ROSALINE (11:07 P.M.): What about it?

POPPY (11:08 P.M.): Does it bother you? People speculating that you and I are dating?

ROSALINE (11:10 P.M.): Only so far as my personal business should be just that—personal. But that's a hazard of the job I accepted a long time ago.

ROSALINE (11:10 P.M.): But if you're asking because of the part where I've never publicly spoken about my sexuality, no.

ROSALINE (11:11 P.M.): I've been out to my family and friends since I was seventeen.

ROSALINE (11:11 P.M.): It's hardly a secret that I'm a lesbian. I just don't talk about it on social media because I don't really talk about anything personal on social media.

ROSALINE (11:12 P.M.): But I'm not interested in hiding, either.

ROSALINE (11:12 P.M.): I've always known, or at least since Lyric attained a certain level of fame that yanked me into the spotlight, that it would be talked about when I dated someone.

ROSALINE (11:13 P.M.): The fact that people are going to act like it's news when I've been out for half my life is actually kind of hilarious to me.

POPPY (11:14 P.M.): That's a relief.

POPPY (11:14 P.M.): That you aren't being outed against your wishes, I mean.

ROSALINE (11:15 P.M.): Definitely not. You can breathe easy.

POPPY (11:15 P.M.): Wait. You said when you dated someone.

ROSALINE (11:15 P.M.): I did.

POPPY (11:15 P.M.): But you've been Lyric's publicist for eight years.

POPPY (11:15 P.M.): Are you telling me you haven't dated anyone in eight years?

ROSALINE (11:16 P.M.): Not publicly.

ROSALINE (11:16 P.M.): I dated a music supervisor for a while, but she wasn't out to her family.

POPPY (11:17 P.M.): Wow.

POPPY (11:17 P.M.): And you want to date me? 😳

ROSALINE (11:18 P.M.): I really do. ♥

October 23

IN MY PINING ERA @claudiaxyz92 • 6h
we need to give those two publicists a ship name. i can't keep calling them those two publicists

LILIANA @evanbuckleystan98 • 6h
replying to @claudiaxyz92
Roppy? Pinclair? Sinterson? Sincoppy?

IN MY PINING ERA @claudiaxyz92 • 5h
💻💅🤡

VICTORIA @pdxprincess • 5h
replying to @evanbuckleystan98 @claudiaxyz92
ooh what about posaline?

October 24

ROSALINE (4:34 P.M.): People on X are attempting to figure out the best way to smash our names together into a portmanteau so that they can ship us.

POPPY (4:56 P.M.): Get the fuck out.

POPPY (4:57 P.M.): What are our options?!

ROSALINE (4:59 P.M.): Someone started a poll. The contenders appear to be Roppy, Pinclair, Sinterson, and Posaline. I'm partial to Pinclair or Posaline, personally.

POPPY (5:03 P.M.): Hm. I like Posaline.

POPPY (5:04 P.M.): Go get on your Love Island burner account and vote for us!

October 26

LYRIC ADAIR @lyricadair • 3h
Today's the day. Santa Ana, my rawest album to date, a

reflection and expurgation of the last two years of my life, is out now. I'm feeling a little overwhelmed about it being out in the world, but I'm ready to let this chapter go. It belongs to you now. Grab your tissues, grab your wine, and maybe consider blocking your ex. xoxo ♥

CASH CURRAN @cashcurran • 3h
Congratulations on another banger of an album @lyricadair. I'm so proud of you, baby 😊♥

LYRIC ADAIR @lyricadair • 3h
replying to @cashcurran
😊😊😊😊😊

ROSALINE SINCLAIR @rosalinesinclair • 3h
It's Santa Ana day! @lyricadair, I know how hard you worked and how much of yourself you poured into this album—blood, sweat, and tears. Couldn't be prouder!

LYRIC ADAIR @lyricadair • 3h
replying to @rosalinesinclair
Love you, Roz!! You're the best! 🎬😊🎧

POPPY PETERSON @poptartpdx • 2h
Happy release day @lyricadair! Today should seriously be a national holiday.

LYRIC ADAIR @lyricadair • 2h
replying to @poptartpdx
Poppy!! 😊👾

'Santa Ana,' a gut-wrenching, no-holds-barred relationship postmortem, is Lyric Adair's best album yet

by Andre Ruiz for *Rolling Stone*
published on October 31

The Santa Ana winds are commonly believed to affect people's moods and behaviors. Like its namesake, *Santa Ana,* the highly anticipated sixth studio album from pop superstar Lyric Adair that released on October 26, is wild, temperamental, melancholic, and at times even wrathful, vacillating between euphoria and desperation, perfectly capturing the storm of emotions that accompanies the end of an intense relationship.

Make no mistake, this is a breakup album. The title track "Santa Ana" is a manic-depressive roller coaster, at times melodic and at others near histrionic, featuring a back track of a flatlining heart monitor. It is sonically and lyrically a push-pull that begs the question of the listener—is the opposite of love hate? Or is it indifference?

Adair's lyricism shines on tracks like "Psyche," a siren-song-like ballad, and "Ember," a veritable dirge that explores the idea of trying to resuscitate a relationship you know is dead, while "A Minute to Midnight" reigns supreme as a powerhouse punch-you-in-the-gut heartbreak anthem demonstrating the star's growth and range as a vocalist.

Despite what it sounds like, the album isn't all doom and gloom and rage. "Silver Lining," the final track on the album, is a dreamy, hopeful, lullaby-like invocation, closing the door on this chapter of Adair's life, not with a slam but with a gentle, reverent snick.

Adair's last album, *TL;DR,* released a little over two years ago and in that time Adair has undergone several life changes. Recently, Adair confirmed her relationship with Portland Pathfinders' quarterback, Cash Curran, making their public debut as a couple at the World Music Awards.

Rating: ☆☆☆☆☆

All's fair in love and war and music: Lyric Adair spurns ex-boyfriend on her new album, *Santa Ana*

by Dominique Eisenstadt
published on November 1

If there's one thing Lyric Adair is great at, it's transforming heartbreak into art . . . and raking her exes through the mud in the process.

Santa Ana, Adair's sixth album, released on Friday to much fanfare. But not everyone's loving the new album.

A source close to Ansel Daily, drummer for the Domestic Noir Plot, and Adair's ex-boyfriend, told *Notoriety Magazine* that, "Ansel's really hurt, honestly. He doesn't think it's fair that the whole world only gets Lyric's side of the story and accepts it as gospel truth. There was a lot of love between them. Just because their relationship ended doesn't give her any right to slander him in her songs and make him out to be some kind of villain. She's just as much to blame for their breakup as he is."

Both Adair and Daily were tight-lipped following their breakup earlier this year, but rumors abounded that the reason behind their split was the latter's infidelity, which Adair references on tracks "A Minute to Midnight" and "Go with Grace."

Notoriety Magazine has reached out to Lyric Adair's rep for comment.

November 26

WHERE IN THE WORLD IS LYRIC ADAIR (TRACKING UPDATES)
@whereslyric • 19h
Lyric flew from Los Angeles (LAX) to Portland, Oregon (PDX) yesterday evening. The approximate flight distance is 833 miles. Flight time is 2 hours and 20 minutes.

Lyric Adair is rumored to be spending Thanksgiving with Pathfinders' quarterback boyfriend Cash Curran—here's what we know

by Jaimie Xin
published on November 26

With Turkey Day fast approaching, fans are wondering whether Lyric Adair and Cash Curran will be spending the holiday together, and if so, where they plan to spend it.

In October, Adair broke the internet when she attended a Pathfinders' game, cheering on Curran alongside his parents from inside the VIP box. Their relationship has been heating up since. The duo, who have been crowned American Royalty by fans, made their official red-carpet debut on October 21 at the World Music Awards where Adair took to the stage, performing the second single from her recently released album, *Santa Ana*, which has taken the airwaves by storm and continues to dominate the charts, monopolizing every spot of the Billboard Hot 100's top 10.

The star expressed her gratitude on social media:

LYRIC ADAIR @lyricadair • 11/3
Are you serious?? I'm utterly verklempt right now. Thank you, thank you, thank you. Thank you for listening, thank you for streaming, thank you for riding this roller coaster with me. 🖤

With another album on the books and a tour yet to be officially announced, though fans are crossing their fingers an announcement will come before the end of the year, Adair appears to have some free time on her hands. Free time some eagle-eyed fans believe she intends to fill with her NFL superstar beau. Not only did her private jet make the trip from Los Angeles to Portland yesterday, her publicist, Rosaline Sinclair, made a rare post to her personal Instagram account, sharing a photo of the Portland International Airport's iconic teal, geometric-patterned carpet, which made a return to the main terminal in 2024 after being removed in 2015.

ROSALINE SINCLAIR @rosalinesinclair • 1d
Embracing the weird and wonderful this holiday season.

Sinclair, Adair's publicist of the last eight years, garnered some attention following her appearance on the World Music Awards red carpet, many viewers taking note of the "undeniable chemistry" she had with Poppy Peterson, Cash Curran's friend and publicist. Chemistry so undeniable that a large number of Adair and Curran's fans are now shipping the two publicists, some even believing that they're secretly dating.

Sinclair originally hails from Portland, meaning there's always a chance she made the trip to the Pacific Northwest solo. However, that seems unlikely. The Portland Pathfinders do not have a game on Thanksgiving Day, freeing up Curran to spend the holiday indulging in a little turkey and stuffing with family. The Pathfinders will be going head-to-head with the Patriots in a highly anticipated matchup on Sunday, December 2.

Lyric Adair and Cash Curran's relationship timeline so far

July 6: Adair's split from Daily is confirmed to *Notoriety Magazine*
August 28: Curran makes a public Hail Mary X pass at Adair
August 29: Adair begins following Curran on X and Instagram
September 21: Curran is spotted leaving the Beverly Hills home of Adair's publicist following an away game against the Chargers
October 7: Adair attends Pathfinders game in Portland, celebrating in a private box alongside Curran's parents
October 7: The Portland Pathfinders and NFL official X accounts begin following Adair and Adair's publicist begins following Curran
October 7: Adair and Curran are spotted getting cozy at a postgame celebration where Curran's teammates were also in attendance
October 21: Adair and Curran make their red-carpet debut at the World Music Awards
October 26: Curran publicly congratulates Adair on her album release, calling her "baby" in a tweet

Representatives for Adair and Curran have yet to respond to requests for comment from *People*.

Chapter Sixteen

November 28

"*Honestly*, Penelope?" Mom fixed Poppy with a glare that could curdle milk. "What were you thinking?"

Poppy paused with her hand on the refrigerator door. She didn't have the faintest idea what she could've possibly done to piss her mother off in the five minutes since she'd stepped through the door. Obviously, she'd done something.

Oh wait, that's right. *She'd stepped through the door.* "I was grabbing a soda, Mom. That's not a crime, is it?"

Out in the den, the rest of the family was gathered, Dad and Jessica and Dillon and their spouses and six collective children; Mom's sister, Donna; and Dad's two brothers, Craig and Mark, and their wives. Her cousins, Andrew, Stacee, Emma, Brittany, and Peter, all older than her by at least ten years, each of them married, their spouses and gaggle of children, Poppy's first cousins once removed, also in attendance. Her niece, Maddie, had brought her fiancé. The Oregon-Oregon State game was playing on the TV, Oregon up at the half, and Poppy didn't want to miss more of it than she already had. She'd only planned to pop into the kitchen for a drink, not have it out with her mother. Best-laid plans . . .

Mom looked like she'd swallowed a lemon. "Do you know how *mortifying* it was for your father and I to learn—from the Winston-Mayfields no less—that our daughter got into a fight on national television?"

Jesus. Poppy hung her head with a sigh. Not this. "It wasn't a fight, Mom. Someone broke onto the carpet, and I stopped them. And honestly, how does hearing it from the Winston-Mayfields make a difference?"

"Because. It's all anyone at the club can talk about. Your poor father hasn't been golfing in weeks."

Boo fucking hoo. What boring lives people led if they were still nattering on about what happened at the WMAs. Even the tabloids had moved on, her tackle old news. "Shoulder season's over. It's almost December. Dad wouldn't be golfing now anyway."

"That is entirely beside the point."

"What exactly is the point?"

Mom threw her hands up. "I want to know what you were thinking!"

"To be fair, it all happened really fast, so I wasn't really thinking as much as I was—"

"*Clearly*. That much was obvious." Mom sighed and shook her head, the textbook picture of disappointment. Poppy just couldn't win. "And to think, this happened on Cash's big night." Mom pursed her lips. "I hope he forgave you."

Poppy closed her eyes and counted to ten. There wasn't anything to forgive because she hadn't done anything wrong. That's what everyone—Cash, Lyric, Rosaline—told her. They had been there. They would know. Mom wasn't going to get under her skin and make her start doubting herself, but maybe Poppy could still make her understand that it hadn't been rash—okay, it had been rash, but it hadn't been *wrong*. "Cash isn't mad, he's—"

"That boy is a saint, is what he is. I hope you realize how very lucky you are that he even gave you this job. God knows what you'd be doing right now if he hadn't."

Cash was no saint, but yes, Poppy was very lucky, and she didn't need anyone to tell her. "I'm well aware of how lucky I am. Trust me."

Mom looked like she highly doubted that. "You could try acting like it."

Jesus Christ. Poppy pinched the bridge of her nose. "If you want to know what I was honestly thinking, it was that Lyric might have been in danger. Okay? That's why I did what I did."

"In danger?" Mom scoffed like it was the most ridiculous thing she'd ever heard. "Really, Penelope, it's not like the woman had a *gun*."

"No, Mom," she drawled, eyes rolling. "She wouldn't have had anywhere to put it."

Mom looked deeply unamused. "Don't be crass." The timer on the oven dinged, and she snatched the oven mitts off the counter. "*Danger.*" Her laugh was mirthless. "My God. You always were such a dramatic child. Always making mountains out of molehills." She reached inside the oven and pulled out a green bean casserole that looked wet, the French-fried onions soggy. She set the casserole dish down on the counter beside the turkey that was resting, not tented with foil, ensuring the bird was going to be bone dry. She ripped off her oven mitts. "I suppose some things never change."

Poppy flinched, hand falling to her side.

It wasn't dramatic for a child to want her parents to pay attention to her. No more than it was her fault that it was only when she accidentally set the kitchen on fire or fell out of a tree and broke her arm that they remembered they had another daughter. That Poppy existed.

She inhaled slowly and then blew out her breath, stealing a few seconds to gather her composure. Someone ought to keep a level head and god knew it wasn't going to be her mother. She had some nerve calling Poppy dramatic. "What exactly do you want me to say, Mom? That I'm sorry? Is that what you want to hear?"

She wasn't, but she just might say it, if it meant she could escape the kitchen.

Mom rounded on her, and Poppy's stomach sank, all too familiar with the pinched look on Mom's face and the brittle look in her blue eyes. "Your actions have consequences, Penelope." Her voice quivered and her chin wobbled the way it tended to before the waterworks started. Her hand flew to her throat. "I would've thought that after what happened last year, you would've learned that. I suppose that was simply too much to hope for."

Poppy's breath left her like she'd been sucker punched in the solar plexus. *Fuck*. Mom could've backhanded her, and it wouldn't have hurt as badly as being told that she was once a fuckup, always a fuckup. That the last year she'd spent working her ass off to get better, *be* better had, in her mother's eyes, been entirely for naught.

Poppy made mistakes. God knew she did. Sometimes it felt like all she did was make mistake after mistake after mistake, but she was trying, and—it's not like she *wanted* to fuck up. She hadn't a year ago and she didn't want to now, and if Mom knew her even in the slightest, she'd know Poppy's biggest fear was letting down the people she loved, being a disappointment. That sometimes she couldn't sleep, the fear of messing up keeping her awake at night. That she'd do anything in her power to avoid that fate. That she was always, always, always going to be harder on herself than anyone else because of it.

She pinched her lips tight to keep them from trembling. It did nothing to stanch the tears welling up in her eyes, threatening to spill over if she so much as blinked.

Mom set her hands on her hips and sighed. "Now is not the time for your histrionics."

"*My* histrionics?" She laughed and a renegade tear slipped down her cheeks. She scrubbed angrily at her face. "That's rich."

Her lips pursed. "Penelope—"

"*Poppy*." She sniffed hard and dragged the side of her hand under her nose. "No one calls me Penelope."

And if Mom paid even a little attention to her, she would know that. Would know that she'd been exclusively going by Poppy since the fifth grade. That the only people who called her Penelope didn't really know her at all.

Mom massaged the space between her brows. "Go tell everyone it's time to eat."

Arms hanging limply at her sides, Poppy stared across the kitchen. What exactly was the point of any of this? What had Mom been hoping to achieve in bringing up what happened at the WMAs? There was no understanding achieved, no resolution, no catharsis. It's like she just wanted to knock Poppy down a peg, make her feel bad.

Suddenly she wasn't hungry.

Mom turned her back on Poppy and reached inside the drawer nearest the stove, pulling out the carving knife. "*Go*, Penelope."

Poppy stalked into the living room and stopped in the middle of the room, loudly clearing her throat. "It's time to eat."

Dillon, wedged between Dad and Uncle Mark on the couch, gestured to the TV. "But the game's not—"

"Take it up with Mom." She whirled on her heel and made

a beeline for the dining room. The sooner they ate, the sooner they'd finish, the sooner she could leave.

As always, Mom had gone all out with the table decor, channeling her inner Martha Stewart, and making hand-lettered placards for each place setting. Poppy circled the table, searching for her seat.

Mom breezed into the dining room and set the plated turkey down in the center of the table.

"Where am I sitting?" she asked.

Without looking at her, Mom jerked her chin toward the formal living room where the kids' table was set up.

Poppy's jaw dropped. "You've got to be fucking kidding me," she blurted, her outburst earning her horrified looks from everyone around the dining table.

"*Penelope*," Mom spoke through clenched teeth and Poppy would bet she was doing it on purpose, saying her name constantly, knowing now that it got under her skin. "The table is only so large, even with the leaf out. There simply isn't room."

Poppy flung out a hand and gestured to her eldest niece, who was three years younger than her. "Maddie gets to sit in the dining room."

Maddie ducked her head and bit her lip, shrinking down in her seat.

Poppy swallowed hard past the growing lump in her throat and tore her eyes away from her niece, glaring at the person who actually deserved her ire. Mom pursed her lips and stared back at her, a placid smile frozen on her face, the tension around her mouth the only sign that Poppy had ruffled her feathers.

She was bitter and she knew she was being unreasonable and a bit of a brat, throwing a temper tantrum and probably confirming what the family already thought: that Poppy was unstable and erratic, prone to fits, hopeless and in need of hand-holding. But she couldn't help it. This was bullshit and if anyone in this room actually gave a fuck about her, they wouldn't be afraid to say something.

A hush had fallen over the table, not a single person meeting her eyes as she looked around the room.

"Yes, well, Maddie brought her fiancé." Mom rounded the table. She grabbed Poppy by the elbow, grip bruising, and steered her toward the door. She dropped her voice to a harsh whisper. "You are making a scene."

"Don't you know," Poppy said, tearing her arm from Mom's grasp, "that's what I'm best at."

A slight furrow formed between Mom's brows, and she shook her head. "I am *trying* to look out for you."

"By relegating me to the children's table?"

"There's no alcohol in here." Mom pursed her lips. "Less temptation for you, Penelope."

She left Poppy standing in the middle of the living room with her mouth hanging open.

Temptation. As if Poppy was going to see a bottle of wine, lose her mind, and tear the cork out with her teeth like a wild animal. As if Poppy really was a child and had no impulse control. Un-fucking-believable.

Gritting her teeth, Poppy crossed the room and threw herself down in the empty chair between Gavin and Alex, her nephews, her sister's kids, preteen boys who were both playing on their Nintendo Switches and ignoring the food on the table.

When in Rome . . . Poppy reached inside the pocket of her maxi dress and pulled out her phone to text Rosaline.

> **POPPY (3:22 P.M.):** I sincerely hope your Thanksgiving is going better than mine.

> **POPPY (3:22 P.M.):** Not that I can imagine how anything could be worse than this.

Her reply was nearly instantaneous.

> **ROSALINE (3:23 P.M.):** Did something happen?

> **ROSALINE (3:23 P.M.):** Already?

Poppy snorted under her breath and Gavin shot her a funny look, unsettlingly similar to the sort of exasperated looks her sister gave her. He shook his head just like Mom did when she was tired of Poppy's antics and returned his attention to the game console in his hands.

> **POPPY (3:23 P.M.):** Oh, you know. The usual. Mom picked a fight, and I did the stupid thing and took the bait. Of course then she told me I was being hysterical. And then I got seated at the kiddie table. Because no one's drinking wine at the kiddie table, so I won't be tempted.

It wasn't that she saw a glass of wine and had an insatiable urge to drink it. Poppy wasn't plagued by cravings, and it didn't bother her being around people who drank. It didn't even bother her kissing Rosaline after she'd had a glass of champagne, that Poppy could taste it on her lips. It was that once Poppy started drinking, she just didn't want to stop, didn't know how to stop, didn't stop.

Mom knew that. Poppy had explained it to her, but either she hadn't really been listening or she didn't care. Maybe both.

ROSALINE (3:25 P.M.): Jesus.

POPPY (3:25 P.M.): Oh, and my niece Maddie, who is only three years younger than me, brought her fiancé and, unlike me, she gets to sit at the adult table.

"Aunt Poppy?"

Her niece Zoe was watching her from across the table.

Poppy set her phone down beside her plate. "Yeah, munchkin?"

"How come you're sitting in here with us?"

Poppy blew out her breath. Great question. "Well, Zoe, do you know what a black sheep is?"

Predictably, eight-year-old Zoe shook her head, pigtails swishing.

That was probably for the best. Educating her nieces and nephews on the finer points of what it meant to be the family failure could wait until at least Mom brought out the pie. "Pass me your plate and I'll fix it for you, okay?"

Rather than sit and stew in a puddle of pity like she wanted, Poppy dug deep for the strength and serenity to get through this day and then did what she did best: put on a brave face and crack jokes to make the younger kids laugh. Every time she got a little too loud, a little too animated, Mom would throw her one of those pinched-lipped frowns from the dining room, chastising her without saying a word.

"Penelope," her aunt Donna called from the dining room and Poppy paused with a forkful of mashed potatoes halfway to her mouth. "Tell us, are the rumors true?"

"Donna, let's not," Mom said, and for the first time all day, Poppy agreed with her mother.

It was one thing to be banished to the kiddie table; the others talking to her while she was at said table just felt like drawing unnecessary attention to the indignity of it all. Rubbing salt in the wound. Poppy would rather everyone just ignore her. Leave her to eat her dry-as-sawdust turkey and soggy green bean casserole and bland-as-fuck mashed potatoes in peace.

Poppy set her fork down with a sigh. "What rumors?"

"Is it true that Cash proposed? That he and Lyric Adair are engaged?"

Maddie whirled around in her chair and gasped. "No way."

Poppy swallowed a groan. "No, they're not."

"Are you sure?" her cousin Stacee asked, eyes narrowed shrewdly, looking at Poppy like she wasn't sure whether she was lying or maybe just dumb and in the dark. She definitely wasn't looking at Poppy like she believed her.

"Am I sure that my best friend isn't engaged?" Poppy struggled to keep the incredulity out of her voice. "Yeah, I'm pretty sure he'd have told me."

"*Pretty sure*," Stacee echoed. "But you aren't positive."

"Jesus fucking Christ," Poppy muttered under her breath, earning a giggle from one of the kids. Her utterance would undoubtedly come back to bite her in the ass when her words got repeated. That was the price Mom would have to pay for putting Poppy at the kids' table. "Cash is *not* engaged. I would know."

"You know," her cousin Emma said, "I always thought you and Cash would eventually get together."

Poppy snorted. "That's disgusting."

"Penelope," Mom admonished. "Cash is lovely. You'd be so lucky."

She rolled her eyes. "Cash is like a brother to me. And he's very, very happy with Lyric."

"What about those other rumors? About you and—what's her name? That publicist." Her cousin Andrew waggled his brows. "She's hot."

His wife smacked him on the arm.

"Rosaline Sinclair," Jessica said. "That's her name. Lyric's publicist."

Poppy froze, the question knocking her off-kilter. If she'd have known that all it would take to get her family interested in her personal life was having her name printed in *People*, she'd have—well, no. She wouldn't done anything differently. "I'm—"

"Don't be ridiculous, Andrew." Mom's laugh was like nails on a chalkboard. "Penelope knows better than to do something as stupid and frivolous as mix her work and her personal life."

Poppy wilted in her seat and dragged her fork through her peas, sending them scattering across her plate.

Ten minutes later, she slipped from the room, grabbed her coat off the hook, and walked out the door. No one tried to stop her. From the way her phone didn't ring even once on the drive home, they probably hadn't even noticed she was gone.

Chapter Seventeen

Amusingly—and confusingly—there was a Pathfinder parked in the driveway when Poppy made it home, the driver absent. After Rosaline had rightly pointed out that his security system was lacking, Cash had upgraded the whole thing, installing a state-of-the-art smart lock with a motorized dead bolt that had received stellar scores across the board, proving itself capable of withstanding kick-ins, drilling, and lock picking. Cash—and Poppy—could lock and unlock the door remotely and they could check the lock status remotely too. Between the new locks and improved security system, Poppy had never felt so safe, the house a fortress. Still, Poppy approached the front door with a small amount of trepidation.

"Hello?"

No one answered and Poppy, still hesitant, slipped out of her boots, leaving them by the front door.

She was halfway up the stairs when the muffled Christmas music reached her ears, drifting down the hall from the last door on the left. Her bedroom. Of course.

Poppy peeked inside the room and pressed a hand to her racing heart. "Jesus." She let out a shaky laugh and slumped against the doorframe.

Rosaline was sprawled across Poppy's bed, a damn sight to see lying on her stomach with her chin resting on the palm of her hand and her feet kicked up in the air, wearing a pair of the tightest dark blue jeans Poppy had ever seen, and a chunky, cream-colored cable-knit sweater.

"What are you doing here?" Poppy asked.

"It's been a month since we saw each other." Rosaline's bottom lip jutted out in an exaggerated pout. Her socks were black and covered in turkeys wearing sunglasses. "You could at least pretend to be excited to see me."

"Oh, I'm sorry, I thought you were a murderer." She padded her way over to the bed, slipping the strap of her purse over her head. "Excuse me for thinking for a second that I was about to get slaughtered while Michael Bublé told me to have myself a merry little Christmas." She tossed her bag on the bed. "How'd you get in here, anyway?"

"I texted Curran. He was kind enough to unlock the door for me." Rosaline rose onto her knees and reached out, reeling Poppy in by the belt tied at her waist. "Now, hush for a second and let me greet you properly."

Poppy grinned and settled her hands on Rosaline's jean-clad hips, tucking the tips of her fingers into Rosaline's back pockets. "Properly, huh?"

"Mhmm." Rosaline's nose bumped hers. "Now shut up."

Her lips pressed against Poppy's, swallowing her laugh.

"Hi," Poppy breathed when their lips parted.

"Hi yourself." Rosaline's cheeks were pink and her eyes fever bright. A slow grin tugged at the corners of her lips. "I wasn't expecting you to be back so soon."

"I wasn't expecting you to be here at all."

"Clearly, considering you thought I was a murderer," she teased, reaching up and tucking Poppy's hair behind her ear.

Poppy poked her in the side. She laughed and squirmed away. Wasn't that something. Rosaline was ticklish. Poppy tucked that fact away for later.

"Hey, I saw a mysterious car in the driveway. I was exercising caution."

"Exercising caution by calling out *hello*?" Rosaline draped her arms around Poppy's waist, palms pressed to the small of her back. "That is such a horror movie cliché."

"I know! Trust me, I was fully prepared to be the big-boobed, dumb blonde at the beginning of the movie who goes up the stairs to investigate and dies a horrible, gruesome death and no one watching even feels sorry that she died because it was such a stereotypically stupid move. Darwin Award–worthy."

Rosaline tutted and shook her head, lips twitching. "The car's hardly mysterious. It's a rental. Did you not see the license plate frame? It has Enterprise Rent-A-Car written all over it."

"Uh huh, and knife-wielding murderers only rent from Budget." Poppy sighed. "No, I didn't even look at the license plate. It's been . . . a day." She pressed the heels of her hands into her eyes until she saw spots. "You never said what you were doing here." She dropped her hands to her sides. "Not that I'm complaining."

Rosaline frowned. "You stopped texting me. I was worried."

Poppy's heart squeezed sweetly inside her chest. "I didn't mean to worry you. I—hold on. You were at your own family dinner, and you left? Jesus, you shouldn't have done that."

"I absolutely should have," Rosaline said firmly. "No offense, but you look like hell."

She couldn't even find it in her to be offended when she knew Rosaline was right. "I'm still sorry I dragged you away from your family."

"I'm not." Rosaline shrugged. "Don't get me wrong, dinner was fine, but it was almost over. I probably would've begged off as soon as the dishes were washed anyway. As much as I love my family, they're best in small doses."

She joined Rosaline on the bed, crawling up the mattress and flopping down against the pillows. "My family is more like . . . you know that poison in puffer fish?"

Rosaline propped herself up on her elbow and stared down at Poppy. "Sure. Tetro something."

"Right." Poppy laced her fingers together, hands resting atop her stomach. "Well, they're like that. Toxic in even the smallest amounts, *probably* safe if you exercise extreme caution, but best avoided altogether because there's always the risk of sudden death." She let her head loll to the side. "It's a metaphor, obviously."

"I hoped." Rosaline smoothed Poppy's brow with a finger. "Want to tell me what happened?"

Not really. She wished she could forget the whole ugly affair. But Rosaline had left her own Thanksgiving early and raced across town to check on her, so she supposed she owed her an explanation. "Mom laid into me almost as soon as I walked through the door."

"Laid into you for what?"

Her laugh came out drier than her mother's turkey. "For tackling that streaker on the red carpet."

Rosaline's face went slack. "That was weeks ago."

"We don't really talk outside of holidays and phone calls on birthdays." They'd forgotten to call her this year. Or maybe the silence had been by design. She didn't know and she really didn't want to spend any more time pondering it. "This was the first chance she'd had to bring it up."

"And she was upset, why exactly?"

"I made a scene." Poppy rubbed her eyes. "On national television, no less. My parents were and still are mortified, my father apparently can't show his face at the club, and—"

"I'm sorry." Rosaline screwed up her face. "*The club?*"

"Golf club. Always gotta keep up with those Joneses." Winston-Mayfields. Whatever. "Basically, what I did was immature and reckless and I'm a disappointment of the first order and when I tried to stand up for myself, I was called dramatic and told I make mountains out of molehills."

Rosaline's eyes were sharp, but her voice was gentle, velvet-wrapped steel. "You're not a disappointment, Poppy."

She scoffed. "Tell that to my mother."

"I'll call her right now if you want. You think I'm kidding?" Rosaline held out her hand. "Give me your phone and I'll do it."

She didn't doubt Rosaline would do it, call up Poppy's mother and give her a thorough dressing down. A petty part of Poppy would kill to see it. "Thanks, but I think having you rush to my defense would do more harm than good."

When Rosaline frowned, Poppy pitched her voice, doing her best impression of her mother: "*Penelope knows better than to do something as stupid and frivolous as mix her work and her personal life.*" She rolled her eyes. "I left, like, ten minutes after that."

"No offense," Rosaline said, "but your mother sounds like a total shrew."

"She certainly has a way of getting under my skin." A wet laugh caught in her throat. "It's mutual, I'm sure. Not that I try, but . . . you know how some parents want their children to be seen and not heard? My parents would rather I not exist at all."

"Poppy." Rosaline's voice was soft and sad, Poppy's name nothing more than a whispered rasp. Poppy had to bite her bottom lip so it wouldn't wobble. "You don't—you don't know that."

"They've never tried to hide the fact that my being born threw a wrench in their plans, that Dad had to put off his retirement, that I put a massive dent in their savings and a damper on their plans to travel once Jessica was out of the house. I feel like—like I was born at a disadvantage, and all I've done is spend my whole life trying to make up for it, trying to make up for the fact that—that I was born in the first place."

"Have you thought about—" Rosaline paused, nibbling on her lip.

Poppy reached out and gently pried Rosaline's lip free from her teeth, brushing her thumb across her mouth. "Thought about what?"

Rosaline grabbed Poppy's hand and hugged it to her chest. "If they make you feel that way, have you ever thought about just . . . *not* going home for the holidays?"

Poppy frowned. "That's the only time I see them."

Rosaline stared at her.

"Oh." Her stomach twisted unpleasantly. "You mean, like, going no contact?"

Rosaline shrugged. "I don't know your parents, but everything you've described to me sounds . . . dysfunctional. At best."

Poppy shifted uneasily. "At worst?"

Rosaline looked distinctly uncomfortable. "Neglectful? Emotionally abusive? Parents aren't supposed to leave a six-year-old home alone to fend for herself."

Hearing Rosaline put it so plainly made Poppy's breath catch. "That was—that was almost twenty years ago."

"There's not a statute of limitations on pain, Poppy. Especially when someone doesn't even apologize for the harm they caused, the harm they *continue* to cause. When they continue to exhibit a lack of care. A lack of basic respect."

Her sinuses stung. "I don't know. It feels like—like, I don't know. Giving up. Quitting."

She'd be lying if she said the thought hadn't crossed her mind. If even today, when she'd parked in her parents' driveway, she hadn't sat in her car for a second, stomach in knots, and thought about how nice it would be to just turn around and go back home and gorge herself on a take-out bucket of KFC. How she could probably do it, and no one would miss her.

But there was something about cutting contact that felt like— failing. As if she couldn't even hack it as a daughter, as if she was so bad at something most people didn't have to work at that she gave it up. Threw in the towel.

Every time the thought crossed her mind, she pushed it aside, flinching away from it, refusing to look at it dead-on. She always concluded she just needed to try harder. After all, Poppy Peterson was no quitter.

Rosaline lifted their joined hands and brushed a whisper of a kiss against Poppy's knuckles. "It's not giving up if you were never given a chance. If you've given it your all. If walking away is going to save you your sanity."

Poppy scrunched her eyes shut. "I just feel like—like no matter how hard I try, nothing I do is ever enough. Never good enough."

That *she* wasn't good enough and never would be.

"That feeling's the worst," Rosaline murmured. "Turns you into your own worst enemy after a while."

Poppy opened her eyes. "You feel like that?"

Rosaline scoffed softly. "Only almost every day of my life."

Not that she didn't believe her, but it was hard for Poppy to wrap her head around someone as successful as Rosaline feeling like she wasn't good enough.

She must've read the confusion on Poppy's face because her

mouth curved up in a semblance of a smile that didn't come close to reaching her eyes. "My parents love me. I've never doubted that, but . . . they pity me too, and that's . . . it's a hard pill to swallow."

"Pity you?" Poppy frowned. "For what?"

Rosaline seesawed her head from side to side. "You asked me once what their *thing* was. I said exceptionality, which I'm sure sounds strange, but it's true. My parents are both amazing artists, top of their respective fields, and it was really important to them that my sisters and I find our niche, the thing that we're best at. My sisters turned out to be wunderkinds. I mean, Helen picked up a cello when she was three and her teacher declared her a musical prodigy. She could read sheet music before she could read letters. Bianca had her first solo art exhibition in the city when she was *eight*. Whereas I was still drawing stick figures and butchering 'Twinkle, Twinkle, Little Star' on the piano when I was ten."

"I think your sisters are the exception, not the rule," Poppy said gently.

Rosaline's laughter had an edge to it that made her chest ache. "Not in my family. If at first you don't succeed, move on, and find what you do excel at. It didn't matter if I enjoyed something, if I wasn't the best at it, it was time to throw in the towel. I got a bronze medal in gymnastics and the next week my mom pulled me out and enrolled me in a competitive swim program instead. I came in second place in the county spelling bee and on the drive home my dad suggested I look into joining mathletes. I spent my entire childhood and adolescence bouncing from one sport and club and instrument to the next at my parents' behest, trying and failing to find the thing I was exceptional at." Rosaline shrugged. "I never found it."

"You did," Poppy argued. "People don't usually know the names of their favorite celebrities' publicists, but you're Lyric Adair's publicity manager and *everyone* knows it. You're the best in the business. You're Rosaline freaking Sinclair. You're a legend."

"But there's not really a tangible way of measuring success in this industry that isn't predicated on your client's success. In my parents' eyes, Lyric is exceptional. She's the talent. I'm support staff. And there's nothing exceptional about being a glorified personal assistant."

She sucked in a sharp breath through her teeth. "They seriously called you that?"

There wasn't a damn thing wrong with being a personal assistant. But that's not what Rosaline was.

"Not in so many words. But . . . it's their tone, you know? The way they gush over Helen and Bianca's achievements, the way they always have. But how, when I share some bit of good news, I get placating smiles and a *That's nice, honey* or *Good for Lyric*." Rosaline stared down at their joined hands. "Like I said, they love me. I've never doubted that. But I've always known that they wanted me to be . . . more. And I just don't have *more* in me. I'm not special. I'm not talented. But if supporting Lyric and helping her take back control of her life and making sure she's happy is my life's greatest achievement, I'll have no regrets. It would just be nice if my parents realized I don't need my own star on the Hollywood Walk of Fame to be happy."

"You're wrong."

Rosaline looked up and frowned.

"Most twenty-six-year-olds wouldn't help a sixteen-year-old stranger file for emancipation from their shitty parents, famous pop star or not. They wouldn't move said sixteen-year-old in with them and practically adopt them," Poppy said. "It's so clear that you'd do anything for Lyric. Most people aren't that selfless, and I don't think most people love like that. Not really. Not unconditionally." People might say they did, but when it really came down to it, when their backs were pressed against a wall, the truth would come out, and most people would falter in their affections. Even parents, in Poppy's experience, didn't always love the way they were supposed to. "Fuck talent. I think that makes you special. I think that makes you exceptional."

Rosaline sniffed hard and let out a wet-sounding laugh as she blinked fast, eyes glistening with unshed tears. "Jesus, Poppy. You're going to make me cry."

"Sorry." She wasn't really. Not for saying what Rosaline so clearly needed to hear.

"Don't be." Rosaline shook her head. "For what it's worth, I think you're exceptional too."

Poppy snorted. Exceptionally talented at fucking up and falling short, maybe. "Thanks."

Rosaline scowled. "I'm serious. Haven't you learned by now that I'm not in the habit of saying things I don't mean?"

She squirmed a little. "I guess that's true."

"You *guess*." Rosaline rolled her eyes but there was a smile playing at the corners of her mouth that belied her irritation. "I see how you are with Curran. The way you'd do anything for him. It's no different than how I am with Lyric. And it doesn't stop there. Screw what your mother thinks, what you did on that carpet was nothing short of amazing. You have such a big heart, and if your parents have their heads buried so far up their asses that they can't see what's right in front of them, screw them. So what if you weren't a part of their plan? I didn't see you coming, but I'm so glad you did, Poppy."

She pinched her eyes shut. "I'm glad too."

Rosaline squeezed her hand. "I didn't mean to make you cry."

"I'm not crying." She was definitely crying. "You're crying."

Rosaline laughed. "Yeah. Little bit."

Poppy dragged in a ragged breath and opened her eyes. "You're staying with your parents, right?"

Her lips twisted and she nodded. "I thought about renting a place, but it seemed silly. But they turned my old room into storage for my mom's art supplies, so I have to crash with Helen in her room. It's only been a day and I'm beginning to regret my choice."

"You could just stay here. Spare me from playing third wheel to Lyric and Cash."

"I don't know, Poppy." Rosaline gave her a sly, sidelong look. "Where would I sleep?"

Poppy wiggled closer and tossed a leg over Rosaline's. "In here, with me. Obviously."

"Presumptuous." Her lips twitched. "Curran won't mind?"

"It's a little late for him to try to protect my long-gone virtue, I think."

She pinched Poppy's side, making her squeal. "You know what I meant."

Poppy laughed. "No, he won't care. Promise."

"Hm, I suppose it would be nice not having to make the drive over here every day," she mused. "Would save me money on gas, at least."

"Mm, frugality." Poppy sighed dreamily. "*So* romantic."

Rosaline's fingers traced the line of Poppy's jaw, her hand snaking into Poppy's hair, gripping the back of her head and tilting her just so, their mouths slotting together perfectly. After a moment, Rosaline's lips curved against hers, smiling into the kiss.

"Is that a yes?" Poppy asked, fingers curling into the hem of Rosaline's sweater.

"Yeah, Poppy." She beamed. "It's a yes."

Chapter Eighteen

November 30

Sent via form submission from Deuxmoi

Pseudonyms, Please: Anon, please
Email: anon@anon.com
Subject: Those two publicists

Message: Those two publicists rumored to be dating after their clients' red carpet debut last month were locking lips in the frozen foods aisle of a Portland Whole Foods. Didn't look like a first kiss, either, and they left in the same car. Anon pls!

**Rosaline Sinclair and Poppy Peterson
spotted dining out in Portland**

by Micaela Monroe
published on December 5

"Those two publicists" as they've been affectionately dubbed (or by their most ardent shippers, "Posaline," a portmanteau of Poppy + Rosaline) were spotted out and about in Portland, Oregon, on Thursday amid escalating rumors that their clients aren't the only ones who are dating.

Peterson and Sinclair first sparked romance rumors during the World Music Awards preshow when they lit up social media with their red-carpet chemistry, leading many to speculate that they might be more than peers.

Rumors escalated following a rare Instagram post from Sinclair, confirming her presence in Portland ahead of the Thanksgiving holiday. As Sinclair is originally from Rose City, that was hardly damning evidence of a relationship with Peterson; however, on November 30, the pseudonymous Instagram gossip account Deuxmoi posted a fan-submitted blind item, claiming that Peterson and Sinclair were locking lips in a Portland Whole Foods.

Now it seems that Sinclair, notoriously private about her personal life, and Peterson are ready to make their relationship public. The two were spotted dining on the covered patio of Lil' America, a popular BIPOC and LGBTQIA–owned food cart pod located in SE Portland. In photos first published by "Page Six," the pair looked cozy, sitting close and keeping warm beneath a patio heater. Sinclair donned a long, vibrant green peacoat over a cropped black top, black leggings, and a pair of black Mexico 66 Onitsuka Tiger sneakers. Meanwhile, Peterson wore a black windbreaker over a mustard plaid skirt and matching vest. She sported a pair of white sneakers.

An onlooker told *People* that Sinclair and Peterson were "absolutely giving couple vibes" and "looked incredibly cute" while noshing on Korean fried chicken from acclaimed food cart Frybaby.

Another source added, "They didn't call attention to themselves, but they were definitely holding hands and at one point they shared a quick kiss."

People has reached out to Sinclair and Peterson for comment.

Seattle vs Portland: Lyric Adair attends her third Pathfinders' game in support of quarterback boyfriend, and talks about her relationship for the first time

by Anika Carter
published on December 8

Lyric Adair has been spotted at her third Pathfinders' game amid rumors that her relationship with Cash Curran is getting serious.

The "A Minute to Midnight" singer, 24, was seen arriving at Pathfinders Stadium ahead of the game with a handful of friends in tow as Curran's team faced off against the division rival Seattle Seahawks. Adair entered the building with publicist and known friend, Rosaline Sinclair; personal assistant, Grey Daniels; friend and producer JJ Murphy; Curran's publicist and close friend, Poppy Peterson; and Cassidy Jones, wife of Portland Pathfinders' tight end DeAndre Jones. Sinclair and Peterson were spotted dining together—and kissing!—days before.

Also in attendance were Curran's parents, whom Adair met in October.

On an episode of the advice and lifestyle podcast *Unhinged with Caitlin McCrory*, Adair opened up about her relationship with the quarterback, saying, "I've never been happier. It's honestly been a breath of fresh air, being in a relationship with someone who isn't afraid to lay it all on the line, someone who doesn't play games . . . unless they're on the field."

When asked about the tweet that started it all, Adair laughed. "I was intrigued. I didn't know who this guy was, but it was such a bold move that I had to respect the—the hustle, you know? I'm so used to doing the chasing that being chased was honestly surreal in the best way."

During a team media availability session following practice ahead of Sunday's game, Curran was asked how he's handling being in such a high-profile relationship. "Of course I don't like having my privacy violated. There are some people that take it too far with the pictures and sharing locations. But Lyric's got a lot of fans, a lot of people who love her and I consider myself lucky to be counted among them. She's so talented and I'm so proud of her and all that she's achieved, especially with this new album. I'm just happy I get to be by her side."

December 11

"Fuck." Rosaline panted, chest rising and falling rapidly. "I can't."

"Sure you can." Poppy grinned down at her. "I believe in you."

"You're evil," she whimpered and dragged the heel of her hand over her brow, wiping the sweat off her forehead so it wouldn't drip in her eyes. "Evil."

"Come on. One more."

Rosaline shuddered softly. "I think I'm going to pass out."

"You're not going to pass out." She held out a hand to help Rosaline stand. "One more lap around the block and I'll make you breakfast."

"Six fucking miles." With a whimper, Rosaline hauled herself up off the curb she'd been sitting on. "I must really like you, Peterson."

Twenty minutes and one lap around the block later, they stood in Cash's kitchen, the ingredients for pancakes laid out on the counter. They were in the middle of hotly debating the merits of chocolate chips versus blueberries—clearly blueberries were the superior addition—when Lyric and Cash stumbled into the kitchen holding hands and sporting matching grins.

Poppy squinted at Cash. She recognized that smile. Knew it all too well, as a matter of fact. It was his *I did a thing I know you're not going to like, but fuck it* smile. The same cheeky, self-satisfied grin he'd worn when she'd confronted him about his Hail Mary tweet.

Rosaline must've picked up on the same thing because she set the bag of chocolate chips down on the counter and crossed her arms, pinning the suspicious-looking lovebirds with a scrutinizing stare.

"What are you two up to?"

Lyric tucked herself into Cash's side. "What makes you think we're up to something?"

"Yeah." Cash rested his chin on the top of Lyric's head. "Can't a guy grab a cup a coffee from his own kitchen? Or is that not allowed now?"

Lyric turned her head to the side, hiding her face in Cash's chest. Her shoulders shook and Cash's smile broadened. He pressed a kiss to the side of her head and whispered something in her ear that made her laugh harder.

As adorable and clearly head over heels in love with each other as those two were, they were definitely hiding something.

"It would totally be allowed," Poppy said. "If you drank coffee, which you don't."

Cash laughed. "You're going to be so pissed."

"*So* pissed," Lyric echoed, still giggling.

"Love that for me." Rosaline scrubbed a hand over her face and sighed. "Okay, spill."

Lyric and Cash stared at each other for a moment, not saying a word, seeming to silently communicate through waggling brows and quirked lips. He shrugged and she nodded, and they both turned to Poppy and Rosaline.

Lyric thrust out her left hand, showing off—oh. Holy shit.

A pear-shaped boulder of a diamond sparkled where it sat on Lyric's slender ring finger.

"Cash proposed!" Lyric bounced giddily on her toes.

"She said yes!" Cash wrapped his arms around her, hugging her from behind.

"You knew I would." Lyric tipped her head back and beamed up at Cash. "You could've proposed with a bread tie, and I'd have said yes, baby."

Engaged.

Lyric and Cash were engaged.

To get married.

After three months of dating.

"Well." Lyric tittered awkwardly. "Come on, you two. Say something."

Problem was, Poppy didn't know what to say. "Wow, you guys. That's, um—"

"Have you two lost your fucking minds?" Rosaline asked.

Poppy winced. It was a fair question, but she wasn't sure she would have posed it quite like that. "Um. I think what Rosaline's trying to say is that this is very unexpected. You took us by surprise."

"That's quite the generous interpretation of my reaction, Poppy." She was clearly agitated, her shoulders tense, practically up by her ears. "You've been dating for three months, Lyric. I have condiments in my refrigerator that predate your relationship."

"My parents got engaged after three dates and they've been married for thirty years. When you know, you know." Cash looked at Lyric like she hung the moon and stars, like it wasn't so much gravity tethering him to the planet but her. "I didn't want to jinx it, but I knew I wanted to marry Lyric after our first date."

Lyric smiled dreamily at him. "I've got you beat. I knew after our first Zoom call. The screen went black, and I sat back and thought, *I'm going to marry that guy.*"

"*Baby,*" Cash whispered, voice brimming with awe.

Rosaline pressed her fingers to the space between her brows and sighed. "It's not that I'm not happy that you're happy. Of course I am. But right now, your brains are swimming in a cocktail of dopamine and oxytocin and—why the rush?" Her eyes bulged and her gaze dropped to Lyric's middle and Poppy's jaw dropped. "Wait. You're not—"

"No!" Lyric scoffed. "Jesus, Rosaline. I'm not pregnant."

"Forgive me for asking the question that's going to be on literally everyone's lips. Get used to it."

"Let them talk," Lyric said. "See if I care."

"Eventually we do want to start a family," Cash said.

"We do. Not this second or anything, but we don't want to wait to start our lives together. For one, we hate being apart."

"Hate it," he agreed. "I'm sick of long distance."

"*So* sick of it."

"Then move in together," Rosaline argued. "You don't have to get married."

"But we're going to get married eventually," Lyric said, the pitch of her voice rising. "Why wait?"

Rosaline threw her hands in the air and spun on her heel, stalking across the kitchen and glaring out the window into the backyard.

"I'm not asking for your permission, Rosaline. You know you're not my mother, right."

A muscle in her jaw flexed. "No, but you sure as hell are acting like a child right now."

"Okay," Poppy jumped in, trying to diffuse the tension before someone said something they were going to regret. Something that wouldn't be easy to walk back. "Have you two talked about where you're going to live or—"

"Of course we have." Cash looked at her like she was the one acting crazy. "We'll live in Portland from August to February, assuming we make it through the playoffs. We'll head down to Los Angeles during the offseason."

Lyric nodded. "There are studios here in town where I can record if I want."

"Or we talked about renovating a guest room. Maybe building out the other side of the basement where the crawl space is," Cash said. "Turning part of the house into a studio."

Lyric gazed across the kitchen at Rosaline imploringly. "I know that from the outside looking in, this seems rash and impulsive, but it's not. Everything you're supposed to talk about before you get engaged? Kids and faith and our families and money and our careers? We've had these conversations. We're on the same page. Rosaline, I *love* him. We love each other."

Cash pressed a kiss to the crown of her head. "Look, I know you don't like me very much—"

"I never said that I didn't like you." Rosaline turned away from the window. "I just want what's best for Lyric."

"You and I have that in common." Cash rolled his shoulders back and stood taller. "I'm not ever going to claim to be what's best for her. But no one is ever going to love her as much as I do or support her the way I will. I can promise you that."

Lyric released a shuddering breath. "Can you just—be happy for us? Please?"

Cash looked at Poppy with so much hope on his face and—she wasn't made of stone.

She lurched forward, rising on her toes, and threw her arms around him and Lyric both, wrapping them up in a bone-crushing hug. "Congratulations. Both of you."

Was it fast? Yes. Too fast, maybe. But it was clear their minds were made up and nothing she or Rosaline said would convince them otherwise.

"Thanks, Pop-Tart," Cash whispered against her temple. "Means a lot."

All eyes turned to Rosaline, who was watching them with an indecipherable expression.

"Roz?" Lyric whispered.

"I *am* happy for you." Rosaline shut her eyes and turned her face up to the ceiling. "I am. I'm just—" She cut herself off with a quick shake of her head. "Poppy and I are going upstairs. We've got work to do."

Poppy perched on the edge of the bed, watching as Rosaline paced the length of the bedroom.

"I'm not *not* happy for them," Rosaline stressed.

"I know."

"It's just . . . three months." Rosaline shook her head. "You know as well as I do what people are going to say."

She did. That Lyric was having a baby. That she and Cash, neither of who had the greatest track record when it came to relationships, were moving too fast, repeating the same mistakes they'd made before. Not that either of them had ever been engaged before, but it was no secret they both tended to fall hard and fast. A fact that worried Poppy and she knew worried Rosaline, too.

"Do you think we could convince them to keep it quiet? Just not say anything?"

Rosaline's footsteps slowed and she looked at Poppy askance. "Keep the engagement under wraps? And what, have them tie the knot in secret? Hard launch their marriage? Do you seriously think that's going to work?"

"I don't know, but it could be worth a shot." She shrugged. "People can't speculate on something they know nothing about."

Rosaline snorted derisively. "Poppy, sweetheart, I adore you, but you and I both know that's not true."

"Yeah, well, it still couldn't . . ." Hold—hold on. "Did you just say you *adore me?*"

Rosaline quit pacing and turned to Poppy, brows raised. "Yes?"

Her heart crashed into her ribs and her lungs refused to work, her mouth opening and shutting wordlessly. *Adore* was not a word she heard used often. Certainly no one had ever said they adored *her.*

"You seem surprised." Rosaline looked deeply amused as she crossed the room and stopped in front of Poppy. "Pleasantly, I hope."

She reached out and tucked her fingers in the pockets of Rosaline's high-waisted leggings. "*Pleasantly* is one way of putting it." A breathless, giddy little laugh escaped her. "I guess I just wasn't expecting you to tell me you *adore me* in the same breath you tell me I'm wrong."

"I didn't say you were wrong. Impractically idealistic, maybe . . ."

"Be still my heart."

With two fingers beneath Poppy's chin, Rosaline tipped her head back, bringing Poppy's gaze to hers. Her green eyes crinkled when she smiled and Poppy's heart thudded extra hard. "I figured you knew, but seeing as you clearly did not, let the record show that I'm pretty crazy about you, Poppy."

"Ooh, on record, huh?" She grinned. "Must be serious."

"Mm, it is." Crawling onto the mattress with her knees on either side of Poppy's hips, Rosaline settled herself on Poppy's lap, wiggling a little to get comfortable. "Now's right about the time you tell me that it's mutual and you're crazy about me too."

Poppy sputtered out a laugh. "Presumptuous, much?"

Arms draped loosely around Poppy's neck, Rosaline dropped her chin, the distance between their faces dwindling. Instead of kissing Poppy on the mouth, she pressed her lips to the bolt of Poppy's jaw. Poppy's lids fluttered and her teeth dragged against her bottom lip. Rosaline's breath was hot against the side of her face, making her shiver. "It's not presumptuous if I'm right," she whispered.

Poppy exhaled sharply. "I figured you knew," she said, echoing Rosaline's words.

Rosaline pressed another kiss to Poppy's jaw. "Doesn't mean I don't want to hear you say it."

"I am." She shivered when Rosaline's teeth scraped her skin. "Crazy about you."

Rosaline sat back and offered her a blinding smile. "That wasn't so hard, was it?"

"Oh my god." Poppy laughed. "You're impossible."

"Nothing is impossible, Poppy." She wrinkled her nose. "Except maybe convincing Lyric and Curran to see reason."

"I still think my idea has merit."

"Sorry, but have you met those two? I bet you twenty bucks Lyric's already been on Etsy looking up shit with *wifey for lifey* bedazzled on it." Rosaline shook her head. "No, we're just going to have to try and get ahead of it."

"Fair enough. I think Cash has probably maxed out his discretion points for the rest of the year." Poppy gnawed on her lip, smiling a little when Rosaline reached out and pried it free from her teeth. "They could—okay, this is going to sound so beyond basic, but what if they just announce their engagement on Instagram? Caption it with as much or as little as they want to say? That would at least give them the opportunity to do it on their terms."

Unlike how the news that they were dating broke.

"It's not a bad idea," Rosaline said, brow furrowed in obvious contemplation. "Gabby over at *E!* owes me a favor. I might drop her a line, hint that she should keep an eye out so she can jump on the story first. Nothing she writes will be defamatory or incendiary. Maybe the other outlets will follow her lead and keep it clean."

"Maybe. Either way, it doesn't seem like Cash and Lyric are too worried. Not the way we are."

"It's our job to worry about them. And even if it wasn't, I still would." Rosaline blew out a breath, ruffling the hair that had escaped the bun on the back of her head and fallen across her forehead. "God, I can't believe Lyric plans to move to Portland." She ran a hand over her face and huffed out a laugh. "Guess I better start looking at properties on Zillow."

"Properties as in, you're planning on moving too?" It probably shouldn't have come as a surprise and yet, until this moment, she hadn't even considered that Lyric moving to Portland meant that Rosaline might be moving back to Oregon too.

"I'm not sure why I'd stay in LA. The sunshine is nice, don't get me wrong, but I can live without the traffic and smog and, to be honest, I miss living somewhere with seasons," Rosaline confessed. "As Lyric pointed out, she can work from anywhere and so can I. And Portland *does* have its charms, after all."

"True. Portland *is* home to the most strip clubs per capita in the nation."

Rosaline laughed. "I was thinking more along the lines of the most *Poppy Petersons per capita*, but sure. Strip clubs too."

Poppy's cheeks hurt from trying to keep her smile in check. "The *most* Poppy Petersons, huh?"

"I'm really only interested in one particular Poppy Peterson. She's enough of a handful."

Poppy laughed. "Well, if during your home search you happen to stumble across a nice, cheap one bedroom, let me know, would you?"

Rosaline cocked her head. "How come?"

"No offense to Lyric and Cash, but I'm not really interested in being roommates with a couple of newlyweds," she said. "Living with Cash wasn't ever meant to be permanent. More of a . . . stopgap until I was ready to find my own place."

"And are you thinking of renting, or . . . ?"

She snorted. "Cash pays me disgustingly well but have you looked at the market here lately? All you people moving here from California are driving up the home prices," she teased.

Rosaline pursed her lips. "I mean. You could just . . . you know."

Her brows rose. She really didn't. "I could just what?"

"You could just . . ." Rosaline shrugged, her gaze set somewhere over Poppy's shoulder. "You know. Move in with me."

Her breath caught and it was a good thing she was sitting down because she was pretty sure her whole world had just tipped on its axis. "What?"

"It was just an idea." Rosaline shrugged tightly, shoulders creeping upward. "If you hate it—"

"I didn't say that," she blurted, not wanting Rosaline to get the wrong idea. "But . . . isn't it a little early to be talking about moving in together?"

"Probably," Rosaline admitted with a wry laugh as she reached up and tucked her hair behind her ears, a self-conscious gesture Poppy recognized. A blush stained her cheeks and the bridge of her nose, but she met Poppy's gaze head-on. "I know it makes me a hypocrite considering I just told Lyric she was moving too fast, but . . . what did Curran say?" The corner of her mouth dimpled into a smile. "When you know, you know?"

Poppy's heart fluttered furiously. "*Rosaline.*"

"It'll probably be months before I buy a place," she said, squirming a little atop Poppy's lap. "But if you're not interested—"

"That's not what I'm saying. I'm just . . ." Still pinching herself that Rosaline wanted to be with her. Because things like this? Things like this didn't happen to Poppy.

Poppy survived on scraps of affection. She made meals out of breadcrumbs. Anything more seemed too good to be true.

But maybe . . . maybe she didn't have to live like that anymore. In constant fear that what she did have would be snatched away. That she didn't deserve to have good things in the first place let alone keep them.

"If you're offering, then yeah." Poppy grinned. "I'd really like that."

An answering smile lit up Rosaline's face and the fluttering in Poppy's chest and stomach increased tenfold.

"Wow. Okay." Rosaline gave a near-frazzled laugh. She pressed a hand to her stomach and the other to her forehead. "Oh shit."

Poppy frowned. "What?"

"We're going to have to tell Curran and Lyric."

Chapter Nineteen

Lyric Adair engaged to Cash Curran following whirlwind romance: "When you know, you know"

by Gabby Fitz
published on December 15

Lyric Adair and Cash Curran are engaged!

The couple—who have sparked nothing but buzz since they started dating in September—shared the happy news on Instagram.

"There are few precious things in life that feel like they're simply meant to be," Adair captioned a photo of her and Curran looking incandescently happy, the sun setting behind them. "Meeting Cash feels like one of those things. I know some people are going to call me crazy, but when you find someone that makes you as happy as Cash makes me, it's not a question of if, but when. When you know, you know. So excited for our forever 💍 @cashcurran"

E! has reached out to Adair and Curran's reps for comment.

PORTLAND PATHFINDERS @portlandpathfinders • 16h
Congratulations @cashcurran and @lyricadair on your engagement! If you're looking for a wedding color palette, might we suggest black and green?? 💍🖤🤍

December 17

"What do you have against March?"

"Not a damn thing," Rosaline said, elbow deep in soapy water. "Only that it's less than three months away. What do *you* have against June?"

"Nothing." Lyric swept her pointer finger along the inside of the brownie batter bowl. She'd nearly licked it clean. "Only that it's six months away."

Rosaline flicked soap bubbles at her, making her squeal. "Brat."

Poppy chuckled and flipped off the oven light. The fudgy Symphony bar brownies—Cash's favorite; Lyric wanted to surprise him and had enlisted Poppy's help—were coming along nicely. Ten more minutes and they'd be done. "She has a point, Rosaline."

Lyric held out her arms. "Thank you." She turned to Rosaline. "See, even Poppy agrees with me."

"Okay, don't go putting words in my mouth. I didn't say *that*."

"Poppy Peterson." Rosaline shook her head and narrowed her eyes playfully. "You're *my* girlfriend. Aren't you supposed to be on my side? The side of, you know, reason."

Girlfriend. God, that was never going to get old. Being Rosaline's girlfriend, hearing her say it. Nothing could stop the smile from spreading across her face. She probably looked unhinged, standing there in the middle of Cash's kitchen grinning for no apparent reason, but whatever. Rosaline had known what she was getting herself into. If she hadn't? No take backs. Poppy Peterson didn't come with a receipt; she was not returnable. "I hardly think it counts as taking a side to simply point out that June is, in fact, six months away."

"Six *long* months," Lyric whined. "We don't want to wait that long."

Rosaline let the water out of the sink and reached for the dish towel, drying her hands. "Everyone is going to without a doubt think you're pregnant if you and Curran tie the knot in March."

"We don't care." Between her epic eye roll and the chocolate smeared on the corner of her mouth, Lyric looked younger than her age. "What's that saying? Truth will out? Given enough time, everyone will see there was nothing to the rumors when I don't pop out a baby in nine months." She paused. "Until the day there is something to the rumors, obviously."

"*Okay!*" Rosaline clapped her hands over her ears and squeezed her eyes shut, expression pained. "One crisis at a time, I beg of you."

Lyric sputtered out a laugh. "I think I should be offended that you consider my having children to be a crisis, but I'm mostly amused by that look on your face. You look constipated."

"One, rude. Two, it's not you having children that I consider to be a crisis; it's the thought of you procreating with Curran that scares the living shit out of me."

"Hey!" Lyric and Poppy said in perfect harmony. They looked at each other and laughed.

Rosaline rolled her eyes. "Curran's a giant. Your babies are going to be massive, Lyric."

Cash wasn't *that* tall, but . . . Poppy had seen his baby pictures. Even as a newborn, he'd looked like a butterball turkey.

"Don't be mean to my future children."

"I'm just worried about your . . . pelvis."

Poppy snickered under her breath at the look of alarm splashed across Lyric's face.

"June still satisfies your requirement of getting married during the offseason. You'll have plenty of time for a honeymoon before Curran has to be back at training camp at the end of July. June gives us more time to plan. Give you the wedding of your dreams."

"You know." Lyric drummed her fingers against her chin. "Cash has a game against the Raiders next week. We'll be in Vegas. We could always take a little trip down the strip and find a twenty-four-hour chapel with an Elvis impersonator to officiate and—"

"Absolutely not," Rosaline growled. "Don't even joke, Lyric. You are not Kourtney fucking Kardashian. You're not getting hitched in Vegas and definitely not by some two-bit Elvis impersonator."

"But what if Vegas is my *dream*, Roz?" Lyric clasped her hands under her chin. "What if Cash and I want to get married at the Taco Bell Cantina? You get Taco Bell champagne flutes and a taco twelve pack and a Cinnabon Delights cakes. They even give the bride a sauce packet bouquet and—" Lyric's composure cracked and she started laughing. "Oh my god, if you could see your faces right now." She clutched her stomach and wiped her eyes. "I can't even."

"Thank god," Rosaline muttered. "I was about thirty seconds away from a full-blown panic attack."

"Anyway." Lyric stretched across the counter to dump the batter bowl in the sink. "It's not like there's going to be much to plan. Cash and I want to keep it small. Just family and a few close friends. Donna, Grey, JJ," Lyric rattled off, ticking off the names

of her manager, personal assistant, and producer on her fingers. "And on Cash's side, he'll want his parents there. Poppy, obviously. A few of his teammates, I'm guessing. DeAndre for sure and his wife, Cassidy..." She shrugged. "Like I said, small. We'll probably just do it here in the backyard—"

"Assuming it won't be pouring rain, considering you want to get married in Portland, Oregon, in *March*."

Lyric rolled her eyes. "Isn't rain on your wedding day considered good luck?"

"Alanis Morissette thinks it's ironic," Poppy joked.

Rosaline laughed under her breath.

"Well, whatever it is," Lyric said, "it's going to be perfect because when it's all said and done, Cash and I will be married. If it rains, we'll just move the ceremony inside. Easy peasy." She rested her chin on her hand atop the counter. "I'm guessing you'll be Cash's best ... woman? That's a thing, right?"

Poppy frowned. Sure, it was a thing, but ... "I think DeAndre will probably be his best man."

Cash had been DeAndre's best man at his wedding; it made total sense that Cash would ask him. Poppy wasn't offended in the slightest.

"Oh." Lyric frowned. "I guess. I just thought, with Rosaline being my maid of honor, it would be kind of nice if you were his ... attendant or whatever you want to call it. You know, for the processional."

Rosaline's head whipped to the side and she stared at Lyric, wide-eyed. "Maid of honor? Me?"

"Duh." Lyric laughed. "You say it like it's even a question, Roz."

"Clearly not, considering you never actually asked."

"I didn't think I needed to. You're my best friend. Who the hell else would I ask?"

"Well." Rosaline sniffed hard, her eyes gone misty. "I'm honored."

"Ba dum tss," Poppy joked and Rosaline's lips twitched.

"Honored *but* it doesn't change the fact that I think March is too soon," Rosaline said.

Lyric slumped over the counter. "Says you, who asked Poppy to move in with you after . . . remind me, how long have you been dating?"

Rosaline pursed her lips. "We're not talking about me and Poppy."

"Maybe we should be." Lyric gave Poppy a scrutinizing once-over. "So. What are your intentions with my best friend?"

"Oh my god." Rosaline pressed the heel of her hand to her forehead. "*Stop*."

"It's a perfectly valid question, Roz."

"Ignore her," Rosaline grumbled at Poppy, looking profoundly uncomfortable. "Lyric is being patently ridiculous. Par for the course with her, truly."

"Excuse you. I'm just looking out for you." Lyric laced her fingers together on the counter and raised both her brows. "Whenever you're ready, Poppy."

She didn't know whether to be deeply amused or legitimately concerned by Lyric's sudden desire to give her the third degree. "You know, I don't remember grilling you when you started dating *my* best friend. You're kind of putting me on the spot here."

Lyric grinned. "No one expects the Spanish Inquisition."

"Touché." Poppy huffed a laugh. "I'm assuming when you say *intentions* you mean *other* than have lots of hot, raunchy sex?"

Rosaline hid her face in her hands with a pained groan.

"I knew I liked you for a reason." Lyric's smile went sly. "You know, I bet we could *totally* get a discount on wedding stuff if we doubled. Split the cost in half, save some cash."

Poppy was about 97 percent sure Lyric was kidding, but that didn't stop her heart from somersaulting at the idea of one day marrying Rosaline.

"Oh sure," Rosaline deadpanned, hands falling and hanging limply at her sides. "Because cash is totally an object here, Miss *I was just featured in* Forbes."

"You don't get rich by paying more than you have to. Besides, you're the one who taught me how to manage my finances."

Poppy cleared her throat. "It's not a terrible idea." She had to bite the inside of her cheek to keep from giggling at the way Rosaline froze in place, eyes big in her face that had gone slack with shock. Poppy was pretty sure she'd even stopped breathing. "If you and Cash would just wait until June to get married—"

"*Ugh*." Lyric threw her hands up. "You two are impossible! Did you rehearse this or something?"

Rosaline recovered swiftly. A little smile tugged at the corner of her mouth as she stared fondly across the kitchen at Poppy. "I can't take credit for that one. That was all Poppy." She toasted Poppy with her mug full of spiced apple cider.

"You two really are made for each other." Lyric sighed softly. "Come on, enough with the jokes. I want to know how you feel about each other. Give me something to work with here."

"Are you so bored with Curran that you're looking for fodder for your next album elsewhere?" Rosaline teased.

"*Fodder*." Lyric jutted out her bottom lip in an exaggerated pout. "You're so mean to me."

"Okay, fine, fine!" Poppy held up her hands. "Honest answer to your earlier question." Lyric sat up straight, eager, and Rosaline cocked her head, long hair loose and spilling over her shoulder. Poppy smiled. "I would love nothing more than to continue to be a pain in Rosaline's ass for as long as she'll have me."

A warm smile crept across Rosaline's face. "You're not a pain in my ass, Poppy."

Her heart swelled and she looped her arms around Rosaline's waist. "I'm not?"

"What is she then?" Lyric asked, watching them wistfully from her perch at the counter.

"She's . . ." Rosaline's tongue swept over her bottom lip. If Lyric weren't sitting there, Poppy would've closed the distance between them and chased it with her own. Rosaline's smile went a little mischievous, like she knew exactly what Poppy was thinking. "She's the best thing to happen to me since I met you."

Poppy melted, insides going as gooey and warm as the brownies baking away inside the oven.

Lyric cooed. "*Roz*, you romantic."

The security system chimed softly, a robotic voice alerting them that the front door had opened.

"Lovely ladies! I'm home!" Cash called out.

Lyric's entire face lit up. "We're in the kitchen!"

The oven timer dinged, and Poppy pressed a quick kiss to the corner of Rosaline's mouth. "It's mutual, you know." She stepped back reluctantly, needing to pull the brownies out of the oven before they burned. "You're the best thing to happen to me in a long time."

Rosaline's cheeks turned Poppy's favorite shade of pink.

Cash poked his head inside the kitchen. "Something smells good."

"Your favorite," Lyric said, tipping her head back for a kiss Cash eagerly gave her. "How was practice?"

"Long. Brutal." Cash sighed and reached inside the refrigerator, pulling out a premixed protein shake, the kind Poppy recognized as being heavy on glutamine for recovery. They tasted like cardboard and overly ripe bananas, the texture gritty and reminiscent of the liquid Augmentin she had to take as a kid when she got ear infections. How Cash stomached the stuff was a mystery. "Coach was on our asses, but at the end he said we look like we're in pretty good shape for Sunday." He reached for the pan of brownies resting on the stove and pulled his hand back with a hiss, licking the tips of his fingers. "Ow, fuck. Why are those so fucking hot?"

"Poppy literally just pulled those out of the oven," Rosaline said, shaking her head.

"You saw me do it, Cash."

Another chime sounded, too soft to be from the security system.

"Could you pass me my phone?" Lyric asked, stretching across the counter, arm not long enough to reach her phone, which she'd left beside the recipe for the brownies.

"Ew." Rosaline handed it to her with a frown. "The case is sticky. I think you got batter on it."

Lyric glanced at the screen. "Five four one. That's an Oregon number, right?"

"Mhmm." Poppy reached inside the drawer beside the stove for a toothpick so she could check that the brownies weren't underbaked. "Eugene, Bend, um, Springfield. Cash?"

He lowered his protein shake and wiped the back of his hand across his mouth. "Medford, too, I think."

"Corvallis," Rosaline said, and all three of them shuddered.

"Weird," Lyric murmured, frowning at her phone.

"Did someone from a four five one call you or something?" Rosaline asked. "Did they leave a message?"

An uneasy look had settled on Lyric's face. "Text."

"Cassidy's got your number, right?" Cash twisted at the waist, cracking his back. "She probably just gave it to one of the other girls."

"I don't think Cassidy would do that," Poppy said. "Not without asking Lyric if she was okay with it first."

In an effort to make her feel welcome, Cassidy had invited Lyric over for drinks with a few of the other WAGs. Over as opposed to out because Cassidy wasn't ready to leave her two-month-old with a sitter.

"No." Lyric shook her head. "It's—it's not from Cassidy. It's . . . really strange."

"Probably spam or something then, babe. I wouldn't worry about it." Cash crushed the drink carton in his hand and tossed it in the recycling can. He paused, brows drawing into a sharp frown. "Unless you mean strange as in threatening."

Rosaline rounded the counter. "What's it say?"

Lyric pressed her fingers to the notch at the base of her neck. "Hi, Lyric. You don't know me, but you're going to want to see this. Sorry to be the bearer of bad news, but I would want to know the truth. xx." She shook her head. "It's not signed."

Poppy shivered and tossed the toothpick she'd used to check the brownies in the trash. Whoever it was knew who Lyric was and somehow, they'd gotten ahold of the private number she kept closely guarded, only trusting it to her closest friends. "That's kind of creepy."

Cash scrubbed a knuckle over his mouth, still frowning. "What bad news?"

Rosaline's eyes were locked on the screen, her lips pursed, and her jaw tight. "There's a link."

"Is it smart to even click it?" Poppy asked. "It could be phishing."

"Just what I need." Lyric sighed. "Someone trying to hack my phone."

Cash crossed the kitchen and stopped behind Lyric, wrapping

his arms around her waist. He kissed the knob at the top of her spine. "We won't let that happen."

"You and what army, Curran?" Rosaline snorted. "It'll be fine. You've got two-factor authentication set up, you've got a photo vault, your software is up to date, and your passwords are all strong and unique. And we'll change them after just in case." She took the phone from Lyric and tapped on the link.

Curious, Poppy crowded behind them, trying to get a glimpse of Lyric's screen.

Lyric's Google Drive app opened and after a few seconds of staring at the triangular emblem set against a back screen, a folder loaded. There were only three files inside, one labeled *tinder.png*, another *tinder2.png*, and a final file called *KasaNightClub.mp4*. Two pictures and a video.

"This is really creeping me the hell out," Lyric murmured, leaning back against Cash's chest. "I don't think I want to open these." She shivered and shook her head. "I don't know. I just have a really bad feeling in the pit of my stomach."

"You could have a stalker, Lyric." Rosaline's index finger hovered over the video file. "*Another* stalker, I mean."

"Hence the *really bad feeling in the pit of my stomach*," Lyric retorted.

"Rosaline's right," Poppy said gingerly. "Staying in the dark isn't going to do us any good."

They needed to know what they were dealing with, what the threat level was, if any, so they could respond accordingly. Increase security presence at Pathfinders' games, contact the police if need be.

Cash pressed his lips to the springy curls at the crown of Lyric's head. "If worse comes to worst, we'll handle it."

With that, Rosaline double tapped on the file. A loading bar appeared, filling quickly.

The video footage was grainy, like it had been overly sharpened, and the camera was shaky. There was no sound, but the club where the video had been filmed must've been noisy, the place packed with people drinking and dancing. The clip was only thirty-two seconds and ten of them were wasted on—

Poppy's heart dropped into her stomach.

The video quality was subpar but there was no mistaking the guy in the corner booth as anyone but Cash. Just like there was no mistaking that the scantily clad woman draped across his lap wasn't Lyric, but his ex, Ashley.

Cash's jaw dropped. "What the fuck is this?"

What the fuck was right. On the screen, Cash fisted a hand in Ashley's long, platinum blond hair and tugged hard. Her lips parted on a silent gasp, a moan maybe, seconds before Cash's mouth came crashing down on hers in a kiss that made Poppy's face burn and her stomach curdle.

She'd never liked Ashley—well, Ashley had never liked *her*. Poppy hadn't had anything against her other than the fact that she didn't much enjoy being looked at like she was a threat all because she was a woman and friends with Ashley's boyfriend.

The video played through twice, set to a loop. After it started to replay for the third time, Lyric set the phone down on the counter with shaking hands and turned to Cash, her face disconcertingly blank.

"When was this?" she asked, voice flat.

Cash raked a hand through his hair. "I don't—I don't even know where this was taken."

"The file says 'Kasa Night Club,'" Rosaline replied coolly. "The place ring any bells, Curran?"

He shook his head. "I don't—maybe? Before we started going to xport, the guys and I went to a bunch of different places for postgame parties. But Ashley and I broke up in January. This video's got to be at least a year, year-and-a-half old. Why the hell would someone be sending it to Lyric? Let alone now?"

"It's not," Lyric whispered, shaking off Cash's arms when she stood. She jerked her chin at her phone, the video still looping repeatedly. "I bought you that shirt. And that tattoo?" She pointed a trembling finger at the dotted lines and tiny stars on Cash's forearm. "You told me you and Poppy got those on her birthday this year."

Bile rose in her throat.

Lyric was right. She and Cash had gotten matching tattoos on her birthday in early June. Constellations, Gemini on Cash's arm for her, Pisces along her shoulder blade for him.

He stiffened as he looked down at his arm. "That makes no fucking sense. I haven't seen Ashley since we broke up." He looked at Poppy imploringly. "Poppy, you know I haven't seen her."

Poppy pressed a fist against her stomach and swallowed hard. She shrugged weakly. "Cash—"

"Don't pull Poppy into your mess, Curran," Rosaline snapped. "And don't ask her to lie for you."

"I'm not asking her to lie for me." He buried his hands in his hair and gritted his teeth. "I'm fucking *not*, okay. I would never ask her to do that."

"And I wouldn't lie," Poppy promised, utterly and completely fucking lost. "I don't know what's happening any more than anyone else here does. This is the first time I . . ."

She didn't know how to finish that sentence. This was the first time she'd seen the video? This was the first time she'd learned that Cash had—no. She couldn't bring herself to think . . . *that*, give it credence, let alone voice it out loud.

"Lyric, *baby*," Cash croaked. The skin beneath his eyes had turned pink and puffy. "Please, you have to—"

"She has to *what?*" Rosaline demanded. "Listen to you lie? Fat fucking chance. Lyric doesn't have to do a damn thing."

"Back the fuck off, Rosaline," he snarled. "I know you love Lyric, but news flash, so do I."

"You've got a funny way of showing it, sticking your tongue down your ex's throat."

"Cut it out, both of you," Poppy said, stepping between them. "Your arguing isn't helping."

Rosaline pressed her lips together in a thin line, looking like it pained her to keep the words in.

Lyric gave a sharp jerk of her head and stumbled into the counter when Cash reached for her. "Don't." She sucked in a shuddering breath. "If you care about me even a little, be honest, Cash. Please just—tell me the truth."

"I'm not lying to you." His eyes were wide and frantic. "I wouldn't do that to you. I *love* you."

"It's a fucking *video*, Cash," she cried. "It's not like I'm imagining things. We all saw you kiss her." Her dark eyes welled with tears. "So just do us both a favor and stop lying. Just—stop."

"No." He shook his head, adamant. "Baby, you've got to believe me. I don't know what that is, but it's not—it's not real. Okay? It's not. I don't know how, but someone—someone must've done something."

Tears spilled down Lyric's cheeks.

"I love you so fucking much, baby," his voice cracked and—*god*. Poppy jammed the heel of her hand against her breastbone, aching. "You've got to believe me. I—look, I can call Ashley. I'll do it right this fucking minute, all right? She'll tell you the same thing I'm telling you."

A hiccupping sob burst from Lyric's lips, and she quickly clapped a hand over her mouth. "Why would I believe either one of you?"

"Because—"

"Save it, Cash."

He shook his head. "Not until you say you believe me."

"I don't!" Lyric sounded like she was a few brief seconds away from hyperventilating. "I can't—I can't do this." She turned to Rosaline. "I can't."

Rosaline nodded once. "Go wait in the car."

"What?" Cash sounded like someone had punched him in the gut. "Lyric—"

She whirled on her heel, all but running from the room.

Poppy reached for his arm. "Cash—"

He ignored her, following Lyric down the hall. The security system chimed, and front door slammed shut a moment later.

Like someone had cut her strings, Rosaline slumped over, hands braced against the countertop. "I knew this was going to happen."

Poppy crossed her arms, suddenly freezing. "What? How could you—"

"Not *this*." Rosaline shook her head. "This is . . . *fuck*. This is astonishingly low. Even for Curran. But I knew nothing good was going to come from this relationship. I knew it and I should've listened to my gut and put my foot down from day one. As soon as I saw that tweet, I knew. I should've tried harder to convince Lyric that Curran was bad fucking news."

"That's—that's enough, okay?" This was still her best friend that Rosaline was talking about. "I know this looks awful—"

"Awful?" Rosaline scoffed. "Poppy, this is *damning*. If a picture is worth a thousand words, that video is worth a million."

Her lips twisted bitterly as if she'd tasted something spoiled. "Literally."

Poppy was going to be sick. "Are you saying you think whoever sent this to Lyric plans on selling it?"

It was bad enough watching the video in the privacy of Cash's kitchen, a special kind of torture watching it with Lyric and Cash and Rosaline. But the idea that hundreds, thousands, maybe even millions of people might see it gave a whole new meaning to the word *violation*.

Rosaline shrugged. "Depends on why they sent it to Lyric in the first place. If it was some Good Samaritan actually looking out for her, or if—"

"Someone could be trying to stir the pot."

Rosaline pinched the bridge of her nose. "*Christ*. If this gets out, do you know what people are going to say? Do you know what this is going to do to Lyric?"

"If Cash said he didn't do it—"

"Are you seriously defending him? *Poppy*." Rosaline sounded horrified and she looked it, too, staring at Poppy as if she'd lost her mind. Maybe she had. Nothing made sense.

She clung to the one thing she did know. "I know Cash."

Cash was reckless and prone to impulsivity, but he was a good person, honorable and decent, always putting the people he cared about first. He didn't lie and he didn't cheat, and she believed it down to her bones that he loved Lyric. He wouldn't do something like this. It didn't . . . it didn't make sense.

Rosaline grabbed Lyric's phone off the counter. She tapped the screen twice, stared at it for a moment, and scoffed. She passed the phone to Poppy. "Maybe you don't know him as well as you think you do."

Reluctantly, stomach churning riotously, Poppy took the phone from her. A screenshot of a Tinder profile stared back at her. Cash's, the profile having been created just last month. Poppy didn't want to, but she swiped to the next and final file Lyric had been sent anonymously. It was a screengrab of an in-app conversation, Cash making plans to grab drinks with the girl he was talking to.

The evidence was stacking up and none of it was good.

If this got out, if someone leaked these screenshots, this video, if they sold it as an exclusive to some tabloid, this would ruin Cash. Ruin his name, his reputation, and depending on the fallout, it might even ruin his career.

Poppy handed Rosaline the phone. She'd seen enough; she didn't need to keep studying the video, torturing herself by rereading the messages Cash had sent the girl whose name had been redacted from the screengrabs. "What are we supposed to do?"

"Poppy." Rosaline shook her head sadly. "Poppy, there's—there is no *we* in this."

"What?" she whispered. "What does that mean?"

No *we* in this. Of course there was a *we*. *They* were a *we*. They were supposed to be.

"You believe Curran," Rosaline said simply, quietly, staring down at her hands around the edge of the granite counter, knuckles white. "Or you want to. And I get it, okay? I do. I can't tell you what to think and . . . he's your best friend." She lifted her head and her eyes met Poppy's, the whites of them shot through with red. "But Lyric is mine. And she needs me to—she needs me. She needs me to have her back. She needs to know I do." She sniffed hard and shrugged weakly, shoulders curling in, looking as small as Poppy felt. "She can't doubt that."

Her eyes burned and her vision blurred. A lump had lodged itself in her throat that made it difficult to speak. "So, what? Lyric and Cash have issues so you and I—" She couldn't say it. "That's just . . . that's it?"

Rosaline closed her eyes. "Yeah." Her breath hitched. "I think that's . . . that's it."

Each blink threatened to spill the tears welling in her eyes. "And I can't say anything to—"

"*Poppy*." Rosaline's voice broke and it felt like Poppy's heart was breaking too. "What would you even say? Think about it. How would this work?"

Poppy tried to imagine it. Rosaline in Los Angeles and her in Portland. Cash and Lyric, the two most important people in their lives not on speaking terms, maybe even unable to be in the same room. Off-limits, Rosaline and Poppy unable to talk about them without it devolving into an argument, old hurts constantly being unearthed, bruises pressed. It would be untenable, the gap between them growing into a chasm too vast to bridge. A slow, suffocating death.

"Everything was—" Poppy pinched her eyes shut and bit her lip, stifling a sob.

Everything had been, if not perfect, closer to it than Poppy had ever dreamed. Not even ten minutes ago they had been baking brownies and joking and Rosaline had called Poppy the best thing to happen to her since Lyric. It wasn't *fair*.

"I know," Rosaline rasped, and Poppy felt her fingers brush over the skin of her wrist, a ghost of a touch. "For what it's worth?" She sniffled. "I really wanted this. I really wanted this with you."

So did Poppy.

"Lyric's waiting," Rosaline whispered. "I should—I should go grab my things. Hers too." She paused and Poppy cracked open her eyes. Rosaline stood a little straighter, her chin rising, piecing herself back together before Poppy's eyes. "Curran fucked himself over. Losing Lyric, whatever the press says about him . . . that's punishment enough. I won't make it worse. I won't call in any favors. For you. I don't want to make this harder for you."

Poppy nodded dully. It would probably sink in tomorrow or the next day or the day after how much that meant, but right now it didn't make her feel any better. "Thanks."

Rosaline crossed the kitchen and paused in the doorway, her back to Poppy. "Don't . . . don't go home for Christmas. Okay?"

The tears Poppy had tried to choke down spilled over, rolling down her cheeks and dripping off her jaw. She nodded even though Rosaline couldn't see her.

"Take care of yourself, Poppy." Rosaline walked out of the kitchen, taking half of Poppy's heart with her.

Chapter Twenty

LYRIC ADAIR UPDATES @lyricadairupdatesunofficial • 12h
Lyric Adair is no longer following @cashcurran.

**Less than a week after announcing
their engagement, Lyric Adair and Cash
Curran seem to call it quits as video of
Curran kissing ex-girlfriend surfaces**

by Jaimie Xin
published on December 21

Mere days after sharing the news of their whirlwind engagement on social media, Adair and Curran appear to have called it quits.

Rumors of trouble in paradise started swirling early Tuesday morning after Adair was spotted outside the Beverly Hills home of her publicist, Rosaline Sinclair, sans engagement ring, looking as if she'd been crying.

Later that same day, a shocking video of Curran kissing ex-girlfriend, Ashley Tibbey, was shared exclusively with *Notoriety Magazine*. While the video has no time stamp, eagle-eyed fans immediately spotted several clues including a recent tattoo that suggest this lip-lock took place after Curran and Adair began dating.

In addition to the video, a Tinder profile belonging to Curran has surfaced. According to the app, Curran created the profile in November of this year.

While a formal statement has yet to be released by any of the parties involved, Adair has removed the post announcing her engagement to the quarterback and wiped any mention of him from her social media.

Representatives for Curran, Adair, and Tibbey have yet to respond to requests from *People* for comment.

VICTORIA @pdxprincess • 15h
I just saw the video. I literally feel sick to my stomach. Poor Lyric 💔 #CashCurranIsCanceled

IN MY SANTA ANA ERA @omgahdaaaaavid • 15h
I was rooting for them so hard 🫠🫠🫠
#CashCurranIsCanceled

UR FAV LESBIAN @imubutgayer • 15h
CASH CURRAN YOU WILL BEGIN TO COUGH IN SEVEN DAYS #CashCurranIsCanceled

DANILA @danianne • 14h
omg this next album is going to be fire 🔥🔥🔥
#CashCurranIsCanceled

LYRIC ADAIR RARES @lyricadairrares • 14h
replying to @danianne
what a shitty, exploitative thing to say. we all love her music, but wtf? she literally just got her heart broken and you're already thinking about the songs that are going to come out of her grief? 😒

X TRENDING BOT @xtrendingbot • 14h
#CashCurranIsCanceled is currently trending in the United States with #LyricAdair and #CashCurran

CHERRY 🫀 @polinlover96 • 13h
not gonna lie, this has me more depressed than when my parents got divorced 😢 #CashCurranIsCanceled

LILIANA @evanbuckleystan98 • 9h
Am I the only one wondering if Rosaline and Poppy are okay? 👻 #CashCurranIsCanceled

IN MY PINING ERA @claudiaxyz92 • 5h
replying to @evanbuckleystan98
I don't have a good feeling about this 👻

PAIGELA @infrontofmysalad • 3h
Man, I have got to stop forming parasocial relationships with celebrities. #CashCurranIsCanceled

Portland Pathfinders suffer bitter loss against Las Vegas Raiders amid cheating scandal plaguing star quarterback

by Edgar Jones, ESPN staff writer
published on December 22

LAS VEGAS, NV—Cash Curran's relationship woes appear to be affecting his performance on the field.

The Pathfinders, favored by seven points, failed to pick up the win, losing 38-34 against the Raiders. Curran, in particular, was off his game, missing four touchdown throws in addition to throwing a game-losing pick in the final quarter of the game.

His mood was markedly melancholy after the game. "It sucks, yeah. We weren't at our best. We weren't cohesive. We gotta clean it up. We gotta do better next time."

"It's all you can do," DeAndre Jones added. "We got two games left and then the playoffs to think about. Consistency is gonna be key for us going forward."

When asked point blank if he believes his recent breakup with pop star Lyric Adair affected his gameplay, Curran took a moment to consider his answer before he replied. "I like to think I'm decent at compartmentalizing and leaving my baggage at the door and stepping onto the field with a clear head, but that's not always the case. I play with my heart as much as I do with my head and unfortunately there's no such thing as concussion protocol for the former."

The Pathfinders are currently the second seed in the NFC West. Their next game will be on December 28, where they will face off against the San Francisco 49ers at home.

December 23

> **POPPY (12:23 P.M.):** Mom, I wanted to let you know I won't be coming over on Christmas Day. Frankly, I don't think you really want me there, so I don't think this will come as much of a disappointment. Maybe you'll even be relieved.

> **POPPY (12:26 P.M.):** I know I haven't always made life easy for you and Dad, but you're my parents. You're supposed to love me anyway. And most of the time, it doesn't feel like you do. It feels like the goalposts for me are different than for Jessica and Dillon; my goalposts are constantly moving. Nothing I do is ever good enough and I'm really tired of feeling that way.

> **POPPY (12:28 P.M.):** Could you please let me know when is a good time for me to swing by and drop off everyone's presents tomorrow?

Read at 12:35 p.m.

December 25

Poppy pumped her arms, weary legs pounding against the pavement. She summoned one final burst of energy and sprinted the last hundred-some yards down the street on aching feet.

"Good run?" Cash's neighbor, Mrs. Eichen, stood on her porch in a bathrobe, holding the paper she'd fetched from the curb in one hand and her son's lunch box in the other.

"Decent." Poppy gave her ponytail a tug, tightening the elastic. "Offer still stands if you ever want to join."

Mrs. Eichen waved her off. "I'm more of a Peloton girl, Poppy. But thanks for offering! Have a great day!"

"You too!"

After a quick cooldown in the driveway, Poppy headed inside, detouring to the kitchen for a bottle of water before limping downstairs to the gym to stretch. Somewhere around mile five, her right sock had slipped and now there was a gnarly blister on the back of her heel, the skin split open, raw and tender and starting to ooze. She was pretty sure Cash kept a first aid kit somewhere down here, otherwise—

"Oh. Hi." She drew up short at the bottom of the basement stairs. "I didn't know you were awake."

Cash was sitting in the middle of the sectional tucked in the farthest corner of the gym in front of the mounted flatscreen he only ever used for watching game tape. And he'd started watching that on his iPad, which he could do anywhere. Poppy couldn't remember the last time Cash had spent time down here outside of his regular daily workouts.

He barely looked away from the screen, offering her the briefest of nods, but even that was enough to tell he looked worse for wear. Unwashed hair unkempt and sticking up at all angles like he'd been running his fingers through it, purple bags beneath his bloodshot eyes, his jaw scruffy with a hell of a lot more than a mere five o'clock shadow. His shirt was wrinkled, the same one he'd been wearing yesterday.

"Hey." He reached for the thermos at his feet and refilled the mug in his hands. "Good run?"

"Fine." She kicked off her sneakers, wincing at the drag against the open skin of her heel. "Missed you, though. Thought you were going to join me."

Cash grunted and Poppy followed his gaze to the flatscreen. Her stomach sank.

On the screen, that god-awful video of him kissing Ashley played on a never-ending loop.

"Cash." She rested her hip against the arm of the couch and crossed her arms. "How long exactly have you been awake?"

"I don't know." He stared muzzily into his thermos. "What day is it?"

Jesus. "It's Christmas, Cash."

"Oh. Huh." He seemed genuinely surprised to hear it. "I tried to sleep. Got an hour or two. I think?"

"Have you been down here all night?"

"Thought I'd get a workout in, try to tire myself out, but then—" He gestured to the screen. "I was just going to watch it once."

"You have to stop this." Guilt was a bear, didn't she know it, but this? This was not healthy. "You've got to stop torturing yourself. You're watching this over and over again, to what end, Cash? Are you—are you punishing yourself? Because that's not—"

"I'm not—" He exhaled sharply and ran a hand over his face, fingers rasping against his stubble. "I'm not torturing myself. This isn't punishment. I'm . . . fuck, I don't know, Poppy. I'm trying to make it make sense."

Poppy chewed on her thumbnail. "I love you. You know I do. But don't you think it's time to admit that—"

"No." He gave a sharp shake of his head. "I'm not going to admit to something I didn't do."

Video Cash stuck his tongue down video Ashley's throat and

Poppy felt just as sick watching it now as she had the first time. How Cash was able to watch it on repeat was beyond her.

"You don't believe me." He sounded resigned.

Poppy pinched her eyes shut. "It's not that I don't want to. Because I do. I really, *really* do. I just—I don't know what to believe, Cash."

She knew the Cash who was sitting beside her. The Cash who'd always seemed to have a sixth sense for when she needed him. The Cash who'd made the two-hour drive from Eugene to Portland one weekend a month, skipping out on the chance to party with his teammates, choosing instead to spend time with her, knowing her parents left her alone more often than not. The Cash who'd picked her up when she was down. The Cash who'd never made her feel like a failure.

It was next to impossible to reconcile that Cash with the one on the screen, blatantly cheating on his fiancé with his ex-girlfriend, not even looking a little sorry for it.

But the Cash she knew, the Cash she loved, had always given her grace.

"You know you aren't your mistakes, right?"

He scoffed. "I don't need platitudes, Poppy."

"It's what you always tell me."

"I didn't do anything." He tugged hard on his hair. No wonder it looked like shit. "I didn't. If I did, I'd own it, okay? I'd apologize. I'd grovel. I'd beg Lyric for forgiveness, but I didn't do it. That?" He pointed at the screen. "That's not me."

"Were you drinking? Because you know that I of all people won't judge you if you—"

"No! Christ, that's not what I'm saying." He stood and began to pace in front of the TV. "That is *literally* not me. It looks like me, I know it does because I've got two working eyes, but . . . It's.

Not. Me." He snatched the remote off the ottoman and rewound the video to the beginning. "Please just hear me out."

Poppy slipped off the arm of the couch and took a seat on the cushion Cash had vacated with her feet drawn up and her knees hugged to her chest. "I'm listening."

She'd always listen.

He offered her a ghost of a smile, wan and weak. "Okay. This is going to sound crazy, but I was reading about deepfakes. About how people can use artificial intelligence to swap faces and—Poppy, I think someone did that to me. At the seventeen second mark, the video glitches. You've got to pay attention to my face, okay? My eyes and my mouth."

Poppy rested her chin on her knees. "Seventeen seconds. Glitch. Watch your face. Got it."

Cash pressed play and the video started. She wrinkled her nose, watching as Cash threaded his fingers through Ashley's hair and—

Wait.

Poppy leaned closer to the screen. "Go back."

Cash held down on the rewind button and started the video from the beginning.

His hand was in her hair. He leaned in and—

The video glitched.

It fucking *glitched*.

"Oh my god."

Cash sucked in a sharp breath. "Did you see it?"

"I saw it. Your mouth looks weird."

He pressed the heels of his hands into his eyes and stood there, breathing in, and breathing out, shoulders trembling.

"Cash?"

He lowered his hands and blinked hard like he was fighting back tears. "*Fuck*." A broken laugh left his lips. "You really saw it?"

"Yeah." She blinked hard and fast, holding back tears too. "I did."

"You believe me?" He tossed the remote down and climbed up onto the couch beside her. "You—you know I didn't do it?"

Cash was a lot of things, but he wasn't a liar, and he was a terrible actor. He couldn't fake this kind of bone-deep relief.

"I do. I believe you." Poppy nodded. "I shouldn't have doubted—"

"No." Cash shook his head. "I know what it looked like. I'm just glad you see it now." He let out a sigh and scrubbed a hand over his face, fingers dragging down the skin beneath his eye, the corner of his mouth. "What am I supposed to do, Poppy? Someone out there's fucking with me. With my life. My reputation. My relationships. *Fuck*."

She took a moment to breathe, to think.

"I'm guessing you've texted Lyric about this."

Cash snorted. "None of my texts are going through. I keep getting a *message not delivered* notification. She must've blocked my number." His eyes darted to her face and just as quickly he looked away, staring at his hands. "I texted Rosaline. Same thing happened."

Her heart clenched painfully. "Ah."

Two weeks had passed since she'd spoken to Rosaline. Not for lack of wanting, but there was nothing to say that hadn't been said, nothing to say that would change a damn thing.

"Do you think—" Cash cut himself off with a wince. "I hate to ask . . ."

Her stomach hardened, muscles tensing, bracing. "Cash . . ."

"I wouldn't ask if I had another option. Something tells me Lyric won't exactly be receptive to another stupid Hail Mary tweet."

Poppy winced. "Rosaline might not even listen to me."

For all she knew, she could be blocked too. A nice, clean break, even if nothing felt particularly nice or clean about it to Poppy.

"She will," Cash said, decisive, sounding a little more like his usual self. "You'll see."

> **POPPY (7:12 A.M.):** Hi.

> **POPPY (7:12 A.M.):** Don't block me, please.

> **POPPY (7:13 A.M.):** Until today, I didn't want to admit it, not even to myself, but I thought Cash fucked up. I saw the video and I didn't want to believe he could do something like that, but the proof was there.

> **POPPY (7:14 A.M.):** I made all these excuses up in my brain. Maybe he was drunk and didn't remember. Maybe right after the kiss he pushed her away.

> **POPPY (7:15 A.M.):** I'm saying this so you know I'm not completely in denial. I saw what you saw. I'm not going to pretend I didn't.

> **POPPY (7:15 A.M.):** But Cash isn't sleeping and he's barely eating. He has hardly moved off the couch since the footage was shared online. He keeps watching the video over again like it's game tape. He's obsessed.

POPPY (7:16 A.M.): I haven't watched it since that night in the kitchen. But today he begged me to because he swears there's a glitch. I didn't believe him until I sat down and watched it. I know it sounds crazy, but at 17 seconds the video does something hard to explain. His mouth doesn't look right. I'm not making this up. If you watch it, you'll see what I mean.

POPPY (7:17 A.M.): I know you probably want to put all of this behind you, but Cash asked me to reach out because Lyric has his number blocked.

POPPY (7:32 A.M.): Merry Christmas, Rosaline.

POPPY (7:49 A.M.): I'll leave you alone now.

Read at 7:58 a.m.

Wednesday, December 26

Subject: Impersonation Report
From: Tinder Help <help@gotinder.com>
To: Poppy Peterson <poppypeterson@gmail.com>

Dear Poppy,

Thank you for your report. Please know we take violations of our Community Guidelines and Terms of Service extremely seriously.

We've reviewed the reported profile and the account in question has been deleted. The email address and phone number associated with the account have been banned indefinitely.

Unfortunately, per our company data policy, we cannot provide any other details at this time.

If you have any additional questions or concerns, please don't hesitate to reach out.

Best,
Molly, Tinder Customer Support

Wednesday, December 26

Subject: Request: Digital Image Analysis Assistance
From: Poppy Peterson <poppypeterson@gmail.com>
To: Matilda Larsson <matildalarsson@uoregon.edu>

Professor Larsson,

I'm not sure if you remember me, but my name is Poppy Peterson, and I took your course called Fact or Fiction several years ago when I was a student at UO. I know this might be a long shot, but seeing as the course you taught was focused on media literacy and evaluating credibility in the digital age, I was hoping you might be able to help me out by putting me in touch with someone who specializes in analyzing digital images for tampering. If not, no worries!

Have a happy holiday season and wonderful New Year!

All the best,
Poppy Peterson (she/her)

Friday, December 28

Subject: Re: Request: Digital Image Analysis Assistance
From: Matilda Larsson <matildalarsson@uoregon.edu>
To: Poppy Peterson <poppypeterson@gmail.com>

Poppy,

I do remember you and hope you're doing well!

As a matter of fact, I do know someone who specializes in digital image analysis with an emphasis on AI tampering and manipulation, if that sounds like what you're looking for? His name is Rodger Schillinger and he's a professor at Carnegie Mellon and a dear friend of mine from grad school. He works primarily out of the Human-Computer Interaction Institute. If anyone can help you out, I think it's Rodger.

His email address is <rodgerschillinger@carnegiemellon.edu>.

I'll drop him a line and let him know to be on the lookout for your email, if that sounds good?

All the best,
Matilda Larsson (she/they)
Associate Professor
Director, Public Relations Program
School of Journalism and Communication
219C Allen Hall
University of Oregon, Eugene

Friday, December 28

Subject: Re: Re: Request: Digital Image Analysis Assistance
From: Poppy Peterson <poppypeterson@gmail.com>
To: Matilda Larsson <matildalarsson@uoregon.edu>

Professor Larsson,

Thank you, thank you, thank you!!! You are a lifesaver! If you ever want tickets to a Pathfinders' game, please let me know and I'll get you box seats!

All the best,
Poppy Peterson (she/her)

Friday, December 28

Subject: Digital Image Tampering (Referral from Prof Matilda Larsson) 📎
From: Poppy Peterson <poppypeterson@gmail.com>
To: Rodger Schillinger <rodgerschillinger@carnegiemellon.edu>

Dear Professor Schillinger,

My name is Poppy Peterson, and I was given your contact information by a past professor of mine at UO, Matilda Larsson.

I'm looking for help analyzing a brief video clip for potential manipulation. I'm not sure if the video has simply been doctored or fully fabricated (I hope I'm using those terms correctly) and if basic editing software was used or maybe AI. I do know it's been tampered with to some degree and has resulted in the spread of some disastrous misinformation.

I'm sure you're extremely busy, but it would mean the world to me if you could help. For convenience, I've attached the video clip. I'm far from an expert, but it looks to me as if there's evidence of tampering around the seventeen-second mark.

Looking forward to hearing from you,
Poppy Peterson (she/her)

Monday, December 31

Subject: Re: Digital Image Tampering (Referral from Prof Matilda Larsson) 📎
From: Rodger Schillinger <rodgerschillinger@carnegiemellon.edu>
To: Poppy Peterson <poppypeterson@gmail.com>

Dear Poppy,

Matilda told me to be on the lookout for your email. I'm not entirely sure if she told you or if you're familiar with the work we're doing here in the Artificial Intelligence Lab and the Human-Computer Interaction Institute, but we're developing deepfake detection software to aid in determining what's real and what isn't in the age of AI. As I'm sure you can imagine, this particular branch of technology's rapid advancement calls for the constant tweaking and training of our software.

I won't lie—I was leery when I received your email. There's a growing trend of suspecting AI interference every single time a photo or video surfaces that paints a public figure in an unseemly light. Look at TikTok—everyone and their mother now believe they're an expert on AI tampering.

On the other hand, I have three daughters who would never speak to me again if they learned I had passed up the opportunity to review something even tangentially related to *the* Lyric Adair. I've examined the video you sent, first manually by slowing it down and studying it frame by frame. The glitch you mentioned around the seventeen-second mark was apparent, yes, but I couldn't be certain if it was the result of the video's compression. However, there were a few clues later in the video that raised several red flags, namely the inconsistency in lighting, a strange absence of blinking that speaks to AI's current struggle to capture the subtleties of human movement, facial expressions that simply seemed "off," etc., so I also ran it through our detection software. Our system has found that there's a high likelihood that both individuals' faces and bodies were manipulated with AI. Attached are the findings.

I imagine you intend to clear Mr. Curran's name. To preempt what I imagine to be your next question, I'm happy to go on the record. At the very least it will win me brownie points with my girls.

Best,
Rodger Schillinger (he/him)
Professor, Artificial Intelligence
Human-Computer Interaction Institute
School of Computer Science
306B Newell-Simon Hall
Carnegie Mellon

Breaking news: video of Cash Curran and Ashley Tibbey deemed "deepfake" by artificial intelligence experts

by Holly Koch
published on January 7

Fans were sent into a frenzy last month after news of Cash Curran's infidelity broke, video footage shared with *Notoriety Magazine* showing the star quarterback engaged in an intimate moment with ex-girlfriend, model Ashley Tibbey, at Kasa Nightclub in Portland, Oregon.

However, multiple deepfake forensics experts have now examined the video and agree that "signs of gross AI manipulation are present."

"There are signs that point to AI manipulation, but it can be hard to spot with the human eye, especially as the systems being used to create these deepfakes get better and better," said Rodger Schillinger, professor of Artificial Intelligence and faculty adviser in the Human-Computer Interaction Institute at Carnegie Mellon. "That's why we've developed deepfake detection software. When a photo or video is fed through, it provides a confidence score that shows whether the media in question has been manipulated. Our lab evaluated the video of Cash Curran making the rounds and gave us an extremely high confidence score. I can say with 99 percent certainty that manipulation is present."

When asked how the general public can better spot AI manipulation, Schillinger said to pay attention to "inconsistencies in lighting, shadows, and color" and "bizarre or awkward facial and body movements," all of which he claims are present in the manipulated video of Curran.

"Whoever created this deepfake did a decent job, but it's clear that his mouth doesn't move the way a regular human mouth is meant to. The joints of his fingers look odd when the video is magnified and his coloring is inconsistent even factoring in the dim lighting of the club atmosphere," Schillinger added.

At the request of the magazine, Jonah Wilson, founder of DeepAI, a generative AI video effects startup, reviewed the video of Curran and Tibbey and came to the same conclusion as Schillinger.

"There are a lot of easily accessible tools to create deepfakes quickly. FaceApp, MyHeritage, Wav2Lip to name a few common ones frequently used by social media users to jump on generative trends," Wilson said. "It's likely whoever manipulated—created, really—this particular video used a combination of convolutional neural networks and autoencoders for facial recognition and body movement targeting, superimposing these attributes onto source video, likely of a real couple in a club. But not Cash Curran and Ashley Tibbey."

In a formal statement issued on social media, Curran said, "It's a relief to have my name cleared, but this has been an absolute nightmare. The harm caused by the creation and spread of this deepfake AI-generated video cannot be understated. I'm not sure we'll ever know who created this video and for what reason other than to be malicious, but I worry about what other harm is going to be caused if this technology continues to go unchecked. Revenge porn, blackmail, false evidence, the spread of political misinformation, etc. Appropriate legislative action needs to be taken to protect people from exploitation."

Fans might be wondering if the screenshots of Curran's Tinder profile were also fabricated. A source at the dating app shared in a now-deleted TikTok that the profile was real but was a "case of impersonation" and the associated account was shut down. According to the same source, the account was linked to an IP address in Ventura County, California. Curran does not, nor has he ever, lived in Ventura County. However, as pointed out by TikTok creator @milesformiles, the Domestic Noir Plot drummer Ansel Daily purchased a home in Thousand Oaks last year.

At the time of publication, Adair's rep had not responded to *US Weekly*'s request for comment.

VICTORIA @pdxprincess • 15h
As the person who started the hashtag #CashCurranIsCanceled, I hereby declare him uncanceled. #CashCurranIsNoLongerCanceled

UR FAV LESBIAN @imubutgayer • 2h
whoops I take it back. cash curran, baby, no coughing for you #CashCurranIsNoLongerCanceled

Chapter Twenty-One

January 17

PORTLAND PATHFINDERS @portlandpathfinders • 1h
SOMETIMES IT ONLY TAKES ONE. FINAL SCORE 7–0. SEE YOU AT THE NFC CHAMPIONSHIP NEXT WEEK, GREEN BAY #PDXvsLA #NFCDivisionalPlayoffs #PathfindersNation

"You played a really great game tonight."

Cash grunted, brooding out the window at the city as it zoomed past.

Poppy deflated like a pricked balloon. Every one of her attempts at making conversation had been met with, at most, monosyllabic answers.

"Cash," she begged. "Talk to me."

"And say what?" He sighed and dragged a hand over his face. Two weeks' worth of scraggly stubble darkened his jaw. "That I *honestly* had myself convinced Lyric was going to be at the game? That I was going to step out on that field and look up and she was going to be there. She was going to look at me and she was going to smile, and everything was going to—" Cash cut himself off with a painful-looking swallow. "I've been telling myself that maybe she just needed a little more time, but . . . she wasn't there, Poppy. She wasn't there and it sucks. Is that what you want me to say? That it *fucking* sucks?"

Cash was acting like he'd forgotten Poppy had spent the last week drowning in the same sea of despair as him.

"You're not the only one who was hoping she'd show." Poppy had held her breath each time the door to the suite had opened, hoping that it would be Lyric. That Rosaline would be with her. "You're not the only one who's disappointed and you're not the only one going through it right now, either. I got my heart broken too, Cash."

His eyes slammed shut. "Fuck. I didn't mean to insinuate that—"

"It's fine."

Their spirits were low, tensions running high, frustration bubbling over. If Cash was anything like her, he wasn't sleeping great, waking in the night to reach for a body that wasn't there, staring at the ceiling and watching the phone, wishing it would ring, aching each time it didn't.

She wanted to believe it could still happen, that at any moment her phone would light up with Rosaline's name on the screen, with a picture Poppy stared at when she couldn't sleep, tracing the lines of Rosaline's face with her fingertips. She wanted to believe, but she wasn't sure how much hope she had left in her after four weeks of radio silence.

Poppy cupped her hand around her eyes and squinted out the window. "I don't think this is the way to the hotel."

She didn't know when it had happened, but they were on the 101 heading north.

"That's because we're not headed to the hotel."

Poppy did *not* have a good feeling about this. "Are you going to tell me where we're going, or am I supposed to guess?"

"Ninety-nine percent." Cash's foot bounced against his knee. "That's what that AI expert said. That he could say with ninety-nine-percent certainty that manipulation was present."

#CashCurranIsNoLongerCanceled was still trending days since the story broke, sympathy pouring in all over social media with cries echoing Cash's plea for legislative action.

"Everyone knows it wasn't you in the video."

"What if it's going to take more than some guy at Carnegie Mellon to convince Lyric it wasn't me?"

Some guy? "Professor Schillinger is the foremost expert on—"

"And he still could only say with ninety-nine-percent certainty that it wasn't me. That's still a one-percent chance that—"

"Ninety-nine percent is as good as that sort of score gets. The article made it clear that it wasn't you. I—I don't know what else I can do to make her believe that—"

"Poppy, no." Cash set his hand on her knee and squeezed. "You're the best defense I could ask for, but I think it's time I do what I do best and play a little offense."

Outside, a road sign welcomed them to Ventura County. The time for speaking in riddles and sports metaphors was officially over. "Where are we going, Cash?"

"Rosaline was right about it being easy to look up someone's address in the county records." He handed Poppy his phone.

"Jesus Christ." On the screen was the Ventura County Assessor property search results for Ansel Daily, his address listed at the top. "This is your plan to fix things with Lyric? Beat up her ex-boyfriend?" She shoved the phone into his chest. "You're going to get your ass arrested and kicked off the team. You're going to be single and jobless and have a criminal record and I'm not going to know how to spin that."

"I'm not going to touch a hair on his head. I just want to talk."

"You want to *talk*?" Poppy demanded. "Cash, we don't even know for certain that Ansel's the one behind the video."

"And I plan on asking him. I deserve the truth and so does Lyric. And if she hears it from him, she'll know for sure it wasn't me in the video."

"Oh, well, good thing Ansel's such a great guy and will *totally* be willing to do all that for you out of the goodness of his heart." She rolled her eyes. "You realize we're talking about the guy who potentially created a deepfake of you for the purpose of ruining your relationship with Lyric and destroying your career, right?"

"He doesn't have to know I'm not planning on kicking his ass."

"Oh my god." Poppy rested her head against the window, the glass cool against her skin. All the many ways this night could and likely would go wrong filled her head as the driver took the exit for Hampshire Road and made a slight right on the ramp to Thousand Oaks. "This is nuts. Totally batshit fucking crazy. You realize that, right?"

"Maybe this works, maybe it doesn't. But if there's even a one percent chance that I can fix this? I have to take it. I have to try." The car pulled into a quiet neighborhood and stopped in the driveway of a single-story stucco house painted the same shade of peach as the rest of the houses on the tree-lined cul-de-sac. Cash unfastened his seat belt. "I'm not asking you to do anything except have my back, okay?" He reached for the door handle. "You can even stay in the car."

As if. Poppy reached for her seat belt. "You're delusional if you think I'm going to sit here and let you go in there and face this by yourself."

Cash told the driver they'd only be a few minutes and met her around the front of the car. "Ready?"

Not really, but Poppy nodded anyway, falling into step beside Cash.

"You realize he's probably going to slam the door in our faces, right? If he even answers it."

"Just trust me." Without warning, Cash rang the bell, then dove behind the pot of bamboo growing beside the front door, hunching to hide.

"*Damn it, Cash,*" she hissed. "What am I supposed to—"

The question died on her lips as her heart clambered into her throat. She could hear footsteps, then the heavy clunk of the dead bolt turning, and finally the screech of the hinges as the door swung open revealing Ansel, barefoot and shirt unbuttoned to his belly, his hair hanging loose around his shoulders.

A lit cigarette hung from his lips and a bottle of whisky dangled from his fingertips. "Poppy Peterson." He exhaled a cloud of acrid smoke in her direction. "Isn't this a surprise?"

"Ansel." She coughed, not even trying to hide her disgust. "We need to talk."

"No offense, but what could someone like you"—he tipped the bottle in her direction—"and someone like me have to talk about?"

Her eyes flitted to Cash's hiding spot behind the planter, then back to Ansel. They really should've rehearsed this. "I want to talk about the video."

Ansel ashed his cigarette against the doorframe. "Video?" He tossed the butt on the ground beside her feet. "What video?"

Poppy glared. Responsible or not, he knew damn well what she was talking about. "The video of Cash that was debunked as a deepfake."

"Oh, yeah. I heard about that."

"And?"

"And what? You want to know if I had something to do with

it?" He laughed and stepped back, a hand on the door. "Do you seriously think, if I did, I'd tell you? God, you're even dumber than you look."

Before Ansel could fully shut the door on her, Cash stuck his foot over the threshold and bullied his way inside the house, forcing Ansel to take several stumbling steps back or be mowed down. "If you won't tell her, maybe you'll tell me."

Poppy had never seen someone go so pale so fast as Ansel did in that moment.

"This is private property. You're trespassing. You're—" Ansel's back hit the wall, and Cash kept him pinned there, palms flattened against the wall to either side of his head. "This is a home invasion."

"I just want answers, man. Did you do it?"

Ansel scoffed. "Fuck you, dude. I didn't do shit."

Cash grabbed the front of Ansel's shirt in both fists and dragged him up to his full height and farther still, until Ansel was squirming on his tiptoes.

"Did you do it?" Cash demanded, giving Ansel a hard shake. "Tell me."

"Fine, fine!" Ansel cried, folding faster than Poppy expected. She'd figured it would take at least ten minutes before he'd crack. "It was me. I did it, all right? Just let me go."

"Why'd you do it?" Cash jerked him higher up the wall until his toes barely brushed the floor. "Did you think it would be funny fucking with me?"

Poppy chewed on her thumbnail, wondering whether she should step in and tell him to ease up, if this was too close to the ass-kicking he had promised not to give.

"Yeah, okay, I—I thought it'd be funny," Ansel stuttered, bare feet thrashing, leaving smudges on the baseboard. "Lyric always gets the last fucking word. I was—I was sick of it." He squirmed harder. "Fuck, dude. Are you happy now? I told you. Let me go."

Cash gave Ansel a rough shove and stepped back. "Am I happy? Fuck you. No, I'm not happy. You put me through fucking hell because you didn't know a good thing when you had it." He fished his phone out of his pocket and swiped his thumb against the screen. "But I'll be a hell of a lot closer to happy after you tell Lyric the truth."

"Wait." Poppy had a better idea.

She poked her head into the living room beyond the doorway Ansel was currently slumped beside and—*aha*, his phone was on the coffee table beside a pack of Parliaments and a lighter. Poppy swiped it, bringing it to the foyer and shoving it into Ansel's chest. "Start recording."

Ansel Daily takes responsibility for Cash Curran deepfake in Instagram Live, shocking fans: "Sorry for the harm I've caused"

by Jaimie Xin
published on January 18

Ansel Daily has claimed responsibility for the deepfake video of Cash Curran that was posted online last month, depicting the NFL quarterback kissing his ex-girlfriend.

The drummer turned to social media to apologize for his actions after rumors of his involvement in the scandal took the internet by storm. "I, uh, wanted to hop on and let you all know that I did a really stupid thing," Daily said, live on Instagram Thursday evening. "I'm the one responsible for the deepfake video that everyone's been talking about. It was a joke, but I recognize now that what I did was wrong." His eyes darted off screen several times during the Live. "I'm sorry for the harm I've caused Cash Curran and Ashley Tibbey, along with . . . I guess Lyric and anyone else hurt by the video."

"Cash is relieved to have answers and hopes that this entire, painful ordeal can finally be put to bed. The harm can't be undone, but he'd like to move forward and focus on repairing the damage done," Curran's publicist, Poppy Peterson, said in response to *People*'s request for comment.

Adair's publicist has yet to respond.

January 24

PORTLAND PATHFINDERS @portlandpathfinders • 10h
RISE AND SHINE! IT'S GAME DAY, PATHFINDERS NATION!
#GBvsPDX #NFCChampionship #PathfindersNation

"How's Benji liking his first football game?" Poppy ghosted her fingers over the downy soft hair on Cassidy and DeAndre's son's head, cooing when he yawned.

Cassidy stroked a finger from his forehead down to the tip of his nose, laughing when his whole face scrunched up tight, making him look like a grumpy little old man. She'd dressed him for the occasion in a teeny-tiny Pathfinders onesie, a miniature version of the jersey she wore, an itty-bitty 89 on his equally itty-bitty chest. Adorable. "He's loving the attention, that's for sure." Cassidy sighed. "And I, for one, couldn't be happier to leave the house. I was going stir crazy."

"Well, if you ever need a sitter, I'm happy to, and I'm sure Cash would be too."

"How's he doing?" Cassidy's lips twisted to the side in a sympathetic smile. "A little better, I hope. What with . . ." She trailed off, the resemblance between her and Benji never more obvious than when her nose wrinkled. "You know. Considering the last couple games haven't been total shit shows, I imagine he's got to be feeling somewhat better."

Or he'd gotten better at compartmentalizing, same as her.

"You know Cash," she said with a shrug. "He's an eternal optimist. He's still holding out hope that everything's going to work out. That Lyric just needs a little more time."

A week had passed since Cash's second Hail Mary play, since he'd tracked Ansel down and, together, he and Poppy had seen to it that Ansel had taken responsibility for the deepfake video in the most indisputable way possible, by issuing a public apology live. As gratifying as it had been, watching Ansel humble himself in front of five hundred thousand live viewers, the fact that neither Lyric nor Rosaline had reached out in the days after made it feel like a hollow victory to Poppy.

Out on the field, the game clock counting down the seconds to halftime hit zero.

"All right, folks," the announcer's voice poured through the speakers. "And that's the half. Pathfinders up by fourteen, the score thirty-four to twenty." The players jogged off the field, heading for the tunnels that led to the locker rooms. "The Pathfinders would like to welcome the Jefferson High School marching band for a special halftime performance."

A hush descended over the stadium as the marching band took to the field, and—

Poppy gasped and the crowd, seeing what she saw, went wild.

Cradling Benji in the crook of her left arm, Cassidy tugged eagerly on Poppy's sleeve.

"Poppy. *Poppy.*" Cassidy bounced on her toes. "Tell me I'm not seeing things."

If Cassidy was seeing things, then so was Poppy, so was the whole stadium. One giant, mass hallucination.

"The Pathfinders," the announcer's voice boomed, "would also like to welcome a very special musical guest—" The drummers in the marching band provided a cheeky drumroll. "Lyric Adair!"

The crowd, already wild, went frenzied.

The camera zeroed in on Lyric as she made her way across the field, smile positively beatific as she waved, stopping on the giant double *P* spray-painted on the turf, mic in hand, the other waving at the crowd. Her smiling face appeared on the jumbotron; she had Cash's number 3 painted on her right cheek.

"Holy shit," Poppy breathed, a laugh erupting from her lips, her eyes stinging and vision blurring as the camera panned to the tunnel where Coach Fitz, the Pathfinders' offensive coordinator, dragged a confused-looking Cash out onto the sidelines.

There was no mistaking the moment Cash spotted her; he fell to his knees then and there, burying his face in his hands for the briefest of seconds before he raised his head, eyes sparkling as he stared at her unblinking, like he couldn't bear the thought of losing sight of her for even a moment.

"Did you know about this?" Cassidy asked, and Poppy gave a wet laugh, gesturing to the mess of tears ruining her makeup.

"Does it look like I knew about this?" She shook her head and gingerly wiped beneath her eyes with her fingertips.

"Hi, everyone," Lyric spoke into the microphone, her voice echoing across the stadium. The green glitter around her eyes caught the light and shimmered. "Hope you don't mind that I crashed your halftime, but—"

The roar of the crowd was so loud Lyric had to pause, lowering the microphone with a bright laugh. Over on the sidelines, Cash had made it back up onto his feet, standing with a hand covering his mouth, grin so huge his eyes had all but disappeared.

Lyric waited until the noise died down from a roar to an eager titter. "Halftime is only thirteen minutes, and I don't want to get in trouble for throwing off the schedule," she said, and the crowd laughed like it was the funniest thing they'd ever heard, the idea that the team, the league, the network, *anyone*, would complain about an impromptu performance by Lyric Adair. News of her appearance was probably spreading like wildfire on social media, people tuning in to the game right now just to watch what would probably go down as one of the most talked about moments in NFL history. "So, without further ado, I'd like to sing one of my favorite songs of all time." She grinned sheepishly, scuffing the toe of her heel against the turf. "This is 'Time After Time' by Cyndi Lauper. I'd like to dedicate it to this guy. You might've heard of him." Her smile was radiant. "His name is Cash Curran."

With a nod from Lyric, the marching band, led by the bright, percussive snare drums, launched into the beautiful, bittersweet ballad.

"Talk about a grand gesture," Cassidy murmured.

"Lyric was worried she'd be too late."

As if her heart had sprouted wings, as silly and impossible an idea as that was, the sound of Rosaline's voice sent her chest aflutter.

Cassidy shot her a sidelong glance and a lopsided grin. "I think Benji's hungry. So, I'm just gonna go whip my tit out somewhere that's, you know, not here, and let you two talk."

She scurried off, Benji fast asleep in her arms, leaving Poppy alone with Rosaline.

Talk. There were a million things Poppy wanted to say, but she wasn't sure whether she should say any of them, if Rosaline would want to hear them, so she kept her mouth shut.

Rosaline stepped into the space Cassidy had just vacated at Poppy's side, facing the field. Poppy wiped her sweaty palms on her thighs and stole a peek at Rosaline from the corner of her eye.

She looked . . . well, she looked beautiful, but that was nothing new. Rosaline always looked beautiful. She looked beautiful all dressed up and she looked beautiful in the morning with bed head. Looking at Rosaline, even just from the corner of her eye, made it hard for her to breathe.

Rosaline stared out at the field, watching as Lyric crooned the song's second verse.

"Did you two come straight here from the airport or something?"

Rosaline turned her head and looked at Poppy and, if she had thought it was hard to breathe before, it was next to impossible now, Rosaline's eyes meeting hers steadily. "Yes, but . . . Lyric was worried Curran wouldn't want to see her. I told her she was being ridiculous."

Down on the field, Cash had already crossed the thirty-yard line, making his way toward the middle of the field where Lyric stood. "He'd wait forever for her. He told me."

Lyric reached the chorus, singing about falling, catching, waiting.

"What about me?" Rosaline said seemingly out of nowhere, glancing out at the field and back at Poppy, bottom lip trapped between her teeth. "Am I too late?"

Every last thought inside Poppy's head vanished; it took a moment to register what Rosaline was asking. Only, she couldn't possibly be saying what Poppy thought she was. "I guess that depends on what you mean."

She refused to assume, couldn't stomach the idea of getting her hopes up only to have them dashed. Again. And not to be petty, at least Poppy didn't want to be, wasn't *trying* to be, but Rosaline had called things quits between them. *She* had ended their relationship. Poppy understood why, but if Rosaline had something to say, she needed to be the one to say it. Poppy wasn't even going to try to fill in the blanks. Trying to read Rosaline was as frustrating as it was futile, 90 percent of the time. Poppy liked it so much better when Rosaline just told her how she felt and left out the guessing.

"I'm saying I'm sorry." Rosaline's throat clicked when she swallowed. "I shouldn't . . ." She trailed off with a frustrated sigh. "I shouldn't have let their relationship dictate ours. It was shortsighted and impulsive of me, jumping the gun like that. I should've . . . I should've done a lot of things differently, I realize."

What Rosaline was saying was exactly what Poppy had spent the last month dreaming. The difference was those were dreams. Dreams didn't have to contend with real-world logic.

"What if he'd done it?" Poppy's voice quivered as she asked the question, dreading the answer, but needing to know. "What if the video had been real? What if next time, because God knows there probably will be . . . what if next time Cash really is guilty?"

Cash wouldn't cheat, but he was only human, same as Lyric. Whether it was next week or ten years down the line, any number of things could happen that might spell doom for their relationship.

Was Rosaline going to break up with Poppy every time there was trouble in paradise between Lyric and Cash? She couldn't go through this again.

To her credit, Rosaline seemed to give the question the deliberation it was due. Wearing a subtle frown, she looked out at the field. Cash had crossed the forty-yard line, his footsteps slowing the closer he got to Lyric, almost like he was savoring every step, committing the moment to memory.

"It would be hard," Rosaline admitted. "I won't lie. But Poppy, these last few weeks have been hell and I realized I'd rather face the hard things *with* you. I know I told you there was no *we* in this, but that was a mistake." It was with an almost shy sort of reverence that Rosaline took Poppy's hand between both of her own and clasped it against her chest. Her heart was beating so hard Poppy could feel it against the inside of her wrist where her own pulse pounded. "There is a *we*, or at least I really want there to be, if you'll still have me."

If she'd still have her. Poppy choked. "Rosaline—"

"Before you say no." Rosaline's grip tightened on Poppy's hand like she was afraid Poppy would try and steal it back. "I spent the last eight years believing Lyric needed me to take care of her, and maybe for a time she did, but she doesn't need that now. She doesn't need me like that. She doesn't need me to protect her or fight her battles for her. And I get that, I do. But I've spent almost a quarter of my life, half of my adult life, believing it was the only thing I was good at." She stole a glance at Poppy from beneath her lashes and brought their joined hands a little higher, closer to her lips. She buffed a kiss across the back of Poppy's knuckles and smiled, the corners of her mouth drawing and dimpling sweetly. "But I think I could be really good at loving you, if you'd let me."

Rosaline's voice didn't falter and neither did the expression on her face, unflinchingly open and earnest, her words a confession and oath rolled into one perfect package. They flooded Poppy's chest with liquid warmth so hot she nearly looked down to check and see if she was bleeding through her jersey.

Happy tears sprang to her eyes. She leaned in, breathing in the scent of Rosaline's perfume, drinking in the way Rosaline trembled softly when Poppy brushed a soft kiss against her lips.

"I think you'll be exceptional at it, actually."

Epilogue

One year later

Portland Pathfinders headed to Super Bowl for the second year in a row following win against the Philadelphia Eagles

by Edgar Jones, ESPN staff writer
published on January 31

PHILADELPHIA, PA—The Pathfinders brought their A game to Lincoln Financial Field last night, pulling off a stunning win against the Eagles.

Even with two of their best cornerbacks and a safety on the injured reserve list, the Pathfinders' defense held firm, refusing to give an inch in the second half.

Quarterback Cash Curran and tight end DeAndre Jones, or the "dream duo" as they're often referred, started strong in the first half and finished even stronger in the final quarter, leading the Pathfinders to a 45-21 victory in the NFC West Championship, cinching their spot in the Super Bowl.

The Pathfinders will face off against the Patriots on February 14 in Las Vegas, Nevada.

February 14

Eileen Curran watched with hungry eyes as Lyric listened intently to Benji's nonsensical babbling. "Lyric, sweetheart, it won't be too long until I get to hear the pitter-patter of tiny feet inside *my* home, will it?" she pried. "Whenever I ask Cash, he tells me to mind my own business. But he's my son. He is my business."

It looked like it physically pained Rosaline to keep her mouth shut.

Lyric, to her credit, simply laughed and bounced Benji on her lap, shooting Rosaline and Poppy a brief *Are you hearing this?* look. "We're not even married yet, Eileen."

Cash's mother pouted. "But—"

"Mrs. Curran?" Cassidy smiled sweetly. "I think DeAndre's mom wanted to ask you about those yummy little cheesy tarts you made for Lyric's bridal shower."

Cassidy Jones was an angel.

"Oh, the Welsh rarebits?" Eileen beamed. "Of course. I saved the recipe to my photo gallery."

Cassidy took Benji from Lyric. "Perfect."

"You see," Eileen chattered as Cassidy led her across the VIP suite Cash and DeAndre had—together—spent an absurd amount of money on so their families wouldn't have to sit in the stands at Allegiant Stadium, "the magic is really in the combination of *good* English mustard—it's important that it be *good*—and Worcestershire sauce . . ."

Lyric breathed a sigh of relief as soon as they were far enough away to be out of earshot. "God love her, but that woman is like a dog with a bone." She rose from where she'd been crouched playing with Benji and dusted off the backs of her legs. "I'm going to run to the bathroom before she comes back and starts finding new and inventive ways to ask me about when we're going to start raw-dogging it."

Rosaline recoiled. "Ugh. *Lyric*."

The sound of her tinkling laughter floated across the room, receding when she slipped inside the suite's private restroom and shut the door.

Rosaline rested her head against Poppy's shoulder. "I understand that deep, deep, deep, *deep* down, Cash's mother is excited, but I don't know how Lyric's managed to keep a level head while planning this wedding."

Poppy stroked her fingers through Rosaline's hair. "Lyric's over-the-moon excited too. I think that helps."

"No one is as excited as Eileen Curran." Rosaline slid her arms around Poppy's waist. "The other day at lunch, when you were out shopping with Cash—lucky you, by the way—she asked me my opinion on cotton versus chiffon."

"The fabrics? You can't really compare them. They're totally different."

"No." Rosaline lifted her head, expression grim. "The colors. They're shades of cream, Poppy, and they look identical. Because they *are* identical."

"What did you say?"

"I told her the truth." Rosaline pursed her lips. "I had to endure a ten-minute lecture about how they were completely different, and did I wear glasses? Because maybe I need to get my eyes checked. Didn't exactly endear either of us to one another, let me tell you."

Poppy pressed her lips together so she wouldn't laugh. "You do squint when we watch television at night."

She touched her fingertips to the outside corners of her eyes. "Do not."

"You do." Poppy nudged her hand aside and kissed the skin right below Rosaline's brow. "It's cute."

Rosaline harrumphed.

"Look on the bright side, she's not going to be *your* mother-in-law."

"As good as," Rosaline grumbled. "Whatever you want to call it, she's going to be family, what with Lyric marrying Cash and . . ." She trailed off, looking out at the field where the halftime performance was wrapping. The Pathfinders were currently ahead, thirteen to twelve, and this was shaping up to be a nail-biter of a game. "Well, you know."

Following the clearing of Cash's name and Lyric's epic performance during the playoff's halftime show the previous year, they had agreed to take things a little slower than they had before and work to build the trust that had been missing between them. Officially, they never called off the engagement, but they did agree to wait, conversations of March versus June forgotten, the date set for the following year.

Lyric had moved up to Portland in the spring and in July, Rosaline had purchased a gorgeous three-bedroom Tudor on the Alameda Ridge with a stunning view of downtown and the Willamette River that was only a ten-minute drive from Cash and Lyric in Laurelhurst. Poppy had moved in the same month.

Now, almost a year later, Cash and Lyric's wedding was right around the corner, happening in June, the week after Poppy's birthday.

"I know what?" Poppy teased.

They'd talked about it, getting married, and had agreed it was something they both wanted. At some point. Poppy wasn't in a rush; when the timing was right, they'd know it. And until then, she was perfectly, incandescently happy with life the way it was.

Rather than answer, Rosaline continued to stare out at the field, a contemplative frown creasing her brow.

"We're in Las Vegas."

Poppy laughed. "Yeah, being at the Super Bowl sort of tipped me off. That, and all those slot machines in our hotel."

"No, I mean, we're in *Vegas*," Rosaline stressed, her arms tightening around Poppy's waist. "We could—" Her tongue swept across her bottom lip. "We could get married."

A laugh escaped her. "Funny."

Married in Vegas. *Sure.*

Rosaline stared at her with wide, guileless eyes and Poppy's jaw dropped.

"You're not kidding."

She shook her head.

"Tonight?" Poppy double-checked, needing to make sure she wasn't imagining this moment. "You—you want us to get married tonight? In Las Vegas? What about that thing you said months ago about two-bit Elvis impersonators?

"No Elvis impersonator," Rosaline vetoed. "But everything else? The time? The place?" She shrugged. "I'm going to marry you one day anyway." She smiled. "Why not today?"

Poppy's head spun and her heart raced, as breathless and lightheaded as she'd been after finishing her marathon. "Cash and Lyric are going to be *so* pissed," she blurted. Why her brain went there, she had no idea.

The corner of Rosaline's mouth curled. "It'll be the ultimate *gotcha* moment when, in a couple of months, Curran and Lyric, reveling in their newlywed bliss, ask us when we're going to tie the knot and we get to tell them we not only beat them to the altar, but that we did it in Vegas."

"You are *evil*," she breathed.

"You love me." Rosaline said it simply and earnestly, her voice steady and her gaze warm. It wasn't a question, not now, and maybe it never had been. It was a statement, a fact, the truth, absolute and unequivocal.

"I do."

The smile that lit up her face was brighter than the whole of Las Vegas Boulevard at night. "Is that a yes?"

Poppy grinned. "Yes."

Acknowledgments

To my fabulous editor, Shannon, thank you for taking such care of these characters. Emily, Jen, DJ, Catherine, and the entire team at Avon, thank you, thank you, thank you for everything you do. Sarah, you're the best agent I could ask for, and I am so extremely grateful to have you in my corner.

Mom, you're the best and I love you, but please don't read this book.

Last, but never least, thank you to my readers. None of this would be possible without you.

Praise for Alexandria Bellefleur

'What a treat! *Playing for Keeps* is filled with top-tier tension, sparkling banter, and deliciously sweet heat. Poppy and Rosaline's story will grab you from the very first page and refuse to let you go—I couldn't put it down! I adored every moment of this heartfelt, sexy romance. I dare you not to read it in one sitting'

Grace Reilly, *USA Today* bestselling author of *Wicked Serve*

'Alexandria Bellefleur's writing is as sparkling as champagne, bubbling with taste in every word. . . . Bellefleur provides sweet, bubbly romance, each romantic moment providing depth, excitement, and balance'

Buzzfeed on *Count Your Lucky Stars*

'Alexandria Bellefleur is an author to watch. Her writing is joyful and heartfelt, and her voice sparkles with a delightful mix of wit, humor, and good-natured sarcasm. I can't wait to see how she wows us next!'

Mia Sosa, *USA Today* bestselling author of *The Worst Best Man*

'[A] distinctly modern frolic, charming and effervescent and entirely itself'

The Washington Post on *Written in the Stars*

'Everything I want from a rom-com: fun, whimsical, sexy'

Talia Hibbert, *New York Times* bestselling author, on *Written in the Stars*

Do you love contemporary romance?

Want the chance to hear news about your favourite authors (and the chance to win free books)?

Kristen Ashley
Ashley Herring Blake
Meg Cabot
Olivia Dade
Rosie Danan
J. Daniels
Farah Heron
Talia Hibbert
Sarah Hogle
Helena Hunting
Abby Jimenez
Elle Kennedy
Christina Lauren
Alisha Rai
Sally Thorne
Lacie Waldon
Denise Williams
Meryl Wilsner
Samantha Young

Then visit the Piatkus website
www.yourswithlove.co.uk

And follow us on Facebook and Instagram
www.facebook.com/yourswithlovex | @yourswithlovex

PIATKUS